Diamela Eltit: Essays on Chilean Literature, Politics, and Culture

Edited by **Michael J. Lazzara**, **Mónica Barrientos**, and **María Rosa Olivera-Williams**

Translated by **Michael J. Lazzara**, **Catherine M. Brix**, **Carl Fischer**, and **Sowmya Ramanathan**

Published by
Latin America Research Commons
www.larcommons.net
larc@lasaweb.org

Cover design: Estudio Entre
Cover image: © Diamela Eltit, "Zona de dolor"
Print version typeset: Lara Melamet
Digital versions typeset: Estudio Ebook
Copy editor: Sam Simon
Bibliography and index: Lisa Rivero

ISBN (Paperback b&w version): 978-1-951634-33-9
ISBN (PDF): 978-1-951634-34-6
ISBN (EPUB): 978-1-951634-35-3
ISBN (Mobi): 978-1-951634-36-0
DOI: https://10.25154/book11

To read the free, open-access version of this book
online, visit https://10.25154/book11 or scan this QR
code with your mobile device:

*Obra editada en el marco del Programa de Apoyo
a la Traducción para Editoriales Extranjeras de la División
de las Culturas, las Artes, el Patrimonio y Diplomacia
Pública (DIRAC), de la Subsecretaría de Relaciones
Exteriores de Chile.*

Work published within the framework of the
Translation Support Program for Foreign Publishers
of the Division of Cultures, Arts, Heritage
and Public Diplomacy (DIRAC) of the Ministry
of Foreign Affairs, Chile.

Table of Contents

Permissions

Individual Works:

Eltit, Diamela. *El Padre Mío* (Santiago, Chile: Francisco Zegers Editor, 1989): "Presentación."

Eltit, Diamela. *El infarto del alma* (Santiago, Chile: Francisco Zegers Editor, 1994): "Diario de viaje (Viernes 7 de agosto de 1992)."

Eltit, Diamela. "National Prize for Literature Acceptance Speech" (December 19, 2018).

Eltit, Diamela. "La explosión del subsuelo chileno o la explosión desde abajo," *El Desconcierto* (October 21, 2019).

Eltit, Diamela. "Directo a los ojos," *El País* (December 1, 2019).

Eltit, Diamela. *Dime cuándo vienes: Cartas de amor, 1893-1917. Rosa Luxemburgo.* Translation and selection by Angelo Narváez León (Concón, Chile: Banda Propia, 2020): "La libertad es siempre la libertad de los disidentes."

Eltit, Diamela. "La pandemia sanitaria y la pandemia política," *La voz de los que sobran* (December 14, 2021).

Eltit, Diamela. "El nuevo texto y su contexto," *La voz de los que sobran* (May 19, 2021).

Eltit, Diamela. "Rezando un rosario de fakes," *La voz de los que sobran* (August 21, 2022).

Chile through the Lens of Diamela Eltit: Prisms of Literature, Politics, and Culture

Michael J. Lazzara, Catherine Brix,
Carl Fischer, Sowmya Ramanathan

Diamela Eltit's literary work emerged on the Chilean cultural scene in a particular historical moment—the 1980s—when the Pinochet regime (1973-1990) had consolidated its project of extermination, censorship, and neoliberal shock therapy.[1] Forced to write in a suffocating atmosphere of restriction and violence, Eltit boldly cultivated a radical, insurrectional poetics aimed at questioning the very underpinnings of authoritarian power and discourse. Her books to date—twelve novels, three nonfiction works, and three collections of critical essays published between 1983 and 2023—offer a searing reflection on the pain of dictatorship and on cultural and political forms of resistance to authoritarianism, imperialism/colonialism, and neoliberal economic policy. To that end, several common threads that bind her literary project are evident within the present collection of essays: a strong preoccupation with the body as text and the text as body; a sustained interest in gender and its constructs; the integration of marginalized voices that otherwise lack visibility or access to the "sacred" space of literature; the fight for

---

1 Some passages in the opening section of this introduction have been modified and expanded from Michael J. Lazzara, "Diamela Eltit," in *The Contemporary Spanish-American Novel: Bolaño and After*, edited by Will H. Corral, Juan E. de Castro, and Nicholas Birns (New York: Bloomsbury, 2013), 320-327.

historical memory; and a constant desire to problematize the political, the artistic, and the social through a questioning of class, race, ideology, and language.

Diamela Eltit completed her degree in literature at Pontificia Universidad Católica de Chile and later pursued graduate work in the University of Chile's Department of Humanistic Studies, where she studied a multidisciplinary and multi-genre, avant-garde curriculum and worked alongside other artists and writers who are now important figures within the Chilean artistic and literary canon. During the dictatorship, Eltit participated in the art-actions collective known as CADA (Colectivo de Acciones de Arte) along with the photographer and artist Lotty Rosenfeld, the poet Raúl Zurita, the sociologist Fernando Balcells, and the visual artist Juan Castillo. The group operated from 1979 until its last action in 1984 and focused its artistic interventions on disrupting the daily flows of life in the city of Santiago that, at the time, was besieged by dictatorship. One of Eltit's closest readers, Nelly Richard, notes in her seminal text *Margins and Institutions: Art in Chile since 1973* (1986) that the strategy of fusing art and life, inspired by more traditional avant-garde practices, was evident in some of CADA's most important urban interventions, like its final 1983 art action "No+," in which the group's members draped Santiago with banners and graffiti, inviting citizens to register their complaints against the Pinochet regime (e.g. "No+ Poverty" or "No+ Torture").

This early period of collective art actions and interventions in daily life had a great impact on Eltit's career as a literary writer, with one foot in the art world and another in social and ethnographic experimentation. For instance, in projects like "Zona de dolor" (Zone of Pain, 1980), Eltit cut and burned her arms while reading fragments of her first novel, *Lumpérica* (1983; *E. Luminata,* 1997)[2]—then a work-in-progress—to sex workers in a working-class neighborhood brothel on Maipú street. Other well-known interventions that would find textual homes in her novels and nonfiction projects include interviews with an indigent man

---

2   In this case and all others in this introduction, we have indicated the titles of works that have been translated into English in italics; the titles of works that have not been translated into English appear in plain type.

later called "El Padre Mío," photographs taken by Lotty Rosenfeld, Eltit's collaborator, of the writer kissing a homeless man on the street in Santiago, and other experiences walking through the urban spaces of Santiago in which she observed and interacted with marginal figures such as the elderly, the mentally or physically ill, and sex workers. These projects illuminate the threads of Eltit's literary style, which combine traditional avant-garde experimentation with an incisive anthropological inquiry into the local, marginal, and invisible corners of the social map.

Eltit published her first novel, *Lumpérica*, in 1983. This text is at once a cry of pain, an act of defiance in the face of power, and a brilliant metafictional exercise in literary theory. The novel offers a glimpse into how Eltit's poetic and literary style crystallized during the early moments of neoliberalism's rise under patriarchal, authoritarian rule. Like the majority of Eltit's novels, *Lumpérica* centers on a female protagonist, L. Iluminada, who occupies a public plaza after curfew that is populated by subjects similar to those found in many of her other novels: vagrants, sex workers, beggars, and people of the night. From the functional standpoint of capitalist productivity, these bodies are "useless" as they attempt to escape the purview of an oppressively white light, a Foucauldian panopticon that symbolizes the dictatorship's totalizing and patriarchal gaze, which defines and confines them at every turn. In *Lumpérica*, Eltit uses theatrical and cinematic devices to turn the public plaza into a literary stage on which its protagonists scream, perform, commune, break gender stereotypes, and unleash erotic urges while under the shackles of military power.

In the following years, Eltit published *Por la patria* (For the Fatherland, 1986) and *El cuarto mundo* (The Fourth World, 1988), which continued her reflection on the fractured Chilean individual and social psyche. While *Por la patria*, as Eugenia Brito suggests, "rewrites the fatherland"[3] in a feminine key, rescuing marginalized voices from oblivion, *El cuarto mundo* delves even deeper into a critique of patriarchy by questioning gender constructs and their attendant violence from the very moment of human conception. As is evident in these novels, Eltit's

---

3   Eugenia Brito, *Campos minados (literatura post-golpe en Chile)* (Santiago: Editorial Cuarto Propio, 1990), 141.

work often problematizes what Giorgio Agamben calls "bare life" by sit-
uating the narration within marginal or residual bodies or subjects.[4] For
example, we hear the voice of the indigenous, female protagonist Coya in
Por la patria at the moment of her conception and the voices of the two
fraternal twins who narrate the beginning of *El cuarto mundo* in-utero.
In selecting the female body as the narrative *locus*, Eltit places the dramas of social reproduction at the center of her broader sociological
exploration of neoliberal subjectivity and the nation under dictatorship.

There are marked stylistic differences between the novels Eltit wrote
under dictatorship and those she wrote after the Pinochet regime.
Despite those differences, we find strong critical continuities between
her earlier works and those of the post-dictatorship period (1990-pres-
ent): *Vaca sagrada* (1991; *Sacred Cow*, 1995); *Los vigilantes* (1994; *Custody of the Eyes*, 2005); *Los trabajadores de la muerte* (Death Workers,
1998); *Mano de obra* (Cheap Labor, 2002); *Jamás el fuego nunca* (2007;
Never Again the Fire, 2021); *Impuesto a la carne* (Printed on the Flesh,
2010), *Fuerzas especiales* (Special Forces, 2012); *Sumar* (Sumar, 2018);
and *Falla humana* (Human Fault, 2023). The common denominator
among these works is their multifaceted representation of power: Eltit's
portrayal of neoliberalism and its effects on meaning, community, bodies, gender, and politics. For example, the panopticism of the dictatorial state that looms large in *Lumpérica* becomes even more diffuse in
a novel like *Los vigilantes*, where a woman trapped in a hermetic space,
hungry and cold, directs a series of letters to a patriarchal figure whose
omnipresent gaze she cannot escape. In the novels of the post-dictatorship period, there is no utopian promise of community that might
suggest a change to the status quo, but rather a sinuous and sinister
democratic pact of silence and a commercial anesthesia that sets in to
consolidate a new political order.

Mano de obra illustrates what happens to subaltern bodies under
neoliberal rule, presenting a vision of the worker as a docile body, cowed
into submission by an implacable and repressive labor regime that
enslaves him at the most basic, biological level. *Jamás el fuego nunca*

---

4   See Giorgio Agamben, *State of Exception: Sovereign Power and Bare Life*,
translated by Kevin Attell, (Chicago: The University of Chicago Press, 2005).

takes up the plight of an alienated female protagonist who works in a hostile city and for the first time tackles the failures of leftist orthodox militancy during the Allende years (1970-1973). While *Impuesto a la carne* reflects "aberrant capitalism" through the story of a fictional mother and daughter who are completely dependent on one other as they are subjected to countless surgeries and medical interventions in a hospital,[5] *Los trabajadores de la muerte* deploys popular myth and tragedy to construct a fragmented, confusing, and dark narrative of a murder that occurred in the 1980s in Concepción, when a woman was killed by her half-brother after attempting to end their sexual relationship.[6] *Fuerzas especiales* tells the story of a female sex worker living in Santiago's *bloques de vivienda pública* (public housing projects) where state protections and services don't exist, leaving the protagonist to fend for herself and her family through sex work in a cyber-café. *Sumar* follows the dispossessed, disenfranchised participants in a public demonstration toward La Moneda, the central government building in Santiago, to protest the state's violent, commercial surveillance. And *Falla humana*, in a neo-baroque style and from the vantage point of an all-seeing owl, tells a tragic story of displacement, amnesia, and violence in a marginalized Santiago neighborhood. In a context where individualism and the market reign supreme, these novels elliptically gesture toward a historical moment in which *communitas* had unquestionable political meaning; they expose the pernicious institutionalization of politics (on the left and the right) and search, tirelessly, for creative lines of flight and forms of survival.

While Eltit's novels have garnered significant attention—in 2018 she was awarded the National Prize for Literature by Chile's Ministry of Culture, and in 2021, the Feria Internacional del Libro de Guadalajara (FIL) Prize for Literature in Romance Languages at the thirty-fifth

---

5   Mónica Barrientos, "Cuerpos anarcobarrocos en *Impuesto a la carne* de Diamela Eltit," *Hispamérica* 42, no. 126 (December 2013): 11.

6   For a more detailed description of the relationship between this case and Eltit's novel, see "The Myth of Motherhood in *Los trabajadores de la muerte*" in Mary Green, *Diamela Eltit: Reading the Mother* (Woodbridge: Tamesis, 2007), 133-151.

Book Fair—her cultural production is by no means limited to her fictional writing. In three nonfiction projects, *El Padre Mío* (My Father, 1988), *El infarto del alma* (1994; *Soul's Infarct*, 2009), and *Puño y letra* (In Their Own Words, 2005), readers see Eltit's social and ethnographic interests creatively intertwining with her literary experimentation. While the literal transcription of a vagabond's testimony comprises *El Padre Mío*, *El infarto del alma* draws on Eltit's long-standing collaboration with the Chilean photographer Paz Errázuriz, which led them to spend time with inmates at the psychiatric hospital of Putaendo, Chile. In both projects, Eltit's attention to the complexities of recorded speech and lived testimony provide a multifaceted reflection on the ways in which bodies at the limit—between sense and nonsense, life and death, center and periphery—negotiate power and forge survival and community against all odds. *Puño y letra,* on the other hand, uses the court reporting genre to capture the idiosyncrasies of a legal trial against the accused and later convicted secret police agent Jorge Arancibia Clavel, but focuses on the perspective of his lover, Hugo Zambelli, to critique the judicial system and overall blending of politics and spectacle. In all these projects, Eltit draws upon both the testimonial and ethnographic traditions to present a kind of photographic negative of the Chilean social sphere during and after the dictatorship, commenting on the impunity of official powers and the staging of lies that many victimizers and accomplices perpetuated. In such texts, the literary rubs against the grain of official history to remediate, repair, critique, and restore complexity to historical memory as a narrative process.

Eltit's Essays

While Eltit's novelistic and nonfiction work provides a remarkable and evolving vision of Chile over the past decades, she offers a different vantage point through her prolific and rigorous cultivation of literary essays. Most of the essays in this book come from three collections: *Emergencias: Escritos sobre literatura, arte y política* (Emergenc(i)es: Writings on Literature, Art, and Politics, 2000), *Signos vitales* (Vital Signs, 2007), and more recently, *Réplicas Réplicas*/Replies (Aftershocks, 2016). These are complemented by Eltit's contributions to newspapers, magazines, conferences, and other cultural proceedings. In addition to showcasing her incisive gaze as a reader of the Western literary tradition—with essays that address the work of figures as diverse as Ernest Hemingway, James Joyce, Severo Sarduy, José Donoso, Gabriela Mistral, and Marta Brunet, among others—Eltit's essays also attend to important intellectual contributions in the present, such as Cherie Zalaquett's *Sobrevivir a un fusilamiento* (Surviving a Firing Squad, 2005), a book about the survivors of forced executions for which Eltit wrote the prologue. They also give us a glimpse at the local and transnational dialogues she fostered with important writers, artists, and intellectuals of her time, such as the cultural critic Nelly Richard or the U.S.-American scholars Francine Masiello, Gwen Kirkpatrick, and Mary Louise Pratt. In this sense, Eltit's essays embody the breadth and voraciousness of her work as a literary reader who unflinchingly critiques local and global politics—from the Chilean dictatorship and transition to democracy to the "War on Terrorism," market fanaticism, and continued colonial domination—while also consistently searching for networks of meaning, dialogue, and possibility within the symbolic and material practices of literary, visual, and cultural representation.

This collection allows English-speaking readers to delve into debates about Chilean public life, in which Eltit has been a key participant. Here, we find Eltit's key preoccupations as a writer and intellectual: the neoliberal marketplace (as a way of organizing Chilean public life and as a space for thinking about literary production); the different bodies excluded from those spaces (a diverse group of people including sexual minorities, convicted criminals, indigenous people, women, and the mentally ill); and Chile's *poderes fácticos* (powers-that-be), an intransigent, conservative force historically focused on the accumulation of wealth and the impediment of egalitarianism of any kind. Some of these issues existed long before the dictatorship, and many of them have persisted during and after the country transitioned to democracy: a transition whose promises persist in constant conflict with the realities of inequality, sexism, and other forms of exclusion.

What spaces for resistance exist in this context? For Eltit, the role women must play is key, and, in this regard, English-language readers will find her focus on the imbrication of women's struggle for greater recognition and rights with overarching struggles for democratic egalitarianism quite familiar. Indeed, there are a number of commonalities between the Chilean experience, as Eltit describes it, and those of other countries: the exclusion of rigorous, intellectual women's writing from the literary sphere; the interconnectedness of different forms of social exclusion (of women, of indigenous people, of queer and trans people, of the incarcerated) and the need for solidarity among them; the need to revisit national literary canons to make them more inclusive; and intersectional questions about how women's experience differs depending on their race and class.

Eltit's work has not been translated into English as widely as other Chilean authors such as Nona Fernández, Benjamín Labatut, and Alejandro Zambra—not to mention Isabel Allende and Roberto Bolaño. While this volume is an attempt to remedy this lack, it's also worth asking about the reasons why her work has been less translated. Is it due to the supposed intellectual "difficulty" of her work, an often-floated epithet that—as she points out—is a sexist designation that some (mostly men) have used to marginalize her within the Chilean literary field? Is her work destined to be the exclusive territory of academicians, including the four translators who have rendered it in English here? On the contrary, it is our hope that showcasing Eltit's essays will help English-speaking readers understand the deservedly prominent place she occupies in her country's literary canon, as well as its political and cultural spheres. These translations seek to make Eltit's formidable ideas accessible to English-speaking readers, but they refuse to domesticate the complexities of her writing style.

Translating Eltit

Translating Diamela Eltit's essays presented a complex set of challenges that stem from her work's sophisticated poetics and dense layers of meaning. In the translation process, we discovered constant signifying frictions between the forms of her poetics and the meanings of her words in English. These were, in a way, analogous to how she depicts her own encounter in a marginalized area of Santiago with the vagabond she calls "El Padre Mío." Reflecting on that encounter in "In the Intense Zone of the Other Me," she asks:

> Under which grammar should I organize his words? I wrote his text over and over implementing different nuances: with separating periods or without. I debated about the use of capital letters. I remember that the versions I typed repeated and repeated from a place of microscopic detail, because in some way, that written discourse required a certain visuality, or at least I thought it needed an exact visuality that could allow for the brilliant and captivating flow [. . .]

We grappled with similar questions and debates while engaging Eltit's texts. Within her essays, there were noticeable features of her style, formatting, syntax, and punctuation that we approximated through a variety of approaches to preserve her poetics while still conveying her arguments in English.

Eltit structures her arguments by building layers of analysis. As the scene of each text unfolds one detail at a time, she compels the reader to appreciate the complexities of the issues she meticulously analyzes. While she deftly harnesses the sentence fragment as a consistent element of her syntactic style, we were highly aware of how such a practice chafes against the clear stylistic resolution that the norms of English writing seem to demand. Using fragments to pace arguments, she establishes a captivating rhythm as her points emerge, often landing her claims with a strong left hook. Many of Eltit's pieces have an aural quality in which repetition and rhythm stand out as hallmarks of her style. The English language generally shuns such repetitions, so we weighed at length whether and to what degree we should preserve them in translation. In Eltit's lengthy sentences, antecedents and subjects sometimes get lost in the milieu of syntactic and lexical ruptures, breaking free from the normative chains of academic, literary, and journalistic styles.

Eltit often utilizes correlated semantic fields of words constructed together or juxtaposed against one another, such as *gesto, gesta,* and *gestión,* which can be difficult to convey with the same lyrical quality and equivalent meanings they have in the original Spanish. She uses double entendres frequently—not only in the body of her essays, but also in their titles; this presented an additional hurdle: that of finding suitable English titles without losing the nuance of her clever wordplay. Yet because such linguistic constellations and wordplays are imperative to her work's poetics and literary politics, we were judicious in how closely we relied on English editorial standards in our translations, as we did not want to risk losing the layered, rhythmic unfolding of Eltit's poetic argumentation by excessively editing her style.

Idioms and figures of speech unique to the Chilean dialect appear frequently in Eltit's essays; these, too, are hard to approximate in English without losing cultural specificity. There is also a *Chileanness* to the texture of her work that is difficult to capture, at times requiring footnotes so as not to sacrifice context (though we tried to use footnotes sparingly). Loaded words such as *roto*, *loca*, and even prominent institutions such as *Carabineros* challenged us to find suitable equivalents. We had many lively and enjoyable discussions about how much to add or subtract from the original, which translation strategies were most appropriate to each context, and how to strike a balance among all the elements and connotations in play.

Eltit is known for her shrewd, analytical, and biting critiques communicated in a conversational and direct tone. We preserved the conversational, even oral quality of her writing to the greatest degree possible. However, the content is challenging. It wasn't lost on us that we were four academics translating her work. As a cultural critic, Eltit writes along the periphery of high art, but in an ethical way that takes into account the many spaces and systems of power and oppression that operate around her. She is acutely aware of her privilege and the complexity of her poetics, and she takes care to elevate the subaltern subjects with which her writing is concerned into the same spaces in which her discourse circulates. Eltit reads marginal figures and examines how they subvert dominant codes and signs while still existing within them, all while raising these "others" into the sphere of high theory where their marginalization and its causes are laid out methodically and inexorably. As translators, Eltit's engagement with marginalized subjects made us confront the ethical challenges of rendering her writing in English both as a political opportunity and as a risk. The acclaimed translation studies scholar, Lawrence Venuti, writes that translators have "a choice concerning the degree and direction of the violence at work in [their] practice."[7] We navigated questions about representing inequality, identity, violence, and marginality in Eltit's texts as a team while maintaining awareness of our own positions in relation to the texts and their content, endeavoring to make our process both ethical and self-critical.

Women writers who have been marginalized within the Chilean literary canon are a major theme of Eltit's work. Concentrating on the concept of *género* (gender and genre), both meanings are inseparable in her literary politics. She questions how genres limit genders and how genders limit genres, pointing to the ways in which women writers constantly bump up against a glass ceiling in literary production. Eltit's essays illustrate the arbitrariness of the boundaries between *literary* and *academic* essays and often incorporate stylistic elements of both. At times we struggled to embrace Eltit's experimental style and depart from the standardized academic modes of expression to which we are accustomed. We considered, for example, the use of numbers in both structure and content in "Chalk It Up to Their Circumstances" and discussed whether to preserve the enumeration in the original text's framework or to tailor the translation to a more conventional format. Ultimately, the discomfort we experienced when making such decisions proved just how adept Eltit is at challenging the limits of *género* and of literary convention.

Beyond her experimental style, there is an ethics to Eltit's art that channels her dissatisfaction with the status quo through poignant and well-aimed critiques of Chile's sexism, racism, classism, homophobia, and corruption. Her cynicism, disappointment with the (current and past) state of affairs, concern with the passage of time, and stoicism are characteristics of her work that harken back to the Baroque. In all their "baroqueness," the essays in this book respond to the moments and environments of their production. Readers must therefore understand each essay as a snapshot of a significant moment in the unfolding of Chile's political, social, and cultural history. Taken together, these essays chart evolutions in Eltit's thought, particularly as she looks inward and outward, responding to Chile's cultural milieu over the course of three

---

7   Lawrence Venuti, "Translation as Social Practice: Or, the Violence of Translation," *Translation Perspectives* 9 (1996), 197.

decades. As we commemorate the fiftieth anniversary of the 1973 coup, these timely translations underscore the need for greater interlinguistic accessibility to Eltit's work, whose overarching themes of marginality, authoritarianism, and hegemony stand the test of time and harbor a call to action that has long outlasted the dictatorship.

A Brief Overview

This book is divided into three parts, each of which contains Eltit's essays on art, literature, and politics from the dictatorship years to the present. This structure aims to give readers an idea of Eltit's evolution as a reader, writer, and thinker while also offering insight into how the political and cultural landscapes have changed over several decades. By including within each section texts from a range of historical moments, we hope that readers will see the implicit and explicit threads that underlay Eltit's literary and cultural concerns and sense the connections she draws between past and present—the complex threads that bind history and contemporaneity.

Part 1, "Specters of Dictatorship," contains Eltit's exploration of the effects and afterlives of authoritarian rule in Chile through the lenses of politics and culture. Fourteen essays, originally published between the mid-1990s and the present, reflect on the overall dynamics and key moments within Chile's post-Pinochet transition to democracy (1990-present): the 1973 coup, the saga of the disappeared, the struggles over memory, Pinochet's unexpected detention in London in 1998, and the fallout from the massive protests that have taken place in the country in recent years, particularly the October 2019 *estallido social* (social explosion).

When the dictator Augusto Pinochet relinquished the presidency after being voted out by a narrow margin in the October 1988 plebiscite, Chile began its transition to civilian rule, which was negotiated such that the military would retain significant power and Pinochet would remain a senator-for-life. The country thus became a "protected democracy," a polity chained to a neoliberal economy that was inspired by the "Chicago Boys," who preached and inflicted a largely unfettered free-market model that for years was nurtured by the Center-left governing coalition that followed the dictatorship: the Concertación de Partidos por la Democracia (Coalition of Parties for Democracy). Despite myriad measures taken by the transition governments to attenuate poverty—and despite conservative celebrations of Chile's economic prowess on the world stage—no government since Pinochet has managed to change the fact that Chile remains one of the most socioeconomically unequal countries in the world. As a result, citizens have taken to the streets to protest realities such as the privatization of education (in 2006 and 2011); discrimination against women, sexual minorities, and indigenous peoples (in many moments); and the neoliberal model as a whole (in 2019). Today, Pinochet's constitution—the Constitution of 1980—is under fire, and the country is engaged in a contentious process that seeks to replace it. To be sure, the quest to safeguard the human rights of underrepresented groups and stem inequality will continue to be an uphill battle. This is true for several reasons, among them that the dictator died in impunity despite being arrested in 1998 in London, that conservative factions still hold great political and economic sway, and that the neoliberal model remains intact.

Acutely attuned to this context, Eltit's essays confront us with the untamed "specters of dictatorship" that the transition has not managed to keep at bay. These specters emerge in her memory and critical thought and form the basis of her sustained and incisive analysis of Chile's political and cultural scene. Eltit, for example, reads the violent theatricality of the September 11, 1973, military coup ("Two Sides of La Moneda"), blending her memories of that day with a biting critique of the neoliberal model that, along with the fallout from the dictatorship's massive and systematic human rights violations, has been the regime's greatest legacy. In later texts such as "Screen Memories: On Public Images and the Politics of Disremembering," written around the time of the thirtieth anniversary of the coup (2003), she returns to the unfinished business of memory and acerbically critiques the Chilean media for whitewashing the past, commodifying it, and ignoring the real specters with which Chile still must reckon. In "Twist and Turns, Riots and Returns," she hones in on the symbolism of the first government of Michelle Bachelet (2006-2010) to signal the promise, drama, and even disappointment that came with the historic moment of Chile's

election of its first woman president. In a way, we might say that the figure of Bachelet herself evokes the specters of dictatorship: the daughter
of a Chilean Air Force general killed by the Pinochet regime, she spent
time in political prison, later rose to become Minister of Defense, and
even won her second term as president (2014-2018) by running against
Evelyn Matthei, the daughter of Fernando Matthei, who led the Air
Force at the time Bachelet's father was killed. As she evokes the dictatorship's specters, Eltit not only zeroes in on the protests that happened
in the streets at many junctures throughout the dictatorship and transition, including during Bachelet's governments—protests by families
of the disappeared or by citizens demanding greater degrees of equality
and rights—but also on the protests staged by artists and intellectuals
such as those of Colectivo de Acciones de Arte (CADA), to which Eltit
belonged in the 1980s. In "CADA 20 Years," she explains how, in fact,
the art actions collective in which she participated played a key role
in creating and disseminating the public language of "No+" (no more,
never again) that would eventually take hold in society and serve as a
tool to topple the regime.

We should note that the sections of this book are not closed thematic systems. On the contrary, Eltit's cross-cutting reflections on the
specters of dictatorship in Part 1 dialogue closely with topics that take
center stage in Parts 2 and 3. "Nomadic Bodies," for example, asks
complex, ethically challenging questions about how power operates on
and through the bodies of female, leftist militants who became traitors
and collaborators during the Pinochet regime. A similar set of questions about bodies, power, and marginality resurfaces in other essays,
though explored in nuanced ways and in different contexts. Likewise,
the theme of "Communities," which is the focus of Part 3, comes to the
fore in Eltit's memories of her early collaborations with other artists and
intellectuals through the interdisciplinary work of CADA.

In Part 2, "Bodies, Gender, and Power," Eltit offers an extended
exploration of the idea of "women's writing": Is it a biologically deterministic category, or should it be maintained as a useful organizational
rubric? Is "gender" a better way of organizing Chile's literary habitus of
difference, or does it undercut the specificity of women's artistic production? The essay "On the Work of Literature," in this sense, asks a
series of questions not just about what it means for women to write, but

also about how to create socially committed writing within the specific context of Latin America, where access to the written word is itself a mark of elitism. An assiduous reader of Bourdieu and Foucault, Eltit points out how the literary field creates these labels only to ghettoize Latin American women and limit their position as writers.

To be sure, Eltit's critique of the literary market is part of a larger economic analysis, which is another key aspect of Part 2. Her understanding of Chile's neoliberal regime, which took shape in the 1980s just as she began to gain visibility as a writer, is inseparable from her approach to gender and literary production. The market's focus on accumulation—of profits, of products, and of the bodies that serve as its raw material—often leads to forms of expression that fall into easy, schematic clichés of romanticism, especially where women's writing is concerned. Eltit unceasingly advocates for a different kind of writing: one that is complex and nuanced and that doesn't restrict women's freedom of expression and movement. "Telling It Like She Sees It," for example, whose paragraphs are numbered to maintain the spirit of the essay's original title, "Contante y sonante"—suggestive not just of the economic reality of counting "cold hard cash" but also of the importance of speaking and making oneself heard—focuses on the difficulties working women (writers or otherwise) experience when seeking to make a space for themselves in a world where they're consistently paid less for the same work that men do.

Responding to critics who have branded her work as excessively "difficult," due to her often-coded, allegorical language, Eltit points out the underlying sexism of that tired critique. Indeed, she shows how Chile's literary field has long been sexist—in two essays she brings up Hernán Díaz Arrieta, also known as Alone, who for decades was Chile's chief literary critic—and points to the fact that when men write in a difficult style, they're often seen as groundbreaking intellectuals. "Women, Boundaries, and Crime" examines the conditions of production surrounding Alone's boosterism of María Carolina Geel's *Cárcel de mujeres* (Women's Prison, 1956), in whose prologue Alone practically took credit for the novel's existence. Meanwhile, in "Wandering around among Signs," Eltit points out that Alone's highest praise for Marta Brunet's *María Nadie* (Maria Nobody, 1957) was that she "wrote like a man." Eltit perceives the continuity between the reception of Geel's and Brunet's work and that of her own: on the page and in life, women's actions and words continue to be "cast into doubt," as she writes in "Errant, Erratic."

Eltit responds to this sexism by taking a revisionist approach to Chile's literary canon, with essays about the works of lesser-known women writers, such as Geel, Rosario Orrego, Mariana Cox Stuven, and Eugenia Brito, as well as more established ones like Gabriela Mistral and Brunet. Her aim is to reformulate how women's writing is understood in Chile, to broaden its scope and reclaim words like "passion," "gesture," and "dilemma"—often used in the context of *novelas rosas*, the genre most stereotypically associated with femininity—which point toward an intellectually rigorous, complex form of female expression.

Eltit also shows interest in the contributions of women beyond Chile's literary sphere, such as Camila Vallejo (in "Camila Vallejo: Mission Accomplished"), Elena Caffarena (in "Gender, Genre, and Pain"), and Natividad Llanquileo (in "The Mapuche on Trial in Cañete"). Like these women, Eltit wants to deepen Chile's democratic sphere and make it more inclusive. In this sense, she affirms—as did Julieta Kirkwood and Caffarena before her—that women's rights are inseparable from democratic progress in Chile overall.

Part 3, "Communities," is best encapsulated by Eltit's own assertion from this collection's final essay: "Contact with others is what matters most to me." As such, this section features the writer's extensive reflections on her collaborative projects, starting with a discussion of her early days participating in CADA and touching upon her longtime collaborative relationships, primarily with Rosenfeld and Errázuriz. Not only does Eltit describe collective work as necessary for evading censorship during the early years of dictatorship, but collaboration later emerges as one of the pillars of Eltit's practice of literary writing. In several essays, the writer cites trust, camaraderie, and the politicized intellectual exchange she experienced while developing projects such as *El padre mío* or *El infarto del alma* ("In the Intense Zone of the Other Me"). With a particularly triumphant tone, she also discusses the consolidation of long-term collaborations with other female writers, artists, and intellectuals as an astounding accomplishment given the highly individualistic nature of the literary market. In "Co(labor)ation," for instance, she expands upon how collaborative work is received with bewilderment by readers or spectators who try to classify or categorize authorship, unable to embrace the work's defiance of individualistic cultural and editorial standards. She also acknowledges the effects and experiences of women collaborators: on the one hand, she sees collaboration as a form of resistance to the competition and envy typically ascribed to the feminine ("Ethics, Aesthetics, and Politics"), while on the other hand, she recognizes that collaboration becomes "naturalized" when it comes to women, whose contributions are seen as "secondary" to the patriarchal politics defined and controlled by men. In this sense, collaboration can be seen as a form of resistance to dominant forms of cultural labor, though it is also inevitably shaped by the politics of individualism and competition it seeks to resist.

Part 3 also looks beyond direct collaboration to the less tangible forms in which Eltit forges community with other cultural, political, and literary histories. The collection showcases her keen reading, writing, and citational practices of the work of her direct collaborators—Paz Errázuriz ("Gazing through the Cracks" and "Chalk It Up to Their Circumstances"), Nelly Richard ("Nelly Richard: Locations and Dislocations'"), and Francine Masiello ("Ethics, Aesthetics, and Politics")—while also uplifting her extensive appraisal of her contemporaries: cultural agents, such as the Chilean painter Juan Domingo Dávila ("Too Bad You're a *Rota*") and the Chilean writer Pedro Lemebel ("The Queen of the Block"). In her readings, she pays attention to how Dávila unravels visual cues to problematize the social meanings associated with the *roto*—a paradoxically celebrated and abused figure of Chilean popular culture—just as she skillfully deconstructs Lemebel's neo-baroque poetics, which offer a sonic and literary critique of the policing, performance, and proliferation of masculinities during Chile's transition to democracy. Beyond Chile, Eltit's sharp skills as a reader can also be seen in her approach to the work of the Marxist critic Rosa Luxemburg, whose love letters emphasize the vital connections between sentimentality and politics that Eltit consistently underscores. In this sense, the essays in Part 3 highlight Eltit's attention to community through her commitment to maintaining direct and indirect dialogues with contemporary, historical, cultural, and social others.

Throughout the different sections of this book, Eltit's attention to community consistently emerges from an ambivalent and paradoxical territory: within the literal and figurative margins, she seeks forms of radical alterity that are capable of reframing difference and reimagining belonging against the grain of neoliberalism's individualism, consensus, and exclusivity. In "At the Edge of the Written Word," Eltit reviews the Chilean novelist Carlos Droguett's *Patas de perro* (Dog Feet, 1968), focusing her analysis on the novel's protagonist, Bobi, who is half-boy and half-dog. Eltit finds remarkable value in Droguett's literary gesture of capturing a problematic, ambivalent, defiant figure like Bobi—a social, moral, and physical aberration—within the culturally coveted space of the novel, characterized by its own forms of consensus and erasure. Whether in her attention to women's forced nudity in the psychiatric hospital or to *santería* ceremonies in the Bronx, Eltit's interests lie in community not as a cliché or fetish, but as a radical form of politics—an "astonishing [mode] of carrying out a contaminated, cultural resistance" ("Latin Scenes in New York")—whereby creativity, survival, and resistance endure despite all of our rational expectations and against all odds.

PART I

Specters of Dictatorship

Two Sides of La Moneda

I ask myself: How can we talk about Chilean political history when that history is at once personal and embodied? And how can we do so without becoming entranced by testimony's vertigo or the predictable exercise of taking an "intelligent" or distanced look at events that live on chaotically—without beginning or end—in memory and whose traces linger in a kind of transversal timelessness, regularly and noticeably assaulting our senses? I think about how to talk about this as someone who doesn't come from a background in the social sciences or politics or from a specific discipline that painstakingly examines political events and the connections among them. From where I sit within the realm of literature, I think that perhaps the key to approaching that history, a history marked by the events that took place in Chile on September 11, 1973, may lie within the word *golpe*.

I say *golpe* in the multiple senses that the word evokes within each individual's psyche, with the varied resonances that the word takes on within each subject's inner life. I say *golpe* thinking, for example, about a scar—or a hematoma—or a fracture—or a mutilation. I say *golpe* as the fissure between one time and another—as a surprise, an accident, an assault—as pain—as an aggressive game, as a symptom. *El golpe*, the prominent and recurring childhood landscape whose repetition takes the form of falling or being attacked, is perhaps the primordial memory. It is the first habit the flesh internalizes, just as the body emerges materially as a body or differentiates itself from another body—the other: that worthy opponent cast as the enemy from the very moment the *golpe* occurred.

If we take *golpe* to mean the coup d'état—the event itself, a form of politics meant to settle the score between two different political paths—then it means, in one way or another, going back to that first moment, going back to the initial impulses, the first fears, even harkening back to the moments in which uncontrollable rage first erupted.

Undoubtedly, the September 11th coup did not affect all of civil society in the same way. Those with symbolic, political, or economic links to the military celebrated it. I'm talking about those with links to the armies of tin soldiers who, enacting their well-studied wartime epic, detonated the process of halting a political project out-of-sync with their own, and who, in response, set out to create a violently authoritarian system. When I think about that system now, I can't help but associate it (I repeat)—beyond the many meanings it may have—with tyrannical children, with a kind of power that sought to become absolute and that spread its desire to bring order to reality—including civil society—with meticulous military precision that bordered on insanity.

They staged an incessant, multi-pronged attack on difference. The surgical split between us and them, pure and impure, patriots and extremists, unleashed a monotonous and sustained binary that disciplined bodies. The body, as a site of politics, became a tragic and exemplary site of discipline—a primitive territory of torture, crime, and disappearance.

I want to return to September 11th and its overwhelming staging: the inaugural moment marked by signs that would proliferate over the next seventeen years.

On that day, the soldiers with their medal-laden uniforms, their sooty faces, their weapons poised to attack, became the definitive embodiment of a wartime atmosphere that seemed smack out of a Hollywood movie that had been abruptly transposed to the neutral and delineated city of Santiago. The image of the soldier armed to the teeth, volatilely scanning the landscape through his rifle scope to hunt the enemy, mirrored and reinforced the rigid, numbered military decrees. Within that maniacal, endless order, the decrees notified the population of one order after another that they'd have to follow. Aside from the emphatic voices and the decrees transmitted on the radio, outside, soldiers patrolled the cities' streets vigilantly: in attack mode, mounted on tanks and trucks, with poses that made it impossible to measure the (cinematic) projection of their real desire to eliminate any "enemy" that crossed their path.

President Salvador Allende's voice could be heard, amid some interference, on two radio stations that had yet to be seized. Those stations transmitted what would become his final broadcast from the presidential palace. That speech—beyond its dramatic character as a historical document—called upon the workers, invoked the future of democracy, and asked for calm resistance. Amid the prudence that Allende asked of his supporters, one could perceive the depressive gestures and deflated tone of a leader faced with a coup d'état that by that time he—and all of us—knew had become unstoppable.

Beyond the military decrees and the soldiers, there was the imminent bombing of La Moneda, located in the very heart of the city: the government seat against which the war planes would launch their missiles. The military would drop their bombs right downtown with the goal of ousting President Allende definitively—and of ousting along with him a swath of democratic history that, as the military would soon assert, should be understood as a "Marxist cancer" to eradicate.

And beyond the military decrees, the soldiers, and the imminent bombing of La Moneda, which they said would happen at noon, an undetermined number of planes flew at low altitudes over the city. The sound of those planes was maddening; it seemed as if at any moment they might crash into the roof of *some* house (*my* house, my *neighbor's* house)—how can I explain it?—*every* house.

Then there were the gunshots. Intermittent rounds from machine guns started forming part of the city's soundscape—from the air and on land. In the coastal cities—by air, land, and sea—the armed forces touted their spectacular power, which unfurled to conquer the enemy hidden in every corner, in every crevice, and in every hiding spot throughout the country. Little by little—as a result of the planes flying overhead, the machine gun fire, the warning before the bombs, and the sooty faces—that enemy began to take root in a little part of all of our minds, in the minds of each of us who was horrified by what was happening. Amid that horror and pain, we had already turned symbolically into the very extremist enemy they were hunting: the extremist enemy who had destroyed the impeccable and legendary Chilean order, the enemy who had to be eliminated to restore the contaminated nation to its original purity.

That September 11th, even before the bombing at noon, the mise en scène had already taken shape through many signs around the city: a war-like atmosphere became an unavoidable montage. Fascism—which before could only be found in small-scale situations—became concrete, pervasive, and encrusted in a city full of new signs that proclaimed a re-founding of the nation: an obligatory and selective re-founding whose messianic enterprise required staring at bodies and dissecting them under the military's microscope.

By noon, La Moneda was literally burning on all four sides; the bombing had been consummated, and the government palace was aglow with flames. The new regime was founded on that burning spectacle; it superimposed itself on the scene. It would continue transmitting radio decrees: sober proclamations not meant to inform the people but rather to notify them of the successive measures and actions being taken to fight a battle that had already been won. Emphatic and—why not say it—grating military anthems cut off all radio broadcasts to stage a patriotic atmosphere layered atop the coup's irreversible immutability.

Television channels incessantly broadcast cartoons, which can't be read naively in the context of consolidating extreme authoritarianism. They blocked information tragicomically. Donald Duck and friends invaded our screens. In that sense, cartoons became the official images of the regime's early hours. Under the pretext of distracting kids, the regime simultaneously revealed a pedagogy—an ironic will to infantilize the population—and gave a glimpse of the hierarchical gaze that the newly emerging powers harbored. They willed to keep civil society under a state of control and infantile dependency, subjected to those cartoon avatars whose distorted voices spewed edifying morals at the end of each episode.

In those early hours, the military declared martial law. The city was emptied of all bodies that weren't military bodies. Any nonmilitary body could be murdered because it was already prohibited to move about the city. The city was divested of its public character and became instead a field of landmines. The state of siege opened a new fissure that, over seventeen years, would persist with varying degrees of intensity: dividing and segregating by radically altering how bodies inhabited public and private spaces, the inside and the outside, safety and danger.

We couldn't occupy the streets. Yet, even more importantly, we couldn't move freely outside at all because the outside no longer belonged to us; it had become stripped of its communitarian face. The outside became an outlawed territory left to our imaginations, which in those circumstances, could envision nothing other than the imaginary of blood and war.

Sometime later that afternoon, the cartoons were replaced briefly by objective and distanced information communicating that President Salvador Allende was dead, that he'd committed suicide inside La Moneda palace. It was scant information, transmitted with palpable indifference and meant to politicize the new hegemony and present military rule as dominant and impenetrable.

TV replaced radio and became the mouthpiece, in between cartoons, for the new Military Junta's decrees. The decrees ordered people to turn in their weapons. They called on Popular Unity's political leaders to surrender at specific military locations, and they summoned the population to denounce extremism patriotically. Extremism was a word that acquired an extensive, generic connotation: in a matter of hours, it would become forcefully and malevolently cemented within the new national lexicon.

By that afternoon, the solemn national anthem burst onto our television screens and interrupted the feverish flow of events. The anthem provided a framework in which the Junta, for the first time, could address the same nation that it had already been governing, tacitly, since the early morning hours. Like in a suspense movie whose architecture is carefully constructed, uniformed men from the military's four branches appeared in front of the TV cameras, seated behind a bombastic table, to deliver the new government's inaugural message.

For some of us, it was the first time that we'd publicly seen a face that, from that moment onward, would never go away—that of General Pinochet, who would lead the new Junta. He was hidden behind dark sunglasses that concealed the direction of his gaze: an impossible gaze to detect behind those shades, which served as another kind of shield. He and the Junta blessed a new, rigid atmosphere and legitimized it through a new, public language that mirrored the military's decrees: identical in its abysmal austerity, its imposing tone, its dry and obstructionist wording. That language spewed from the deadpan face of someone who seemed like an archaic father, a man whose convincing, angry theatricality seemed resigned to take any measure necessary to prove the omnipotence of his patriarchal power.

The bodies of the soldiers who carried out the coup seemed, in the waning hours of that afternoon, like the final element needed to round out the scene: the mise-en-scène of a political performance that would play on for the next seventeen years. There they were, seated behind an official table: four uniformed men spinning their choppy and confusing discourse, calling for an end to political parties—an end to practically everything—to pave the way for a new era: the era of order. All this took place in the waning moments of one of the most decisive and chaotic days of the century in Chile.

Once the military had taken control, televised images of the four heads of the armed forces were thrust into people's homes. The military had seized public spaces by systematically inculcating fear into citizens and by relegating civil society to the domestic sphere—to spaces that were, in fact, doubly domesticated because the state of siege imposed a strict curfew and the military had suspended all civil rights.

In those hours, outside spaces turned foreign and clandestine because the radically occupied city proffered signs of death. Many women and men were detained throughout the country and taken to military facilities or sports stadiums. A considerable number of men were executed while the coup was happening. More than one person died inside their home from stray bullets fired haphazardly by compulsive, perverse soldiers who later faded into complete anonymity. We knew about those deaths because, even though there was no news media, the charged atmosphere of those hours encoded the news within its very syntax.

A precipitous, violent learning process swiftly altered the signs of culture. Alongside signs of a culture of death, a parallel culture of survival emerged. To survive in that environment, we had to learn to read signs differently if we were ever to move beyond mere survival and manage to live amid powers adverse to those of us who had been raised in an anti-dictatorial context.

To read those new signs meant lucidly internalizing events as they were happening. It meant being able to analyze military power—which was allied with an important civilian apparatus and even with international forces—as an explosion of incalculable proportions that ran contrary to all logic. It meant reading, amid that boundless and seemingly unjustifiable explosion of power, how the military mounted its (political) discourse to sustain outrage and legitimize it through twisted rhetoric.

Later, over the course of seventeen years, interpreting those new signs meant inhabiting, reading, and rereading the meanings of centralized power; it meant never forgetting the historical relationships among bodies, power, and defenselessness. It meant staying attentive to the fact that behind the enslavement of bodies lurked an unspoken economic desire, a savage form of reorganizing capital. This was about powerful people clawing back wealth at the expense of emaciated bodies—especially the bodies of popular subjects pushed to the limits of poverty, abused in unbelievable torture sessions, and subjected to endless mental humiliation.

The scene of September 11th was, above all, a scene ornamented, sooted, and bedecked with patriotic values that, in fact, only sought to implant radical capitalism camouflaged behind stereotypical discourses. Those discourses incessantly cited the fatherland, order, and the integrity of the Chilean family, while clandestine detention centers and mass firings of workers who opposed the system proliferated. TV programs called for people to denounce their comrades as a gesture of patriotic valor. The "we" (the civilian-military alliance) became pitted against the "others": the enemies apparently *out to get them* by who knows what means.

The only visible discursive axes were the binary construction of "us" versus "them"—a purposeful equation that sought to detonate a hidden agenda: to progressively dismantle the state through a persistent, refined, and complex operation against a civilian population unable to muster any gesture of opposition. Behind the repression, behind the terrible human rights crisis, lurked an unbridled adherence to liberalism that would ensure the dismantling of the state and become at once victory, truth, and essential dogma.

Given that Chile gloriously persists today in an economic arrangement theoretically underpinned by a kind of relativism that makes it possible to buy and sell—and to buy and sell some more—and to have the right (that is, the *obligation* and *duty*) to take on debt (a clear manifestation of pseudodemocracy), it remains important to remember that on September 11th the (historic, hysterical) bombing of La Moneda took place. The bombing of *that* Moneda: the other one.

(1997)

Translated by Michael J. Lazzara

1974

On March 28, 1974, Santiago Avilés, a painter, and Nicolás Flores, an upholsterer's assistant, were found dead in an irrigation ditch, riddled with bullets after being detained in a raid on the Quinta Bella shantytown.

A host of unending abuses became institutionalized, precisely that year.

1974 unfolded in a blur, in an immovable way, as if the landscape had become petrified and the only perceivable movement was of bodies. No, not of bodies—of legs surreptitiously trying to make their way toward a new reality. That dismal year, the year of the Buenos Aires car bombing, ushered in a deliberate and systematic period of torture, bullets, murders, people being fired from their jobs, disappearances, and new rules.

Yet it was also a glorious year for many Chileans who gushed over Pinochet's directness (his threatening and coarse lexicon). It was a more-than-extraordinary year for the civilians who collaborated with the government. Oh, the impressive impunity of those civilians! Their profitable subservience to Pinochet!

We called that cruel puppet a Pinocchio, the protagonist of a terrifying story.

That infamous (and twisted) year we lived quarantined, carving out space in our minds to resist the dea(r)th. All the while, the corner shopkeeper was happy—happy with his array of merchandise, his prices, the position of his shelves, his clients' neutrality, the superficial peace that encased his street corner. His shop was run-of-the-mill, like you would find on any street corner, teeming with fascist jubilation (and rigid exaltation of the patriotic order); it was part of a present perched upon a disgraceful State of Exception.

The year the bomb went off in Buenos Aires was when we stopped speaking. We talked, but we didn't say anything.

Many had left, and others were still leaving. Carlos, my childhood friend, was already in Paris. In Paris! People kept leaving and, in a move that could be considered unjust, we started to resent them in our minds. The displaced threads of exile wove resentment onto a map we'd never before imagined. The forced displacement of people beyond a bare-ly-imagined border started to demarcate an all-too-decisive scene: in reality, a sharp and irreversible division was forming between those who stayed and those who left.

Many of us vaguely understood that our bodies were destined only to amplify what was happening on the inside. We stayed, we persisted, we were nameless. Disgraced and deprived of epic recognition, we were a confused mass of people prepared only to endure.

That year, Jaime Guzmán, with his puny physique and his ultra-right-wing, Catholic soul, finished drafting the Declaration of Princi-ples. Pinochet, failing to hide his perverse satisfaction, would declare himself Supreme Chief of the Nation.

Yes, Supreme Chief of the Nation. It was almost unbelievable. In a rewriting of the most pedestrian history of tyranny, he re-dedicated the building that housed the military junta by inscribing the dates 1810-1973. He and the regime proclaimed that the nation had been founded anew, and in that way they demarcated the birth of the Second Republic: the Military Republic.

That year, a rigid imaginary lent itself to a painful, patriotic farce. With the most perfect anachronism, those in power inflicted a basic military pedagogy. Yet that simplistic totalitarian education covered up a sordid backroom deal because, in 1974, DINA (Dirección de Inteli-gencia Nacional, or National Intelligence Directorate, the dictatorship's secret police force) would become more than just recognized. Yes, in that unnamable year, in a radical move, DINA won its autonomy and received funding to do its dirty work.

Manuel Contreras—the military officer who made our already-in-firm landscape even more vile and whose name is now unavoidable—began to assert himself as a figure who would secure his place forever in the darkest annals of history.

A web of acolytes paid by the State (protected, legitimized, and listed on the rosters) would play out all their destructive fantasies. They acted and overacted. They delighted in the bodies they captured, subjecting them to the cruelest of tortures, until they decimated those bodies and minds.

Abjection met its match in El Guatón Romo, one of the dictatorship's most notorious torturers. What didn't he do? What didn't he do? Or rather, we should say: "What didn't *they* do?" Because every one of those acolytes, most of them from the military, made sure they inflicted the most maniacal forms of violence. And they enjoyed it.

(I'm convinced of that—that they enjoyed it. They enjoyed the planning, the destructive sessions, and the basic feeling of absolute domination they achieved.)

That year, thanks to DINA's institutionalization, a scientific program of annihilation began that was nothing if not efficient. The initial period of spontaneous repressive actions came to an end. Bodies would now be carefully watched, militarily diagrammed, and technically conquered.

Behind the scenes, deep in the marrow of the State of Exception, they orchestrated a scenario that would become the future norm. No longer would a border divide the legitimate from the illegitimate. That border didn't exist because, right there in the heart of the State, any "exceptional" tactic of annihilation would be valid.

(Today, the totalitarian reality of 1974 seems shocking or impossible to me. It seems like—how should I say it—an uninhabitable nightmare.)

They gutted the public apparatus amid overwhelming, senseless, and protracted unemployment that had no end in sight. More and more officials bloated the state bureaucracy by occupying public offices. Those officials, supported by high-level functionaries appointed by the system, grabbed hold of civilian spaces the only way they knew how: by wielding military power. It was that same power that operated in the barracks, that same power that in that year shot through civilian institutions and turned them into spaces teetering between embarrassment (because of the idiotic orders the bureaucrats issued) and the creation of a scene more extreme than anything that the masterful aesthetic experience of Franz Kafka could have foretold.

Nineteen seventy-four was perhaps the most pedagogical year. It was the year in which we really learned. Our bodies became completely subjected to the new order. We understood that from that point forward we'd be living at the limits of duplicity, on a never-ending razor's edge with no solid ground. Bodies would have to circulate along that movable edge, or more accurately, on the appearance of an edge—because underneath that edge (which could be modified or frozen on a whim) there lay another cruel and duplicitous reality full of death and pain.

We moved through public spaces with neutral, unchanging expressions. Many of us knew what was happening. We understood that we were becoming a passive part of the landscape. Faced with that knowledge, to feign apathy was our only weapon—though we knew that our outward neutrality would be a double-edged sword because the regime would reinforce its cruelty in (or upon) our apparent apathy. On the other hand, that same apathy became our tool: the only political recourse we had that year.

(I'm talking about holding back our emotions. I'm talking about radically relinquishing any inkling of citizenship.)

Relinquishing it: I mean that we didn't express anything, when, starting in 1974, the Program of Minimum Employment (known by its Spanish-language acronym PEM) took root and the streets filled with men and women pushing rocks from one place to another. Yes, enormous rocks. And the pay they received—as the authorities stipulated—equaled one-third of the minimum wage. All the while, the workers, chained and enslaved to a kind of genocidal salary, were "rebuilding"—or so the authorities proclaimed—the Chile that today fills us all with pride.

(At that exact cost: a third of the minimum wage.)

What anger it caused to gaze upon those opaque, taciturn, humiliated workers on display in the street with their emaciated bodies—so humiliated they wouldn't lift their gaze from the rocks—because, by 1974, the social project had been completely subjugated. The PEM arrived to reinforce the punishment the regime had been inflicting on the working class and to emblazon upon our retinas (my retina) both the shame that stemmed from those proletarian bodies' cruel fate and the terrible conviction that, when faced with forced labor, we all had to acquiesce.

Contaminated from top to bottom by violence, we forced ourselves to survive by inhabiting that violence. But we also gravely attacked our own political being. In that precise year, we had to learn to crush the strong sense of dignity our education had instilled in us.

We learned to destroy ourselves. We were an enormous contingent wandering through the city; traversing public spaces; dealing with traitors; fading into the woodwork; fighting to survive economically; desperately seeking to turn ourselves into insignificant, gray beings because we consumed within ourselves—in some material piece of ourselves—the wrath and pain.

(. . . Consumed it in a piece that's still there. My chronic body, from that year forward, could never be cured. I carry the scar that hides the moral wound that cut irrevocably through my soul.)

In that year, 1974, we were forced to forget the rituals of a past in which thought was possible: to forget that the streets belonged to us, to forget important words that could incriminate us, to forget the aesthetics that organized us, to forget every millimeter of rebellion. It was a desperate and tragic task, but nonetheless urgent. The streets became foreign; words, forms, rebellion all disappeared from the horizon as if they had never existed. It seems impossible, doesn't it?

In 1974, emblematic leaders were murdered; they, too, would become part of an amnesiac process charging toward a violent and cruel objective. That year, the fate of MIR, the Leftist Revolutionary Movement (Movimiento de Izquierda Revolucionaria), was sealed. With Miguel Enríquez's implacable death in a Santiago neighborhood, the members of DINA, an organization that had been established and funded via Decree 521, boasted with a pride that could only seem repugnant when compared to the resistance exhibited by the outnumbered leader of MIR.

Yes, 1974: the same year that the bomb went off that would do away with General Carlos Prats and his wife, Sofía Cuthbert, whose body was savagely mutilated.

(Only modesty keeps me from describing the effects the bomb had on Sofía Cuthbert.)

It happened right in the middle of the capital of a neighboring country and, still, it seemed so far away to us, so distant. And so it was, because in 1974 our opaque and painful reality had fully taken shape.

(2005)

Translated by Michael J. Lazzara

CADA 20 Years

Just as rereading certain texts provides new meanings to the reader's present, or the detailed observation of an old photograph brings about a sudden understanding of an almost-lost event, rethinking an artistic activity after 20 years is thrilling. This is especially so when the closest thing to that past could be sketching an ever-changing version of artistic acts that remain halfway between memory and forgetting and are activated by an inalienable political passion. Thus, I do not intend to establish a narrative thread here that points to a "truth," but I want to weave certain threads from the past into a flexible and provisional tapestry.

Twenty years have passed since the eruption of CADA onto the public stage. When I speak of a public stage, it is simply a figure of speech, or a mere reference. In reality, 20 years ago, an attempt was made to build a stage similar to what today would be called a microspace: a place that was going to be erected in a fragmented way, like other precarious gestures of resistance, while the most intense and bloody times of the military dictatorship continued on.

In my case, recalling the emergence of CADA (Colectivo Acciones de Arte) in 1979 can acquire extremely testimonial overtones. Having been a member of an art group that left behind a series of materials that remain unofficial, that lack of official recognition constitutes (it must be said) a risk, a merit, a dearth, an enigma, and a problem, among other things. But at the same time, it can allow us to critically read sociocultural signs of the transition to democracy's hegemonic discourse. Of course, it is an arbitrary critical exercise to put into circulation something that comes out of a stubborn vocation to commemorate.

In Chile we already understand that the act of memorizing, of detailing, of agitating the times becomes ridden with conflict when we search in the furrows of the past for ways to interpret the cultural knots of the present.

On the one hand, the current system (*so* bourgeois, *so* appeasing, *so* blinded by fear), prevents us from seriously and systematically entering into historical memory in a complete and sustained manner, since this blockade legitimizes the existence of political forces that require forgetting to guarantee the viability of the present. On the other hand, on the margins of the ruling party, writing about memory constantly needs to rebuild and reassemble its resources due to the multiple difficulties that beset it. The expense of the expression, the expression we expend, are some of the difficulties. So is the use and abuse of a certain rhetoric that turns memory into a mere aesthetic resource, an intellectual game, a fetishization that gradually gets separated from its particular historical context. The writing of memory can thus become yet another possible cultural market, that is to say, a writing that can be narcissistically captivated by its own peculiarities.

If CADA were desired as the mise-en-scène of multiple kinds of politics, and if it had begun as the result of a radical aversion during an equally radical dictatorship, it would be necessary to explore some of the gestures that defined it. I mean that they defined a group that proposed a cultural strategy that was none other than the production of an analysis of the rejection of rejection: an aesthetic symptom that revealed the dimension of discomfort and a sign produced to demarcate the clear contours of resentment; delimiting uncomfortable, but always provocative, places for establishing work that was also intended to be critical and unstable amid these critical subjectivities.

Discomfort, resentment, aversion, and rejection of rejection are the places most stigmatized by a present that (mis)understands plurality as a haven of diversity. These aspects should coexist without making their tensions explicit: flowing in the midst of a territorial paradise capable of turning differences and even disagreements into parallel forces without the slightest possibility of confrontation about the structures that make them irreducible to each other.

Raúl Zurita, Lotty Rosenfeld, Juan Castillo, Fernando Balcells, and myself formed CADA in 1979 in a perhaps impulsive act, somewhat unaware of what was to become an impossible-to-define artistic experience. Its theoretical apparatus developed hesitantly, sustained especially in the interdisciplinary encounter of creative forms whose only border was established by the urgency of the national political situation.

Rather than creating a detailed theoretical debate, the group focused on doing, making, and convening.

Luz Donoso,* Pedro Millar, Hernán Parada, Patricia Saavedra, and Paz Errázuriz, among numerous other artists, joined the call of CADA to establish themselves as crucial members who performed politics in the city or, perhaps, micro-politics of the city.

CADA sought to turn the city into a metaphor. It materialized the city's hunger through successive gestures, that is, the imperative to create a new circulation whose flows would displace the cruel, persistent militarism that controlled citizens' bodies: bodies that were repressed or overwhelmed by the violent sociopolitical apparatuses with which the Chilean dictatorship tested its limits.

Today I think that CADA's work was dedicated to establishing a cultural production that unceasingly, passionately expressed discontent, criticism, and open dissent: not only concerning the reality of dictatorship, but also in terms of other artistic practices. Some of the topics that marked its brief course included the idea of the street in opposition to the museum, reproduction versus the unique object, the relevance of the popular subject in opposition to univocal bourgeois dominance, the sustained struggle for the recovery of civic life, and inclusivity over exclusion.

Over approximately five years of collective work, the city became the canvas for an art experience that constantly sought to correct and perfect itself. This was until the city, occupied and pushed by the vertigo of the political circumstances of its citizens, had to take the conceptual coherence of the group to the extreme: to the point of producing its dissolution.

I have already said that the group's stated objective was to conceive the city as a cultural battlefield, as a political calling, and as a text and a context. Milk arose around the city, with the hungry, maternal metaphor that it entailed. The milk that had already been cited with powerful consistency in the poetic work of Raúl Zurita was reformulated in a new device: literal milk. For that very reason, it generated a distance precisely with the literality of milk to transform itself into a sign of demand that operated by transforming the request for milk into a historical calling. In short, I am talking about the urgent need to establish new circuits for better political nutrition: the restoration of democracy in the country.

With the work entitled *Para no morir de hambre en el Arte*, CADA was born. It was a time when reality, perhaps too fragmented or self-absorbed by the political regime, was marked by the uncertainty of what the meaning of cultural artistic work was. Using milk as a "medium", the first "art action" (the name taken, I think, from a conversation with Eugenio Téllez) was set into motion. It was an art action, as Eugenia Brito would have said at that time, that was organized around milk as a signifier.

Nelly Richard, Carlos Leppe, Carlos Altamirano, Eugenio Dittborn, Francisco Brugnoli, and Virginia Errázuriz were the closest interlocutors but also the most critical members of the group. As tends to happen in hyper-fragmented zones, these differences produced exhausting and passionate sessions of artistic debate. We already know of the tensions that circulate and define minority practices, sometimes atomizing them. Therefore, what I want to say is that these debates concerned only Nelly Richard and the artists who radicalized their works and their discourses at that time, and who pointed out that in the work of CADA, there were conceptual cracks or artistic deviations that inevitably undermined the effectiveness of the group.

I have to say that these sessions, for the most part, tended to be filled with questions and observations that sometimes implied strong objections, and that, despite the divergences, these meetings were mostly called directly by CADA. I also mustn't forget, of course, the space for debate opened by Francisco Brugnoli in the "Visual Arts Workshop." I am interested in highlighting CADA's attitude toward deliberation to contrast those proceedings with the dominant culture of the present that, curiously, tries to evade and obstruct critical debate. In this way, it consolidates the hegemony of those artistic practices and discourses that are most functional to the dominant political project.

I am talking specifically about the obligation to consensus established by the Concertación de Partidos por la Democracia (Alliance of Parties for Democracy) in its long transition to democracy: a consensus that does not affect the political and economic right, but rather the discourses coming from the various lefts that cannot explicitly state their disagreements with the political model.

Paradoxically, today we are facing an impressive political operation that, in part, can be read as a way of steadfastly safeguarding consensus. I speculate that it is a consensus operation that must avoid the further creation of public media in which debates can take place, like the press and television, in order to be sustained. This is because the existing media belongs to the economic right, which is the spokesperson validated by the Concertación in its nine years of existence.

Of course, I do not intend to point out that the dictatorship era, in any sense, can be compared with this transition to democracy. What I simply want to indicate is that fear of critical discussion seems to be one of the sustained foci that runs through the dominant systems.

What were the problems, starting in 1979, that CADA provoked among the group of cultural producers that Nelly Richard would later call the *Escena de Avanzada*?[8] I think that these questions, doubts, and skepticisms were the result of a complex confluence of signs that were knotted together by non-homogeneous arguments.

To some extent, when working with video in a rudimentary way to organize its records, CADA was directly related to a technology that was received in the group's critical sphere as ambiguous. CADA's use of video as part of its artistic project was seen as a way of obtaining a record that would act as a reference point, allowing for the organization of a memory.

As far as the renunciation of the unique object, and the occupation of the street in direct actions that quickly dissipated, video played an invaluable role. At the time (and it already seems that I am evoking a time of prehistoric technology), the use of this medium was completely elitist. This was seen as a contradiction: video was at once a mechanism that broke with bourgeois convention and of the most sophisticated materials of capitalist production. However, even when considering the possibility of a contradiction, the group validated the reproducibility of video.

Another of the criticisms (I cannot compile them all, partly because they are dissolved in memory) referred to CADA discourse as linked to "the majorities" or to an explicit relationship with the Brigada Ramona Parra. These were the anonymous groups of graffiti muralists ascribed to the Communist Party until 1973 that generated a sustained and recognizable visual syntax of a realistic and pedagogical nature in the city.

Indeed, "majorities" is a term that must be questioned today. The majority is associated with common sense, negotiation, consensus, domination, and homogeneity. However, it is necessary to remember that

---

8   The term for the artistic movement was coined by Nelly Richard in *Una mirada sobre el arte en Chile* (1981).

during the 17 years of militarism—and even acknowledging the support that this regime achieved in a sector of civil society—the dictatorship was sustained by violence carried out by a minority against that "majority" to which it alluded. CADA literally represented the groups completely repressed by the official powers of the time.

In another sense, the Brigada Ramona Parra had and, in my opinion, continues to have a relationship with CADA, albeit not one of a linear nature. I mean connections such as the collective character, the occupation of the city, and the defined and definitive politicization of its signs. Certainly, their artistic operations are different and, in a certain way, could be considered divergent. From another point of view, however, there is a thread (I mean the tireless thread of desire) that, in a fragmentary and nomadic way that was lacking in power (because it lacked a political party) like CADA, was linked to the previous artistic-political occupation of the city. It turned citizens into readers, suddenly assaulted by a space that appealed to their political marrow and to the public and unstable nature of their condition.

After the milk, as much discourse as material, as decomposition, as support and as something molded into the memory of the delirious route of the row of milk trucks crossing the city to park in front of the National Museum of Fine Arts (I mean the ten trucks from the Soprole company that formed an unusual industrial sculpture), the CADA group, with the work of *Ay Sudamérica*, managed to get six small planes to fly over Santiago, from which 400,000 flyers were dropped over its most overcrowded neighborhoods.

I do not intend to give an account of each and every one of the procedures used by CADA to shape its art actions; perhaps I will only indicate that a part of the actions involved intervening with their materials and using them as an artistic canvas, such as with the anti-dictatorial magazines that circulated. These magazines, like *Hoy*, *Apsi*, *Análisis*, or *Cauce*, survived thanks to a brilliant set of strategies.

In my opinion, the most radical proposal of the group came in September of 1983, with the work "NO +."

Exactly ten years into the dictatorship in Chile, CADA designed NO + as public graffiti.

The + sign was the contribution that the group offered as an economy, as a twist, as a challenge, as something that thinned an atmosphere that had become oversaturated by the wear and tear of old political graffiti. Indeed, this fixation with the + sign maintained a relationship with the notable work of Lotty Rosenfeld, except that its directionality was different: to achieve a flow that would allow for the internalization and mobility of the + sign towards a explicitly dissent-based political transversality, openly in conflict and definitely discontented.

A sizable group of Chilean artists tirelessly tagged the streets, inscribing the motto everywhere. In an equally tireless way, the public began to complete the graffiti with their own demands, based on their particular symptoms. Thus, expressions of subversion and resentment began to consolidate themselves in the city.

After a while, graffiti murals with the slogan "NO +" proliferated around the city on their own. Later, we were able to observe how "NO +" was the motto that accompanied the end of the dictatorship, from all spaces of citizen resistance.

Perhaps due to the rigor of relentless pursuit of their objectives, the group later dissolved while NO + continued its expansive movement, no longer tied to any authorship.

It was an extraordinarily exact ending for a group that sought an intensive and extensive connection between art and politics. It was art and politics that ended up annihilating the continuity of the group whose work contained its own end.

Stopping at the social effectiveness of NO +, it was an experience between art and politics that after 20 years still seems movingly possible and impossible at the same time.

(1999)

* **Author's Note:** Lotty Rosenfeld carried out an art intervention in December 1989. It was a video installation (*Cautivos*) on the wall of a hospital located on the outskirts of the city of Santiago. In the vastness of that space, she created an aesthetic design by strategically using lights (in the theatrical manner) and showed three video pieces on a loop that brought together images and speeches that alluded to the ideological debacle that was happening throughout Latin America and in international spaces.

* **Editor's Note:** About an exhibition of paintings by Juan Dávila

* **Editor's Note:** About the painting of Roser Bru.

* **Editor's Note:** About a showing of artistic embroidery by Carlos Arias.

** When CADA celebrated its 20th anniversary, I couldn't help but remember the works of art by Luz Donoso and Hernán Parada. Their groundbreaking and epic artworks, created at undeniable personal risk, brought the faces and objects of a series of disappeared persons into the public sphere.

Translated by Catherine M. Brix

Screen Memories: On Public Images and the Politics of Disremembering

(May-September 2003)

Television stations proliferate. They compete to show exclusive, never-before-seen images of Popular Unity, especially the government's fall, consummated by the bombing of La Moneda. It's impressive to verify the flames beating violently against the palace's powerful cement blocks. The scene repeats.

The conflagration repeats incessantly.

Thirty years on, images of President Salvador Allende's government fill our screens.

Thirty years. And even though I understand that the market's massive, evanescent thirst drives this return to the past, I observe the black-and-white hue that shapes the figures: images that seem—how shall I say it—lightly supersaturated, overblown, out-of-focus.

And too late.

So many years had to pass—slowly, quickly, ambiguously, and at extreme cost—to make this swath of history official. But that's not how it is. It's just a mere bacchanal of images superimposed on each other until they explode. They don't let us see anything, only that explosion of images.

Yet something can be seen. With the same strangeness that now-definitively-obsolete technologies provoke, these images seem to be conceived in a discordant rhythm, imbued with a certain clumsiness from the vantage point of the modern gaze. Therein, I think, lies time's true density: in that technique and, of course, in the conversion that allows us to envision the frenetic movement of technological time's passing. There, in that curious anachronism, the past's materiality takes shape: that definitive past that for millions of us embodied a true social catastrophe.

It's that technique we must examine. We must situate ourselves squarely within it to try to understand precisely the velocity of that time—if it were possible to do so. I'm talking about the need to articulate a technical gaze.

But what was the velocity of that time like?

(The parades of never-ending bodies pressed together. The savage energy that oozed from the marches. The multitudinous crowd emphasizing how necessary it was to make the bit of power they demanded official. Yes, power. I evoke a resonant and monotonous slogan that today might seem extremely naïve: *"Crear, crear, poder popular"*/ "Create, create, the people's power." But it was poetic—and because it was so poetic, it was political.)

Surely, it's too late, and surely that time will be unrepeatable and unrepresentable in all its paradoxical and conflictive reach. The passage of time has already taken shape with its nervous gesticulations. Relentless.

Exaggerated silence took hold; in a similar way, we now have a superabundance of images. Deliberately rational and serene analysis—and a certain sensibility—are required for historical time to crystalize. But it hasn't been like that. We've had too many years of aggressive silence. Those in power have exacted the most pure and simple violence. This violence is part of a repressive political program that's been carried out on each and every front. I'm talking about multilateral complicity orchestrated to impose silence—in a selfishly sinister way, I have to say.

Yes, I have to say it. Although common sense is efficient and contains some wisdom, it's also an overtly repressive instrument of domination that obstructs and compresses. Common sense and its twin—the commonplace—are equal and detestable.

Yet it's not a matter of common sense. More accurately, shielded and hidden behind common sense, a political specter inhabited our power structures that the powerful refused to confront. In the age of the image, images vanished to the point of non-existence. In that way, the powerful unleashed a multipronged, perfectly synchronized operation of concerted silence.

First, the dictatorship succumbed, then the Concertación.

Now, something akin to a carnival proliferates—right at the very moment when those images have lost all effectiveness and have been launched into the unrelenting, fragmented market, reduced to the inertia of their parts.

Too late, or perhaps we should say *sufficiently* late, we've embarked on a tourist's journey into the past, administered by a television industry that belongs to the economic right. That industry is not at all neutral. Witnesses abound and step up to attest—all compressed together, between cuts, with their decontextualized or foolishly careful and opportunistic interventions. And there are adversaries—and warnings.

The analysts, victims, and architects of the coup blend together in the same format: they all inhabit an identical site, in a desperate attempt to build potential equilibrium. Ah, yes, the hateful sensibility of equilibrium. They promote objectivity as artificially as they can, and they try to make everything seem unobjectionable. Yet, in reality, everything gets (con)fused.

Allende rises to become a protagonist: Allende-the-man. Details about his family proliferate: his likes, his defects, his inclinations, and his abilities. Yet, it's not really Allende-the-man who matters most, but rather the political project he led and its effects on the citizenry. That's what gets left on the cutting room floor of every TV station: the forces, the political flows, the economic interests, the truth about how dominant imaginaries were altered, and a commitment to clarify the axes upon which power flowed historically.

(They also ignore the magnitude of the scientific, effective, incessant intervention that the United States orchestrated to detonate the coup. They bracket it—precisely—within a convenient parenthesis.)

Still, none of this seems important or consequential now. It's all about general storylines that erase shades of meaning; it's about visual narratives that render the details irrelevant.

For there are no political details: only anecdotes proliferate, and a sense of the prolonged assault of historical domination.

These thirty years and their commemoration are completely controlled.

But it's a subtle, complex form of control. Precisely because images and discourse now get produced, the long silence is even more salient. Muteness turns into evidence. As different instances of discourse come to public light, they become part of a political technology that strives to kill off certain images—a technology that annihilates images through excessive repetition.

Thirty years on, the commemoration is a feast for the new masses, for those alienated by the increasingly toxic light of their TV screens. Or it could be the opposite: memory dosed out like a strong medication to pacify the will and quiet (bad) consciences. The sponsors of every documentary can smell profit. The thirtieth-anniversary trend unfolds; it's the perfect political whitewashing to ensure the topic is fleeting.

All over the streets people buy t-shirts that bear Salvador Allende's image; peddlers sell them at the top of their lungs, amid a host of other products. We see the t-shirts there: they flank pedestrian thoroughfares while the vendors anxiously await the next product fad that will help them mitigate their precarious subsistence.

The streets. Documentary programs stitch together images—especially—of a city teeming with people on every side: thousands of citizens' bodies coming together to support a political project.

(In reality, it was about giving more body—a quantity of presence that now seems useless to try to reproduce—and more street, and more political ownership of a radically different political project to a part of the citizenry that systematically demanded, defended, and celebrated that project. The political frenzy broke down the walls that divided people and established new, turbulent borders. A humid, contagious passion engulfed a huge swath of the citizenry.)

The streets have now become normalized, filled with a different kind of rush. Bodies occupy the city pragmatically. The current, mediocre political pact obliges people to walk purposefully as individuals. Obedient citizens move from here to there, driven by an imperative to satiate their own needs. They walk around completely domesticated. They walk around shackled by salaries they can't negotiate. They walk around tied to their unstable salaries—their bodies rotted out by a workday that doesn't allow a millimeter of dissidence.

(Every one of them faces the ferocious precarity of their salaries. All the while, in the background, there are thousands upon thousands of marginalized people: the dramatic byproducts of the social bacchanal, people walled off within their own epic narrative; they are the others, the segregated, those who can't, who won't, who just-can-not, who live out their days branded, swinging like pendulums between drugs and crime.)

The streets are monotonous, anesthetized, and lethargic. Citizens today move through the new, present-day reality with a modern gait. Their bodies give shape to the triumphant era of obedience and conformity. Nothing really surprises us anymore. The citizenry's apathy only cracks when some scandal erupts—the gibberish that the media administer brilliantly—and brings a necessary political respite. Indeed, it's the media that controls and directs bodies. It's the media that allows passions to erupt and infiltrate a corner of the voyeuristic eye.

The citizenry appears as mere spectators who feed improbable, fickle surveys that yearn to measure a scandal's impacts. Yet how quickly they forget. How quickly! Nothing is sufficiently solid. Ah, how they turn their backs on the characters who until just yesterday they spent all their time scrutinizing. How swiftly those ultra-manipulated citizens forget their heated discussions. For an instant, a dangerous indifference floats in the atmosphere. We must quell indifference. But the media is already plotting its next juicy story.

Right now, the TV channels compete for our attention on this thirtieth anniversary. La Moneda palace burns and burns on every program. President Allende's cadaver enters on a military wagon repeatedly. His blurry, lifeless body foreshadows the explosion of half a skull, the annihilated disappearance of a face.

(The violent effects of the shrapnel on his body foretell the deluge of blood that would come in the years to follow.)

That harbinger-blood doesn't gush in any documentary. Instead, the wound appears in the survivor's testimonies. In other sequences, it manifests in images of the National Stadium or the mind-boggling images of prisoners.

But the National Stadium's prisoners file by too quickly. This isn't intentional, I think. No, it's not. In their wake, we intuit a fleeting shadow of shame that evades the cameras. The vagueness of those images downplays the National Stadium's infamy. We must linger on the absolute precarity of those images and digitize the (diffuse) prisoners who occupy the bleachers.

Yes, we must isolate a freeze-frame of the face of the specific prisoner at the back of the bleachers whose gaze exudes an opaque glow of stupor. We must do it. We must project his frozen image until it explodes. We must make his countenance explode in our faces so that we can recapture the National Stadium's drama: the way people suffered in the stands, the disgracefulness of that multitude of bodies confined in a sports arena.

The multitude of political prisoners who were detained in the National Stadium and in Estadio Chile may seem like an intelligible phenomenon within the context of the coup's exceptionality, but it isn't.

We need to revisit on a conceptual level how the dictatorship's detention centers were operationalized, who gave the order to create them, what plan of action guided them, and how a system of incarceration came about that was half clandestine and half carried out under the open sky. The media downplay those scandalous images; they dilute them such that they come across as just one more episode, one of many.

El Estadio Chile. El Estadio Nacional.

Perhaps it would be useful to focus on the notion of the stadiums, on the stadiums' revealing names that foreshadow the long siege of detentions to come.

Prisoners were subjected to the sight of empty fields, confined by force within rigid bleachers, with nothing to see on the horizon other than themselves: what was at play there, and perversely so, was nothing more than their own lives subjected to the random spectacle of their gaunt bodies.

(Torture. Summary executions. Bullets pulverizing organs. People committing suicide in the National Stadium.)

Yet today we know so little—so little about each one of those lives, and less about the instant of their deaths.

And, as if all this social depravity weren't enough, the prisoners still linger in Chilean society, their deaths segregated by repulsive hierarchies.

Yes, because the social imaginary, shot through with issues of race and class, forged a rift between first-class and second-class victims. How sad and petty.

The thirtieth anniversary has come and gone.

And it was just a passing fad.

(2005)

Translated by Michael J. Lazzara

"They Executed Me in Chena"

The Italian writer Primo Levi (quoted by the philosopher Giorgio Agamben) affirms: "[...there is] no one [who] ever returned to describe his own death."[9] Of course, in the most literal or physical sense of the term, Levi, a survivor of the Auschwitz concentration camp, is exact and rigorous. Basically, Levi's statement accounts for the place of the witness: that singular witness that emanates from the event's very center and stands as a key figure in the construction of not only legal procedures, but also collaborates in the configuration of the archives that constitute history.

For Primo Levi (who turned to writing about and describing the Auschwitz camp), the radical witness, or the final or total witness of the crimes—considered today as crimes against humanity—is impossible, because he is dead. He is the one who entered the gas chamber or exploded internally, becoming immersed in the massive, disaggregated, robotic figure who, in the concentration camp and due to his bodily pose, was (paradoxically) known as the *Muselmann*.

From the specificity of the Chilean situation, and due to the rupture's scale in relation to the ethical and legal implications caused by the coup, I now ask myself: would it be pertinent to rethink this condition of impossibility in the face of the existence of witnesses who were indeed murdered? I mean, those who physically confronted the ultimate device of human destruction, the firing squads. I think they constitute an extreme exception insofar as they were murdered and yet continued living.

---

9   Giorgio Agamben *Remnants of Auschwitz: The Witness and the Archive,* trans. Daniel Heller-Roazen (New York: Zone Books, 1999), 33.

Making the evidence explicit here regarding the extreme situations to which these witnesses testify compels us to put ourselves in the place of that which is *inhuman* and yet also carries the *human*. I mean, it allows us to reveal that exact limit where what is understood as "human" is stretched to show an inhumanity that belongs to it and that, moreover, it exerts. It also means entering the most disturbing area that an existence coming to its end can reach through the institutionalized violence of the firing squad, which opens a scenario that inescapably marks the end of life. In that sense, it means to become dead and, in the same condition of being dead, reemerge as alive.

This witness then slides between an inside and an outside, in a moving terrain that connects him with both life and death. It is an *in-between* life and death, and this transit through an ambiguous, unclassifiable zone makes it difficult to register him under the singular and stable concept of *survivor*. It is not possible to understand him this way, since his survival happened through his murder, a material murder, an *active* execution recorded by history, and an explicit and recognizable form of extermination—beyond any simulation. I mean that for each of these witnesses, this is not a question of a simulated execution, nor a frequent, atrocious torture exercised and produced through the parody of a simulated death, nor a habitual practice or tactic to which extensive testimony has been given. This book, *Sobrevivir a un fusilamiento: ocho historias reales* by Cherie Zalaquett, introduces situations that speak of an inevitable chain of events: they were shot by representatives of the state and, given that they reached that condition, it must be understood that they were murdered and that they remained alive. Simultaneously.

Moreover, each of these radical witnesses—the most extreme in the history of Chilean testimony—is the effect of a policy or, as Michel Foucault has pointed out, of a biopolitics and a social moment in which their human condition was called into question. They were consigned as mere living species (just pure biology) that had to be eliminated. Their end, which was concretely orchestrated by the institutional bullets that destroyed them, did not involve legal sanctions for the Chilean state-sponsored marksmen. According to *that* state, these witnesses had lost their status as humans.

After more than thirty years, Cherie Zalaquett brings the stories of Chileans who must be understood as *executed* to the public stage. With undisputable certainty, her crucial book places at least two instances of state terrorism on the collective table: there were executions (operated in these particular and simultaneously devastating conditions), and there were the *executed*.

What I am trying to point out is that Cherie Zalaquett's book becomes a detailed testimonial archive of the existence of the methods, forms, nuances, and mechanisms that these methods of execution acquired, to the extent that it is the executed themselves who in this book come to serve as witnesses of their own deaths. As Enrique Patricio Venegas points out, "But the only thing I know is that they killed us on the slope." "They executed me in Chena," says Daniel Navarro, while also indicating what has, until now, remained inexpressible, the primary evidence of his comrade's death: "There were three *carabineros* observing where they had executed Silva."

Furthermore, the publication of this book exposes a legal deficiency: how could these situations be legally classified? Moreover, is there a *precise* legal nomenclature that encapsulates the figure of someone who was institutionally executed and who, despite his execution, lives? In another area, it shows a gap regarding reparations to the victims of state terrorism, since these witnesses not only suffer the experience of being victims of torture but, further, their lives elapse in parallel to a situation or a *position* of death.

Thus, these witnesses' accounts show how the tragedy that the 1973 coup d'etat initiated is ultimately presented as *irreparable*. I mean, there is no possibility of legal or monetary reparations that can compensate, let alone objectify, the multiple and complex dimensions of human devastation exercised over seventeen years of military control in the country. This difficulty allows us to affirm that beyond (or among them, or concerning) economic and legal matters, a situation persists that requires the reinforcement of thinking that does not annihilate the horror: the *inhumanity* of the *human*. Rather, it must be laid out on the social surface as latency, like an active layer below the surface that concerns us, lies in wait for us, and especially, compels us.

Regardless of *personal* experiences and beyond the direct participation in history, the coup d'état must be understood as a synthetic space of violence that, on a different scale, continues to repeat itself again and again with varying intensities in each of the systems that govern us. In this sense, the executed citizens' speeches are also alarm bells to which we should listen, since they correspond to discourses at the limit, extracted from a traditionally speechless space. They come from the site of a double silence: the silence that death brings and the social silence that surrounds powerless citizens.

The effects of state violence in Chile have been measured following a summative guideline: so many tortured, so many disappeared, so many sentenced to death, and so many murdered. There are eloquent numbers to account for the cruelty, and numbers that consolidate figures and feed statistics. However, measuring violence through numbers as a privileged methodology also produces violence. More precisely, it reproduces violence to the extent that there is a process of de-subjectivation so definitive that it re-annihilates concrete lives and renders them invisible, synthesizing them in a purely arithmetical agglomeration.

Systematically, citizens who were grassroots militants and sympathizers affiliated with the most deprived sectors of the social scale are lost within the numbers or made into (nothing more than) a number.

This is how history is written: history modulated over an anonymous surface that has become the human infrastructure on which processes, social epistemologies, and their events are articulated. Notably, this hierarchical way of constructing history has allowed the processes of subjectivation to take place only in the upper echelons: in that area secured by bodies that carry class, political, or economic privileges.

However, the second half of the 20th century's social narratives sought to relax an open practice of segregation by integrating *other* discourses or *othered* discourses. They would leave marks or traces of their difference beyond the norms imposed by networks of cultural domination and even participate in the dominant networks' production of meaning.

As a democratizing mechanism, testimony came to the social scene to inscribe itself as a *political* possibility to establish territories of speech endowed with greater discursive reach. Such territories of speech would make it possible to arrange those subjectivities banished from sectors of power into a *network*. In this way, they would achieve an expansion of inscription's devices and registers from *one* language that is always the same—official, rigid, and marked by hegemonic interests— to *languages* in order to make the dissemination of diversity possible.

This particular witness, the victim of state terrorism, has acquired a multifaceted potential: not only describing his situation as rooted in a particular history but, crucially, this description as a transversal model that crosses times and territories. This transversality manages to establish, as a whole, the coordinates in which the social contract—founded on the value of life—is suspended. This opens the way to a domain in which life, guarded by the state, ceases to have meaning for the state guarding it.

From this perspective, I return to the Italian writer Primo Levi. His first work, *If This Is a Man*, gives an account of Aushwitz's organization. Published more than half a century ago, in its layout one can read how beyond obvious differences, there are territories shared with the book *Sobrevivir a un fusilamiento: ocho historias reales*. Both texts reveal an institutional, programmatic, totalitarian vocation that is aimed at devaluing both life and death. In this abysmal devaluation, the witness forms a proliferating chain that traverses eras and agendas to indicate precisely the (lack of) value that life can achieve. From that place, the derisory space that death acquires or, as Giorgio Agamben assures: "[...] having realized the unconditional triumph of death against life [...] of having degraded and debased death."[10]

Thus, this book can be understood in a register analogous to the work of Primo Levi: in this particular case, as a document endowed with unprecedented *depth*, given that it integrates those narratives that dodged annihilating bullets and avoided being added to the increasing numbers. Their common voices (in the broadest sense that this term carries) are there to demolish or perhaps rethink what is understood as *common*: they are voices that become exceptional due to the exceptional nature of their conditions of enunciation.

In this text, José Guillermo Barrera Barrera, Blanca Esther Valderas Garrido, José Calderón Miranda, Manuel Antonio Maldonado, Alejandro Bustos González, Enrique Patricio Venegas Santibáñez, Luis González Plaza, and Daniel Navarro González share the situation of those who were executed.

---

10 Agamben, 81.

Residents of the rural world: José Calderón, Alejandro Bustos, and Daniel Navarro, from Paine; Manuel Maldonado, from Lampa; José Guillermo Barrera and Enrique Patricio Venegas, from Curacaví; Luis González, from Puente Alto; and Blanca Valderas, from Entre Lagos, come from agricultural culture and its history. This is a history that can be inscribed as the bearer of feudal echoes in the 20th century's productive means, to the extent that the feudal structure's tattered banner is inscribed in the very matrix of the condition of *inquilinaje*.[11] Thus, one of the communities that these stories describe is the place of the wage-earning peasant and its particular configurations of meaning.

In each one of the narrations, whether as current testimonies or collected from legal protocols, a segment is organized to consolidate *astonishment* regarding the sudden experience of being present during the incomprehensible or unthinkable moment when the Rule of Law is completely withdrawn, introducing a domain in which the same representatives of the Rule of Law transform into agents of extermination. *Astonishment* runs through these narratives about the exact moment in which the seemingly impossible occurs: the rules are shattered, and the exception becomes the norm. "Despite tremendous suspicion, no one thought to mention that they were taking us to some hideout to kill us," says Alejandro Bustos.

This shock is recurring. Beyond the arrests and even despite the torture, what these witnesses are unable to clearly integrate into their reasoning, however, is their imminent fate of being executed. They *don't want* to understand; or, to be exact, they *can't* understand the scale of the social breakdown in which they found themselves trapped. They don't understand it because they have a *clean record*. There is no imaginary for them that includes this exercise of power. In a situation that could be considered ultra-perverse, the bodies that confront them—mainly *carabineros*—maintain certain ties with some of the witnesses. This makes it impossible to predict that their perpetrators were already part of the squadron bound by a lethal decision, despite any pre-existing relationships.

---

11 *Inquilinaje* in Chile is derived from the encomienda system in which tenants work for a landowner. See Pérez Porto, J., and A. Gardey, "Inquilinaje" *Definición.de*, 30 Mar. 2021, definicion.de/inquilinaje/.

Daniel Navarro recounts the degree of disorientation that some witnesses experienced in the face of what can be understood as a comprehensible *not knowing*: "It was Sergeant Soto of the Carabineros, who had previously been in Huelquén; he liked soccer and always invited me to play for his team."

"Sergeant Soto, sir, why don't you help me?"

Daniel Navarro was not capable of assimilating that the person with whom he had played soccer, citizen Soto, was already someone else: a state official who not only was *not* going to help but was there to execute him from his position as Sergeant, Sergeant Soto.

In his book *Remnants of Auschwitz,* Giorgio Agamben alludes to a truly terrifying aspect in a different but not entirely distant register when he examines the operation of that concentration camp and attends to the testimony of one of the survivors. The survivor was part of a special commando of Jewish prisoners whose function was to take their companions into the gas chamber. Between the breaks that this work allowed them, the SS soldiers organized soccer matches with the members of this squadron. In this regard, with completely lucid and current political insight, Agamben indicates: "But also hence our shame, the shame of those who did not know the camps and yet, without knowing how, are spectators of that match, which repeats itself in every match of our stadiums, in every television broadcast, in the normalcy of everyday life. If we do not succeed in understanding that match, in stopping it, there will never be hope."[12]

That is what it is all about for us: first *listening* in the finest sense and, at the same time, being aware of what is understood through hearing, in order to then *understand* the soccer match that Daniel Navarro and Sergeant Soto once played. It is about approaching the shame of that match that would be sealed by the firing squad.

Another doubling occurs in these witnesses just because they are inside death or among death itself: their ability to witness the death of some of the others executed. Indeed, while executed themselves, they are the only ones who can account for the final images, grimaces, pain, and dying gestures that conclude the scene of their comrades' executions. In

---

12   Agamben, 26.

this way, a group of these deaths is restructured in order to fracture the category of a mere number that had codified them. These voices arise to remake the end of a life that had been denied the category of human existence. Because these images are published and because their end is described in detail, both their lives and deaths acquire a resonance that had been lost in the accumulation of numbers.

It is then a matter of *restitution*, a leap, or break in the chain of (de)valuation that consumed their lives. This process of fragmentary and dramatic description of their last gestures—the subjectivation of their last moments—returns them to that sphere of lost humanity. Even despite the horror, it makes them live and die with a decency that had been hidden.

Luis González says, "At that moment, Jaime Bastías, who was a 17-year-old boy, crying, terrified, hugged me in the middle of the gun-fire."[13]

Patricio Venegas talks about the funeral rite that he managed to set up for his half-brother, Justo: "In that darkness, feeling my way through, I found my brother's body. The impression of seeing him was so shocking. He was missing half his head! I closed his eyes and kissed him goodbye."

Solitary and in solidarity, it is up to Alejandro Bustos to accompany Orlando Pereira's most human agony: "I don't know how the waters carried us to the shore or how I was able to drag him to that sandy bank. And there he told me: 'Put on my sweater so that it covers your body because I'm gonna die.' I could see blood gushing from the little holes in his chest where the bullets were, and blood running down his arms. 'Lay me down, please, lay me down.' I held him in my arms, and his mouth filled with blood. He lay shivering on my lap. He whispered to me to ask his wife and his children to take care of themselves, and especially, of his daughter Sarita, whom he loved so much. Then, he drowned in blood, jerked, and he died in my arms."

---

13 Eltit's original text specifies "17 años" in this quotation, which differs from the 2015 "In the Intense Zone of the Other Me", where the boy is described as 16 years-old. Zalaquett's text states, "[...] Jaime Bastías Martínez y Rigoberto Julio Díaz, de 17 años [...]" (80).

It is that moment—the moment of the hug, the kiss, or of becoming the support of a body in agony—which gives meaning to both life and death. Despite the tragedy, in its midst it is possible to initiate rites for some of those who die. Even amid the most extreme elements or precariousness, these rites recognized that a *fundamental event* was taking place. Thus, they were able to overcome the biological fate to which they were left by the state.

From what Michel Foucault calls thanatopolitics, Giorgio Agamben asks himself: "How is it possible that a power whose aim is essentially to make live instead exerts an unconditional power of death?"[14] Putting this question in the Chilean sphere, this book raises problems that attempt to at least provide a trace of an answer: it is possible and it is conceivable to attend to the complicity that was established, by way of the state, between part of the civil classes and the military world.

The State of Emergency, which was the mechanism that was called on in order to produce institutional disaster, permitted the union, and in some cases, a mixture of actions that wove both realities together. A sector of civil society invested itself with the *sovereign* power that the military had established for itself.

These citizens operated at times when *the law* was suspended by *martial law*, as if the exception to the law resided *within* them or *for* them—as if the suspension of the law were there to mark their own sovereignty and authorize their *outsideness of the law*.

Without a doubt, this blurred complicity further deepens the ominousness and comes to highlight the "unconditional power of death." In the same way that the arrival of the plague triggered anarchy in the medieval city due to the quarantine that enclosed it, here the state of siege authorized a lethal form of anarchy through the civic-military association.

Considering that the group of executed who testify in this text comes from the agricultural world, it is necessary to remember how and to what extent the feudal lord, a figure of the Middle Ages, is embodied in the image of the *patrón de fundo* whose multiple powers are deployed

---

14 Agamben, 84.

over the bodies of the *inquilinos*.[15] As a matter of fact, agricultural production generally maintained strong feudal echoes, social forms of such a pure patriarchalism that their relations were only sustained with the violence by which territorial dependence was ensured.

I think that civilians' entry into these execution practices explains how the symbolic power of the *patrón de fundo* was embedded in civilians, regardless of the fact that in the specific cases, those involved did not hold or maintain that position in reality. What I want to point out is the validity of superimposing the image of a totalizing figure: the feudal lord. Separated from history, the image had to be inscribed in agricultural operation, spanning the times and generating power relations with expressions marked by omnipotence.

From this place of agricultural production—precisely in the center of the place where social relations take on their most archaic profile—the agreed association between military forces and a group of civilians makes *possible* for the exception raised by martial law to become a bacchanalian power that exceeds even the exception itself.

In each of these zones, there is a looming figure that can be defined as *the exception within the exception*, due to the active participation of civilians who uncover an immeasurable territory: the possibility of imagining that the responsibility for some of these executions belonged to the sovereign power of civilians, who *in* or *from* the center of martial law, made an extermination pact with representatives of the state.

Alejandro Bustos does not hesitate to offer an account of this association: "The *carabineros*, along with the civilians Claudio Oregón, Antonio Carrasco, and Darío González walked on top of us, crushing us." Furthermore, on the trip to the execution, Alejandro Bustos reveals the scope of this fusion and its bacchanalia: how after the barbecue and the drunkenness with which they commemorated (and this could be

---

15   A patrón de fundo is an owner of extensive lands, associated with latifundistas under the inquilinaje system. The tenants are called inquilinos. See Faúndez Becerra, Claudio. "Los Patrones de Fundo." El Mostrador, 29 May 2019, https://www.elmostrador.cl/noticias/opinion/columnas/2019/05/29/los-patrones-de-fundo/. Accessed 10 July 2023.

the subject of extensive analysis) the festivities of the *fiestas patrias*,[16] the civilians and carabineros consummated the end of the party that had brought them together on the bodies of the prisoners: "There were two vehicles: the Carabineros' green ambulance-type van, and the Carrascos' cream-colored Fiat car. At the entrance to the checkpoint, I saw a caravan of vehicles: Claudio Oregón's yellow truck, Pancho Luzoro's white truck, and the green Ford truck belonging to Jorge Sepúlveda, Ramón Huidobro's son-in-law. And a red truck that I didn't know whose it was. They had already eaten the barbecue and now they were going to slaughter us."

Today human rights organizations are growing and spreading continuously. Their growth indicates precisely that these rights are being permanently, systematically, and constantly violated. What is understood as "human" is always at risk due to acts carried out by the very communities in which humanity is embedded. The technological and economic globalization of hypercapitalism, although complex and confusing due to its paradoxical ability to fragment, has consolidated at least one concept for Western culture: the configuration of crimes against humanity that are considered imprescriptible.

Chile is one of the bearers of that stigma. Yet to avoid the effect of a simple nomenclature that could turn into a bureaucratic expression, it is necessary to *understand* how it works and internalize this expression's meaning in a concrete way. This requires an understanding of vulnerability as a situation that belongs to us and in which violence can be exerted constantly.

In this sense, the witness to crimes against humanity is a key figure who never prescribes, or, in other words, whose voice is also imprescriptible. He is there precisely to indicate that abjection exists.

Thus, the voices of the witnesses who appear in the book *Sobrevivir a un fusilamiento: ocho historias reales*, by Cherie Zalaquett, do not belong only to the past and to the horror of that past, but they also

---

16 The fiestas patrias in Chile include the September 18th celebration of Chilean Independence and the September 19th celebration of el Día de las Glorias del Ejército (Day of the Glories of the Army), which celebrates the armed forces, notably with a large military parade in Parque O'Higgins.

especially concern that which we desire as the future. Their speeches exist to give us knowledge that we cannot and *should* not give up, since they come from the most feared and mysterious place: the site of death. Perhaps instead it should be called: the site of a perverse form of death, the insignificance of life, the dual blast of the bullet and the state.

(2005)

Translated by Catherine M. Brix

Signed, Sealed, Delivered

One of the constant questions that systems have posed to writers lies in the pertinence of establishing a social commitment to the problems of their time. The response, naturally, has been plural, dynamic, and has generated diverse and even contradictory attitudes toward the subject. Frequently, speaking of committed writers is associated with political militancy or with the production of literature that exalts an ideology, a work that actually focuses on thematizing the writer's commitment. However, it is also important to remember that commitments to history can be articulated in unexpected, and equally impactful ways.

Leonidas Morales' edition of *Cartas de petición: Chile 1973-1989*, shows that the work of literary criticism can intervene politically in history and the present. Literary criticism can fight to make a concrete contribution to the future of society without renouncing the complex specificity that the uniqueness of its disciplines confers upon it.

What this book proposes to us, in one of its aspects, is that certain forms of writing that literary frameworks consider peripheral, such as letters, can be narratives that signify beyond the status that culture assigns to them. The letters compiled by Leonidas Morales acquire a dramatic texture in this book because they resound like the voices of a Greek chorus accounting for the magnitude of a tragedy.

It is a contemporary, popular chorus, a tight and tense ensemble of Chilean voices that contain the extent of their pain, sheltering it within epistolary courtesy. This contained pain specifically constitutes the book's dramatic nucleus. What is truly moving is that these letters seek to establish a human dialogue amid a radically inhuman situation. Amid injustices and horror, they nevertheless manage to address those responsible for their hardships and request, with good manners, that they restore the fragments of their pulverized civil rights.

The publication of this book confronts us in an unavoidable way with the effects of the 1973 coup. It places us in the center of life or death situations that have no justification. Prison, executions, and disappearances become repeated motifs within the letters. These letters capture the reality of permanent and extreme abuses carried out under a pervasive state of emergency, as well as the vileness of repeated thefts from the victims of human rights violations. Within an already cruel context, these robberies only exacerbate the injury committed against people who were defenseless. These thefts prove that the violence was not only political but also that money and looting were part of the regime's plan of extermination.

In this sense, Leonidas Morales's critical work will occupy a specific place in his field. The precision of his cultural proposal impeccably connects literature and politics. Starting with a theoretical concern about the place that the letter, as a genre, occupies within literary production, this book approaches the epistle as a historical document that we can read not only as "intimate" correspondence, but also as an account of the vicissitudes of an era narrated in the sober voices of its own protagonists. The power of writing allows protagonists to tell stories that until now were submerged in the margins of the system.

This book goes out of its way to present the dignity and integrity of these letters and position them in the public sphere. It transforms each letter into an irrefutable document, while enabling the emergence of a textual corpus that, beyond individual differences, tells a story. From letter to letter, from situation to situation, from style to style, it is possible to identify a narrative thread that brings us closer to the anguish that the dictatorship inflicted on bodies.

By compiling a group of voices that express their demands, Morales's work allows us a close-up look at movements and strategies deployed by the centers of power. The choice and distribution of the letters chart a painful journey through the years of the Chilean dictatorship and reveal the repressive techniques that the authoritarian regime deployed for almost two decades. They were years with no ceasefire for a considerable number of Chileans whose biographical and family trajectories were irreversibly affected.

Of course, social memory was irrevocably affected, too.

Historical memory has been one of the major conflicts of the transition to democracy because of how difficult it has been to generate a coherent attitude toward the human rights violations committed. This book acutely takes a position on memory that is political, ethical, and aesthetic. In that sense, the very publication of these letters, collated with a will to merge politics with culture, becomes an act of memory and a passionate protest against the forgetting that political interests agreed upon.

These letters combat forgetting for many reasons. First, they document the military regime's ominous procedures and the social damage that comes from not yet having full access to justice when faced with abuses. Second, these letters are not an abstraction: their material words are signed, sealed, and delivered. Third, the book presents the victims' writing and the poignant institutional red tape they battled. Fourth, the letters show an effort to reason despite being immersed in an irrational situation. Fifth, they lead us to think about the degrees of loneliness, lack of protection, and the frightful asymmetry of power that our unfortunate comrades had to face. And finally, they show how despite all the adversity that surrounded them, the families searched for understanding, a possible channel to recover the bodies or obtain news about the whereabouts of their loved ones.

They wanted to know. They were looking for remains. They did not resign themselves to the definitive loss of their relatives, and these letters bear witness to that. This tragedy needs reparation. I think that the publication of this book also aims to achieve reparation since it contributes to the construction of a broad and undeniable memory by conceptually organizing the correspondence and circulating it as a clear historical document.

In this sense, the connection is important that Leonidas Morales makes between these letters and the letters of petition that indigenous peoples submitted to the Spanish crown's authorities. Indeed, history has linked sites of military rule to signs of violence. The conquest as a founding space required the sacrifice of a significant part of the indigenous populations. Centuries later, the refounding that the dictatorship sought was established on the basis of the physical or psychological extermination of militant bodies.

Cartas de petición: Chile 1973-1989 forces us to reflect lucidly on the illegitimate concentration of power. It reminds us how and to what extent terror and violence were unleashed on a considerable number of citizens, mostly from the working class, who had their lives or an important part of their history expropriated. However, this book's ethical contribution is its understanding of a collective national problem. Although time has passed, the stories in these letters remain valid and speak eloquently of the horrors of the past. Yet they also warn us about the social instability that the always trembling future holds for us.

(2000)

Translated by Catherine M. Brix

Stigma(ta)s of the Body

It is possible that the book *Tejas Verdes* is one of the most significant testimonial texts to be written about the 1973 coup's devastating scale. It is significant because, while maintaining extraordinary finesse, it gives multiple accounts of the senselessness of an ostensibly unilateral violence.

The author, Hernán Valdés, tells us of his imprisonment in the Tejas Verdes regiment, the place that gives his work its title. Despite the publication of numerous testimonies about the situation of political prisoners, this book stands out in particular because of its epic tale—its proclamation and demand—which moves and articulates itself through corporeal materialities. It is organized by observations that exist beyond a traditional melodramatic register and that, nevertheless, are thrust back upon us as drama, fear, anguish, absurdity, and, most importantly, as a deliriously aggressive situation provoked by the excessive abuse of power.

Tejas Verdes can be read as making a cut, an interruption, as the first consolidation by a definitively repressive system of an indeterminate number of bodies: heterogeneous bodies that flowed together into the prison camp after making distinct biographical journeys. The military coup managed to homogenize and standardize them through a persistent technology of suffering. Suffering united these different citizens under the label of political prisoners.

Its author, an intellectual and a writer, gets arrested for no reason other than his affiliation with *Unidad Popular* (Popular Unity), which opens up the first point of conflict in the reading. It is not a question of a leader's arrest. It is not even clear whether he is an organized militant. Rather, what will inevitably drive Hernán Valdés to Tejas Verdes is the suspicion of an error (or the error of suspicion), a misunderstanding or, most reasonably, the possibility of a paranoid denunciation by some fascist neighbor.

The insufficient space for containing the prisoners takes the shape of a fence around the body, like an assault on the subject's privacy. The first impact that the book makes is to show how a broad process of unlearning takes place: unlearning bodily behaviors, placing the body in a no-man's-land, sharing sweat and exhalations, and especially, giving up any semblance of modesty. It means abandoning the culture with which one's own body is endowed, going back on an entire hygienic custom that dictates bodily cleanliness, and coming to coexist collectively with what is most archaic: filth, shit, and urine. It means living with others as one: like anyone, like nobody, like nothing.

The text describes this unlearning in detail. What at first is presented as impossible becomes an everyday practice. Hernán Valdés insists on detailing the microscopic spaces of confinement and there, in the center of that space, his stubborn refusal to unlearn stands out. He masterfully narrates how the body refuses to assume its new acultural condition as mere flesh, as captive prey. Constipation represents a great symptom of rebellion: Valdés retains his excrement as a method of preserving his status as a subject. This is until the moment when his biology simply overflows and he shits in public, becoming just another prisoner and a mere survivor in a world altered by the uncertainty of destiny.

This process of describing apparently minor details is the principal strategy that runs through this *testimonio*. What we understand as the "I" experiences a dismantling, a radical renunciation of all awareness of what we understand as intimate. The book's plot is composed of a collection of surrenders and dispossessions. Every day seems to bring one more setback: a final loss in which the protocols of the body are processed and rearranged due to the simple fact of being alive, of remaining alive.

It is not a complacent text; on the contrary, Hernán Valdés tells us about how groups work in the midst of crisis and the way in which solidarities are shaken and shredded. He shows us that despite sharing the same terrible situation of confinement, the prisoners' passions, preferences, and antipathies explode with even more force on account of the obligation to remain (there).

Hunger, overcrowding, filth, and multiple losses are the most visible punishments that run through the space and set its tone. These experiences become even more hellish than the specific moment of torture for

Valdés. They will represent the prelude to freedom, after he survives a useless session of perverse and elaborate corporal torture.

The testimony ends abruptly with the prisoner being freed in an unknown, random location. Thus, the question that is established and remains floating as we read the book is: Why? Faced with this question, we have only a single answer: Just because.

The reprint of this book in Chile by the Lom publishing house brings us back to a time that continues to reveal great ambiguity even today. Now that the 25th anniversary of the coup d'état in Chile has passed, that era has been reinstated as trauma, as a dispute, or as silence. It is no doubt impossible for Chilean society to collectively read, or establish, or carry out a lucid practice of memory.

It is not enough just to *attribute* this silence, and this difficulty, to the implementation of the neoliberal economic model and the hegemony of the market and capital, or even to the fascist enclaves that openly persist amidst the transition to democracy. Rather, it is necessary to think about *what* silences this silence.

Certainly, it is a manifold silence, overflowing with signs, permeated with nuances, and filled with conflicts. But along one of its edges, I perceive that the figure of former President Salvador Allende is what calls for a certain sacrifice of memory.

Salvador Allende, despite any differences of opinion about his project, is no doubt the most proactive political leader of the 20th century in Chile. His long struggle to obtain the presidency of the republic coincided with the installation of international progressivism and the battles of minorities against central powers to register new forms of public recognition.

Allende's project was fundamentally based on greater social justice. When he triumphed in 1970, he led the popular segments of society to an unprecedented role in our history. His speeches, his facial features, and his aesthetic occupied public space as a legitimate government. This obviously caused commotion among established conservative circles.

However, Allende's economic proposal attacked capitalist interests and drove the prompt mobilization, from all angles, of a multi-pronged sedition that even transcended borders. I prefer to dwell now on the centralism reached by popular bodies during the so-called "thousand days of Popular Unity."

Amid a long and sustained cultural span governed by a conservative right, there was a spectacle of popular bodies displaying their needs, their aggressiveness, their strength, their demands, their desires, and, especially, their aesthetics. This was the great, embodied utopia that ran through that time. The *roto*, a "broken" figure disparaged by central powers and a term long used by the bourgeoisie to name people of humble origin, was no longer reverted to a minus sign but, on the contrary, gained a proud and dignified degree of cultural capital. In this new sociopolitical situation, the *roto* emerged, revealing its numerical force, *mestizando* the social landscape, and publicly mocking the tics of a bourgeoisie that was exposed in an open and legitimized parodic and political reconstruction carried out by its "other" for the first time.

The strong territorialization of the city boomeranged to call the concentration of long-entrenched economic forces into question. The so-called *barrio alto* and its dominant culture were challenged by working-class expressions that counteracted any accusations of their impurity with denunciations and ridicule of the suspicious, deadly sterility of the wealthy.

The outbreak of a hybrid *latinidad* filled the public sphere, putting the control and the long historical discipline that had constrained and relegated popular presences in check. The rupture of a white model opened itself up to mestizo features, imperfections, and unpolished speech. This time, they reached a social status that became prestigious.

Work itself became visible: no longer as mere infrastructure but as the center of a public narrative it could exercise on its own. It was a narrative that confronted a bourgeois order, thus achieving unprecedented social parity. This is not, of course, to affirm here that the Popular Unity government "effectively" managed to achieve a social equilibrium. What I want to point out is how, despite the asymmetry (as)signed to popular worlds, a public setting was being consolidated in which it was possible to inscribe difference, politically and aesthetically speaking. This took place through the opening of central powers that became participants and allowed for—indeed, privileged—the emergence of popular and working-class sensibilities.

Salvador Allende was the one who made this opening possible in the public space. His government had managed to alter social imaginaries completely and materially by promoting a democratized cultural modality: the true and recognizable revolution of the so-called "Chilean road to socialism."

Speech was pluralized and thus the hegemony of so-called "good taste" was broken, behind which the bourgeoisie had protected their interests and had exercised their multiple and sustained forms of discrimination. The proliferation of new symbolic parameters allowed bodies to inhabit and influence public spaces, flowing massively across the map and altering the social spectrum.

With the death of Salvador Allende inside the Palacio de la Moneda, the violent machinery of a destructive power against institutions was set in motion. It is this mechanism, its violence, and its sadism that the book *Tejas Verdes* recounts from its exceptional narrative position: nothing less than the installation of a power that sought to seal and close off the marks of the past at one of its edges.

It is from that moment onward that the working-class subject was expelled from public spaces—banishing its aesthetics, its politics, its ethics, and its discourses along with it. Popular bodies were progressively eradicated from public spaces. It is an eradication that goes through the end of the dictatorship to forcefully give rise to the dominance of a class-based culture. It paved the way for the hegemony of an economic bourgeoisie that has been building itself up as unique and inexorable, thanks to strong support from different political establishments and their established pacts during these eight years of democratic transition.

Despite the social expectations that surrounded the return to democracy, harassment and discrimination against popular bodies persist today with undeniable clarity. They are bodies that only exist to the extent that they comply with a double standard: as a labor force and as consumers subject to perpetual debt, thus provoking new forms of control and depoliticization through the programmatic assurance of consumption and debt.

The popular subject, a privileged central figure in Salvador Allende's political plan, now wanders through the social imaginary only as a criminal, and as a cruel and dangerous actor. This is thanks to multiple technologies that, in the face of inequality and the absence of real programs to achieve greater social equality, imbue the figures with a violence that is incubated within the system itself.

In this sense, the figure of Salvador Allende is controversial and uncomfortable, since any analysis and any memory of the Popular Unity era necessarily implies a review of the popular world and its participation in social spaces. And yet, that seems to be a great aspect of oblivion, given that the great political maneuver upon which the consensus that surrounds us today has been established is by forgetting. Forget those bodies, bury their aesthetics, strip them of power, and reduce their meager economies to exhaustion by superimposing upon them the bourgeois structure as the only possible model of a way of living.

For this reason, the 25 years since Allende's death were a limit point that bordered on the absurd: the weakly festive spectacle of the National Stadium came to replace the thousands of former political prisoners that once, and without possible repair, were housed by the sports venue. Pain was exchanged for a toneless party. Hesitant political speeches maintained their ambiguities. Crime statistics populated the media alongside the same faces that Salvador Allende—the great martyr sacrificed for the diverse public—had thought would populate the large boulevards: where the free man would walk to build a better society.

(2008)

Translated by Catherine M. Brix

Nomadic Bodies

I feel compelled to make clear that this text responds to a personal question. For that reason, it doesn't contain permanent answers, only the creative, dynamic exercise of cultural conjecture born from reading certain books that, because of the conflicts they broach, confronted me with a scenario that doesn't cease to be problematic. I'm interested in trying to describe these problems, to capture in writing thoughts that have circulated chaotically in my mind, with no beginning or end, erratically, in recent years.

The books I will analyze were met with an alarmingly minuscule, almost nonexistent reception in Chile, and the silence surrounding their publication was, in my opinion, an effect of neoliberal politics—an effect of the self-censorship and repression through which individualism's rampant propaganda quells any ethical contradictions that stem from the recent past, with the goal of stimulating the free market economy, plunging citizens' bodies into the violent eternal-present of consumption and debt, and generating, through a rational defense of the market's barbarity, notable social exclusions and massive cultural marginalization.

And so, I propose to offer readings of two autobiographical texts and a news story that unsettled me to the point where I had to ask myself why I was feeling so much upheaval and in what sense a part of my being was strongly committed to those stories.

I'm talking about Luz Arce's *El infierno* (The Inferno) and Marcia Alejandra Merino's *Mi verdad* (My Truth), both published in 1993. The two books tell the stories of female, leftist militants who, in 1974, during the dictatorship, were captured by the military's secret service (DINA, Dirección de Inteligencia Nacional, or National Intelligence Directorate). Later, after being subjected to torture, they started collaborating with their captors until they eventually achieved the rank of military officials within the same secret service organization that imprisoned them.

The Inferno features a prologue written by a priest named Father José Luis de Miguel, and Mi verdad was published by a human rights organization during the transition to democracy, specifically during the first Concertación government that President Patricio Aylwin led.

During the dictatorship, Luz Arce and Marcia Alejandra Merino had already become notorious for having participated in raids that aimed to capture their party comrades. Survivors' testimonies verified those raids and cited the women's active presence in torture sessions. To be accurate, we should add one more name to the list: that of María Alicia Uribe, a MIR (Movimiento de Izquierda Revolucionaria, Leftist Revolutionary Movement) militant whom the authors of the two autobiographies mention innumerable times. According to Luz Arce and Marcia Alejandra Merino, Uribe still serves in the army to this day. In short, the three women took their place within the social imaginary as informants and traitors.

I think it's necessary to point out here that the initial phase of the transition to democracy, 1990-1994, brought an invitation from the Catholic Church, which was amply supported by the government, for all Chileans to reconcile. In fact, the first attempt to recognize publicly the status of detained-and-disappeared citizens came from a government commission on "Truth and Reconciliation" that proposed material reparations to the victims' families. That commission didn't propose legal measures to punish those guilty of disappearing people; instead, it merely served to acknowledge that the dictatorial state had victimized people. The commission collected and shared testimonies, but the sources remained anonymous. Despite that anonymity, Luz Arce gave an extensive testimony that was printed with her name on it in several national press outlets.

As a participant in that history (I lived in Chile throughout the seventeen-year dictatorship), I read Arce's testimony, and it didn't leave me indifferent. To the contrary, once clandestine knowledge had been officially recognized and betrayal under torture publicly confirmed, a question arose in me that I found impossible to answer: How to approach speech provoked under such conditions?

I didn't know then that this would be just the first of a series of questions that, years later, would proliferate incessantly when I read the two autobiographies—to the point of nullifying my original question.

My questions drove me to the extreme of writing a series of texts about the books, of which this is just one more.

I want to pause to point out my conviction that all autobiographies are born of a process of writing memories, and, for that reason, they shouldn't be read literally as truth; more correctly, autobiographies are performances of the self, biographical stagings in which the "I" who speaks in the text is, at bottom, a fiction. I'm not talking about the traditional opposition between truth and lies, but rather about a genre that foregrounds the exercise of constructing an other-place, a separate place from which to speak, one that allows us to read the autobiographer's choice, the fiction that the "I" fabricates.

This point is strategic for approaching Luz Arce's and Marcia Alejandra Merino's books because a desire to clarify political "truth" drives their writing and justifies the construction of their first-person voices, which serve as the bearers of that truth. And thus, a desire for "truth" justifies the desire of the "I" who speaks, in accordance with autobiography's conventions. To put this in somewhat parodied language, the gesture would be something like: "When I write, I don't write, rather I immerse myself in my 'real' reality, which becomes truth; by extension, the institutionalized form of the book captures an institutionalized form of writing, which is autobiography, that legitimates my truth."

And so, self-validation and the essentialism of the "I" merge within the autobiographical genre, thereby diminishing the complexity and multiplicity of the first person-voice, eclipsing the unstable nature of "truth" and obliterating the materiality of writing itself.

In reading these books, I've sought to delve beyond their surface content to find their deeper meanings: to tease out those meanings within the unevenness of speech, within the desires and hidden fantasies that the two texts are reluctant to acknowledge because of the impulses that compel their authors to write. I've worked to deconstruct the autobiographical "I," or, better yet, to read the "I" as a spectacle, as part of an ambitious staging that, at times, reveals the texts to be pretexts for the most important aspect that lies at their core: the hidden meanings in-between the lines of every page.

In the first place, I think that these books posit a fundamental problem regarding the body and identity as dynamic, ductile, vulnerable categories—especially when the subject, in this case the female subject, is caught up in the web of dominant power, specifically within a zone of that power that requires violence, whether parodic or explicit, to preserve hegemony.

Luz Arce, a socialist militant, belonged to a minor wing of the Socialist Party that embraced paramilitary activities. Marcia Alejandra Merino, a MIR militant, also received military training because of the nature of her party, which promoted armed struggle as a strategy to achieve socialism. Both women had experience analyzing documents, and Luz Arce, specifically, took on the rather clandestine task of capturing information and relaying it to the Political Commission of the Socialist Party.

In this way, between 1970 and 1973, both young women put their bodies at the service of an impending, potential war. They performed theatrically on a parodic stage: the dreamlike Latin American imaginary of the seventies, in which women's bodies broke with their long-standing cultural status of inferiority and became identical to those of men, all in the name of building an egalitarian, collective future.

For these women to inhabit the kind of feminine body that dominant political discourse promoted—the discourse of the effervescent and recently-elected Popular Unity government—they had to reject traditional Latin American discourse. They had to cast off the weight of tradition by pushing to the extreme new ideas about romantic and family relationships and about the real practice of motherhood.

Nevertheless, at the heart of this parodied performance of masculinity—which subordinates the intimate and personal to the public and collective—these autobiographies allow us to read the fissures within this new mode of being. Luz Arce was the mother of a young son whom she had to entrust to the care of her parents while she trained like "one more man" in a game of war. In Latin America, the epic and historic act of abandoning a child was always the father's domain. In this case, the mother's sporadic presence doesn't make her a "bad mother" or leave her stigmatized for her indifference; instead, she responds to a higher and unprecedented motherly calling insofar as her absence becomes a form of sacrifice that finds ideological justification in political discourse. Her absence would honor her child and help secure his future life in a more just society.

Luz Arce's parents—grandparents through and through—played a classic role vis-à-vis her maternal crisis: the family continued to provide the support system that shaped Luz Arce's being. For her part, Marcia Alejandra Merino maintained an extremely strong and (reading intently between the lines) almost symbiotic relationship with her widowed mother. In both cases, bourgeois family structures remained untouched because the two women remained dependent on their families, who exercised a form of control, a clan-like power over the women's parental bodies.

Daughters to the core, Luz Arce and Marcia Alejandra Merino, both from lower-middle-class families within the extremely classist country that is Chile, jumped at the chance to become active participants in history; they took their place within the undeniably powerful domain of militarization. Their autobiographies recount how they gained access to that domain. Rung by rung, they climbed the ladder: Luz Arce from secretary to driver for a member of her party's Political Commission, then from driver to armed guard for President Salvador Allende, and then from armed guard to analyst of classified materials. Her meteoric rise caused one party leader to ask her "how far she hoped to go." Faced with that question, Luz Arce reflects: "What I understood as 'full commitment' was being interpreted as an attempt to climb the ladder." Shortly after this, she recalls the image of Che Guevara: the martyred, male figure with whom she identifies both her work and identity.

Here, then, we see the first symptom of a disaster that, later, will plunge both women into a sort of identity crisis. As women who depend emotionally on their families, they seek refuge and act solemnly within a discourse of self-sufficiency and change driven by male bodies. In this context, they must display double or triple the ideological commitment of men, compete, and show off their skills, all in hopes of a political promotion that will bring them prestige.

Yet theirs was a kind of *macho* prestige, a cross-dressed imitation of Che Guevara. Or perhaps the women were androgynous, fugitives from their own bodies who had to persuade themselves and others at every turn that their femininity didn't matter, privileging instead the triumphant, explosive, and powerful revolutionary body performed through a staged battle of discourse more than through action.

They were offensive bodies on a battlefield that was inoffensive because it was unreal; theoretical bodies involved in a linear enactment of political discourse that allowed them to subvert their roles abstractly;

bodies prone to authority, situated at the heart of power that military training represented.

Reading the beginnings of these autobiographies reveals the women's gargantuan struggle to forge their identities by questioning traditional gender roles. To enable their epic participation in history from within the dominant power structures they wished to access, they had to place their biological bodies at the service of masculine cultural codes.

However, the military coup of September 11, 1973, thrust both militants' bodies into another space, the ambiguous space of clandestine life: a physical-and-mental, anxiety-inducing space that allowed them to hang onto the fiction of their epic struggle but without social prestige, opportunities to climb the ranks, or any palpable future. Faced with this new scenario, their contacts change, the presence of their political boss (or bosses) becomes intermittent—which confuses them given that they articulate their own identities always in relation to their superiors—and the political power to which they aspire vanishes.

When she recounts the moment in which life turns clandestine, Marcia Alejandra Merino makes an initial reference to money. Marcia Alejandra Merino—clandestine, working intermittently, equating her identity to that of a Soviet revolutionary, disconnected from a political movement crushed by the coup d'état that had previously given meaning to her life—launches her first veiled critique of her political party when she contrasts two comrades, a couple without money, with another *compañero* who had quite a bit of cash. Her comment can't be interpreted innocently in an anonymous, disintegrated, clandestine, and for that reason, undetectable setting. She mentions money right as power shifts to the military, right as the dream of Socialist revolution turns into a nightmare.

The two women are taken prisoner in 1974. Marcia Alejandra Merino, apparently the better trained of the two for war, couldn't withstand torture and collaborates almost immediately. Luz Arce does manage to resist but is attacked brutally, relentlessly, raped repeatedly, wounded by a bullet, beaten, hung, and shocked with electricity. She starts collaborating with her torturers when they arrest her brother, another bit of evidence that proves that the family always took priority over the revolution.

The two books become more complex in the parts that come after the militants' arrest. *El infierno*, the title of Luz Arce's book, is undeniably accurate because of the barrage of extreme descriptions it contains of the violence inflicted on her body.

Having made this point, I can't help but pause to note the relationship between the body and violence that marked Chile's social reality for seventeen years. Torture as a fascist instrument of power and pillage, the body as finite matter, confession as staged confrontation between truth and lies, between life and death: all of this forced me to read these texts in an explosive, shattered way.

How can one remain unscathed when faced with human rights violations of such magnitude?

After the women's capture, the figure of the secret service agent takes center stage in their narratives. This figure is personified through several characters and includes people of different military ranks—lieutenant, major, commander, general. Yet beyond individual ranks, the chain of command has but one objective: political destruction through bodily aggression against the prisoner.

I think it's necessary to clarify that political prisoners were not recognized publicly or in any official way; consequently, they virtually lost their legal existence given that they were held captive in clandestine places. Such a Kafkaesque form of nonexistence, where people were detained in a kind of indeterminate limbo, was part of a cruel scene designed to exacerbate fear, to couple nothingness with death.

In torture, the body becomes fully itself through pain. Bodies are pitted against one another, they confront one another in an unequal distribution of power whose goal is to make the prisoner talk—to obtain, through the destruction of the biological self, the truths hidden inside bodies. Torture and confession come together in a unique scene aimed at provoking confession.

Yet behind the brutal scene of confession, we can read a will to destroy the captured subject's identity; here, confession is no more than a symptom of a pulverized identity, an outward manifestation of the severing of a person from their own history through the magnification of bodily suffering. It would seem, then, that torture's most important goal is to depoliticize bodies by forcing them to give up thought and reduce them to their most basic survival instinct.

The body becomes an archaic body, subjected to a ritual of pain such that the confessionary act—that is, the speech act—becomes a means of stripping away speech. It therefore doesn't seem to me that torture is directly linked to extracting information from prisoners, but rather to a fascist scene of mental annihilation, or of destruction, especially psychic destruction. The torturer decides whether the prisoner lives or dies; he or she becomes a kind of god who desecrates the prisoner's body, nullifies it. Emptied of her being, the speaking subject paradoxically loses her identity. She "breaks."

This expression repeats within these autobiographies. When Luz Arce and Marcia Alejandra Merino say in their texts that some prisoner gave up names, they say: "She broke." And what breaks or is fragmented is no less than everything that ties that person to her political core. She is left exposed to the void, to her own nothingness—and to the ideological price of being dispossessed of herself.

Luz Arce and Marcia Alejandra Merino confess and then collaborate. Undoubtedly, confession and even collaboration are to be expected in extreme situations such as those that these two women lived. So, with the understanding that the problem that arises from reading these books has nothing to do with questioning the prisoners' confessions or even their dramatic collaboration (which cost numerous party comrades their lives), it is, nevertheless, from that moment onward that their stories take an extraordinarily heavy twist.

The world they narrate twists and turns until it's turned upside down; it shuts down and begins anew. It's precisely that new beginning that caused conflict and raised questions for me as I read. From what place could I judge the situation of women who had been raped, tortured, and imprisoned in a brutal context that I had lived from another place? Did reading their emotional stories from an intellectual vantage point break the bond of gender between me and them? Why not forget these impure stories and act as if they'd never existed? Wasn't it, in a way, advantageous that a writer who had never been a militant in a political party herself would become a reader of the cruel crisis of two female militants?

These unavoidable questions continue to nag at me even though, from another angle, I think that undertaking a reading like this is a different kind of political act—a kind of militancy to find meaning.

This is because, in my opinion, what is at stake in these autobiographical texts are the relationships among power, the body, female gender, and ideology—and these, at the same time, are deeply connected to the current power structures of Chile's transition to democracy. They have profound cultural and social resonance in the society I inhabit today.

Luz Arce and Marcia Alejandra Merino were co-opted by the military's secret service, DINA, and for almost a year they remained in a state of limbo where their willingness to collaborate was tested repeatedly. Over that year, the contradictory aspects of their gender identities resurfaced. If at the beginning of their political histories, their struggle to become subjects had to do with receiving affirmation and climbing the ranks of a political hierarchy that would recognize their androgynous-masculine merits and thereby allow them to achieve higher status within that power structure, the year they spent in prison (1974-1975) again put them in a situation where they had to gain new knowledge: this time knowledge of the military's ranks.

After they betrayed their comrades and gave up names, addresses, and on-the-ground knowledge about their political parties, Luz Arce and Marcia Alejandra Merino entered a new life stage. They redirected their energies toward the specific objective of becoming officers in the secret service. To do that, they sought the protection of older officers, men who, with their impressive power, allowed women to live by capitalizing on the most classic site of encounter between males and females: sexuality.

When the narratives reach this point, parameters change. A careful reading allows us to see that the women are now truly committed to the military intelligence networks. They become intellectual and emotional participants in the military's conflicts and internal struggles. Each of them—along with their respective coworker-captor-lovers—again takes up, let's say, a political ambition.

Outside the prison, they continue to work for DINA, led by the sinister Manuel Contreras, and they achieve their objective of becoming officers. Even though they say in the text repeatedly that they feel like prisoners, their narratives can't help but point out their professional successes within the questionable organization to which they belong. Despite the double fear that envelops them—fear of the military and fear of the reprisals they might face from their former leftist comrades—they still feel a certain pride when they distinguish themselves within a masculine world; they recover their identities through a brush with dominant power structures.

When DINA disbands, the women panic. They openly take Manuel Contreras's side. The former prisoners experience Contreras's fall dramatically because they see their slice of power teeter and fade. Thanks to their old DINA contacts, they are able to join the Central Nacional de Informaciones (National Information Headquarters, or CNI), the new intelligence service that the dictatorship created to whitewash its image and deplorable human rights record internationally.

Curiously, even though the women lived freely for many years, their narratives contain no "outside" beyond the social, sexual, and political fabric of the military intelligence apparatus. One the one hand, the absence of any outside might have to do with the fact that they are forced recruits; but, on the other hand, it doesn't seem off base to me to associate that lack with military tradition. The military is characterized by its social hermeticism; generally speaking, the military keeps its distance from the civilian world.

This observation leads me to venture the hypothesis that these women were committed to their new institution and enjoying their newfound military identities. Beyond the emotional quality of their stories—and considering their self-definition and examination as free prisoners—I can't help but think that for fifteen years, Luz Arce and Marcia Alejandra Merino dedicated themselves to achieving social and economic status within a sector of the armed forces that allowed them to be—once again—participants in centralized power.

Although Luz Arce retired from service around 1984, she stayed connected to the military world in one way or another until 1990. Marcia Alejandra Merino stayed until 1992. And the third prisoner, María Alicia Uribe, is still there.

The transition to democracy began to take shape with the 1988 plebiscite and became tacit in March 1990 with the transfer of power to the Concertación de Partidos por la Democracia (Alliance of Parties for Democracy), led by the Christian Democratic president Patricio Aylwin. It's an alliance of center-left parties (excluding the Communist Party) in which the Catholic Church plays a major public role. Neoliberal politics remain potent and on the rise. The middle classes are especially obsessed with the drive to consume, which fuels individual-ism and a lack of collective political projects.

Chile's transition to democracy is the result of a consensus-based pact between military power and the political right. This pact couldn't result in anything other than historical amnesia regarding the period from the 1970s to the 1990s, forgetfulness forged in the name of a dem-ocratic future. Yet the protagonists of the current political pact are the same actors who lived through Chile's recent history. And so, the cen-ter-left (especially the Socialist Party) must coexist with its enemies and dialogue daily with those who were their captors and possibly even their torturers.

Without getting into political details that aren't my place to discuss, I must admit that it seemed strange and even alarming to me that the publication of these autobiographies fell on deaf ears. Why were these polemical and overwrought narratives publicly silenced? What was it about these texts that made it such that groups so often referenced within them, like the Socialist Party, offered no reading at all?

I can only explain this silence by citing the delicate power relations that the texts reveal. Luz Arce and Marcia Alejandra Merino published their books at a moment when centralized power had shifted to a new democratic regime. Moreover, two prestigious institutions that under-pin democracy endorsed their books: the Catholic Church and a human rights organization. Bracketing the content of their narratives, I should note that the 1978 Amnesty Law also protected the authors; curiously, their narratives contributed no significant information about human rights violations that happened after that date and, for that reason, the women remained sheltered from any potential judicial reprisal. Conse-quently, if we follow the thread of their lives, is it not legitimate to think that publishing these books was but another move to become part of the dominant power structures? Don't their narratives conform to the domi-nant discourses of forgiveness and reconciliation? And lurking under the apparent courageousness of their stories, don't we find that these devo-tees of power display a shocking vocation to inhabit spaces of power?

Luz Arce and Marcia Alejandra Merino compulsively present themselves as traitors in their texts. However, betrayal—a social phe-nomenon that carries great symbolic weight in our culture—requires a dramatic episode to leave its mark. Reiterating betrayal nullifies its impact, voids it of drama, flattens it. In my opinion, the label of "traitor" that the authors pin on themselves is inaccurate; it serves to cover up the conflictual relationship they have with their own feminine identities, their fascination with traditionally masculine spaces, and their competitive desire to secure a ubiquitous presence in those spaces.

In another sense, a strain of feminist theory has rethought the notion of betrayal that has been traditionally ascribed to minorities, women, gay people, and indigenous peoples. The most obvious Latin American case is that of La Malinche: the *chingada* who, in the light of feminist theory, becomes the *chingadora* of patriarchal power (to put it crassly), someone whose "non-being" allows her to move freely through different spaces, with no need for loyalty because any social commitment would lead her into an inevitable state of non-belonging and indifference.

Although this reading is quite interesting—and although debunking prevailing stereotypes is a necessary cultural practice—I also think that the "non-being" ascribed to women is questionable today because theoretical discourse and cultural production about the female gender have gained legitimacy throughout the twentieth century and have become a significant political platform. Ethics and aesthetics have merged to give birth to a diversity of discourses that, despite their unstable cultural inscriptions, have managed to upset dominant culture. To some degree, women's long-standing, subordinate position has been challenged as well, disrupting the monolithic cultural category of masculinity.

I foreground this matter because it strikes me as politically complicated to unpack dismissively the symbolic social meanings of something like betrayal. I think that when betrayal (of the other, the community, or the self) becomes relativized and loses its ethical weight, that move bolsters capitalism's savage effects and fuels its broad, unstable, and suspicious repertoire of ambiguous, mutable ethics and aesthetics; it also justifies the unwieldiness of capital and consumerism's unequal oppressiveness, which aim to violate the social body by depoliticizing it.

With that parenthesis, I want to return to the bodies of Luz Arce and Marcia Alejandra Merino. They want to be seen as traitors; they label themselves as such. Yet betrayal is not the main issue. Betrayal is divested of its dramatic effect through repetition. Their bodies, instead, are little more than spaces through which power flows wildly and mutates chameleonically. Their books are a bold attempt to inscribe themselves into centers of power. In an exhausting way, the authors create a symptomatic, expressionist painting whose very center dangles over a void, over an empty space where power recycles meanings of the feminine, twists them, and renegotiates them infinitely.

The drama of these autobiographies is therefore not betrayal, but rather the political neurosis of masculine tradition that makes it impossible for the "wrong" body to fulfill its desire. The nomadic character of these stories is connected to a bad reading of social codes and, more specifically, to a deep crisis of the determinants of gender, one that the authors are only capable of resolving through a process of reversal: to be masculine at all costs. To be masculine is nothing more than an operation fueled by the sheen that centralized power holds for them, the result of an acritical, ideological appropriation. Luz Arce—and this is predictable—converts to Catholicism. She seeks an advisor (here we find the necessary image of the protective superior whose power she also challenges), the figure of the suffering Christ replaces Che Guevara, and her testimony before the National Commission on Truth and Reconciliation casts her in the role of a martyr.

And so, to hazard an answer to my earlier question about why these books were met with silence, I would say that—speaking at arm's length—I see symmetries with how power is exercised in today's Chile: that is, thorough forgetting and the normalization of certain political understandings that legitimate consensus, modernization, and the frail border between neoliberalism and progressivism. All of this becomes systematized through the mentality the women project in their books. They seek identities they can only find in the centers of power, and they deploy memory as a rhetorical strategy to establish an ideological discourse that gives them access to privileged social spaces.

I therefore feel that the extreme, radical violence that these texts convey is rooted in the dynamic and intelligent ways in which the subjects manipulate the ethical and aesthetic limits of their connection to others. By perversely toying with those limits, by resorting to commonplaces of psychoanalysis, by re-torturing their own bodies, and by invoking the family, love, sexuality, and politics, Luz Arce and Marcia Alejandra Merino set a social trap that, curiously, links them to a feminine tradition that new forms of cultural discourse have blocked. The overt victimhood to which they appeal can't move readers who, in one way or another, can't manage to recognize in them a feminine aspect that would absolve them of responsibility. And if we read the texts even more rigorously, they contain evidence of a failed masculinity that never adapts to its own rules but that, in one way or another, cites classic forms of adhering to centralized power. In this way, the texts' legibility becomes illegible.

To be clear, Luz Arce and Marcia Alejandra Merino forge their discourse upon terrain that's as misunderstood and manipulated as their own life stories. They publish stories that, within the framework of the Chilean neoliberal project, can't be deciphered beyond the reductive way in which they're told. I mean that they can only be read as the hysterical histories of two traitors.

And, beyond all potential relativism, betrayal—as we well know—begets silence and, especially, revulsion.

***

As I read these autobiographies, I came across an image that stuck in my mind. I remembered news that I read in 1974, the same year in which Luz Arce, Marcia Alejandra Merino, and María Alicia Uribe were taken prisoner. It was a hard-hitting story, at once marginal and mysterious, that recounted the collective suicide of the Quispe sisters (Justa, Lucía, and Luciana) in the Chilean highlands. The Quispe sisters, descendants of the Coya ethnic group who lived isolated in the highlands, hung themselves from a crag, tethered at the waist, after slitting their animals' throats and hanging their two dogs.

I'm still unclear about the extent to which it's possible to draw a conceptual connection between these two trios of women. Nevertheless—and with apologies for presenting an unfinished reflection—I think that when placed in tragic symmetry to one another it's possible, despite differences, to identify some consistencies. To evoke the thought of the Mexican poet Rosario Castellanos: there must be some other way of inhabiting the world for these women. I think, in fact, that another way of being (politically) exists that doesn't push bodies to the extreme, or extremes. Yet still, the Quispe sisters' silent, compelling, funereal lyricism continues to speak to me, obsessively, about society, there in the private fragments of memory that comprise my cultural imaginary.

In the Andean highlands, the remains of the indigenous cultures that make up the "Andean World" barely survive. The Atacama people, the Coya people, as well as the Quechua and Aymara peoples continue their economic exchanges; they constantly move from here to there with their animals, which support their livelihoods. The men emigrate to seek better opportunities, which means that most of those left behind in the small pueblos and farm towns are women.

Within this dramatic landscape, in isolation, the diverse survivors of ancient indigenous cultures maintain their traditions, rituals, and festivals. Life in the highlands progresses secretly, nomadically, torn between past and present, between one world and other, different, extinct worlds.

The Quispe sisters' suicide was picked up by the tabloids. A photograph showed the three mestiza women hanging in the void, bound at the waist. In the background, one could see the dead animals and, next to them, their two hung dogs. The texts that described the event were unreliable, ambiguous, and sensationalistic, and they most certainly offered contradictory interpretations. Either this had been an act of passionate resolve or the product of a psychosis that plagued all three sisters. They lived alone, and a goat herder passing by became witness to the scene.

At the edges of the photographs, it was possible to envisage a space full of overwhelming solitude. I read in these photographs an unfolding of the hyper-marginal scene of an ancient tragedy: a scene in which one could see the effects of a dramatic, concerted decision whose multiple meanings could never be deciphered. Three *mestiza* women had committed suicide in the highlands, and their deaths transmitted a series of complex codes. An entire language saturated their funeral rite: a language honed with extreme precision.

The violent theatricality of their deaths conveyed a carefully plotted pact whose syntax proved impossible to decode. Because of the careful rituality that enveloped it, their collective suicide became a form of social discourse that made it possible to integrate death into both a long, collective history of deferrals and *mestizajes* and into their wounded, autonomous, familial present. It was a funeral rite that combined bodies, secrets, economies, silences, loneliness, landscapes, and ethics. It wasn't just about the will to end their lives but also about demarcating their territory, the site in which their highland identities were rooted.

That's why their dead animals and hung dogs played a central part in the ritual, legitimizing their life stories and the theatrical ornamentality of their deaths.

Although the Quispe sisters staged a terrible death scene, a certain oblique vitality permeated the photographs. In my opinion, this paradox was possible because of how their suicide spoke. On the one hand, it was undeniably a protest, but on the other hand—and this strikes me as crucial—it also spoke of a power that, though marginal, was all theirs. They exercised it, through their death ritual, in a way that was entirely their own.

Far away, in a distant, geographic microcosm, the Quispe sisters voluntarily decided to abandon this life; yet the method they chose to fulfill their desire birthed a new symbolic microcosm shot through with ethics and aesthetics that channeled the stories of their lives and deaths. Through their elaborate ritual, they left behind a sign that spoke to their permanent possession of and dominion over their lands and goods. At the same time, they held onto their radical right to abandon it all, to take it all with them, or to put an end to it all.

And it seems important to me that you know that the only material goods the Quispe sisters (Justa, Lucía, and Luciana) possessed were twenty goats, two dogs, and their own bodies. Nothing else.

(1996)

Translated by Michael J. Lazzara

Twists and Turns, Riots and Returns

My perception of certain aspects of Michelle Bachelet's government is not based on a *scientific analysis*, per se. Here I only intend to go over some cultural signs, to think about those signs, and to doubt those signs.

In my opinion, Michelle Bachelet has become an international benchmark for women's movements, but her specific experience—her biography—in relation to traumatic memory in Latin America is also noteworthy.

She is not only a woman president, the first in Chile and perhaps the most renowned in the history of Latin America. She is also—as experts have repeatedly pointed out—considered a person capable of overcoming adversity: the death of her father as a consequence of the torture received at the hands of his own comrades-in-arms; the imprisonment and torture to which Michelle Bachelet was subjected together with her mother in clandestine camps of the dictatorship; and the experience of exile.

From another perspective, Chilean women (who voted en masse for a socialist woman in an unprecedented way) identify with Bachelet. She was separated, head of her household, a *single woman* who was able to weather love and family dilemmas and get ahead in life: first as a doctor and later heading up important government agencies. From that place, Bachelet is the perfect daughter of the cultural revolution of the 1960s: a modern woman who sought to *stand* within the social space and for whom that *standing*, although it took a toll, also allowed her a radical entrée into the most important sectors of power.

Without denying any of the characteristics that are credited to her, however (while avoiding a political romance novel), I think that Bachelet is a disciplined woman as understood by Foucault: modeled by rationalism, capable of interacting with frightening powers, and strategically preserving the most absolute respect for hierarchy. That has been possible because Michelle Bachelet was an expert in military structures, the most strategic space of all, in which the arc of the hardest power has solidified: she belonged to them.

As the daughter of an Air Force general, her childhood and early youth were directly and indirectly associated with schedules, regulations, ranks, promotions, and adaptations to territorial changes. Her father's assignments not only moved her around Chile but also to the United States, where she completed part of elementary school. In this way, and from that place, Bachelet organized what could be defined as her first rebellion: being part of *la familia militar* and, without denying her affective ties and the close relationship with her parents, building a position on the other front where the crisis broke out within the structure of the Armed Forces. I want to point out, however, that this was possible thanks to a knowledge of the organic discipline of militancy and ongoing involvement in the ups and downs of contingent politics. At that moment, Bachelet would enter a space that was also absolutely masculine. It was a space that would not have been so successful (I would guess) if it had not been preceded by the stratified wisdom that her text and family context gave her.

On the other hand, Bachelet studied medicine, a field that was traditionally a masculine arena and at first, she wanted to train as a psychiatrist, but later she specialized as a pediatrician. While she was in exile in East Germany (the primordial site of the communist experience) she continued to forge a path that would not have been possible except by strictly observing order and orders, taking refuge in the most absolute discipline.

Later, during the government of Ricardo Lagos, she took charge of the Ministry of Health in the context of an unprecedented and even unusual presidential *threat*. The President of the Republic told her publicly, and in an authoritative tone, that she had three months to end the lines at the clinics that served the most destitute population in the country.

Bachelet concentrated on finding mechanisms that would make it possible to offer better organized care, an objective that she was only partially able to achieve. After the governing Concertación had produced a kind of *gap*, or a *vacuum*, or an *absence* of leading figures, due to excessive presidential personalism, Bachelet came to occupy her most decisive, foundational, and high-profile position: Minister of Defense. Aside from the sympathy and even the popular fervor that certain innovations achieved, her appointment opened space for a complex and intricate ambiguity.

The Ministry of Defense was inseparable from the image of Pinochet. It was not just about a woman as the head of the Armed Forces or even, in other words, *about* the Armed Forces; it was rather that a historical and social context had to be considered in which the Armed Forces had been inextricably associated with state terrorism and caused the deepest social drama of the 20th century. Thus, the appointment of Bachelet could be understood as a way of breaking or piercing the Armed Forces themselves by feminizing them (humiliating them or subduing them, one could say) when they came under the command of a woman.

Yet, in another version, it was also noteworthy that it was about a woman with a particular story: a woman who was the daughter of an Air Force general who died as a result of torture received within his own ranks. In this sense, the arrival of *this* daughter came to mark the most concrete form of an insistent call throughout the transition years: the call for the reconciliation of all Chileans. Such a reconciliation could not be carried out, in part because the forgiveness being requested was couched within an ostensible demand for legal impunity. In this way, Bachelet became a living example of this imperative and another of the recurring premises of public discourse was also fulfilled: "We must look forward."

In contrast to the Association of Families of the Detained-Disappeared, a group made up mostly of women who (relentlessly) sought reparation for the past, Bachelet, as head of the Armed Forces, seemed to embody another perspective: biography (memory) as abstraction and social epic. Meanwhile, her active body entered the most acute labyrinths of a present that was unable to pacify its signs.

Another possible reading was that her appointment would ultimately benefit the Armed Forces since she could be understood as the "prodigal daughter" who returned to her place of origin. With her return, she cleaned up the image of the Armed Forces, which had been sullied by the destructive and illegitimate blemishes that their high command had produced throughout 17 years of dictatorship. It was, then, a reconciliation that would take place within the Armed Forces, since they too could be understood as the lost sheep that returned to their institution (their institutionality) to insert themselves into the new stage opened by the democratic transition.

Nevertheless, during the 1990s Michelle Bachelet had specialized in military subjects, taking courses on military strategy at the Academia Nacional de Estudios Políticos y Estratégicos (ANEPE) where she obtained first place and an honors scholarship to take courses on continental defense at the Inter-American Defense College in Washington, DC along with 35 other uniformed personnel. In this way, she not only signified a series of political meanings but, in addition, she had become a specialist in the field that she was going to command. She had a wealth of direct experience regarding the operation of military power. However, what seems fundamental to me is that she had acquired specific knowledge that validated her conceptually to occupy the position that, ultimately, would lead her later to the presidency of the republic.

In another sense, politics as praxis progressively deteriorated in the public imaginaries that saw politicians as inoperative signs, as people guided by a lust for wealth or mere figments of the social imagination. In fact, the possibility of an inclusive democracy was in crisis, since more than 80% of young voters did not participate (and do not participate) in the electoral system. However, one politician escaped this public scrutiny: President Lagos, whose public image grew and was notably amplified in public polls to such an extent that there was no "man to overshadow him." That was so literal that only two women managed to emerge as presidential candidates: Michelle Bachelet (a socialist) and Soledad Alvear (a Christian Democrat). An unexpected and even incredible plot twist had taken place. These women were the only ones who achieved support from a citizenry that alternated between the Concertación's centrist project and the right. The right hoped to finally seize the only thing it lacked: political power.

Of course, if one thinks more carefully, what was happening was that this unexpected scenario appeared to be the most reliable way to captivate an electorate already weary or disenchanted with the Concertación. Novelty once again prevailed in order to awaken debates and passions that had fallen into oblivion. The two women were the final trump cards wielded by the conglomerate's masculine power to continue exercising control over public spaces.

Furthermore, it turned out to be exciting to watch two women go head-to-head in the fight for power; Soledad Alvear was doomed from the start, of course, since Bachelet's popularity was already completely unbeatable.

One of the pillars of Michelle Bachelet's presidential campaign was the reformulation of the pension system. It was there that her administration proposed to change a structure that would otherwise lead to the economic ruin of thousands if not millions of citizens. She also offered a *basista*[17] proposal, emphasizing the importance of citizen involvement in decision-making. But towards the end of her campaign, she took a noticeable turn when she began to deepen a discourse on women: not from the point of view of mere social welfare, but openly denouncing historical segregation that she proposed to change.

In this sense, there was a turning point in Bachelet's public discourse. Never before had she stated that she held what might be called a *feminist position*. Perhaps for this reason, her turning to the core of the gender issue—inequality in each and every social sphere—was understood in some sectors as a way of consolidating support or capturing the attention of voters in the segment of the population that was often most reluctant to vote for progressive parties: women. Throughout her campaign, which was managed entirely by well-known men from established coalition parties, voices from the right insisted that Bachelet did not have the "ability to lead." On the sidelines, it was insinuated that she had not been able to maintain a traditional family (although that could not be said openly, since most children are born out of wedlock in Chile). For this reason, the right-wing candidates insisted on incessantly displaying their own families as trophies. Of course, there was no shortage of predictable references to her physical appearance, through recurring sarcastic jokes about her weight, as well as a detailed investigation into her personal life.

The left, made up of the Communist Party, the Humanist Party, and sectors that were critical of the Concertación, focused on the question of the neoliberal economic model and its aberrant legacy of inequality. Their speeches were organized around social exclusion and its violent

---

17 Sergio Villalobos-Ruminott defines *basismo* as, "a movement that challenges the hierarchical structures of political parties and other representative organizations and insists on horizontal decision-making processes (*basismo*), based on a commitment to democratic de-centralism" Sergio Villalobos-Ruminott, "The Chilean winter," *Radical Philosophy*, Jan/Feb 2012: 12.

remains. For them, Bachelet only represented the continuity of the same model. In their eyes, ultimately, there was no significant difference between the Concertación's project and the right's.

The day that Michelle Bachelet was elected as President of Chile, a multitude of women took to the streets to celebrate her triumph and theirs—that of all women. They did so by symbolically wearing presidential sashes, and Bachelet did not disappoint them. In her first public speech to her constituents and the media, she emphasized her status as a woman and reiterated her promise of a cabinet with gender equality. And she followed through.

In my opinion, during her first year of office, Michelle Bachelet has already become part of the political history of women's movements due to her decisive emphasis on gender equality in her administration. From my point of view, this crucial resolution (which she had no obligation to adopt) is not only part of a specific political logic but, especially, is in keeping with her own paths and experiences. These shaped an enlightened outlook in her, but also one that was cold and analytical. I am referring to each situation that, with absolute certainty, Michelle Bachelet personally experienced: the traditional discrimination against women in the public and private spheres. My hypothesis is that Bachelet, given her understanding of the social codes, was able to inhabit (and endure) those spaces. However, when she was elected President of the Republic, her greatest gesture and feat was to stage what has historically been the greatest demand within feminist circles: equality between the sexes.

Her gender-equal cabinet has an example or a precedent in the Spanish government of José Luis Rodríguez Zapatero. However, carrying out this political operation in Chile is completely radical. Like many other countries, Chile is culturally structured under the incessant conventional signs of machismo. We must very carefully consider that the gender-equal cabinet, as well as important positions within the state, entailed the tacit expulsion of a considerable number of men who have had to (also tacitly) relinquish their space to women. Thus, Bachelet's decision generates political tension within her own coalition, because for once in history, a marginalized group had overcome or had transcended its barriers. Yet this ascent implies, naturally, that grudges will surely be visible in future distributions of roles.

Indeed, the government of Michelle Bachelet did not set out to modify the structure of the neoliberal economic system. As long as that does not change, inequality continues to be the biggest political and social problem weighing Chile down. The economic program that the Concertación has strengthened (inherited from the Pinochet dictatorship) seems immovable, despite the internal costs it exacts. That is a debt that accumulates, taking violent tolls and generating visible traces of resentment in the present.

That territory, that of the economy, has remained static and must be read within the carefully designed framework of consensus. Despite this severe limitation, Bachelet has maintained an uncompromising attitude (to date) toward her values. The Ministry of Health's decision to deliver the morning-after pill free of charge in clinics to all women over 14 years of age, without notifying the minors' relatives, has generated conflict not only with the political right but especially with the Chilean Catholic Church. Undoubtedly for them, Bachelet represents everything that the most zealous Catholicism stands against: a woman president, who is separated, secular, socialist, and has a Marxist background. On the other hand, this dispute is not simple since this institution is one of Chile's central de facto powers. She must contend with the messages of the bishops and the cardinal himself insisting on the preservation of life, their rejection of the pill, and any state measure that might compromise the pre-eminence of the traditional family, and naturally, a strict ban on youth sexuality.

Certainly, this first year has had many eventful milestones. The opposition and even some voices from the Concertación itself speak constantly of "disorder" in the executive branch, emphasizing that supposed "inability to lead" with which they intend to discredit Michelle Bachelet. The most definitive social complaint that she has had to face was the national strike of high school students. Known as the "Penguin Revolution," the students protested inequality in education, which generated sympathy and support among citizens and forced Bachelet to respond to their petitions.

Of course, one must consider the death of Pinochet, which occurred months after Michelle Bachelet took office: the first woman President of Chile, the daughter of a General who died in prison, the same woman president that maintained a permanent dialogue with human rights associations and the Association of Families of the Detained-Disappeared during this time. Pinochet died of a series of illnesses. Yet in a related story that appeals to another narrative, it could be assured that he died of fright before the apparition of this unprecedented scenario: a scenario that his hierarchical regime of terror was never able to foretell.

(2007)

Translated by Catherine M. Brix

The Pinochet Machine

I recognize—I must admit—that I never thought seriously or deeply about Pinochet's death, partly due to a kind of unexplainable superstition: I thought that if I thought about him, he'd never die. Yet as the years passed, he lingered there: persistent, stubborn.

I preferred not to think about him because, if I did, it would open an irreparable door to resentment and grief. That's why when the dictator, who had transformed into Senator Pinochet, was detained in London, I was able to experience the marvelous feeling of something akin to justice, or perhaps revenge. His detention struck me as a portentous event because, strictly speaking, the trip he took to London to be cured is what wound up taking him down; his own spine knocked him over. I think that's what brought about his downfall: the spinal column that had propped him up completely fell apart.

People mocked him. And although his prison was luxurious, cameras observed him from every angle and repeated an unthinkable image in the news: that of a dictator pacing around a patio from which he would not emerge for over a year.

Pinochet got weaker that year. Young people—neoliberalism's adolescent children—started to swear that he was a freak, a questionable character right out of a comic book. After London, human rights trials followed. Pinochet lost his status as senator-for-life, and, consequently, one of the most shameful episodes of the long and difficult transition to democracy ended.

However, there wasn't a single judge who could convict him. Not even the entire political system could convict him. Yet although he was never convicted, his image deteriorated. His followers became fewer, older, and more caricaturesque.

The political right took distance from him: the General's image was no longer profitable; it cost the right votes and branded it for life. This was especially true when the Riggs Bank accounts appeared containing millions of dollars that Pinochet had socked away under a series of false names. That wounded the political right—not the crimes, but the theft. Apparently, the political right knew about the theft. The dictator's entire family is ostentatious; it always was. The family has so much money that came out of nowhere—well, not out of nowhere, from the public coffers.

His followers no longer only maligned the "communists" (as they called all of Pinochet's opponents), but they also accused the right of being traitors, of having used and abused Pinochet for their own economic gain.

Pinochet, who never would die, got sick: a heart attack and pulmonary edema. His followers, about a hundred people, prayed for his health. And, as on other occasions, he got better. He walked around his hospital room; they were even going to release him. Yet suddenly he died; he took a turn for the worse, as the doctors said, and it was impossible to revive him.

A media frenzy ensued: Pinochet once again filled each and every screen. Pinochet had died, but his death unleashed that fervor that accompanies televised corpses. Thousands of Pinochet supporters came out of the woodwork and waited for hours to see the dead man's face. The political right appeared and showed its true face. After years of silence, they came out to capture votes.

Pinochet didn't have a funeral like other heads of state. Thousands of people celebrated his death, and various human rights organizations decried that he had died without any legal conviction.

When I found out that Pinochet died, I naturally thought he was dead. Some hours later, I thought it was better that Pinochet had died before we did—that we survived him.

Yet, over these hours, I've also been thinking about the dead, the disappeared, the prisoners, the tortured, the exiled. I've been thinking that Pinochet is latent: a machine that keeps churning, a machine of destruction and abuse whose every facet bears the name Pinochet. I've been thinking that the same political right that showed up for his funeral has a secret identity named Pinochet and that the army incubates Pinochet in its weapons and medals. We've survived one Pinochet, but there's another, and another, and another. That's why we'll never rest in peace. Never.

(2006)

Translated by Michael J. Lazzara

The Explosion of the Chilean Underground or the Explosion from Below

I see images of the recent social outburst in Santiago, allowing us to read a series of signs. I see tanks. I relive the curfew in my memory. While in the United States the debate focuses on the continuity of Trump due to an unprecedented presidential style marked by multiple ineptitudes, images of Santiago arise alongside a fury that is both present and, at the same time, an accumulation of past grievances.

It is not just about the abusive pension system, or about the problems of Chile's privatized waterworks, or about the existence of pollution that disproportionately affects specific social classes, or about healthcare, education, or housing. It is not just about working conditions. It is about millions of lives lived on credit, and the non-existence of young lives on the periphery.

This moment already has its image and its writing. It seems to me that the fiery passion we see must be read as a social temperature that rose and rose because the political establishment as a whole has been incapable of controlling the completely profit-driven corporate greed that runs throughout the system.

Politics has been transformed into quotas, elites, and transactions. Congress is in an ambiguous place, with endless re-elections, plagued by questionable friendships mediated by various interests, without the slightest "aura," in the sense coined by Benjamin.

The left-wing parties (with the possible exception of the Communist Party), governed by the desire for power (and money) for their leaders, left their citizen bases behind while poverty was viewed with suspicion and equated with criminality.

Inequality is part of the neoliberal reality, thanks to a shameful naturalization of an ideology in which there are (a few) worthwhile citizens and a multitude of other bodies seen as worthless.

White-collar crimes are seen as minor: almost a footnote in the system. Today, the church is a focus of sexual scandals. This particular institution's crisis has been deepening recently, but the central issue is the huge, decades-long failure of the political parties, absorbed in disputes over positions or representations in the midst of ever less representative voting bases.

The fare increases to the metro system was the straw that broke the camel's back. A kind of Instituto Nacional[18] uprising was unleashed that spread throughout the city's underground, barreling through tunnels with unstoppable speed.

This speed was increased by the lack of leadership and credible voices because the peripheries are seen as having no story, no dialogue, and no future. The poor and very poor middle class and the "wretched of the earth" (as Fanon would say) live as distant from the centers of power as if they inhabited an unknown housing project in an unknown dimension.

While Santiago burned, the president played his fiddle in Vitacura.

(2019)

Translated by Catherine M. Brix

---

18   The Instituto Nacional, a prestigious public boy's school in Santiago, was notably overrun and occupied by its students during the 2006 "Penguin Revolution." Students demanded educational reform, which was encouraged by mass protests throughout Chile, and eventually resulted in two national strikes after negotiations with the Bachelet administration broke down. This mirrors the impetus of the 2019 *estallido social*, in which students organized under #EvasionMasiva protested the increase in metro fares by jumping over the turnstiles, eventually leading to national protests and demands for constitutional reform.

Straight to the Eyes

These are tragic days. Protestors have died. More than two hundred people have suffered severe trauma to the eyes; many of them have lost vision in one eye, and Gustavo Gatica, a young student, was blinded by two shots. The police aim their steel-laden pellets directly at people's heads. Thousands of young people have been rounded up in police stations, and there's word of accusations of sexual abuse.

The revolt can't be stopped. A moment comes when that which is latent materializes with surprising precision. High school students' calls to boycott subway fares set in motion an unprecedented chapter for Chile. From my perspective, that action stirred a dramatic tension that had been lingering underground and that, on that day, rose to the surface. A call to dodge payment—in a society that had already paid dearly—caused subterranean energies to flare up and break through the mirage of prosperity that shrouded the Chilean economic model.

As this scene of anguish and discontent unfolded, political elites plummeted because they had lost touch with the citizenry. Party leaders and Congress no longer represented the people, who cast them aside.

Subway fare increased by thirty pesos, though not exactly by thirty pesos. Instead, citizens insisted that the pesos represented thirty years—or, perhaps, forty-six.

Inequality was a factor that the neoliberal model, which the dictatorship entrenched, considered a marginal cost. Yet ever-increasing inequality rendered millions of citizens invisible; it pushed them to the peripheries where the overwhelming task was to find ways to survive the savage model. Chilean life persists on credit: a considerable segment of the population has access to food and medicine thanks to debt and abusive interest rates. We should remember that the word debt comes from *debita*, which means "to have without having."

Today a few owners of the world amass wealth at shocking rates. In Chile, a select group accrues wealth just as obsessively. It's like a kind of Diogenes Syndrome in which tons of money piles up in a platinum vault, fueled by the sacrifice of millions of workers' bodies and the insatiable pillaging of our land. Local economists place wagers on growth, but for whom? We must remember that in Chile the one percent accumulates wealth equal to that of five million workers. These are statistics, I know, but this is an overwhelming one because it encompasses real lives, real poverty, and an appalling system: a system that for decades managed to eliminate the "us" as a sign of community and replace it with a competitive "I" obsessed with climbing the social ladder.

We must add to the mix the great feminist movement of young university-goers in 2018, which garnered massive support. When the twenty-first century feminist movement burst onto the scene, it demanded equality and asserted that the neoliberal apparatus had an extractivist effect on women's bodies, subjecting them not only to salary differences but also to double or triple work without pay. Unlike *MeToo*, the Chilean feminist movement demanded an end to the mistreatment that the aggregated institutional powers had naturalized. It centered the body as a political instrument and opened dialogue about how to redistribute wealth. The feminist movement participates actively in marches and town halls.

Despite all the violence, mutilation, and death, I know that a form of emancipation is taking place. As a writer, I also know how neoliberalism affected Chilean literature: it unleashed an exaggerated, acritical dependency of writers on the media. Chile only has two newspapers, and of the two, just one contains a cultural supplement that dedicates space to books. Digital newspapers, which are quite valuable, haven't managed to integrate thought on artistic happenings consistently. At the same time, the selfie trend promoted first-person writing—some quite interesting—to the point of saturating our tiny market. It ostracized fiction, which, in my opinion, is capable of offering decentered, dynamic perspectives.

In recent decades, traditional literary disputes have become minor power struggles. Everyone spends their energy chasing the charted road to success, deferring a razor-sharp critique of what lies beyond selfie culture. People were able to take distance from that critique because, on the surface, everything was working. It was about publishing everywhere possible or about how many times one had been translated. It was about being "recognized."

What I want to signal is that neoliberalism is an invasive machinery: it penetrates, divides, and destroys communities. It seeks to normalize profit. It domesticates bodies and literature. It foments insecurity. However, there are Chilean writers who resist, not just in the street but through the written word.

I think, as always, that the only true success comes with finishing the book one is writing. Yes, because one writes simply because of the urgent need to write.

(2019)

Translated by Michael J. Lazzara

Reciting a Rosary of Fake News

The prevailing hegemony has used and continues to use multiple mechanisms to reproduce its mandates, mechanisms based on the indissoluble equation between wealth and power. Right now, a violent siege on the citizenry has ramped up to stop the existence of a new Constitution. Hegemonic powers have thrown themselves into promoting the *Rechazo*, the Rejection, so that Pinochet's text remains intact.

Hegemonic powers set in motion a machinery articulated through well-defined forms. First, they silenced the social uprising. They did it by taking advantage of the quarantine and by putting extreme voices on TV, a medium that was clearly in decline even before the imposed confinement. Second, they sought to portray as mere crime the important and impressive protests which highlighted the oppression, exclusion, inequality, machismo, and injustices that devastate the Chilean population. They sought to make people forget the explosive uprising and turn it into mere *pop*.

This double machination meant destroying the legitimacy of the constitutional convention's representatives and ensuring that people forgot that those representatives had been democratically elected. It also meant burying their own irrelevant vote (that of the right) and concentrating instead on injecting into the social imaginary the idea that the protestors came out of nowhere. Doing that allowed them to make egregious statements of a classist, racist, and, of course, sexist nature, which flew in the face of the parity of the convention's demographic composition.

Obviously, if the representatives of the constitutional convention were branded as inept, hostile, radical leftists, communists, and "Indians," the text they wrote would never be accepted. Moreover, according to these right-wing voices—which became entirely fused with the old neoliberal progressivism and that deployed simplistic, almost illiterate language—the text was simply "bad."

This right-wing campaign, widely copied from the electoral play book of Trump and Bolsonaro, has made *fake news* its most recurring theme. The idea of plurinationality has been used and abused to insist that the new constitution would turn indigenous peoples into "first class citizens." This *fake* spin is horrifying and embarrassing because the indigenous peoples that came before us have *always* been considered outcasts throughout the entire history of the republic. The new constitutional text, written by popular mandate, advocates for the recognition, restitution, and the correct location of diverse indigenous peoples on the political and ethical map.

Gonzalo de la Carrera[19] emerged from inside the Trojan Horse, spurred on by his destructive disease, and had his say. He intended to erase everything: to erase the crimes of the (his) dictatorship and to kill off the detained-and-disappeared for a second time because their names appeared in the electoral records. But it's essential they remain there; they will be there forever as a presence and an absence because they are neither alive nor dead (and that is indeed terrible). They are part of a political category that Pinochet bequeathed to us.

Gonzalo de la Carrera is the mirror image of the Kasts. He embodies the right wing and its zombie supporters (men and women) who, like a good army ravenous for status, lined up for a photo-op with Kast during the first round of the last presidential elections. To that group, we must now add the right wing that calls itself center-left and that acts like wrapping paper that covers and adorns the hard right with a flashy ribbon. I am referring to the *amarillos*:[20] current and former authorities

---

19   Gonzalo de la Carrera is a representative of Santiago's affluent 11th district, which includes the neighborhoods of Las Condes, Vitacura, Lo Barnechea, La Reina, and Peñalolén. He is a member of the ultraconservative *Partido Republicano*, founded by José Antonio Kast.

20   Referring to Movimiento Amarillos por Chile, a political party founded in 2022 by Cristián Warnken. The centrist party criticized the *estallido social* of 2019 and was also critical of the Constitutional Convention, calling for its members to support the *Rechazo*. Other notable members include the ex-Christian Democrat, Mariana Aylwin—the daughter of former President Patricio Aylwin, and Minister of Education under former President Ricardo Lagos—and former President Sebastián Piñera's Minister of Health, Jaime Mañalich.

of all kinds who cover up the right's true face—hide it. Yet, it's the same package: one, unique, the very same.

We already know that hegemony captures and injects its precepts and principles into the social imaginaries that it penetrates and subdues. Gramsci already referred extensively to culture in all its variables as the most likely venue for sustaining hegemony; Bourdieu precisely addressed how symbolic power works by generating effects of reality, which equate to violence.

Right now, the entire right is lying in wait. Their tools are visible, while others hiding in their shadows, recite the complete rosary of *fake* upon *fake*.

But what about the youth, the urban poor, the women? ...

Apruebo. I approve.

(2022)

Translated by Catherine M. Brix

The New Text and Its Context

Pinochet's Constitution ended in an objective way more than four decades later. The end has come for a hegemonic text that allowed for an incredible privatization of natural resources (water, the sea, mining) and an unprecedented accumulation of wealth. The 1980 Constitution: the driving force of privatization and the sponsor of debt, which mortgaged the bodies of workers like so much collateral. Amidst the ruins of workers' rights, it pushed thousands of bodies toward the street and into informal employment.

Yet today I cannot help but think about how *before* or *behind* that privatizing, illegitimate Constitution—implemented without a voter registry, approved, and re-approved during the transition—there came a time of dictatorship marked by oppression, repression, crime, political imprisonment, and torture.

The end of *that* Constitution should revive the memory of an unprecedented social victimization in the 20th century: a memory fiercely controlled and diluted during the transition by means of the mall and garbage television propagated by banal people spreading gossip and nonsense; of a society that was manipulated by the climax of the market, consumerism, and debt.

I think it is a moment to *hacer memoria*—to exercise memory—to inscribe that memory in the present, and to endlessly reflect on how greed can destroy fragile politics. It is a moment to rethink the category of the detained-disappeared person as an irreparable situation.

In my view, the celebrated writing of this Constitution with gender-equal representation among delegates stems from the sum of two social moments. On the one hand, there was the so-called "Feminist May" of 2018 that managed to politicize women, starting with the university students: it was that feminist micro-revolution that led to gender parity among the Constitutional Assembly's constituents. On the other hand, there was the massive, incessant, nationwide, so-called "Outburst of October 18th," which made the end of Pinochet's Constitution possible.

Neither the Feminist May nor October 19th initially demanded the end of the Constitution.[21] They came about due to marginalization, poverty, the excesses and violence of the system, and of course, the inequality caused by a model maintained by a large part of political representatives. Nevertheless, terrified by the force of the citizenry, the political leaders agreed to a Constitutional Assembly. An agreement was signed for an Assembly with seats *OCCUPIED* by the two-thirds majority that the right and part of the center-left thought they were sure to get in order to push through their initiatives. And yet, best of all: they did *NOT* get them.

It was the women in the street, along with men, who unleashed the scenario that we are experiencing today. Traditional politicians are not the instigators of this event: it is the citizenry and its defiance. Of course, there had long been political movements, students, social leaders, enlightened associations, and popular television stations who never gave up. But all these energies came irrevocably together between the years 2018 and 2019. Furthermore, there was significant unrest in the Mapuche communities in the Araucanía region.[22]

Nevertheless, these celebrations cannot take away the fact that what is happening today comes at the cost of the dead, the injured, the mutilated, thousands of political prisoners, and the victims of sexual abuse by the *Carabineros*; international human rights organizations have recorded all of this clearly and unanimously. The villager Camilo Catrillanca, Ms. Fabiola Campillay, and the college student Gustavo Gatica are all symbols of this era. Their cases speak for themselves, yet they also represent dozens of others who experienced the same macro-violence of the 21st century. The unprecedented violence of the *Carabineros*

---

21   The original text notes both October 18th and 19th as significant dates of the *estallido social*. On the 18th, massive protests brought Santiago's metro to a halt, and on the 19th, former President Sebastián Piñera declared a state of emergency in response.

22   "Popular" from "poblacional" referring to "población." In Chile "población" refers to poor neighborhoods/slums.

is still meted out without any limit, albeit this time under a democracy that has overstepped its own boundaries.

We must celebrate but also express sorrow for what happened: for the existence of law enforcement's Special Forces who are still not held accountable for their violence, infiltration, bombs, and bullets.

Yes, celebrate the triumphs, but lucidly analyze the texts and contexts. Examine how pasts operate as presents. Understand the existence of opportunistic politics of forgetting. Protect the integrity of citizens in the near future, if neoliberal voracity can be controlled.

(2021)

Translated by Catherine M. Brix

PART II

Bodies, Gender, and Power

Errant, Erratic

Juan Carlos Lértora has asked me to discuss some of the issues that seem to repeat themselves, both in my books and in current events.[23] So, I will try to return to some matters of recent concern for me, but I would like to point out that this should be placed in a certain context: I think what I write here should be understood as separate from the novels I've written, because they're part of a creative *oeuvre* that follows its own rules. Not only am I unaware of those rules; I can't be held responsible for them. Just as I could never rewrite so much as a single page of any book that I've already published, I think that there are questions in my writing that exist in a space that's entirely beyond me. And that is perhaps what keeps my desire to write alive: that voice that escapes me, and that often surprises or even mortifies me.

I should also say that even though my thinking and maybe even my writing follow a particular logic, my own certainties are constantly in a state of flux. So whenever possible, I tend to avoid making any grand authorial declarations. I avoid them because I think that if this kind of thinking has any meaning, it has to do with a personal process that allows me to make changes and modifications as needed—instead of establishing a discourse that gets congealed into ideology, or paralysis, hampering a mental process that I prefer to keep fluid.

I will thus speak about the following matters only provisionally and partially.

---

23 This text was solicited by Juan Carlos Lértora for a volume he was editing of critical articles about Eltit's novels, entitled *Una poética de literatura menor: la narrativa de Diamela Eltit* (Cuarto Propio, 1993).

Writing Under Dictatorship

The really hard thing was *living* under dictatorship. To live in a dictatorship is unspeakable, part of a story that seems to me never-ending. I cannot say everything I'd like to say about this, but I did find that writing and thinking were forms of personal salvation in that situation. It's something so delicate, even inexplicable, that it's hard to talk about without resorting to clichés. How could one ever define the effects of a negative, sordid, threatening form of power? Learning to live with powerlessness, putting up with the daily humiliations of working as a government employee under the dictatorship, struggling not to give in to the comforts of indifference, surviving amidst desperate and frustrating economic scarcity, among other situations: this was what I experienced for many—too many—years. My writing took place in that context—obsessively—not because I thought I was making any kind of material contribution, but because it was the only way I could salvage my own honor, so to speak. When my liberty—and I use that word more in a symbolic sense than literally—was under threat, I just decided to take the liberty of writing with liberty. Of course, those of us who were publishing during that time didn't exactly find a favorable environment for nonconformity in the cultural sphere. But that isn't the heart of the matter, and it never was. Why would they have offered those kinds of freedoms in a territory under so much surveillance, so much threat? Publishing under dictatorship was, without a doubt, a no-man's-land. But due to the kind of work I do, I will always be maneuvering within a fairly reduced space. And that's fine. Anyone who publishes a book might expect certain gestures of welcome from the cultural sphere, but for me the major litmus test was when my novel *Por la patria* came out in 1986—to absolute critical indifference.

I wrote four novels during the dictatorship, and that's the social space that I claim as my own. However, writing was hardly a relief, even for one moment, from the humiliations, fear, pain, and powerlessness I felt on behalf of the victims of that system. Writing in that space had to do with my own personal motivations and passions. It was my secret political resistance. When you live in an environment that is crashing down around you, bringing out a book might just be one of your only options for getting by.

But I should also say, as a more positive memory of those years, that I had the privilege of being surrounded by a number of writers and visual artists who were important interlocutors for me, including Raúl Zurita, Nelly Richard, Lotty Rosenfeld, Carlos Leppe, Eugenio Dittborn, Carlos Altamirano, and Eugenia Brito (to name just a few). Alongside them, I was able to think through the answers to a series of questions. Perhaps the most important question was about the possible relationship, and the real distance, between art and politics and between art and society. The search for an answer is ongoing, I think, for each one of them, and I hope to keep that question alive in myself.

Marginality

When I began writing *Lumpérica*, I completely enclosed myself within a particular domain of meaning. I can't say that I chose that domain, at least not consciously, because I didn't experience a particular moment of decision. Later, when the book came out, I saw for myself how marginal it was. That was when I understood that there was a recurring thread in my books: spaces, characters, or meanings that could be linked to particular kinds of marginality. But what has maybe been most meaningful for me was that I've been able to organize certain structures of meaning around marginality. I think that what we understand as marginality, and what has marked my own margin as a writer, has to do with structure. The word in all its centrality or non-centrality, its aesthetic resonance, its play and its mockery and its twists, is the greatest challenge I've had to confront in the writing process. I don't aspire to a splendid process of telling stories, which is something that lies outside the realm of my interests. It's more important for me to submerge myself in as much ambiguity as the habit of writing can possibly provide, and then, from there, to create a bit of meaning.

I'm interested in the artisanal aspects of writing a novel—by which I mean looking for one word, and then another, finding just the right one for the page—and the slowness of organizing meaning. It's a certain notion of time. (When I'm writing, my own life is annulled, and my own death is suspended.) I'm interested in the paradoxical and intertwined stages of creation and death that come into play there, constantly colliding with the meaning and the senselessness of an undertaking that is so ambiguous, and yet at the same time so concrete.

This is all just to say that I write only because I like to. Writing is my passion, and if I'm going to write, I'll write what I like. That is why my only limits are my own shortcomings, which are, of course, ongoing and wide-ranging.

To date, I have chosen not to create a monolithic novel, based on any kind of rational structure. Rather, I have chosen a more wandering path, which has allowed me fragmentation, plurality, nuance, and edginess. I think Juan Carlos Lértora says it better than I do when he talks about "dispersion." That which is dispersed always constitutes itself as a margin, because it questions the centers and their pretense of unity. My place in literature has involved working with material fragments and excerpts of voices, vaguely exploring (as would a vagabond) different genres, masquerades, simulacra, and verbalized emotions. I truly appreciate those spaces, but that doesn't mean that I think they're the only possible spaces for literature; on the contrary, I believe that the process of writing is manifold and that the important thing is to construct certain aesthetic spaces that carry the weight of meaning. I think that's the center of the literary dilemma.

The Margins

On the other hand, I have resigned myself to the idea that I only have the brain that I've been given and that I only have the syntax that I use. I acknowledge that my place of aesthetic and social intervention lies in transitory areas where power, or the norm, or the consensus (or whatever) tends to settle scores in unfair, injurious ways. In this sense, my observation of dominant cultural codes that are *Chilean*, for lack of a better word, has been exemplary. By this, I mean behaviors that I find restrictive and reductive, and which—under the anachronistic aegis of classism or economic voracity—weave a tapestry of conduct that is stereotypical at best, and repressive at worst.

But behind this lies one of my only hard and fast convictions: the knowledge that I belong to a country marked by inequality and a number of social problems. It is on behalf of the punishing struggles experienced by Chilean men and women that I offer what is perhaps my only gesture of political and social rebellion: writing in a way that undermines comfort and counters the signs of convention. I might be wrong about the things I've said, and it may also be true that the feverish, commercial rhythms of our time can work against me, but I still believe in literature more as a disjuncture than as a place where readers can find answers to make them happy and content. The (ideal) reader I aspire to reach is more problematic; she has inadequacies and doubts and is plagued by uncertainty. It is there that the margin—all the multiple possible margins—provide pleasure and happiness, but also disturbance and crisis.

Given that I was not born with a silver spoon in my mouth, and that I find myself compelled to provide for my family and for myself on a daily basis, I am always going to be on the side of workers. I believe in discipline, but also in the right to legitimate protest for those who are subordinated. Perhaps that is why I am open to reading symptoms of defenselessness, whether social or mental, from my own experiences growing up outside the *barrio alto*, subjected to family crises, as the daughter of my father and his hardships. My own political convictions—unrestricted, and perhaps even grand—are in solidarity with those spaces of abandonment, and I aspire to a greater social equilibrium and for more flexibility in the apparatuses of power.

Being a Woman Writer in Chile

I think of writing as a social instrument that can't be gendered. Its mise-en-scène, so to speak, has historically been exercised by men, but that's just a detail: a significant detail, maybe, but a detail nonetheless. It seems reductive to me to read texts in a bipolar, straightforwardly biological way, as either feminine-female or masculine-male. I'm interested in bodies, but in bodies *of work*, independent of an author's particular gender. Lately, I've been thinking that the issue lies in how gender is constructed. From there, it becomes clear that the value we assign to the masculine sex has to do with how power is administered; that which we understand as feminine is subordinated and remains peripheral to power. I know this may sound simplistic, and maybe it is. I'm aware that this is a very complex issue, and I don't think of myself as a specialist. I'm only trying to think, and think about myself, in terms of my particular—and indeed precarious—perspective.

That's why I'm interested in the norms surrounding the writing of novels, for example. There are female writers who are masculine, metaphorically speaking, in their approach to certain codes, and there are male writers who operate in a more peripheral position vis-à-vis power, locating themselves closer to the category of the feminine. I'm not speaking of sexual orientation so much as about social conventions such as gender. And, of course, there is a spectrum of positions and fluctuating borders. I say this because it seems clear to me that it's possible to play with the construction of certain bodies of writing, imbuing them with particular signs. The kind of body of writing that emerges, and the meanings attached to it, is strategic. This also has to do with our willingness to read particular literary themes as symptomatic of our affiliation to a work. For example, a novel in a conservative literary canon that's about political non-conformity isn't necessarily critical if its modes of production go unquestioned. A novel that presents itself as feminist, or feminine, or as women's writing, wouldn't be transgressive solely by virtue of its focus on current problems. So, my idea is to read the texts and find the political points they're making.

On the other hand, I think that works of art are political to the extent that they manage their material in accordance with the meanings they create. My understanding is that certain works of feminist theory try to seek out gestures of crisis or resistance or subjectivity in certain texts written by women. And that's important. But there's another critical approach that values, from a sociological standpoint, any literary work written by women. I find that approach unconvincing because it could lead to a ghettoization of women writers, placing them on the periphery such that they compete amongst themselves and make no impact on the system as a whole.

However, there's another factor as well: the social and cultural space that a woman who writes must inhabit. Her real life as a writer. And that's a major problem. I will talk about myself here because it's not my place to do otherwise. What I will say, then—and this isn't important to my own situation—is more of a didactic exercise. I have experienced discrimination that has been camouflaged behind certain gestures. The comment that a work "doesn't make sense," which might confer an air of prestige or defiance upon male writers, has functioned as a slogan of determinism and exclusion when applied to me. Since I've sought to maintain a particular cultural discourse focused on the dilemmas that writing itself presents, I have garnered the paradoxically bad reputation of being perceived as "very intellectual." And that "very intellectual" is not in any way a compliment; it's about rejecting a certain form of communicating. But in the end, this is one of the rules of a particular cultural game. I don't think that there's necessarily bad faith at play here; I just read in it one of the unconscious ways in which women's actions and words are cast into doubt. It seems that people expect women to respond to dominant models of speaking and writing. Many of those models seem very fragile to me, in that they have been so simplified that they have become devoid of nuance. The romance novel is not the only possible space for a woman to write, whether it's about unrestricted abnegation or sexual emancipation. It seems more important to me to create a constellation of thinking that connects the individual to the public sphere, and the subjective to the social.

I do what you might call triple work. I'm a worker who lives on a monthly salary, I have a family I'm responsible for, and I'm a writer. There are several roles involved here, and there are dissonances among them. It's not easy. Because of that, my great challenge is to balance these different spheres—to the extent such a thing is possible—and take advantage of the time I have to write. In any case, not every pitfall a woman writer faces can be attributed to outside forces—men included. Many of these pitfalls can be found in the psyche of the woman herself—an effect of the culture into which she was born. There are parts of me, however uncomfortable they may be, that have to do with the conventions I grew up in, and I imagine that they will stay with me until the end. I think I at least partly understand the culture I inhabit, in all of its good and bad aspects. Women are hardly the only minority in society, either; there are ethnic, sexual, and economic minorities too, all of whom experience similar conflicts. Although I feel committed to all the symbolic and political struggles to improve the situation of women, I don't have the power or the ability to change national habits, nor do I wish to turn myself into some kind of fanatical preacher trying to correct people's public or private deeds. The only way I can respond to the different ironic, malignant, or unjust details that women must contend with is to try to write my books freely, without complacency or any pretension of redemption, and then fight to get them published. What else can I do? I write because I like to write, and the truth is that I'm just one woman writer among many.

(1993)

Translated by Carl Fischer

On the Work of Literature

The Impossible

From my perspective, work in the field of symbolic creation—that is, the literary process—entails the inability to precisely discern the laws that govern writing. Such laws determine narrative decisions, themes, and aesthetic approaches, among other things. It's impossible to define those laws because the symbolic organization involved in literary writing is so extensive—and therefore so hard to grasp, so multiple—that any attempt to capture it is nothing more than a reductive, empty gesture. It becomes a simplified parody of the energy that makes it possible, an asphyxiated reference to its landscape, and basically a simulacrum of the process.

However, what I do think is possible is an approach to *part of* the work of literature; that which—aside from narrating a particular plot—also entails political choices in the usage of language and writing.

It is possible, in my opinion, to examine the political genealogy of a work, as long as certain conditions are met. We must accept that language is not innocent and that it is indeed charged with the peripatetic interplay of history (meaning "History," with a capital H, intersecting with the concrete traces of a biographical history that has a social narrative). We must open ourselves up to thinking that the literary (as writing) contains symptoms of excess—it is wide-ranging, with a certain metaphoric range. And we must admit that literature entails trying to uncover the precise meanings of language through the effectiveness of the text as a social intervention.

To interrogate that approach, to determine a literary position, I believe it's necessary to think of oneself within a wider field: a field formed by diverse kinds of writing and a range of political positions. One must confront, for example, the cohesion or interruption inherent to a particular sentence, or the saturation of signs, or certain verbal games and codes, in order to explore the meanings that get constructed. What stories are created through a debate with the language that articulates them? Which syntaxes move, bump into one another, and emerge in the broad territory of language?

Distance and Otherness

If it's true that I write with a social word—at once another's and my own, inherited from others and always ambiguous, simultaneously malleable and calcified—then it means that I am embedded at the center of an incomplete landscape and in work whose only satisfaction comes from feeding my obsession with the word. And my job, my political intention (in the sense of my particular literary politics), is connected at its edges (the edges of the written word, the great raw material of literature) with uncertainty. This is a self-imposed journey whose unstable route ends with a story that is foreign to me even as it belongs to me—and I will lose it a second time, once it's published. It's foreign to me, first of all, due to the otherness of the language I inherited, marked unquestionably as it is by my social and family background. This otherness is deepened by the subterfuges and shortcomings of my own abilities, by the hesitations inherent to the words I choose. It's an otherness that never manages to extinguish the syllables that I was supposed to reject. That sense of being overwhelmed by the expressions that came before me. The hardened fixity of the only place that it can construct.

But it is an uncertainty that also leads to pleasure. It's the pleasure of using words to build a material setting in which words can be desired in an artisanal way. It is a place of writing—its assembly, its volume—that comes as a liberation, preventing oblivion and sustaining memory as a counterpart to the orality that flees to the extremes of time.

However, my own literary practices force me to establish another discourse, a cultural discourse, that speaks for my work. This second discourse, which stands upon the perceptions of the first (that is, upon an uncertainty), is useless for understanding or *illuminating* one's own work (in all its intentionality and its failures). But it can work toward generating a supplementary word: that of the author and her cultural determination. It's a discourse that has to come out, even if it goes unreceived, because it alludes to the cultural conditions of one's work, and to one's subjective perspective in the context of a social reality. I will thus speak from where I'm standing. I will speak from my cultural experience as a woman writer from Chile.

What to Write, and What to Publish?

I think that publishing in Latin America has a double valence. On one hand, we have the pleasure of an enclosed writing, absorbed in its own boundaries, protected by its codes, judged according to the verisimilitude of a landscape, and subjected to a hierarchy by national habit. But on the other, we have writing exposed to the signs of a crisis that comes from the fragmentation of its cultural production. I am referring, of course, to Latin America's ongoing lack of integration, wherein the Spanish language spreads out, taking on multiple and unexpected meanings as it crosses national borders. This is a historical fragmentation that leads to the creation of certain literary categories by the few publishing companies able to operate in multiple countries; they can dictate reading habits by promoting one particular written product over another. Those tactics can end up reducing the legibility of other forms of writing. By rejecting certain texts or enclosing them within certain stereotypes, they end up impoverishing the ways in which the centers of cultural power read Latin America.

Writing from a Latin American perspective, in my opinion, is an activity whose dominant impulse is literary creation itself, in all its regional varieties. It is an act of establishing oneself—in an archaeological way—in one's own territory and alongside the impulses that go along with that territory. This is work that gets diminished by the effects of an ongoing (im)politics that limits what one can say or, rather, limits the cultural destination of what one says. It impedes the symbolic flow of certain discourses, depriving them of their ability to interact with other kinds of writing. These editorial boundaries prevent the deterritorialization of the word.

The Context that Speaks

Speaking from that boundary, from a specific border, and as an inhabitant of a continent designated as poor and consigned to (chronic) poverty, I find myself confronting a changing set of discursive parameters: the discourse around me is shifting from one of social reparation to one that is more economic and pragmatic. An economic discourse that sees the market as the sublime restitution of everything we lack. I have witnessed how that market hegemony brings with it the implantation of a series of social images that anchor themselves in the public sphere and become institutions. Their installation of a particular way of life leads to the mandate to consume.

An image that appeals to common sense (that is, everyone sensing the same thing) quickly turns into a commonplace, which is none other than that of the market. Images that seek to impose a (social) body modeled upon the dynamics of supply and demand. Bodies that circulate within the logic of media publicity (propped up by the advertising industry and its large-scale purchase of commercial space). Bodies whose success hinges upon the implantation of these images in the collective body.

The politics of consumption are hardly new, but what *is* new, I think, is the fact that it's beginning to affect Latin America's social discourse and political programs. It's generating certain kinds of bodies, placing them under their auspices and promoting them with industrial brands—syntactical brands—as bodies set apart by the overwhelming speed of fashion. The body itself then becomes a kind of fashion, under siege as it is by the discourse of advertising slogans. These bodies are held captive, captivated, by the promise of superficial erotic pleasure: the erotics of consumption. This is a "new era" for Latin American bodies who see their faces, their aspirational identities, and their histories mirrored back to them in the symmetrical bodies the triumphant market offers them.

But then we look to the other side of this project: the protracted marginality of Latin America, where more than half the population lives in extreme poverty. A population that is condemned under this new order to try and survive without images, to a material existence without a common ground. They are expelled from the words that name their aesthetic and are prevented from recognizing themselves in the cultural production of their region. Because of these new discourses, the concrete marginality of a broad swathe of the population of the Americas finds itself confronting a reality outside of any discussion. It's literally out of circulation.

And this cultural remainder—this omission—carried out by a dominant discourse that is economic above all else, implies a linguistic remainder, an amputation from the popular symbolic universe, a cutting-off of the senses. This minority of persons living in extreme poverty is, like all minorities, condemned to a kind of extinction—its large numbers notwithstanding. I'm talking about a symbolic extinction, because their bodies are hidden from the public, their desires are submerged, and their cultural future is under threat.

The First Word, the Third Word

The turbulence of the market affects literature as well. Latin American publishers, who are responsible for some of these symbolic materials, struggle to keep up with this new order. To stay in business, they try to promote a literature that builds, and is built upon, the *common sense* of the turn of the century. Theirs is a literary discourse whose images promote the transparency of fashion, the self-assuredness of speech, and the linguistic materiality of the consumer classes. This is a literature that seduces with the vertigo of being the latest (and the only) product, a literature that maintains the tone of the *common place.*

But if Latin America is a place of opacity, if its official discourse is the result of a battle for language, if the memory of its past defeats (or its triumphs, for some) is *mestizaje*, if its race-based hierarchies are what distinguishes it (I'm referring to a particular kind of facial appearance), and if its regionalization is the origin of its popular language (the codes of its slang, its spatial history), then how is one to turn the word, in the so-called "third world," into one's first and only commercial product? I don't know. But this is the dilemma that the (literary) marketplaces have placed before us, because it's definitely about the implantation of a new political project.

The Imperative of Context

And what is a feasible cultural discourse? I think it is that which provides context alongside text. A cultural discourse must point out the social conditions of a given action, because the result of that action—a book—is part of a larger project that determines, based on sales, a hierarchy of editorial decisions.

One central aspect of that context, it seems to me, is the fact that I am a woman who writes. I hardly think it's necessary here to repeat information about the social realities of Latin American women, but I will point to the omissions, exclusions, and fragmentations that have characterized a cultural history that has assigned unequal roles to the different genders. This inequality is no different from other unjust social decisions that have been made based, for example, on ethnic differences or on the rigid economic categories that rule all public places—not to mention public fates.

In this way, I feel that there is a persistent periphery in our continent, confronting a central power, and organized in a fairly deterministic way. I'm thinking, for example, of the effect of social genealogy, or of the ideological positionings of gender (which result from a fixed relationship with sexuality). These are structures that affect the way we live: surreptitiously or openly, subtly or violently, but always efficaciously. These hierarchies are made possible by the conventions that the system follows, allowing it to manage not only the abstraction of civil power, but also bodies, desires, and outcomes. It is a system of power that has entrenched itself in history, based on its repeated struggle to establish the monotonous consummation of that model.

One of the strongest counterparts, or at least counterpoints, to this, as far as questioning convention goes, has been the contributions made by feminist theory and action. I use the word "contributions" because they have to do with thoughts and actions that have achieved tangible results in terms of psychic and public breathing room for women. However, it needs to be said that these ideas come from countries that are considered to be "developed," and as such, those of us who belong to countries that are colonized, or dependent, or in any case net receivers of "first world" products and productivity, should receive these ideas from a certain cautious distance, as far as how the assumptions they make are delineated, outlined, and positioned in specific realities.

And what I'm saying doesn't mean that the dilemmas of gender, class, and ethnic division can be regionalized, per se, but they do risk getting overshadowed when certain categories are administered internationally throughout history. This history is no more or less full of conflicts than any other, but it carries the sign of difference, relative not only to habits and living conditions but also to the fact that a certain protracted scarcity of living (as happens in Latin America) has a psychic impact, marks social relations, and situates its desires in a world of artisanal improvisation, separated from the technologies of production.

Even so, it's clear to me that contemporary feminist theory has been paramount in its interrogation of existing structures of power. Its strength and efficacy are no doubt linked with the urgency of its demands. And this strong interrogation can be located within a larger theoretical field involving psychoanalysis, politics, and even economics; it has remodeled circuits of thought, revealing the excessive arbitrariness of ideological constructions and placing gender at the center of how we think.

Meanwhile, feminist actions—that is, its concrete international organizations—have managed to create a dialogue with institutions of power, opening up spaces for minimal–but–important social actions on behalf of the family and the public lives of women.

Admittedly, international feminist organizations have suffered crises: their ranks have been polarized and fragmented, and their demands have been weakened by the pragmatic considerations necessary for conducting political dialogue. And as a movement, feminism has been dismantled as an organic body (a dismantling that is understandable if we think of feminist action as a critical space that seeks to reformulate the administration of power). Still, its achievements, though potentially reversible, are impossible to ignore.

Feminist action cannot correspond to feminist theory in a linear way beyond particular actions and a determined reading of its assumptions. We understand that a particular text can be read, unread, or read poorly. And it is precisely in the results of reading—that is, in terms of feminist action—where I find it all the more important to clearly outline contexts. Our continent, even in its regional differences, carries the mark of the artisanal, in my opinion. In the context of this practice (a word I use in the sense of the artisanal nature of writing, for example), concrete thinking and living are ways to name a woman who carries in her body a particular way of connecting with reality.

One way this becomes legible is through motherhood, which we could think of as a form of artisanship specific to women's bodies. A relationship that can perhaps be considered enjoyable in terms of the power of a body that incessantly "creates." And that "creation" defines Latin American women by their multiple gestations. Notwithstanding the ideological meanings that are often placed upon motherhood as a category, or the social problem of overpopulation, I would like to turn to the moment of gestation, of the authority of a body. To think of that body as a creative projection. A body that is particularly active in social sectors that have the greatest needs.

But to think about that body means, in my perspective, establishing a reflection, a reading, and a revision of one's own story in a way that takes other bodies into account—specifically those bodies that are in a state of subjection relative to those in power. If, at a symbolic level, the feminine is that which is oppressed by those in power, I think that it is permissible, in principle, to extend that category to all those groups who share that positionality because the condition of vulnerability—whether symbolically or materially speaking—is not exclusive to the (social and biological) bodies of women.

I am thinking, for example, of solidarity-based feminist theory and action, which can contain and extend its thinking and its work toward an interdisciplinary framework that brings meaning to the direction that our social future is taking.

Literature and the Feminine

The effects of international feminism are making themselves increasingly known in the field of Latin American literature. Designations like "Women's Literature" or "Women's Writing" or "Feminist Literature" are becoming more and more familiar to those of us who write. These terms are the result of the breakdown of a literary history that has been organized to center literature written by men—women's writing is then figured as peripheral.

The creation of these categories has generated an interesting and valuable critical and theoretical discourse, broadening our reading practices and our perspectives on literature itself. It is an area of thought that offers new criteria for understanding women's writing, based on the (dis)order of particular lexicons, the visual figure that presents subjectivity, or the eroticism of work on a textual body. And this area of thought, it seems to me, is particularly relevant in that it forces us to carry out a more exhaustive and complete interrogation of those texts as a whole.

However, I should also point out insistent attempts to oversimplify these matters, which sometimes perpetuate exclusions. I've noticed that the designation "women's writing" is overused, and when that happens, it results in the creation of insidious and calculated competition among (women's) writing; in those disputes for hegemony, the other hegemony—the traditional one—remains unchallenged. Although this tactic doesn't obscure women's writing, it does divide it and confine it to one privileged referent: the fact that it is created by women. This does a disservice to the intensity of feeling that the textuality of a literary work is capable of enacting.

I may not be a specialist in this matter, but I think of writing as a social instrument. It has been historically used by men, and the suspiciously low number of women who have made use of it to create literature has possibly limited its ability to produce meaning. I am thinking about this at a hypothetical level: repressed writing might have been able to alter, broaden, or change the way things are done centrally, producing movement, or at least a shudder, in the production of literature, to perhaps make its development more dynamic. This can take place as much in men's writing as it can in women's, of course.

What I do think is that broadening literary codes is more important than broadening the thematic content that can be read in a particular work. To put it in a different way, I don't think being a woman is enough to guarantee that a work of literature can make changes to existing structures, just as it's clear to me that some literature produced by men is basically a capitulation to market forces.

I'm still fascinated by literature that problematizes its own zones of production, using its symbolic order to broaden the senses. I perceive a literary diversity, in the same way that there are diverse modes of producing literature, and multiple conflicts that ensue.

And although the obstacles in the path of every woman who writes (part of that intransigent social order in the literary world) are as obvious to me as they are offensive, I should say that I remain focused on the variety of works and on the fundamental aesthetic order that a politics of writing can shape.

(1993)

Translated by Carl Fischer

Telling It Like She Sees It

1. The political effort to undo women's longstanding subjugation materialized in their emergence as social subjects within the public sphere under the rubric of feminism. The convoluted context in which this movement emerged is hardly worth detailing here; I will simply say that its strength is linked to the production-oriented changes that would affect the social sphere at the onset of the industrial revolution. Just as new modes of production would call upon bodies to monotonously manage machines at a massive, serialized scale, it would also generate new subjects.

2. A politics of equality was key to feminism when it came on the scene: it was a succinct way of naming a movement that sought to account for the female-subject's lack, despoliation, and devastation within both the symbolic and literal organization of power. The drive for equality, which first coalesced around the fight for women's suffrage, was a fundamental way of demonstrating the extent of the inequalities and obstacles that women experienced. Feminism was a strategic term in that it could expose all the forms, techniques, and actions of "rhizomatic" domination, to use Deleuze's term, insofar as that domination lacked a clear beginning and end. Indeed, it proliferated incessantly, adopting different guises and hiding behind institutional discourses to consolidate and perpetuate its coercive practices in the realms of the family, religion, the law, and the state. These practices were the most expeditious ways of cultivating, transmitting, and propagating the inequalities that feminists denounced.

3. The word "feminism" took on extremely negative connotations. Since the 19th century, it has been uncomfortable and aggravating for many,

and the powers that be have wisely used this to highlight feminism's unbecoming and belligerent aspects, thereby diluting or dismissing the politics it proposes. The early emergence of feminism was seen as inappropriate or anomalous, sectarian, impossible to countenance, and—above all—incapable of achieving solid, broad coalitions with any other protest groups. Whereas the feminist struggle did not achieve an effective insertion into the public sphere due to the relentless attacks upon it, socialist or communist or anarchist movements—to name a few of the more controversial ones in recent memory—were able to obtain a certain amount of power.

4. Irony, caricature, opprobrium, and cooptation were the most effective instruments for fragmenting and neutralizing feminism's epic, egalitarian aims. Because of this, and with the same vigor, the word feminism had to be rethought, and the issues of its concern were repositioned under the broader, atomized, and somewhat neutral auspices of "gender." In French thought, moreover, the struggle for equality was modified by the theory of difference. This led to a misunderstanding: the urgent need for social equality came to be understood as the desire to be equal and identical to men rather than as an active, egalitarian way to inhabit the social sphere.

5. This name change—this restoration of a façade—greatly weakened the political efficacy of feminism. The possibility of inhabiting the social world as equals came to be understood as the obligation to inhabit it on differing terms; but a basic, structural inequality was established *on top of* this difference.

6. Women travel along an openly hostile social horizon that the passage of time has not been able to repair or reformulate. Over the years, one characteristic of their domination remains unchanged: the means of production, and the majority of the world's wealth, belong to men, while women are paid unequal salaries that allow others incredible profit. Institutional discourses strategically exacerbate this situation. Throughout the Western world, women make—we make—less than men for the same work. The economy—whether in cycles of growth or contraction—sustains itself upon this asymmetry. Today's global

economy is founded upon the exploitation of a huge population (there are more women on earth than men), and the irregularities we experience are the same—the differences between the working class and the executive class notwithstanding. These salary inequalities are lucrative enough to sustain entire global systems. Yet it's important to understand that one has to be considered less-than, not to mention officially counted as less-than, in order to be paid less. And this "less-than" is such an iron-clad, exhaustive, and all-encompassing construction that it comprises everything from the real to the symbolic spheres in order to achieve its aims.

7. Money as the lamb of god, or the mother of god, is the definitive economic, operational factor that keeps women at a disadvantage in every situation in which they find themselves. This, of course, relegates women to an always-specular relationship with men, who in turn inscribe and describe women.

8. As the weaker figure in the gender binary—subject to the economic operations of power and forced either into dependency or to defend themselves at every turn—women are culturally and arbitrarily constrained within their gender. This gender system is designed by men, made to their measure, and always tautological. Aside from any theoretical discourses that might remedy or reverse this, women's spaces are inevitably limited and controlled precisely by the masculine power that subjugates them.

9. In this sense, it's interesting to recount how women's writing has developed in Chile. Rosario Orrego, considered to be Chile's first female writer, published her book *Teresa* in 1870. A contemporary of Alberto Blest Gana, Orrego—whose literary work was skillfully rendered and carefully executed—addressed the very tensions upon which the incipient, fragile nation rested. Rosario Orrego created an active, politically committed female protagonist, who would give up love, marriage, and procreation—the forms of capital most commonly assigned to women— for the cause of anticolonial liberation. However, this project was discontinued. Later, Mariana Cox Stuven wrote the liberal novel *El diario de Marie Goetz* at the turn of the 20th century, using the pseudonym

Shade. In it, she wrote about a woman, unhappy in her marriage and objectified into a purely decorative role, whose only possible escape was multiple amorous fantasies. That was the same path that the elaborate, suggestive writing of María Luisa Bombal would later pick up on: the escape of a bored, bourgeois woman into a fantasy world that was amorous, idealized, and evocative. Marta Brunet's solitary writing, meanwhile, registered the amplitude of the senses that modern women experienced in their vexed relationships with money and the public sphere. Using the many techniques of literature, Brunet created a complex woman: she told it like she saw it.

10. Karl Marx once emphatically said that religion was the opium of the masses. To paraphrase Marx, I'll venture to state, with the same level of emphasis, that love is the opium of women, as far as how different institutions and their propaganda apparatuses have organized things. Let me repeat that: love is the opium of women. A sizable proportion of literature produced by women focuses on love and sentimentality, with a touching side of obedience. The ups and downs, the complaints, and the amorous insurgencies of these themes were written as if they "belonged" in the domain of women, in an essentialized, naturalistic way. As if this were the only kind of writing that could pertain to women.

11. On the growing, invasive horizon of the literary market, women's writing has never ceased to use relationships with men, whether tortuous or providential, as a vehicle for examining social issues. Their focus on men—whether present or absent—is but an entry point for scrutinizing women's ways of life, their bravery, and their will to remain agents in their lives regardless of the whims or rejections of their loved ones. From there, they open up spaces for a delicate erotic to emerge, always in accordance with recent institutional openings. This has been the most effective way of setting apart and segregating one particular type of literature. Women's writing, as the market understands it, has worked to repair omissions, but it has also exacerbated its own ghettoization. It is left to men to use literature as a venue to explore meaning-making. Women's writing is pushed to the sidelines as a lesser product, a merely decorative byproduct.

12. The market performs a process of castration—an operation of compartmentalization and segregation—that reduces literature to biology or, one could even say, to genitality. It ignores the symbolic depth and the political work that literature does with signification. Dramatics are assigned to women with their corresponding thematic, but the *logos* itself—and all the textual dilemmas it entails—belongs to men. The production of meanings, signs, and paradigms continues to be associated with masculinity; femininity is for reproduction.

13. The free market—that matrix of ultra-capitalism—has incorporated difference into literary commerce, turning the political dilemmas of gender into marketing strategies that appeal to its customers: women. Women read women. But we need not examine this sentimental—and, therefore, conservative—filiation as an interrogation of the so-called romance genre; instead, those texts are part of the apparatus of domination promoted by a masculine system. We must think of it as a systemic effect; the system is designed to exclude by including, positioning products perversely in order to dismiss them, thereby maintaining traditional power structures intact.

14. This brings me back to the beginning of this extraordinarily complex, baroque, and mystifying political problem. What happens in the literary sphere can be observed in the networks of domination that control many different social fields. Inequality is a constant menace, ready to act and hide behind its usual impunity. Public discourse in the media—in the newspapers that the economic right-wing controls, for example—constructs a sexist cultural imaginary that could also be considered deeply anti-democratic. These spaces violently and dictatorially generate an aberrant, neoliberal political utopia based on the centrality of men (as a system or as a group of individuals) who publish criticism, write literature, and enter into petty factional arguments among themselves. Yet beyond this, it's important to rethink the concept of gender. For now, it's insufficient as a political resource, and it's a superficial, amorphous, malleable concept. It may be better to return to a Marxist understanding of gender, founded upon the concentration of capital. To give but one example of why this is important: just 500 people in

the world control more wealth than the monthly salaries of 416 million poor people, most of them women. This is a global reality, and it is a concrete way of examining how meaning is made in today's world.

15. I'll repeat a point that seems crucial to me: for the same work, as women, we earn less. We are less-than in salaried terms, and this fact cannot be divorced from women's value in the symbolic sphere. Within the literary sphere, this difference institutes domination and castration that resignify us as "less-than" within critical—or pseudocritical—discourses. Entire maps and geographies of literary power can be drawn with existing strategies, technologies, and tactics. Some tactics are basic, easy, and frequent, like irony or open mocking, but these also tend to be the weakest, clumsiest, and easiest to disregard.

16. My proposal is for us to position ourselves, literarily and politically speaking, at the center of an all-too-eloquent problem: Chile is one of the most socially unequal countries in the world, and the literary inequality experienced by women needs to be understood and situated in that unsatisfactory context. We must also rethink the notion of difference. The fight for social and symbolic equality is an incontrovertible, political, and democratic aspiration. Gender's polarized configuration as a concept has become obsolete in light of the recent proliferation of gender and sexual identities. However, that first wave of egalitarian feminism—even with its anti-religious, restless charge—still seems more intense, more productive, and more political than the notion of gender, or at least the vacuous, commercial idea of what is most commonly understood as such.

17. Without discounting the contributions of feminist and gender theory being produced in the powerful metropolitan countries that head up the process of globalization, the possibility of a more local understanding of these concepts seems increasingly necessary to me. We are the ones who can best comprehend our own national context where the public reception of women's literary work is indisputably taking place. The sexism of the present isn't going to end; on the contrary, the economic system that attempts to disqualify the literature of women whose work lies outside the spaces traditionally assigned to them by hegemonic

power—spaces of sentimentality and self-referentiality—will only grow stronger. The notion of gender seems weak or timid to me, so I prefer to go back to that crucial moment when egalitarian feminism took center stage. And, looking ahead, literary inequality will only continue its inexorable and implacable ascent.

(2008)

Translated by Carl Fischer

Women, Boundaries, and Crime

Passion, one of those territories in which humanity comes up against its own limits, is a topic upon which works of art, and particularly literature, have perennially expounded. Masterful narrations of inexplicable, guileful, ungovernable, sentimental dramas populate the great works of Western literature throughout history. Since *Oedipus Rex* and its focus on an irrevocably tragic destiny, we can read about every imaginable domestic transgression and trace the emergence of a literary subject in crisis: whether guilty or innocent, she is perpetually *in extremis*.

It is precisely because of literature's symbolic power that criminality—as the ultimate transgression—has been able to surpass the barrier of legitimate horror that a particular unmediated reality can provoke and inhabit in another sphere of intelligibility: that of literary fiction. When criminality inhabits the space of literature, we can sense the drama through which a politics of emotions takes form.

The feminine subject has always been configured in history and culture as the subject of passion par excellence, due to how distantly she was positioned, culturally speaking, from scientific thought and rational consciousness. Women have been the protagonists of numerous narratives of passion, most of which have been linked to suicide. Many other narratives by women have focused on sentimentality: on the terrible fate of impossible love.

I want to take this opportunity to write about a book that focuses on a different universe: that of women and crime. *Cárcel de mujeres*, published in 1956 by the Zig-Zag publishing company in Santiago, is a work of indeterminate genre.[24] At once a *testimonio*, an autobiography, and a

---

24 All parenthetical citations within this essay refer to María Carolina Geel, *Cárcel de mujeres* (Santiago de Chile: Editorial Cuarto Propio, 2013) (editor's note).

work of fiction, it is about the prison experience of María Carolina Geel, a writer who served time for killing her lover in the tearoom of a luxurious Santiago hotel.[25] This crime became a touchstone of sensationalistic journalism in Chile due to its public nature and the involvement of a well-known writer. With the publication of *Cárcel de mujeres*, María Carolina Geel's crime was repositioned within the mediated space of literature, and thereby softened by the prestige of a book published by the most prominent press of the period.

It's a unique book for multiple reasons. First, we have to examine its prologue, written by an influential Chilean critic who was employed by the country's most powerful and conservative newspaper, *El Mercurio*. Hernán Díaz Arrieta, known by the *nom de plume* Alone, had achieved enormous power by either canonizing or eviscerating literary works in the pages of *El Mercurio*. His was the key voice in establishing hierarchies of value within the field of Chilean literature. For that reason, his prologue to *Cárcel de mujeres* was more than a mere gesture; it represented major support for María Carolina Geel, restoring to her the status of author while relegating her criminal act to the realm of fiction.

A close reading of Alone's prologue, written in the 1950s by a critic firmly ensconced within the conservative establishment, reveals a fascination with the connections among crime, writing, and incarceration. By sublimating the carceral space, Alone views imprisonment as an idyllic site for literary production; he even compares Geel's situation to that of Oscar Wilde and Cervantes. He goes on to incite the imprisoned narrator to write, using examples taken from European high culture: "Write, narrate, just tell us what you know, because even if you're the one this is about, you're not omniscient" (8).

With no shortage of theatricality, Alone involves himself in the epic story of María Carolina Geel's imprisonment. He focuses on this kind of writing due in part to his fascination with the fact that hers is a text

---

25   María Carolina Geel is the pseudonym of Georgina Silva Jiménez, who published *Cárcel de mujeres* as well as *El mundo dormido de Yenia* (1946), *Soñaba y amaba al adolescente Perces* (1949), *José, o el pequeño arquitecto* (1956), and *Huída* (1961). Her academic study *Siete escritoras chilenas* was published in 1949 and enjoyed multiple editions (editor's note).

about the "privilege" of writing while in prison—a privilege that Alone himself seems to wish he could also enjoy. In fact, one might understand from Alone's prologue that he is the first to have received the unedited pages that went on to comprise the book—a book for whose existence Alone advocates. We might also say that the book is the result of a cultural pact between the critic and the writer and therefore circumvents any social sanction that might come from committing a crime.

Moving between philosophical disquisitions and psychological references, Alone's prologue works hard to allude to the plurality of the subject—focusing on one fatal, unforeseeable piece of it that alleviates Geel's responsibility for her actions. Alone situates María Carolina Geel within the ontologically mysterious place of non-responsibility.

Alone alludes to a certain "somnambulism" throughout the text (in the sense of something faint, or dream-like), which paradoxically works in *Cárcel de mujeres* as a bulwark against the chaos of criminal insanity. His prologue goes beyond a traditional book presentation, in the sense that the critic occupies multiple places at once. He moves between philosophy and psychology, before positioning himself as the champion of the text, a hybrid book that was written at Alone's request; he had written letters to the author to "convince" her of the need to redeem herself, and thus her crime, through writing.

The prologue insists that by killing her lover, María Carolina Geel actually caused her own death because that act led her to an undetermined place of "unreal pathways, detached amidst phantasmagoric streets and houses" (14). So, it is Alone who must respond, since "those who remain alive have an obligation to extend a hand to those who find themselves sinking, without any desire to come up and breathe" (14). Yet given that the prologue is part of the book, it would seem that the critic becomes an inhabitant of the women's prison. He takes his place amidst criminals and in a conventionally feminine space, either as a man linked to power or—considering that he is a figure who is transformed by the book's emotional language—as a more feminized subject.

Then there is the narrator's hybrid voice, a voice that refuses to name itself and that takes on two different tasks: on the one hand, it describes the other female prisoners, and on the other, in an exercise of sharp difference, it positions Geel as someone who has been eternally trapped in the prison of her own mind.

The book eschews the predictable dynamics of confession and abso-
lution. In fact, the text systematically avoids the word "murder." Instead,
it works to establish the power of writing as a weapon and a strategy for
obtaining a sort of social acquittal.

The voice of the story's protagonist reveals her lettered background
while inhabiting one of the spaces most frequented by non-lettered
subjects: the prison, where common criminals are held. Even though
lumpen subjects are conventionally viewed as unable to reflect upon
their own impulses and grudges, here we encounter a voice that is wise,
ethical, and aestheticized, outlining the violently wide-ranging inner
lives of those who inhabit the prison.

The difference, of course, lies in writing—in the total power that
comes from constructing a subject endowed with a full subjectivity
while writing about others using an external and purposefully superficial gaze. In this way, the protagonist sees herself in dualistic terms: not
only is she the narrator of the story but she also stands at a conceptual
distance from the rest of the prisoners. The prison is a micro-space full
of thieves, sex workers, and alcoholics whose actions are identical to
hers. Each character has a coarse, crude identity that confirms her own
fixed, subordinated social position.

All textual strategies aside, though, the prison is a space of initiation for the narrator. But this initiation is multifaceted and complex
since the protagonist finds herself in an ambiguous position. On the
one hand, she takes the prison as raw material for her writing and as a
place where she can observe others. But, on the other hand, thanks to
her social status, she can inhabit a privileged area of the prison in which
inmates can pay their own way. So, she manages to stand apart from it
all, isolated from daily contact with the other prisoners. She thus lives
in a prison within a prison, and these multiple levels of confinement
allow her to imagine herself in a sort of self-isolation as if she were in a
convent rather than a jail cell.

This fiction of being in a convent allows her to imagine the prison
as a cloister from which she can observe the depraved world of female
prisoners from a distance. This degeneracy ends up becoming part of
her own process of self-expiation, in which she forces herself to observe
an impure, imperfect universe that reminds her of the gravity of the
crime that put her there in the first place.

However, imprisonment is not what causes the narrator the most anxiety. Rather, it is having to coexist, albeit from afar, with other criminals whom she caricatures as monstrous figures. They aren't necessarily representatives of "evil" in the religious sense, but they are figured in her writing as psychically and socially inferior.

In this way, she forcefully establishes a bourgeois perspective rooted in classism and a certain intimate view of herself. The work projects an image of femininity characterized by acute sensitivity, extreme discretion, and even the intelligence of coming to terms with new surroundings to legitimize the integrity of the text itself. The narrator experiences the horror of what she learns in prison with tranquility and even acceptance. Indeed, a fine sense of irony can be found throughout the text, particularly in its character descriptions. Here, the great paradox lies in the drama of confronting, albeit obliquely, those who have a more rudimentary sense of morals. The book's narrative is thus primarily about the punishment of being stuck with other female subjects in their most abject state.

The narrator's alter ego is constructed as a nun, given that the prison is run by the religious congregation of the Good Shepherd. Geel describes the nuns as "women who must mask their shy personalities and harden their refined, aristocratic customs when facing others for whom there is no law but violence, and no principle but desire" (57).

In this group of religious women, the narrator meets her match in Mother Asunción, who tries to initiate Geel in the love of Christ. Although the narrator's agnosticism precludes any encounter with God, she finds in the nun a kindred spirit, someone who, like her, is also a victim of the women prisoners. The protagonist dwells on the nun's sacrifice—a sacrifice ringed by an aristocratic halo—given that the nun dedicates her life "ceaselessly to those situated by life on the complete opposite side of any moral mandate" (57).

In this way, the prisoner and the nun forge an alliance. The nun has a double function: she can offer moral redemption through Catholicism, but she is also in charge of enforcing the prison's laws. Her powers—at once sacred and profane—figure her as the incarnation of both God's law and the justice system in which she is the warden. Thus subordinated to masculine power, the nun becomes the representative of that same power among the women who are subject to her strict surveillance. The protagonist allies herself with this figure, who is herself subordinated to the central powers; yet even amidst her subordination, the nun dominates the prison space.

Indeed, the protagonist situates herself within the same realm as the nun; the difference is that her own position isn't linked to religion (for she isn't a believer) but rather to a shared position of power based instead on social class. Her formation within the strictest of bourgeois mores allows her to acquire an attitude that borders on mysticism, especially when she decides to isolate herself in the cloister of her own thoughts. Still, the mysticism that appears throughout the book—a double withdrawal from the prison and reality into the fiction of the cloister—is strongly connected to the profane.

Despite being doubly or even triply isolated, the protagonist still keeps a controlling watch on the feminine subjects populating the prison. Her gaze becomes a panopticon (evoking the work of Michel Foucault in *Discipline and Punish*), an all-powerful eye that incessantly observes the prisoners without being seen by anyone. It is a view that controls, classifies, and captures the bodies of the women, only to re-penalize them through constant judgment.

The symmetry of the gaze allows the protagonist something that the law forbids: to judge without being judged. Her body doesn't circulate—it is confined, like that of a novice—but it observes the customs of the incarcerated women as if from behind an opaque screen. These women become the raw material for her writing in a text that legitimizes the plight of the imprisoned. Contrary to tradition, the warden is not the one stigmatized throughout the story; her fellow inmates bear the brunt of stigma, not because of the magnitude of their crimes, but on account of the psychic and moral degradation accentuated by the narrator's censorious and castigating gaze.

This degradation is linked to sexuality, of course: sexuality that lies at the heart of the protagonist's real initiation into prison life. Accusations of homosexuality are constantly leveled at the prisoners, and the protagonist is overwhelmed with angst when she hears of it. Although the narrator understands lesbianism not as a sexual orientation but as a perversion necessary for emotional survival within the prison, she constantly moralizes about it, as with the following reflection that takes place after she hears an erotic conversation between two inmates: "I violently pressed my hands against my ears... Why in the world should people suffer over something that others would simply consider innate?" (38).

She doesn't want to hear, but she does listen; she doesn't want to see, but she structures herself around the gaze. Beyond what the text makes explicit, the protagonist obviously has an avid curiosity, a thirst to find out about everything that is going on in the prison, albeit always from a position that remains hidden from the prying eyes of others. Her new knowledge is mostly related to the transgression of dominant sexual mores. This stark, brutal sexuality wounds the protagonist's sensibilities, and she becomes terrified of her own sexuality: "Suddenly, I was struck by something that marked me for the rest of my life: the woman was talking about sex" (23).

Shame and repression coalesce in the story such that questions arise about the protagonist's own latent homosexuality. Indeed, whenever she glimpses, hears, or even imagines sex talk or sexual acts, she obliquely reveals her own desires, even when they're masked by her professed need for "diffidence, non-vulgarity, fear of men, yearning for an atticism that I was never able to find. Solitude" (24).

This fear of men and of (male) vulgarity is what leads her to seek refuge in the pagan territory of the women's prison, as if her crime were the only way for her to reach this purely feminine space: a prison irrevocably linked to the explicit confirmation of lesbian urges. Writing these urges down and naming them become forms of consummating them. But giving them a name and a form also means degrading her own desires, letting the lesbian substance emanate from an other-body that mirrors her own, in a way that the critic Alone wisely describes as follows: "Even if you're the one this is about, you're not omniscient" (8).

Homosexuality is the kind of licentiousness that the prison allows once all other social norms have been transgressed. Even when surrounded by homosexual acts, the narrator evokes the man who led her to commit her crime. The protagonist repeatedly insists on the need to put boundaries between herself and the day-to-day life she previously led, emphasizing her lover as her only link to the outside world. But her need to isolate herself is not borne of timidity or mysticism; it comes from the fact that she sees the outside world as a mediocre place, a reality she can hardly bear due to its inelegance and lack of complexity. She thus positions her lover as part of that mediocrity: he represents the outside world, a link to her former life, and this sustains her, albeit with a tinge of condescension that surrounds everything she considers to be weak: "...and I, without noticing, was inspired by the genuineness of his simplicity, that is, by that inferiority of his that in some way made him superior to the demonic world of intelligence" (79).

She tolerates the inferiority of her lover, unintelligent and possibly from a lower social class, as long as the pact between them is respected. But the pact is broken, according to the narrator, when her lover, who had been married, becomes a widower and then proposes marriage to her. She turns him down, motivated (as ever) by "the terrible moral misery that marriage induces in all human beings" (77). Although she acknowledges that her lover was actually going to marry a younger woman—something of which the protagonist professes to be unaware—her story discounts this crucial fact as a possible motive, as if passion and jealousy were part of the indignity of the world to which she no longer belongs.

When she refuses to admit that jealousy was the motive for her crime—which would make hers nothing more than a mere crime of passion—her reasoning turns ambiguous and vague. Within that ambiguity lies the possibility of a fateful outcome: a predestined course of events that could involve them both. The crime would thus become an act shared by both victim and criminal, foreshadowed from the time at the beginning of their relationship when he went with her to buy a gun.

The gun mediates their relationship: out of the 400 men she works with, it is he who chooses to go with her to buy a weapon. This early interaction, tinged with a magical air, helps convince her that her lover is somehow an agent in his own death. She was only obeying his desire, and in this sense, the roles are reversed, and the fragile line dividing victim from criminal becomes blurred. Although their first attempt at purchasing a weapon is unsuccessful, it does lead to a relationship between them in which using the gun gets deferred to a later date when, for no apparent reason other than a vague, hoped-for breakup, a shot gets fired and the protagonist's long-standing desire for isolation—to go unnoticed—is fulfilled.

However, she paradoxically needs scandal and publicity in the form of the banal judgment of others so she can tell the story of herself as a different prisoner motivated solely by unbridled passion. In this way, she can overcome her own lack of self-control, her own criminal impulses, and that assemblage of feelings she's unable to acknowledge within herself—let alone integrate into her life harmoniously.

Cárcel de mujeres is thus the result of an extreme experience, but it's also a ploy aimed at glossing over certain details that the narrator would rather ignore. Given that the practice of writing is characterized by the ambiguity of its own signs, Geel allows us to glimpse the fragile foundations of her story easily. We see her voyeuristic eye that—even as it discredits others—offers us a peek at its desire for an encounter with that woman whom it finds contemptible. This is perhaps because what the author really finds contemptible is her own same-sex desire. She thus focuses not on the legitimacy of difference but on a story of obstinate social inequality. This somewhat reactionary politics of the eye is analogous to a particular way of handling memory. It is a memory that cannot recognize abandonment and jealousy as criminal motives in order to politicize those motives in the service of a feminist cause, thereby revealing them as the byproducts of a well-thought-out, monotonous system of domination. Instead, the narrator makes use of a vague kind of philosophy to make herself look good while sidestepping the explosive passions that led her to commit her historical, hysterical crime of passion.

(1999)

Translated by Carl Fischer

Gender, Genre, and Pain

It's important for me to question, first off, the conditions that academic essays must meet to be considered good quality. There's an overly narrow standard that disrupts the creativity that essays should have. I'm not proposing that we start making things up or that we should avoid the important textual references that enrich essays. Instead, I'm questioning the institutional practice of placing strictures upon the essay, of subjecting it to rigid guidelines that repress, or oppress, its narrative possibilities on multiple theoretical and aesthetic fronts.

A dangerous consensus has materialized regarding the protocols of what people consider academic writing. These protocols end up privileging an academicism that restricts writing, when that writing should instead try to advance the academy based on the multiplicity of techniques, objects, and problems that characterize the educational field.

My question, then, is about the limits of the writing process. The increasing growth in graduate programs has led to the establishment of a strong didactic component to writing, with the imposition of one sole way of writing about culture. It's quite strange that an advanced educational training should lead to a contraction in discourse: it's similar to those techniques that taught handwriting through rigid, repetitive practice. That metaphor of standard handwriting is also useful for thinking about the patterns that published academic essays follow: such exercises lead to homogeneity not only in terms of form, but more concretely, they lead to a fossilization of the senses.

All analytical thought can be understood as a form of fiction, not in the sense of some kind of delirium or metaphoric break with the universe of the real, but rather because we have to think about interpretation as the need for a liminal space that only the imagination can provide, grouping together or dividing up different texts to generate a space that allows interpretations based on a rigorous set of reading operations.

The academic essay is part of an intensive practice of bringing different kinds of readings together. It entails having the audacity to add yet another interpretation into the mix. Essays contain a multitude of signs that come together in complex ways, generating tensions between the self and the other. They are undulating, unstable zones: abyssal spaces that show that at the edge of oneself lies the extension of the other, which is no longer neither self nor other, but rather part of a network of meanings that revolve around—and uphold—citations, in the broadest and most ambiguous sense of what it means to cite.

I cannot help but wonder how such an extraordinarily homogeneous consensus around the (baroque) requirements for academic essays came to be, and how that consensus led to journals that turn vibrant analyses of cutting-edge, emergent subjectivities into uniform, interchangeable objects.

One thinks of the robotic gesture of creating a market for writing in which clear branding guarantees large-scale, unquestioning, and acritical consumption.

The task for readers in the literary "field" (as Pierre Bourdieu would call it) is to highlight the twists and turns of different readings, with the risk of establishing analogies based on a poetics, and politics, of the letter. The constraints imposed by consensus harm the "field" of the essay—which would otherwise be a passionate and exciting discursive practice. This is especially true when it comes to the important, uncertain territory of research carried out under the auspices of Fondecyt, the Chilean government research agency (all the more so if one takes into account the fact that this valuable institution will soon be under the auspices of the Ministry of the Economy).

We must broaden these rules not only from the perspective of those who work outside the academy (people whom one might expect would advocate for such a thing), but especially from the perspective of those who work within it, to avoid a kind of mass production and promote the rise of more critical subjective forms. This is not at all about skirting any norms, of course; it's about opening up gaps and escape valves within this form of writing. Such spaces wouldn't do any harm; instead, they would transmit minoritarian impulses that would guarantee pluralism.

I want to make my thinking clear. I'd like to talk about how I managed to organize a field of research whose formal research methods don't abhor uncertainty or eccentricity. I've been interested for several decades in the development of women's writing: the feminine—as a cultural decision, as a field of obedience and disobedience, as a destination, and as a challenge—has been an active, ongoing part of my cultural work. A key dimension of my Fondecyt-supported research has been articulated based on those ideas, and my results show that dilemmas continue to follow an inexorable, asymmetrical course that has both marked Chile's transition to democracy and caused pain in social groups characterized by the non-normativity of their gender identities. Indeed, this reflection wouldn't be possible without the intelligent work of the poet, critic, and researcher Eugenia Brito, and her thesis student Rocío Alorda.

How can we think about the dilemmas of gender and genre for certain Chilean bodies that passionately inhabited the first half of the 20th century? It was a time marked not only by the persistence and ambiguities of colonial thinking but also by industrialization, which brought more women into the workforce. The female gender has territorial specificities beyond its consistent subordination throughout the history of the world. After all, every place on earth, whether part of Western culture or not, has created its own network of meanings for different bodies based on different variables, ordinances, and cultural dynamics.

It's possible to speak about "universalism" to the degree that being part of the female gender means navigating different kinds of subordination. However, that diversity expresses the universality of subordination and a kind of mobility that provides an opening for rupture or a breaking point.

Theoretical discussions about gender are ongoing. The 20th century brought with it a number of approaches to thinking about, and politically promoting, what some call the "gender issue." The role of women has been analyzed, examined, and rethought from every possible angle. So-called first-wave feminism, which advocated for women's civil rights, opened up new spaces for dialogue with progressive forces (as difficult as it must have been) in ways that were not just political but also theoretical.

That expansion of feminist thought and action generated a multifaceted reaction that sought to caricature gender-based knowledge and experience and promote the rejection of the term feminist, especially among women who feared being discriminated against based on the very category that paradoxically advocated for non-discrimination in the most historical sense of the term.

In Chile, the 1980s were feminist years, during which we actively struggled against the dictatorship. In a way, those feminisms were understood as foundational in the country precisely because of the silence imposed on women's history by academia and in schools, which erased the oppression and the historical struggle for women's rights. But later, during the transition to democracy in the 1990s, the expansion of feminism was curbed by the fragmentation of its leadership as people joined the public sector or were relegated to irregular, minoritarian forms of representation.

However, certain academic projects and local critical works have kept their focus on women's historical and cultural production while also maintaining dialogues with current theoretical debates about gender.

Two works offer us a particular glimpse at women's social imaginaries and the social construction of the female body during the first half of the 20th century. One is the correspondence of Elena Caffarena, the leader of the feminist Chilean Women's Emancipation Movement (Movimiento pro Emancipación de la Mujer Chilena, known by its Spanish-language acronym MEMCH) from 1935-1940. The other is the correspondence between Gabriela Mistral and Doris Dana, compiled in the volume *Niña Errante*, published by Lumen in 2009 (and translated into English by Velma García-Gorena as *Gabriela Mistral's Letters to Doris Dana*, published in 2018 by University of New Mexico Press). Both texts offer literal and symbolic approaches to the relationships among gender, genre, and pain.

I begin with two observations that may seem banal at first glance. When examining the extensive archives of Elena Caffarena (whom I had the honor of meeting and interviewing at several points during the 1980s and 1990s), I became interested in one particular detail: a fissure of sorts in one of her most important texts, in which—as part of a legal argument—she argued for the restoration of universal suffrage following its revocation by government authorities. There, she invoked the Law of the Permanent Defense of Democracy, which the Gabriel González Videla administration (1946-52) had used in 1948 to suspend the constitutional rights of all members of the Communist Party and send many of them to internment camps in the remote northern Chilean town of Pisagua.

Along with other leaders of the time like Amanda Labarca, Elena Caffarena was known for her fight for Chilean women's right to vote. It was somewhat paradoxical, then, that in January 1949, just days after the passing of universal suffrage (note that Caffarena was not invited to any official government celebrations of it), this right was revoked. But Caffarena, a lawyer by profession, personally defended her rights in an historic letter addressed to the *Conservador de Bienes Raíces* as part of her appeal to the Election Tribunal. She used the letter to make a wide-ranging political statement that was vibrant, intelligent, and well-founded. She basically made the point that she was not part of the Communist Party (she was an anarchist, officially), and thus her account of the sociopolitical and gender situation of her era was also an impressive display of her cultural knowledge.

However, one section of her letter read as follows: "If this were years ago, and my health weren't seriously compromised, I would have already made a decision." When she wrote those words, she was just 46 years old. I was amazed that Elena Caffarena would make such a reference to her body in that document, especially when I myself had witnessed her excellent physical and mental state during the final years of Chile's dictatorship, and even later, in the nineties, when she remained completely up to date on even the most minute details of the transition to democracy. I was intrigued by the mention of personal, physical details by a public leader who had been trained not to make emotional arguments. Elena Caffarena lived to the age of one hundred: an entire century of life, with all the experience that entails.

From a different angle, and with a different structure of feeling, I now turn to the poet and essayist Gabriela Mistral. Mistral, one of Chile's most canonical writers, was known for frequently mentioning the state of her health and advanced age in her writing, even when she was fairly young. Her eloquent correspondence consistently alludes to different illnesses and physical problems, as well as to the effects of aging. In fact, she didn't personally claim her prize for her poem "Sonnets of Death" at the 1914 "Floral Games," an important literary contest, despite the invitation she received from then-president Ramón Barros Luco. In her place, she sent her young friend and literary admirer Isauro Santelices, with whom she had corresponded for a long time. In a letter to him, Mistral explains that she chose to receive her prize in absentia because she considered herself an "old woman." She decided instead to witness the award ceremony anonymously as a spectator. She was just 25 at the time. A large part of her correspondence from throughout the twentieth century has now been compiled and published by experts.

As a longtime reader of her letters, I was completely familiar with Mistral's way of representing herself. But the correspondence that appears in *Niña Errante* had a broader impact in the public sphere because it made her lesbianism—which different cultural and political officials, thinking it harmful or dishonorable, had kept secret until then—fully legible.

I was fascinated by the Chilean state's reaction to this. Until then, it had exalted Gabriela Mistral's maternal side, emphasizing the pedagogical task of memorizing her poems about caring for children, while also pointing incessantly to her platonic love for Romelio Ureta, a young man whose suicide supposedly prevented her from having any kind of love life. These twin aspects—her platonic love and the maternal desire she apparently sublimated into a love for the children of Chile, which she expressed through her poetry and her work as a public school teacher—were extolled in textbooks that the country's Education Ministry had widely distributed for years.

However, in the twenty-first century, this story of thwarted motherhood and impossible love—which she herself promoted as part of her biography—took something of a "turn of the screw," in the words of Henry James. The Chilean state acquired the parts of Mistral's archive that until then had remained in the custody of Doris Dana's niece, Doris Atkinson; this made it possible for her correspondence to be organized and published.

As the twenty-first century wore on, Gabriela Mistral was transformed from a pained victim of impossible love cut off by death into a 60-year-old woman whose letters revealed a passionate affair with Doris Dana: a young, educated American lesbian to whom she later bequeathed her possessions and her literary estate. More than fifty years after her passing, the government at the time, as well as new academic approaches to the body and sexuality, made it possible for her sexuality to be accepted.

At the time, I heard a lot of commentary about the publication of her correspondence, most of which celebrated the importance of undoing these weak, idealized myths about Gabriela Mistral. But much was also said about Mistral's numerous health complaints—namely, about the detailed accounts she gave of her many symptoms. Some said that those complaints, which they considered excessive, diminished the book's impact.

As a connoisseur of Gabriela Mistral's correspondence, I wasn't surprised by this aspect of the book, aside from the fact that it was fairly evident in the final letters that her illness was affecting her mental state. It was unfortunate that the editors decided not to include a warning explaining why the letters from the final period of her life came across as erratic.

It seemed necessary to situate the epistolary genre as a form governed by a very specific set of protocols. Or, to put it differently, it was important to call attention to the official rhetoric that structured her letters. I'm referring to her strict formatting: the date, the greetings, the farewells. The letters' spontaneity is diminished by their conditions of production and the courtesies that had to be followed at the time.

It also seemed necessary to emphasize that one of the primordial forms of epistolary courtesy involves inquiring about the other person's health as a way of opening up a broader dialogue. The body thus occupied a space that we might call organic—organic matter as a strategy of verbal exchange. In that sense, Gabriela Mistral's letters were hardly outliers for their time, notwithstanding the literary flair she lent to emphasizing her symptoms and dramatizing what was wrong with her.

Meanwhile, I had the privilege of studying Elena Caffarena's correspondence with MEMCH members all over Chile thanks to her granddaughter, the historian Ximena Jiles. She and fellow historian Claudia Rojas gave me a copy of these documents, which are now held by the Chilean National Library.

In some of those letters, which mapped out the construction of Chile's most ambitious women's organization, multiple MEMCH members named different illnesses that limited their range of movement. These women seemed to have internalized the fact that they could, and indeed should, talk about their various physical symptoms, even as they blazed a trail to greater social autonomy.

I couldn't help but think—in a somewhat less literal sense—that it was important to listen to the pain of those women and try to understand it in a critical, more poetic way. At the same time, I thought about how the practice of sending handwritten or typed letters has died off with the advent of new systems that have made communication more instantaneous. The bureaucratic, depersonalized epistolary form is still in use, of course, contributing to burgeoning archives around the world.

From a no less muddled perspective, I thought about how the transition from the twentieth century to the twenty-first, coupled with the expansion of neoliberalism, had erased the practice of inquiring about another person's health from the norms of epistolary communication. I even thought about how today, asking about another person's health might be seen as uncomfortable, or even invasive. The neoliberal body is a working-body without organs, unless it has been absorbed within the system of *organic consumption*—by that, I mean the smaller-scale network of state-based hospitals and clinics. Health as a topic of correspondence and social communication has become little more than a memory. One's organs—the lungs, the heart, the ovaries, and the kidneys, among others—have been extracted from the conventional sphere of communication, and the idea of pain as a conversation starter has become repressed. The body has become an external facade, and the word as a space inhabited by illness became a relic of the twentieth century.

Meanwhile, despite the pain they experienced and the damage aging caused to their bodies, the powerful cultural images of Elena Caffarena (who talked about all this in her forties) and Gabriela Mistral (who spoke about her old age when she was just twenty-five) show that their (ill) health never prevented them from being extremely productive; it also never kept them from being leaders. Based on this literal interpretation, as well as on the idea of emancipation—one of the founding principles of MEMCH that has lately made a return to intellectual circles thanks to the ideas of Jacques Rancière, who thinks of emancipation as a method for broadening and deferring the law—I have come to think about this pain (and the inevitable signs of death that accompany it) as being emancipated by social organization, at least in the case of Elena Caffarena and her peers. They echoed this female pain from different areas all over Chile, but their organs resisted it precisely by joining a feminist organization.

In the case of Gabriela Mistral, it's particularly provocative that the pain surrounding—and, perhaps, laying siege to—her correspondence disappears when she writes to Doris Dana as if she were a man. When she parodies masculine speech, her gender performance suspends the tangible, taxonomic aspects of her organs. In this game of identity displacement and inversion, Mistral's epistolary discourse becomes by turns omnipotent, threatening, and possessive. In these powerful—and, let's say, healthy—discursive moments, meaning changes because the poet appropriates a cultural geography that had previously only been assigned to and used by masculine subjects. In this playful, erotic operation, she shows how gender predisposes us to and disposes us of conventional categories. In this radical move, Gabriela Mistral confronts pain but also turns her back on it, thanks to the possibility of moving grammatically through the labyrinth of multiple genders. The word, with its potential for creating multiple meanings, allows her not only to inhabit the pain that surrounds her but also to avoid that same pain through a sort of virtual sense of masculine domination subjugating a woman (that is, the representation on paper of Doris Dana). And, crucially, it subjugates its own femininity, liberating it from itself and setting it free from its (weakened) organs.

I will offer here a somewhat loose interpretation of the concept of contemporaneity as originated by the Italian philosopher Giorgio Agamben. I was sure that I needed to become a contemporary of Gabriela Mistral, of the members of MEMCH, and of Elena Caffarena: not in the sense of going back in time, but rather as a way of working in a place where time can be suspended. In that opaque location where different times come together to mark a space unconsumed—much less consummated—by consensus, I can think alongside Gabriela Mistral, Elena Caffarena, the members of MEMCH, and other contemporaries of theirs who solidified their relevance.

This entry into a suspended time, the urgency of being contemporary in a period disconnected from any specific date, allowed me to think about the theorist Judith Butler with the same intensity with which I thought through a particular history of Chilean illness in the postcolonial era. I was able to think about smallpox—and the resistance by the Chilean population to state-sponsored vaccination campaigns—in the same way that the medical profession extended its domain over women's reproductive lives in its long war against the historical figure of the midwife, replacing her with the more professionalized, medically-trained birthing nurse. That was the same suspended time in which the Chilean thinker Julieta Kirkwood wrote about the unresolved tensions between women and organizations.

It thus became possible to read Gabriela Mistral through the lens of queer studies, whose importance has grown in recent years. We can examine Mistral using Judith Butler's theoretical ideas about performativity, or in conjunction with the lesbian codes of her time, or from the perspective of wordplay, which was the most recognized form of literary production for Latin American women writers in that era. I believe that the private uses of time, and forms of alternating among or (better yet) combining genders to rebel against the binary, continue to be fundamental for a multifocal approach to pain and emancipation in fiction.

(2013)

Translated by Carl Fischer

Globalization and the Production of Subjecthood

I'm interested in connecting globalization and inequality—the latter being one of the most pressing problems of our economic regime and one that has radically and intensely affected our social context. Exclusion is without a doubt one of the most obvious problems of the system. It's a paradoxical situation, since even though globalization is a process of constant aggregation, behind the scenes we see more and more disaggregated subjects who have created an anarchic counterculture based on violence.

In this sense, I'd like to hypothesize about how criminality and its rhizomatic implications—which have no beginning or ending—are necessarily, and by necessity, linked to the globalizing project of ultra-capitalism.

Technological globalization produces multiple, divergent positions: points of view that range from exaggerated and acritical celebration to a form of conservative denialism in the face of any change to cultural hierarchies.

In effect, the present moment is characterized by a massification of images and the democratization of technology such that the broadening of our horizons stands in tension with the real, physical limits of geography.

The vertigo-inducing instantaneity of communication technology has led to a feverish appropriation of de-localized discourses (whether visual, textual, or gestural). Some discourses have moved beyond the virtual space and into the physical realm, forming a new cultural arena.

However, we need to scrutinize the social conditions in which this proliferation of technology is taking place. Embedded within the savagery of capitalism's very brain, technology focuses on incentivizing communication at the maximum possible speeds, which displace or destabilize critical thinking and replace it with superficial, random, and even laughable reactions.

What I want to say is that these frenzied technological advancements are driven—and more than that, manipulated—by broad, traditional strategies of domination. Dominant ideology and its economic rapacity have appropriated these technologies, rechanneling them into their agenda of capital accumulation.

Therefore, examining the globalized present means looking at the correlations between technical instruments and the political-economic agenda of the powers that be.

Of course, these technologies themselves offer countless benefits. We need look no further than how the massification of the television and its integration into the home increased access to information and democratized the circulation of images.

Yet this technology—inevitably subject to ideological and economic structures—also brought about cultural change where it was least expected. The magnitude of the subjugation that this technology wrought upon us, as a way of co-opting and manufacturing public opinion, would come to favor consumption and the creation of identities invested in economic growth.

Our profound scrutiny of this technology has nothing at all to do with whether it should exist. Rather, the question has to do with how unilaterally it's appropriated, with its ensuing lack of diversity, which clearly leads to the creation of monolithic, uniform ways of thinking. In fact, that very uniformity is what capitalist theory zeroed in on when critiquing societies founded upon the omniscient power of the state.

The desire and drive to implant this monotonous way of thinking lie in a paradoxical set of maneuvers: on the one hand, the creation of a homogeneous discourse derived from the free market, and on the other, a rigidly political segmentation of bodies. This segmentation is of such a great magnitude that it needs, and also ensures, a vast terrain of exclusion in order for its project to work.

The final point of a program founded upon exclusion—and this is catastrophic—relies increasingly upon criminality, which feeds and reinforces this project by generating the only form of dissidence the system can allow.

Within this savage form of capitalism, common criminality has multiple functions: it becomes a massive phenomenon that eclipses social movements generated by those who are marginalized and unsatisfied, but it also feeds into an anxiety-ridden and anguished devotion to capital insofar as crime comes to generate the supreme fear of losing private property.

More than that, criminality works to fragment the poor on a large scale by dividing them up—in a slippery, unjust way—between honest consumers and nefarious criminals.

The criminal thus becomes the system's other, and the visible object of its repression of difference. The so-called "firm hand" against crime turns out to be a cover-up for the system's extraordinarily firm hand against legal citizenship: that is, the systematic violence of a debt-based economy and the establishment of a none-too-subtle form of usury, in the form of legalized and legitimized theft.

One key piece of this analytical puzzle would thus have to be about how ultra-capitalism needs common criminality in order to legitimize itself as a project. In a shady cultural move, it imposes and displaces its own violence onto the figure of the criminal and refuses responsibility for the violence of a system that increasingly enacts a severe and growing social segmentation: one that is racial, sexual, class-based, and territorial.

What I am hoping to show is that the system *produces* crime so that it can ensure that its citizens remain anesthetized and submissive, thereby circumventing any substantive political movements.

His or her violent situation notwithstanding, the criminal thus becomes a phantom: an abstract and destructive projection that technology activates and magnifies. The media creates a terrifying social narrative based on potential attacks on private property. And of course, this narrative never admits to the fragility of what we understand today as private property.

In the end, I will point out two fundamental conditions for the supremacy of ultra-capitalism: the replaceability (disposability) of objects and—at the same time—the incentivization of profit through perpetual debt. Goods and services thus become mostly transitory: they belong not to consumers but to business interests.

Economic models based on rentiership—the foundation of everyday life—show the extent to which culture is founded upon ambiguity:

nothing belongs to us, and yet anything can be taken away from us. It is through that non-belonging and expropriation (in every sense of those words) that the criminal becomes a myth, a scourge, a plague that pervades the social space—sustaining and perpetuating it.

(2008)

Translated by Carl Fischer

The Mapuche on Trial in Cañete

It's hard—maybe even impossible—for me to offer a precise account of the universe that the Mapuche people inhabit (as it would be for me to talk about that of any indigenous group). Their cosmovision has a history and a density all its own. It simply cannot be reduced to the paradigms of, let's say, "Chilean" culture. This specificity is currently being reimagined and reworked because in recent decades, Mapuche thinkers have established new ways of interpreting their own history. These new approaches are changing how Chilean academia has understood and constructed the Mapuche. In fact (just to name one microscopic change), one no longer refers, in Spanish, to "Mapuches" in the plural; one speaks about the "Mapuche," which is a way of following the linguistic patterns of their language, Mapudungun.

Still, it is possible today to speak of the dramatic effects of the material and symbolic domination of the Mapuche and other indigenous people by the Chilean state and other powers that be. It's obvious that this has continued to create terrible prejudices within the Chilean population, which lead to marginalization—if not outright derision—of their customs and figures.

One of the pillars structuring the Western world is the idea of the binary (high/low, black/white, good/bad…), in which one pole is deemed superior to the other. This inevitably leads to segregation-based hierarchies that are legitimized through synthesis: that which is superior and that which is inferior. This synthesis is founded upon segregation. It organizes social imaginaries, not just reproducing structures of domination but also collaborating with conservative power. That power sustains itself, in part, thanks to the marginalization—occasionally enforced by marginalized people themselves—of certain social groups that are deemed unintelligible, threatening, or otherwise problematic.

In the Chilean cultural imagination, the Mapuche people have been deemed the inferior pole of many of those binaries due to a lack of understanding of their culture. They have been at constant risk of cultural disappearance, resulting from exclusion and paternalism that date back to the colonial era, as well as multiple attempts (most often by leftists and centrists) to assimilate them. At every turn, these attitudes result in a clear process of marginalization of their social experience.

However, the voracious rise of hypercapitalism has once again positioned indigenous people's long, epic resistance to territorial occupations at the center of global debate. Meanwhile, the expansion of capitalism sustains itself through environmental depredation and the expropriation of the lands of different indigenous communities.

In the face of this newer, more powerful wave of attacks on indigenous people—continuously removing them from their land—the Mapuche people are protesting and defending themselves against this large-scale invasion, this time by large, private, national, and transnational corporations. This invasion, implacable in nature, is based on the purchase of indigenous lands, displacing people (with the complicity of the Chilean state) in order to establish large industrial installations that have already done irreparable harm to the health and well-being of local populations, flora, and fauna.

It is hardly an overstatement to say that it was the Chilean state, not the Spanish crown, that consolidated control over the territory of the Mapuche people. This took place during the terrible, destructive process known as the "Pacification of Araucanía," carried out during the second half of the nineteenth century. We must always remember with utmost clarity that, after all, the Chilean state usurped these people's lands and established the (eloquent) notion of "reductions": small areas of land set up to contain (and dominate) entire indigenous populations. These were the very people who had fought for centuries (with astonishing perseverance) against the Spanish empire, impeding its advancement. This was one of the bloodiest, most lethal invasions in human history.

By the end of the nineteenth century, the republic of Chile had taken over territories throughout its southernmost reaches to allow for the expansion of large *latifundios* that stood upon their ancestral possessions, or in other words, *literally on top* of what had once been their lands.

Today, in the early twenty-first century, the semi-feudal *latifun-dio* system in ancestral Mapuche territory has given way to industry—primarily mining, energy, and logging. Although the Mapuche traditionally come from the south of Chile, and despite the fact that they share a series of rituals and legitimate demands for land, today they are fragmented—even divided—like many other indigenous groups. These divisions manifest themselves in different political convictions and stances among their leaders, but they must also be understood as the result of the strategic processes of separation: the state's political and economic machinations to serve the interests of the economic elite.

The only possible result of this context today is ongoing tension between the Chilean state, the private sector, and the entire Mapuche nation. There is a stubborn impasse there that could only be resolved by a sophisticated restitution process involving community leaders. At the same time, however, the fact that the land in question is so rich in natural resources indicates that these conflicts will not be resolved any time soon. On the contrary: technological and industrial expansions in the area foreshadow more rebellion, as well as more repression aimed at those leading the rebellions.

The Lebu Prison

Visiting incarcerated people, as a small group of us did in Lebu, is no simple task. This is partly due to the resonances that freedom of movement acquires because a visitor (me) can leave. At least in that sense, his or her freedom (mine, that is) stands out in contrast to, even as it highlights, the imprisonment of others.

The jailed Mapuche activists, known as *comuneros*, have fought to be referred to as political prisoners. And that's exactly what they are, whether or not they're officially recognized as such (and of course they have not been). The authorities generally understand this as the case, at least vaguely—particularly the people directly guarding them, who follow a specific protocol in their treatment of the prisoners. It's deference or maybe caution—I'm not sure.

Héctor Llaitul, one of the leaders of the Coordinadora de Comunidades en Conflicto Arauco-Malleco—an activist group created in 1998 that's most commonly known by its Spanish-language acronym CAM—thinks that Mapuche prisoners need to be in a special facility that would recognize their status as Mapuche and allow them to carry out their cultural practices while incarcerated. He is speaking specifically about their access to the land, to incorporate the cultural identity that defines them into the terms of their imprisonment. In fact, the El Manzano prison in the city of Concepción, where they were previously held, allowed them access to a small piece of land where they planted two *canelos*, the sacred trees of the Mapuche people, which were destroyed by the prison guards after the prisoners were transferred to Lebu. The young and vivacious partner of one of the imprisoned activists told me two days after I visited that the guards who ripped out the *canelos* would experience terrible suffering for desecrating sacred Mapuche ground.

A Mapuche prison is necessary because there will be more arrests, Héctor Llaitul thinks. Not just because the Chilean state has such a high rate of indigenous political prisoners but because the movement for land restitution isn't stopping any time soon. Yet Llaitul also thinks that their incarceration, and the long sentences prosecutors are demanding by submitting them to both civilian and military trials—Llaitul himself risks more than a century in prison—are methods that the state is using to harass all Mapuche communities, to reduce the number of people who would join these activist efforts to get their land back.

Llaitul figures that the Chilean state is in total collusion with the private sector, and that the so-called Antiterrorist Law is nothing more than a way to criminalize the Mapuche and cover up rapacious capitalist expansion on their land. Llaitul states that the Antiterrorist Law was actually created with the sole purpose of containing the Mapuche, and that it won't really be used against other groups (anarchists, for example, or *okupas*), despite what the authorities say. The Antiterrorist Law, Llaitul insists, was conceived as an attack against the Mapuche and it exists to empower the financial interests that lobbied for its passage.

Héctor Llaitul thinks, in a word, "territorially." According to him, the Mapuche who live in Santiago should return to their ancestral lands because only there will they fully exercise their identities. He believes that mass migration by the Mapuche to Santiago is a process of exile that needs to end. He sees the cause he leads as completely linked to environmental conservation practices, and he believes that no one can represent that cause better than the Mapuche, given that their relationship to the stewardship of nature is a constitutive aspect of their existence.

Héctor Llaitul defines the CAM as enacting a political praxis of land restitution outside the auspices of the state. His position is anti-capitalist, he says, because capitalism is an attack on the culture of the Mapuche people as a whole.

As Llaitul speaks, his youngest son comes and goes. Babies are passed around. A young activist speaks with his daughter, who is just a few months old. The movement's spokesperson, Natividad Llanquileo, displays her extraordinary charisma. Young, intelligent, and astute, Llanquileo augurs a future of active leadership in the movement. Two days later, I see Llanquileo speaking in Mapudungun with her mother. She introduces us, and her mother addresses me in Mapudungun too. I can't understand her. The family members of the prisoners say that the *carabineros* police and the detective force are studying Mapudungun to spy on them. They say they're attending Mapudungun classes at the university.

It's hard for family members to visit the prisoners because they don't have enough money to cover their transportation costs. It's difficult, they say. They are completely focused on every minor detail of the case. They speak of a set-up; they mention the lengthiness of pre-trial detention (a year and eight months, so far); they allude to torture; they complain about the state's protected witnesses; they object to the range of legal inconsistencies in the cases; and they laugh at the police's different theories as riddled with errors.

The Trial in Cañete

A member of Chile's Investigations Police, or PDI, is summoned to the witness stand by the prosecution. It's the first day I'm attending the trial in Cañete. The strapping young officer on the stand discusses analyzing phone calls between the *comuneros* and a potential buyer for stolen timber in the area in order to substantiate the charges of robbery against the defendants. He says that he's part of a team that has recorded an unprecedented number of phone calls. Under cross-examination by the activists' defense attorneys, he is unable to conceal his anger. Meanwhile, the prosecutors use technicalities to object to the defense's questions, one by one. This leads to constant interruptions. "What do you have to do tomorrow?", an alleged buyer asks an alleged timber seller in one recording. In every conversation played during this part of the trial, we never hear anyone say anything directly; all we hear are fragments of speech that fail to incriminate anyone. The way the detective explains the conversation seems to me to be total conjecture. I'm no specialist, but I do think that even if timber had been stolen, the recorded conversations don't prove it because the detective's analysis has little or nothing to do with what the recordings actually say.

The defense attorneys are basically working pro bono. They've been traveling from Concepción to work on this long trial, living in Cañete for most of the week. As he speaks, the public defender shows that he is highly prepared. He's doing well, I think. In the audience, chiefs—known as *lonkos*—and young mothers with babies in their arms arrive and sit in their assigned places. The otherwise distant attitudes of the defendants only change when they look and wave lovingly at the babies from inside the glassed-in space where they're being held.

The two days of the trial that I attend (thanks to a press pass from *The Clinic* newspaper) are alarming for me, partly because of the shock of listening to the phone recordings. They've even tapped the phone line of a thirteen-year-old girl. I can't help but think about how many phone lines throughout the country are tapped.

The detectives on the witness stand who have been spying on the defendants are all part of the intelligence services. They are literally spies. They also do data analysis. The indigenous communities have been ransacked with an unexpected, evil violence, the defendants' family members say. When they do these searches, I'm told, they take everything. The members of these communities are terrified. In one of the recordings, we hear someone—possibly Llaitul—clearly say that the police "are barging in on the communities."

The detective testifies that he saw a group of armed, masked activists supervising the robbery of timber. The prosecutor asks him who those people were and he answers, "everyone who's sitting here." Later, though, he retracts his statement and suggests that only "some of the people who are sitting here" were involved. I wonder how he recognized them through the masks. These are just details, I tell myself. It's not worth thinking about, I tell myself.

During the recesses, the audience and the family members talk amongst themselves. Natividad Llanquileo looks at her phone (which must be tapped, I think to myself) and says that she has to travel to Santiago. Later, I see her briefly at the house of a dear friend of mine and we have tea together. Natividad is going to Santiago to meet with the new Archbishop of Santiago, Ricardo Ezzati. The defendants' family members and lawyers are saying that the *comuneros* feel abandoned, and that public debate has hardly paid any attention to their cause. They say that after a long hunger strike, the only result was silence. They speak about their loneliness.

The lawyers and family members speculate that the trial will be over by late January; by then, after the testimony, the judges will issue a verdict. The family members and one activist from France who have watched the entire trial speculate that Llaitul and one of the Llanquileo brothers will be convicted—which is the main goal of the trial. Yet what they consider most aberrant and distressing is that the defendants have been judged in a civilian and military trial simultaneously, which is the key condition set out by the Antiterrorism Law. These trials often call on anonymous witnesses, too. Even though the law was reformulated following the defendants' prolonged hunger strike, and they will now only be judged according to civilian law, the trial will still end with a verdict maintaining the structure of the Antiterrorism Law. Legally speaking, this matter is very complicated, so my analysis here is only an approximation.

The accusations against the activists are manifold: illicit association, assaulting the *carabineros* police, assaulting a prosecutor, carrying illegal weapons, and the robbery of timber, among others.

As I write this piece, I wonder whether the judge's verdict will be out by the time it's published. At the same time, right now, I can't help but remember how when I was sitting there, behind a glass window in a neighboring room, listening to the recordings, hearing the detectives talk about timber, timber that was supposedly stolen from a big logging company, I felt the urge to get up out of my seat. I felt like standing up.

Yes, I would have liked to break protocol, go into the courtroom, walk up to the presiding judge, and remind him—ever so calmly, ever so surely—of that famous (and wise) saying: "Thieves who rob from thieves get a hundred years' reprieve."

Of course, it was nothing more than an impulse. Albeit a powerful, sincere one.

After that, we returned to Santiago.

(2011)

Translated by Carl Fischer

Camila Vallejo:
Mission Accomplished

The streets are one of the most effective instruments we have to congregate and articulate social discontent. It is by occupying the city that the public sphere can best express itself. Mass gatherings of bodies are what make the power of people's demands particularly explicit. The city becomes a spectacle of disturbance on a stage that heightens an already-vibrant social vitality and shows the power that vitality can wield.

Without a doubt, though, that space (the streets as the cultural locus of politics) is also a prime location for police brutality. The so-called "public order" is the most visible method the state has for justifying its repressive force. Repression exists to legitimize the idea that, in the end, public space belongs to the police.

Here, I'm interested in thinking about the streets as the place where the figure of the student leader Camila Vallejo took shape. But I also want to trace a genealogy in recent Chilean history, albeit an insufficient one, that might offer an interpretation of her formidable emergence.

The early years of the so-called "transition to democracy" in Chile were truly traumatic. Pinochet continued on as the head of the Armed Forces—as their commander-in-chief. Civilian collaborators with the dictatorship reinvented themselves in congress as bastions of democracy. Underneath this façade, however, fear and uncertainty persisted in the form of self-censorship. It was outrageous to see how memory was repressed. Official forgetting was seen as a means to maintain the fragile institutions of democracy.

The economic regime was intimately intertwined with politics and a frenetic "consumerist fever" broke out. Chile was the world's most intensive laboratory for neoliberalism, which generated a society based on expense and excess. Healthcare, housing, and education became consumer goods—markers of social inclusion and exclusion.

The height of the paradox lay in the fact that Pinochet left the leadership of the Armed Forces in 1990 to become a (non-elected) senator following the 1980 constitution. That constitution, which remains in force to this day, was passed under his regime. Thanks to a constitutional provision, the dictator became a democrat, in an attempt to whitewash his image. Without a doubt, it was a confusing, and even toxic social situation.

The Concertación de Partidos por la Democracia (Concentration of Parties for Democracy), a coalition of center-left parties, left the prior economic regime untouched and even legitimized it by lending a sheen of truth to it—to the benefit of local and multinational business interests. However, the new political scenario did lead to the restitution of human rights in the country. When the Concertación took power, it brought an end to state-sanctioned abuses and crimes, save for certain isolated cases.

Private universities boomed in the 1990s. Capital held by the economic right wing poured into one particular industry that turned out to be highly lucrative: education. Meanwhile, public universities had to raise tuition, and students took out loans with usurious interest rates.

There was a new twist to this dynamic in 1998. Pinochet was arrested in London while he was there for back surgery. International courts issued an arrest warrant for him following a charge issued in Spain by the legendary judge Baltazar Garzón. The image of Pinochet sitting in his backyard while under house arrest was seen on television screens across the world. A mood of generalized stupefaction took over in Chile. The government demanded his return home.

Pinochet was never tried in Chile but he did have to resign his position as a legislator. Although he never spent time in an actual jail, his arrest in London marked a degradation of the power he had held for more than 25 years. In one way or another, Pinochet had controlled and occupied Chile's public spaces for a quarter of a century.

Later on, the parties that made up the ruling Concertación coalition lost the ability to sustain the epochal narrative of themselves as opponents of the dictatorship; they became administrators of a neoliberal economic regime. Lowering inequality became less of a political priority for them than simply reducing poverty.

Without a doubt, the election of Michelle Bachelet as president was a milestone for the Concertación. A charismatic figure whose personal history was marked by the tragic effects of the dictatorship, Michelle Bachelet—the first woman elected president in Chilean history—was beloved and respected by Chileans thanks to her lack of pretensions, her good humor, and her rejection of the pomposities of power.

However, the ambiguous positions of different politicians in Chile vis-à-vis political and economic power led to a crisis: the power of the political right wing was growing. Therein lay the paradox: just as the most popular and beloved president of all time was taking office, her political coalition ran out of steam, in part because she didn't use her unquestionable leadership to lower economic inequality, increase access to social rights, and decrease labor precarity. Nor was there any particular progress in the cultural sphere as far as diversity, pluralism, or citizen dialogue and participation.

Michelle Bachelet's initial project was to construct what she called a "citizen government." However, her allies turned their backs on her; she ended up having to govern in a more vertical way. Her efforts at achieving gender parity—naming an equal number of men and women to her cabinet—had also failed by the end of her first year in office. The extreme pressure from her own governing coalition undermined her attempt to democratize the public sector.

Sebastián Piñera, an entrepreneur who had made his millions in the credit card business, was elected president in 2009. Piñera had been moving between politics and the private sector throughout those twenty years of democratic transition. A representative of the liberal right, he formed a governing coalition with the hard right (itself rooted in an extreme defense of Pinochet), whose focus was on generating wealth for the private sector and defending so-called "family values" and conservative sexual practices.

The massive earthquake (8.8 on the Richter scale) and tsunami that caused damage to half the country in 2010, just days before Sebastián Piñera took office, also meant a more symbolic upheaval. It had been fifty years since the right had been democratically elected to govern the country. The country was partially in ruins, and thousands of people were homeless.

The Concertación had successfully managed a number of social conflicts as long as its leaders had been in office. This success was due in part to its negotiations with the leaders of various protests. By politically co-opting those leaders, it guaranteed something of a "social peace." Any hints of social discontent were quashed thanks to the agreements that the Concertación reached with protestors, as with the "Penguin Revolution" of 2006.[26]

As long as it maintained its hegemony, the Concertación was able to ignore any signs of unease. In its final years, just fifty percent of the eligible population was voting—the rest simply didn't register, spoiled their ballots, or left them blank. Many of those in that non-voting fifty percent were young people who flatly refused to participate in the electoral process. And the Concertación did not address that issue adequately because the votes it did receive kept it in power. Still, the margins were too narrow for the Concertación not to have taken this into account.

Piñera's first year in office was relatively easy. The terrible impact of the earthquake, as well as the rescue of 33 miners who were trapped underground after their mine collapsed, brought him political benefits. The students remained silent that year.

But significant changes were already underway in 2010. There was an uprising in the city of Punta Arenas, in the extreme south of the country, where civil society organizations were protesting the high taxes and excessive fuel costs that disproportionately affected them. Citizens who protested were met with brutal police repression, but even so, civil society organizations continued to make demands and blocked all access to the city until the government gave in. This was the *Puntarenazo*: a harbinger of the most large-scale, massive protests in twenty years. Chile's outlying areas began to protest in a process that lasted throughout 2011 and transcended the local news to reach the global stage.

Sebastián Piñera's inauguration as president was like a dam breaking. The discontent that had built up over twenty years of Concertación governments exploded in one of the areas where the coalition was most vulnerable: education. According to experts, education in Chile costs as much as, if not more than, education in the United States. Students were mortgaging their futures by taking out loans directly with the banks.

---

26 The "Penguin Revolution" (Revolución de los Pingüinos) was a series of protests by high school students in Chile—students who are colloquially referred to as "penguins" because of their black and white uniforms.

A number of student organizations, grouped under the Confederation of Students (known by its Spanish-language acronym CONFECH), called for a strike led by Camila Vallejo, the head of the student union at the University of Chile, the most important university in the nation. For the first time, she garnered a degree of fame, as well as a growing following.

Vallejo, who studied Geography, led the explosive student protests throughout 2011. With uncommon fortitude, she was able to manage an onslaught of media coverage with aplomb, responding calmly and clearly without ever losing sight of the cause she represented: free, quality public education. Her slogan: "Stop for-profit education."

Camila Vallejo was fortunately joined by Giorgio Jackson, the president of the Student Union of the Catholic University (Chile's second most important university). Like Vallejo, Jackson also had outstanding leadership abilities, as well as a way with words that served him well in interviews, debates, and public forums. Notably, he acknowledged Camila Vallejo as the leader of the movement, proving on multiple occasions his loyalty as second-in-command.

The student movement was a coalition of multiple sensibilities that ranged from philosophical anarchism to more moderate leftism. It operated in an interesting way in that it lent a degree of dramatics to the student uprising. The students held assemblies throughout the country to break with any centralism that might have privileged Santiago. The main television channels covered them consistently. Despite its internal differences and even arguments, the coalition remained intact under Vallejo's intelligent leadership. Moreover, its protests, all successful, were able to capture the national imaginary because they were carried out performatively: the students who participated (roughly 100,000 of them each time, on average) followed the logic of their own imaginaries, using costumes, music, dances, and other tactics. Vallejo's perspicacity lay not only in allowing but also in incentivizing these kinds of autonomous gestures and then not interfering with them.

Camila Vallejo's figure generated a number of different reactions, but her beauty was what her followers, as well as her detractors, responded to the most. It was a beauty that was distinct, or distanced, from what she said, because she did nothing to indicate any self-consciousness about how she presented herself. She may have had a nose piercing—an irreverent 21st-century style—but her political discourse was focused and on-message.

Her affiliation with the Communist Party, in a country that has generally been anti-communist, even among its left wing, did not detract from her leadership at all. This paradox was able to sustain itself, at least in part, because Vallejo was able to be self-effacing as a subject tied to any particular biography, focusing instead on her place as a social subject. She refrained from turning her private life into a spectacle. She refused to be trapped by the sentimental discourse that commonly surrounds the feminine, and although she did have a boyfriend (the former president of the University of Chile's Student Federation), she never appeared in public with him and skillfully avoided questions about her personal life.

Meanwhile, the (often forceful) way she had of debating was marked by utter calm. Camila Vallejo never lost her cool, even when she was treated quite poorly on multiple occasions. That particular characteristic—her smiling, unruffled poise—worked in her favor. It won her the trust of those who saw her not as a representative of the supposedly menacing, Cold War-era Communist Party, but rather as a young, beautiful woman successfully fighting for collective ideals.

Camila Vallejo soon became a national and international icon. She was incessantly subjected to media scrutiny as the student protests continued. The students didn't go back to class, multiple campuses were occupied by strikers, and there were ongoing meetings with the authorities to reach an agreement. Most of the country, according to polls, stood in solidarity with the movement that Vallejo led, despite the economic losses that went along with it.

It's quite possible that Camila Vallejo is the most important student leader in Chile's history. The key question is how leadership of that magnitude can emerge and sustain itself in such a male-dominated environment. Her beauty is not to be discounted, but it's not enough; there are many beautiful women who never reach the heights that she's reached.

It's more constructive to focus on how Vallejo administers her beauty in conjunction not only with her formidable intelligence but with a collectively articulated social identity. In this sense, one might speak of the distribution of that beauty in a non-aggressive, and rather inclusive way, because it becomes part of the national patrimony. It's used not for a beauty pageant, but in the service of a historic struggle for social rights.

As the psychoanalyst Melanie Klein shows, Camila Vallejo—perhaps envied for her supposed willingness to take on such an overwhelming struggle—has transformed the negativity of envy into its liberatory opposite: admiration.

There's a connection, of course, between the figures of Michelle Bachelet and Camila Vallejo. Bachelet's ascent to the highest office in the land broke a historic barrier for women in public office. This breakthrough "naturalized" female leadership in politics. This was despite the fact that women occupy a more sacrificial position in the way power is distributed behind the scenes in terms of income distribution, workplace access, healthcare costs, and poverty. It's interesting to think about figures who inspire enthusiasm despite their physical differences. While Michelle Bachelet buttresses herself with a more formal, neutral, and even somewhat frumpy aesthetic, Camila Vallejo makes use of the attractive iconography of her youth: cleavage, a miniskirt, and long hair. Even so—and this is the curious thing—both of them put their bodies on the line, in a sense, because their leadership is based on their charisma. It wouldn't be possible to establish a mother-daughter genealogy between them so much as a captivating, surprising surplus.

It's always possible that the idea of these women in power can function as nothing more than a band-aid solution for the massive problems that women experience in Chile. The most urgent problems aren't solvable, in any case, given that no existing legislation addresses abortion (seemingly unthinkable at this moment), even under the narrowest of circumstances.[27] The disproportionately low representation of women in the legislature is simply mind-boggling. The overrepresentation of men in politics has consolidated what Pierre Bourdieu has called "masculine domination." Money, executive leadership, and wealth accumulation are still masculine spaces, while seduction continues to be located at the center of women's emotional lives—at least in terms of their representation in telenovelas.

---

27 Abortion was legalized in Chile, under three limited circumstances, in 2017.

Camila Vallejo is still writing her own story. The most important question, as far as cultural critique is concerned, is how she'll exercise her leadership. One option appears to be as a member of congress: this won't be an easy path given that it would mean working within an imperfect system that she herself has denounced (due to the ongoing imprint of the military dictatorship on the electoral process). She might end up co-opted by parliamentary bureaucracy. Her membership in the Communist Party, which—like all political parties—has a notoriously sexist structure, could lead her to negotiations that might cut her off from key civil organizations, daily life, and cultural changes. What could easily happen is for her to become just another one of the political elites, losing her connection to the people who saw her as an important social leader.

All of these considerations aside, though, Camila Vallejo is already one of the most captivating actors within the political history of this young 21st century. Her epic trajectory has been completely exemplary.

(2012)

Translated by Carl Fischer

The Actual Pandemic
and the Political Pandemic

I'm surprised that none of the political analysts, or the pundits, or the specialists have thought to view COVID as one of the main reasons for why our social situation is as complicated as it currently is.

This coming Sunday we find ourselves facing the remote and—I think—impossible scenario that Sebastián Piñera's completely failed administration will be succeeded by a hardline, ultra-right-wing leader.

But we need to examine that candidate, who is—among other things—an authoritarian, an admirer of Pinochet (and a fierce defender of the 20% of the population that voted in 2020 to keep the current constitution), and a misogynist. According to him, communism is preferable to feminism; he constantly insults sexual minorities; he is neoliberal in the extreme; he calls for the destruction of the state apparatus through mass firings of public employees and the elimination of various government ministries. He has called for active state repression by the armed forces. He is against environmentalism and he promotes the prison system (except when it comes to the white-collar crime of collusion). He is a false prophet of social peace. He is a fanatic of a sort of indeterminate "order."

I am insisting on some of the characteristics that define him and his supporters—the opportunistic disingenuousness of these beliefs notwithstanding.

Chilean neoliberalism is currently undergoing a crisis and maybe even a real decline. Even the country's greedy business class can see it, even though their drive to accumulate wealth has barely slowed. What exploded in October 2019 was the crisis of Chile's economic model; just a few months later, amid multiple human rights violations, came the explosion of the pandemic.

In just two years, the political situation has taken a major turn. Even though 80% of the population rejected Pinochet's constitution, we later saw the left lose its majority in congress and the nomination of the most extreme right-wing presidential candidate we've ever seen. What happened? From my perspective, COVID interrupted the effervescence of a political debate that was marked by an emancipatory spirit.

The deaths and the medical (Mañalich) violence created a health-care frenzy.[28] Our country had the fourth-largest number of deaths per capita in the world at one point. Fear of death became our primordial condition. An acute process of discipline befell us. Successive lock-downs, which were later extended, annihilated the way communities were organized. Forced quarantines removed young people and adolescents from the public sphere and relegated them to the solitude of virtual get-togethers. Students, ever on the cutting edge, took a back seat. The TV networks, which had been experiencing a freefall in viewership, regained prominence when everyone was forced to stay inside. The social explosion was converted, amidst our isolation and the images we consumed, into nothing more than an instance of common crime. The population, already affected enough by fear as it was, only doubled down on that fear.

The political collapse of the right, which had dedicated itself to the accumulation of wealth and a pseudo-liberal agenda, also constituted a regression of sorts. The right entrenched itself behind its hardliner candidate and took a step back into the UDI-Pinochet era, full of archaic values based on the so-called *patria*, the heterosexual family, and a paternalistic, religious concept of charity with colonial roots.

It's not my intention to deny the historical hegemony of the right, much less forgive the protracted mistakes of the neoliberal center-left that brought about its own destruction. We have to acknowledge the lack of experience and the naiveté of the Frente Amplio as it has immersed itself in retail politics.[29] It is that kind of politics that Izkia Siches has wisely focused on. But let me insist on the fact that in order to best

---

28   Jaime Mañalich was Chile's Health Minister when the COVID-19 pandemic began.

29   The Frente Amplio, or Broad Front, is a coalition of left-wing political parties and movements that supported the candidacy of Gabriel Boric in Chile's 2021 presidential election.

understand this situation we have to factor in the pandemic/lockdown/ fear/death as the fundamental realities of a citizenry already affected by layers of mourning and media manipulation.

I don't think that the supporters of the hardliner candidate are motivated by invocations of the dangers of "Chilezuela" or communism. Those arguments are simply too grotesque. Instead, I'm thinking about the process of discipline and quarantine, and about how voters' imaginaries of women and sexual minorities have been colonized by adverse forces. I'm thinking about the existence of a populist brand of sexism.

But right now, I'm thinking about the large portion of the citizenry that didn't vote. Especially young people. And I'm thinking about how they will go out this Sunday to exercise their right to vote for Boric as a sign of a new rejection of this hardliner candidate: a character who inhabits a ferocious world with a craving for wealth and an altered state of mind, full of non-existent values. He is a denier of history.

As he himself said: "If Pinochet were alive, he'd vote for me."

He said this because the antiquated shadow of Pinochet is his highest ideal.

(2021)

Translated by Carl Fischer

Wandering around among Signs

We are living in a complex, or confusing, or paradoxical time. I know full well that such signs—complexity, confusion, paradox—tend to repeat themselves from one era to the next. But the multiple conflicts of our own time contain certain signs that we can analyze. I am approaching the outlines and paradigms of our current situation in an ultra-schematic way, of course, but it's clear that this is a period defined by the intensification of neoliberalism with all the circumstances and repercussions such a system brings with it. It seems to me that Chile's economic model–with all the costs it entails–is beginning to show signs of a decline that will surely drag on for quite some time.

The present is defined by forces that work incessantly to conserve the hegemony of the market, which its apologists see as the only way to sustain democracy: some say that democracy can moderate the preeminence of the market, while others believe that democracy can change the market altogether by introducing a greater measure of statism, thereby allowing for better harmony and social justice.

The conservative worldview is based on utopias of order that have long been in dispute: the strangest one of these is likely a desire for the restoration of the traditional family. Liberalism, in contrast, focuses on the segmentation of the social universe under the guise of diversity. But conservatives and liberals alike share the same—or similar—convictions about the accumulation of capital. The left—or, as the thinker Nancy Fraser calls it, post-socialism—promotes the end of neoliberalism, the recognition of diverse identities, and economic redistribution by a strengthened state with a social welfare system that can reduce inequality.

Meanwhile, we are living at a tense time of dispute over global power. China is emerging as the new hegemon, its hybrid of capitalism and communism displacing the United States and generating ongoing low-intensity confrontations over technology, property, and territory.

The progress of the Chinese in every area is indisputable. The powerful arms industry—that ever-expanding industry of industries—has found in the Russia-Ukraine war an opportunity to substantiate itself, incited by Russia's autocratic, nationalistic tendencies and exacerbated by the always-active intervention of the United States. This war is taking place within a Europe impregnated by different, antagonistic forces, including an extreme right wing that is showing clear signs of growth.

The crises of war and destruction, as well as issues of poverty and corruption, have generated incessant, massive waves of migration. Migration, along with war and poverty, has long been one of the main motors of history. Today, more than five million Venezuelans are living outside of Venezuela, some of whom have followed dangerous routes that have left them tremendously vulnerable. Another effect of mass migration is the rise of nationalism and racism—the principal structures upon which the extreme right wing has built its power. But it's also important to point out that migration produces major uncertainty: we don't know the real population of many countries due to illegal border crossings and the huge numbers of undocumented inhabitants with no legal rights.

Meanwhile, the invasive, growing practice of drug trafficking in different countries—with all the violence and corruption that comes along with it—cannot be contained by public policy. Not even legalization can stop drug trafficking organizations, murders for hire, or corruption. It doesn't mitigate addiction, either, which affects significant parts of these countries.

We need to think about these tensions, problems, and hostilities within the framework we have, in which radical neoliberalism is ascendant and the state always has a thorny role to play. It is because of deregulation that neoliberalism aggravates these problems, generating segregation and community breakdown. Neoliberalism is based on a fundamental inequality that is generally seen as its inevitable byproduct, even as it generates a surprising accumulation of wealth for the rich, who then turn that wealth into the stuff of mass spectacle.

Of course, neoliberalism constructs subjects and desires, programs people's psyches, defines the circulation of goods, and demarcates territories. That always-uncertain idea of the "I" at its center has generated a segregated, discriminatory reality. And this segregation isn't just an economic method for determining people's consumption habits in the context of a segmented market; it also has to do with the segregation of identities for the benefit of the market—identities that serve as consumer goods for the other identities from which they find themselves segregated. This phenomenon multiplies the number of categories of identity even as it ossifies them, preventing them from evolving and changing, discouraging ambiguity, ensuring that they remain perfectly designed and discrete, and forcing them—following Foucault—into a panopticon that constantly keeps them in place. In this way, it generates surveillance and inequality, founded upon rigid divisions.

A paradox is thus created: we can observe the proliferation of different identities and subjectivities, some of which are repressed and severely punished by existing social mores, but at the same time, these increasingly visible identities are frozen into place instead of achieving the emancipation they have been seeking.

The recognition of different identities is important, of course, but it's a dynamic that replicates the inequalities of the program that recognizes them. Or, to put it another way: this recognition is fragmented by the very market that upholds it.

The matrices of power and domination in our lives follow their inexorable, historical course because they're almost entirely controlled by the universe of masculinity. This scenario includes economics, science, religion, law, technology, war, drug trafficking, and environmental depredation, to name a few of its more visible dimensions. Analyzing these matrices—where women are extremely scarce—means focusing on violence and scarcity in areas of great conflict. There may be some discourse of inclusivity, but we can see where the hegemonic centers are and how the syntax of the world is defined.

Allow me to bring us to the territory I inhabit—Chile—in order to continue my meditation on the so-called "gender issue." I have some tentative questions that may themselves have blind spots or even misconceptions, but I've still decided that it's important to share them. In 2018, a new era of Chilean feminism was born, which politicized our bodies and turned our focus to matters of gender equality. Perhaps one of the most far-reaching aspects of this revitalized movement was the drafting of a constitution by an assembly with equal numbers of men and women: a global milestone, as many social analyses have pointed out. Meanwhile, the current government describes itself as feminist, and its cabinet has been constructed with gender parity in mind. Its central project is to promote gender equity. This, for me, is crucial.

This scenario offers the possibility for a considerable cultural change on multiple fronts. The current state of affairs in Chile is thus marked by the recognition of diverse identities. Under the administration of Sebastián Piñera, same-sex marriage was legalized and, along with it, the state created space for a different kind of family in the social sphere with full equal rights.

These gestures of parity are important for us to observe, so we can think about our own role in the democratization of space. This allows for a form of public representation of the kind of model we aspire to have: representation with a strong state as an exemplary mise-en-scène of equity. These public-facing gestures need to be carefully read vis-à-vis the distribution of power in non-government spaces as well, particularly in finance, science, technology, and large corporations. These are masculine spaces, where women occupy minor roles in contexts where wealth is generated and managed: they don't have management roles, so much as roles in which they're charged with the implementation of directives made by others. Let's not forget that in Chile just 1% of the population holds the same amount of wealth that the next 49% of the population holds. I believe it's important to point out that many people live their lives chained to debt, with levels of interest that are determined by the interests of the wealthiest. The social position of women—whose positions in the social sphere tend to be more precarious—is irreparably and inexorably determined by the relationship between body and debt.

Of course, the actions and administration of the state take on extraordinary importance. Laws mandating gender parity can and should reduce inequality and bring change to spaces controlled by the private sphere, as well as all the organizations and corporations within it. But it's also important to consider that there are inequalities within this space of egalitarianism: not just between men and women but within the genders themselves. For this state-based equality—or, as I've suggested, this mise-en-scène of parity—proposed by the government to take root and spread, a cultural change needs to take place on an intense and immense scale. A rewriting of the genders needs to take place within those genders themselves. This means a rupture of the imaginary that changes, or even breaks apart, the very structure of the gender binary into a plane where such divisions cease to exist. This is a goal that I think we need to pursue as a constructive political horizon. We know that gender and the conditions it entails are imprinted upon girls even before they're born. We know that one isn't just born a woman or a man, but that one is born a gender, so to speak: born into a gender that comes previously formatted. So that's why I think that the current administration and its focus on the recognition of identity is a possible future here in the present, to the extent that it can perform a parity of power in a reality where there is an absolute asymmetry of power. What I'm trying to say here is that a "mature" parity of state is taking place in a context where inequality exists from birth: a symbolic parity that, for now, lacks the structures it needs to take root.

This gesture by the government is important precisely because it allows us to realize what we've been lacking and understand the progress we need to improve the experience of women whose movement through space is disadvantaged even though their identities are receiving increasingly greater recognition. I believe we need to rethink the current liberal order, founded as it is upon rigid, rationalized, and even academically justified segregation, as well as upon the obstruction of community-based mobilization. The Marxian notion of the industrial proletariat has been displaced by industrial production outsourced to India, China, or Guatemala, while in Chile, the growth of the middle class has led to people crossing above the poverty line. These changes have been useful for the market, and especially for neoliberalism, as a way of sidestepping potential class-based conflicts.

But I feel better prepared to speak—always tentatively and with words that are solely provisional for now—from the literary sphere where I have been for practically my entire life. As a reader, I experienced the effects that the binaries of gender and sexuality had on the formation of different canons. This translated into the obligation to read certain things within the framework of must-read novelists. But, as a reader of many women writers, I could understand how the conditions of gender impregnated women's writing through the years. That's how I understood that even as times and political conditions changed, many texts were populated by a kind of excessively programmatic romanticism, related to relationships and breakups that were represented in a schematic way: emphasizing either their success or their failure.

Emotions lay at the center of these texts, in which the love object was made into a divine, Marian creature constantly subjected to subordination. Just as we can't deny that the colonization of women's imaginaries leads to cultural models in which hegemonic power goes unquestioned, it also seems impossible for me to deny that these same emotional technologies exist in the context of gender and genre. These technologies trace paths of subordination for women in literary texts as well, which of course are permeated by the most traditional gender norms. I think it's possible to read from that perspective: from the understanding that writing, like other aspects of the social arena, obeys rules, acting them out in the literary world and functioning as a builder of imaginaries. Or, to cite Foucault: gender and genre are constructed using technologies of discipline that automatically reproduce themselves. This disciplining of gender and genre operates on multiple fronts in literature. But a considerable number of women writers are able to evade, elude, or transgress this shortsighted pedagogy of the letter, and enter into the terrain of a more destabilizing variety of meanings and poetics. These generate a strange sense of the real in fiction, or they generate a realism that denounces the very categories it enunciates. This is a way of opening writing up into new, politically charged territories that make literature a place that can problematize the flows of literary production itself.

In this sense, I have been attentive to differences. I watch for moments within a literary work where genre and gender grow charged and leap ahead, thanks to precise literary strategies. I've noticed this, for example, in Rosario Orrego's *Teresa* (1870), and in Marta Brunet's *Doña Santitos* (1926) and *María Rosa Flor de Quillén* (1927), which explore and excavate complex forms of power and lead us to exciting methods of (de) liberation. Other works, meanwhile, take on the prejudicial condition of the norms in which gender and genre are constructed; but by accepting them as evidence, through a careful administration of literary material, they can produce coherent narrative spaces of persistence and resistance, as with *María Nadie* (1957). Let's not forget that the most important Chilean critic of Brunet's time energetically praised her by stating that she "wrote like a man." This was Alone, who brought attention to her work by openly pointing out that men's writing was superior; he considered women's writing insufficient. Or maybe he just felt that "writing like a woman" was deficient—the stuff of cliché. I can't help but think of

Alone right now. Let's look at him in the context of the present moment: the idea of "writing like a man," for starters. I can't help but connect it to today's market-based commercial platform of "women's writing."

For several decades now, literary movements based on emancipation have focused on that which has been diluted in, or outright erased from, the literary sphere. The push to make women's literature more visible has been a constant, but in my opinion—after years of examining the effects of this push—I think that designation has become a literary category that has been used by the system in a duplicitous way. It functions to accumulate different types of writing only to subordinate them into a traditional, antiquated canon. That denomination "women's writing" operates in a biblical way, like Adam's rib: a vestigial bone that can be removed without damaging the powerful superstructure in any real way.

Over the past few years, I've become increasingly sure that one possible way of democratizing the literary field—of moving beyond this idea of Adam's rib—is to de-biologize writing by valuing its resourcefulness and the power of its methods, such that the sexes of different authors become little more than biographical data. Sisterhood cannot be understood as biological complicity in the literary field because that would require abandoning its cultural origin, the idea of literary difference, and aesthetics as the center of production. We would have to renounce the questions that literature generates, replacing them instead with a kind of corporate defense of women that would risk the replication of subordination. I think that the passions of literature lie in risk, as a form of intervention and literary alter(c)ation.

I have to admit that it is with some trepidation that I ask whether the idea of "sisterhood" as a univocal response to these questions isn't the result of its own sort of (m)othering. In this sense, I also think that we need to de-maternalize the social apparatus that positions women as the bearers of a kind of sacred duty, thereby exposing them to social, job-based, and parental exploitation—not to mention self-exploitation. We know full well that reproduction is something that women can do—whether they choose to do so or not—and that this has been the principal way of domesticating them and exercising violence over them throughout history. But I would venture to say that the mother is dead (to borrow from Nietzsche's audacious declaration), at least in terms of how we understand her as a biological phenomenon. The intervention of reproductive technologies has changed how women bear children and their so-called "biological cycles." Today, women over 60 are becoming mothers, and the commercial successes of sperm banks and egg donation are well-known. Uteruses can function as a sort of organic small business, which poorer women can rent out. So, the idea of a child as "the fruit of thy womb, Jesus" is passé. Women's reproduction has become yet another industrial force. And yet the figure of the mother continues to be linked to the "natural," in every sense of the word. Same-sex couples can have children without mothers, or with two mothers. However, I believe that the historical—or even prehistorical—idea of the mother continues to be relevant; this relevance omits the growing profitability of reproductive technology, intensifying the idea of sacrifice. And, not coincidentally, this liberates the father from the sacrificial discourse imposed by culture. It's interesting to observe how the market strategically positions certain literature that emphasizes motherhood precisely at a time in which motherhood is undergoing one of the most intense periods of change in the entire history of reproduction. Meanwhile, the literature of technologized motherhood, or surrogacy, is accorded a lesser status.

I will conclude this talk by evoking Augusto D'Halmar, one of the most incisive writers in Chilean literary history. D'Halmar skillfully portrayed the ways in which conservative power controlled our imaginative horizon. His 1902 novel *Juana Lucero* is important because it shows how a poor woman with no relations—with no mother and an absent father, and whose domestic labor is understood as an entrée for access to her body by her employers—becomes the center of a story of violence and sexual abuse. *Juana Lucero* is a naturalist novel in the vein of Émile Zola, but it's also possible to read it in a more local register, and when we do so, it seems incredibly current. I also want to cite D'Halmar's *Pasión y muerte del cura Deusto*, from 1924, which is the first—or at least one of the first—works in Latin American literature to include themes of gay love and attraction.

For the moment, though, I will focus on a short story that allows me to think about the matter of artificial insemination: "En provincia," published in 1914, about the acquisition of seminal fluid for the purposes of conception. The story is about an infertile man—a concept that is often absent in cultural discourse since infertility has largely been seen as one of the more dramatic problems of female existence. Even though infertility can now be remedied thanks to reproductive technology coupled with economic power, culture preserves it as a female defect and tragedy. In this story, however, the infertile man makes an agreement with his wife to use a male employee as a sperm donor so that his wife can "give him" a child. The employee, who understands that he is being used and falls in love with his boss's wife anyway, serves as a surrogate for his employer, as part of a relationship in which power is vastly imbalanced.

In this sense, Augusto D'Halmar proposes and exposes infertility in a space that culture and literature rarely traverse; a similar situation of surrogacy occurs in José Donoso's *El obsceno pájaro de la noche*, but it's portrayed in a vague, oneiric way. "En provincia," on the other hand, is ahead of its time: it fearlessly examines surrogate fatherhood in an arrangement dictated by the economic power of a man's boss where the woman and the blindly naive employee come together to conceive a child and save the father from cultural disgrace.

Reading these literary texts—with all the dynamics of domination, enigma, and force that they portray—allows us to travel back in time, viewing the past as the present, examining subjectivities, power, and submission. They allow us to think beyond, or outside, even the hardest and fastest of rules.

(2022)

Translated by Carl Fischer

PART III

Communities

Col(labor)ation

For practically 25 years now, I have worked in collaboration with Lotty Rosenfeld. First, as members of CADA (Colectivo de Acciones de Arte, or Collective Art Actions Group, 1979-1985) during the height of the military dictatorship when we worked alongside Juan Castillo, Fernando Balcells, and Raúl Zurita; then, we threw ourselves into pondering the relationship between art and politics by designing a set of urban interventions that critically questioned art's traditional media and the dictatorial violence being inflicted on the Chilean social body at the same time.

The work, realized collectively and without individual authorship, was my first experience of an aesthetic opportunity to set authorship aside in favor of work created by a group. Without a doubt, the political urgency we felt during those years made the notion of the group and the launch of a collective practice conceptually indispensable. I am referring to the "tough" years of the military dictatorship, a time when the collective was viewed with suspicion.

In the context of CADA, Lotty Rosenfeld and I began our collaborative work. In 1981, we did a project that eventually won a competition: an installation called "Traspaso Cordillerano" (Cordillera Crossing). It was an attempt to merge the practices of literature and visuality, a project in which we sought to erase disciplinary borders by claiming the work fully and jointly through "dual" authorship.

After CADA finished its work, Lotty Rosenfeld and I relied on our experience and shared trajectory to continue experimenting with collaborative projects and to keep the questions we faced alive as artists working under the neoliberal context with its consumerist demands. Basically, our unanswered questions evolved and continued to unfold around the formation of dynamic, aesthetic scenarios that reflected and projected critical cultural meanings.

Independently of these collaborations, Lotty Rosenfeld systematically continued with her work in the visual arts, as I did with literature.

After almost 25 years, our collaboration has remained uninterrupted. Moreover, part of our artistic practice remains linked through new and diverse works.

Today, our collaborations take place in a primarily "professional" setting. Lotty Rosenfeld creates documentaries about different topics requested by institutions, and I act as a scriptwriter. This necessitates systematic exchanges between us through frequent and exhaustive meetings where we fine-tune the work's progress.

The results of this collaboration have been multiple and gratifying, mainly because we have achieved a friendship and working relationship over a considerable number of years without estrangements. Often, carrying out creative projects damages personal relationships because of insurmountable differences. I believe, partly, that this was not the case for us because of CADA, the precursor, which methodologically solidified a productive practice in a context of political urgency. The social situation was so pressing that we set aside the personal when faced with the need to produce under such conditions.

We lived within a difficult and adverse political situation, which engendered a labor politics: a wager on behalf of artistic production that we developed over many years. This has allowed us to work so fruitfully together over the years.

However, I do recognize that our collaboration has been put to the test on countless occasions. So, I now propose to delve into the terrain of the problems we faced.

Perhaps this is a somewhat paranoid attitude, but I do not think the neoliberal system—I'm speaking of a general system and a nonspecific form—is inclined toward shared labor. This is partly because capitalist structures are founded on individual work and, beyond that, the notion of the author and authorship are inscribed within the artistic system as ordering and hierarchical blueprints. Thus, collaboration and its diffuse borders threaten and disrupt the system because somehow they introduce a kind of impurity that "devalues" the work by putting the comfortable and verifiable limits of individual production in crisis.

Collective works, in one way or another, are received as a curiosity, an experiment, a unique experience that must be read within the framework of a broader universe. More than a creative expansion, these kinds of artistic productions fall paradoxically short; they linger in the in-between, in an imprecise and unanalyzable border territory.

On the other hand, analyses applied to collaborative works seem to concentrate not on the work itself but on which characteristics might permit us to define authorship, which, to be precise, is what the works are intentionally experimenting with. This reading, ultimately from the outside, leads to a confusing domain in which collaboration and its resistance are called into question.

As I noted, for twenty-five years Lotty Rosenfeld and I worked on various projects. Many of them took place outside of systems and artistic institutions. During the dictatorship, we threw ourselves into tasks grounded in solidarity politics (generating posters, slogans, scripts, and stagings) that circulated publicly without authorship or any indication that they had been created collaboratively.

Our work in those years was completely anonymous, free to embrace a clandestine, anti-dictatorial grammar. Its productivity lay precisely in its capacity to intervene politically: in how a poster, an inscription, or a specific concept born from aesthetic knowledge could be inscribed effectively within the political circuit.

In this sense, and from this place, I would venture into another area of conflict: the problem of gender.

I'd like to mention certain collaborations that were indispensable and necessary to us from an ethical standpoint. Our works were absorbed and appropriated by political organizations that requested that we contribute textual or visual imagery to specific interventions.

However, when it came to collaborations with male artists, political organizations made their authorship known, and what's more, the fact that those artists signed their works helped to measure and bolster the social outcry enabled by the ascribed authorship.

In our case, the different projects seemed to resonate with a more antiquated form of welfare labor culturally attributed to the female subject. In a way, our collaborations were perceived as equivalent to domestic work, a less significant or "natural" form of solidarity meant to magnify true political labor. And insofar as our authorship was not culturally recognized, its contributions to the intersecting fields of art and aesthetics was erased.

There is no doubt that the political organizations that asked us to do certain projects perceived our collaboration as "natural" and secondary, due solely and specifically to the problematic behaviors linked to gender asymmetry: this was about two women that worked collaboratively, and, in that sense, the prestige or the possibility of symbolic prestige that could be attributed to the posters, slogans, or stagings that we created was practically nonexistent.

We were called upon for our *responsibility* and *favorable disposition*, which in no way constituted bad faith on the part of those who solicited works from us; yet these political instances embodied and enacted certain cultural stereotypes that place women in a subordinate position, especially if we understand political work as belonging to the masculine sphere. There, immersed in that male-dominated world, our works were received with a vague outlook as *support for the cause*.

Yet that situation, of which we were keenly aware, didn't lead us to quit nor to seek *recognition* as we developed these anti-dictatorial interventions. As I pointed out before, this is partially because of the way we worked; that is, our labor politics allowed us to understand how gender conditions affected every facet of our collaboration.

Our collaboration and political activism, beyond its particularity and exceptionality, is a useful and productive metaphor for a zone of conflict, full of unexpected ups and downs, which we've had to confront repeatedly.

I don't mean to dramatize the practice of collaboration because none of these social difficulties turned out to be definitive obstacles to our projects. The limitations of gender have served as a lucid driving force: as one more political factor for confronting and comprehending social spaces in which traditional power structures continue to heavily shape cultural traditions.

But, let me return to the beginning, to the main difficulty: that the system impedes (because it is impeded by) collaborative work, and doubly so when it involves women. Now, when it comes to women who support, let's say, fierce or sharp-witted forms of discourse, they tend to be met with a not-so-subtle dynamic of devaluation. Their works are easily cast aside, not included in artistic circuits, or avoided completely. They become avoidable, especially certain artistic projects considered to be dark or cryptic, such as ¿Quién viene con Nelson Torres?, a work that

Lotty Rosenfeld and I created together and that I mention as just one example.

Yet what is most critical, at least in my view, lies in collaboration itself as a political effect and a political weapon for building culture. I am referring to persevering in a minoritarian and certainly ambiguous practice; in an association marked by small accomplishments, not without its misgivings, that slowly weave together a cultural modality or *position* in one way or another. In reality, the work of collaboration points toward expanding and growing imaginaries that, when combined, generate an*other* space. This is radically different from individual work because it materializes in doubly surprising and amazing ways.

However, what is most important is that Lotty Rosenfeld and I consolidated a practice and a method that has taken root and allowed us to practice a kind of creativity in which nothing exactly "belongs" to either one of us because what each of us produces is rearticulated, lost, and diluted, and all that is left is the emergence of a production whose ambivalent effects are just as strange as they are familiar.

(2005)

Translated by Sowmya Ramanathan

Gazing through the Cracks

A first look at Paz Errazuriz's work would confirm that her obsessions and passions lie in the search for a different kind of body. These bodies stand before a lens that aims, frames, and captures them; in turn, they unleash an unexpected form of violence, the longing for their most-desired poses, a single moment of glory to defy their own transience, and the sheer fragility of their destinies.

That first look at Paz Errázuriz's gaze turns decisively toward bodies that permit a glimpse of the energy that inscribes them on the periphery of a city they scarcely inhabit—due to their old age, cosmetic appearances, or amidst the complex intimacy of dance—and within urban spaces that cannot contain them. A sense of certainty characterizes her photography, through which Errázuriz repairs the (social) belonging of dismembered bodies; in other words, the photographer restores these bodies to a hierarchy that hegemony denies them, as silhouettes that are considered guilty: of an organic misery (old age in the asylum), symbolic crises (transvestites),[30] dramatic nomadism (the circus), or obscure, vulgar violence (fighters and boxers).

These social bodies exist on the brink of collapse. They delineate a space of urban catastrophe that lacks even the slightest hint of value, beyond briefly arresting the *social* gaze. Consider the fighter's small, fleeting triumph in front of his neighborhood fans; the social compassion of public welfare and asylum, which take in the elderly to *perform* charity; the twisted spectacle of a popular circus; or the transvestite's bids to passersby on the street.

---

30 While "travesti" or "transvestite" is the original term Eltit used, Eltit's more contemporary writings choose the now more widely accepted term "transgénero" or "transgender" instead.

These bodies *at the limit* seduce us upon our first glance, but if we manage to move beyond this, we discover another image: of bodies that elicit signs of social neglect. Whether torn away from or clinging to their devalued precariousness—assigned to them by the institutions that shield them from the world—these bodies attest to an inadequate social fabric. Such inadequacy, in turn, highlights these figures' eccentricity.

Paz Errázuriz's gaze is, thus, mobilized by playing with codes. On the one hand, she restores the presence of urbanism's legendary figures to the frame. Yet the crucial aspect of her work lies in how her gaze transcends physical deficiency, mental decline, and the mysteries and dilemmas of sexuality. This raises some real questions about the axes of social power that regulate our spaces and bodies, draw limits between populated territories and social wastelands, and control the circulation of desire everywhere.

Physical spaces captivate the viewer like enigmas in Paz Errázuriz's work. We witness a scene through the cracks: through chipped paint on the walls or rooms that've had a rough go of it. This deterioration doesn't elicit feelings of compassion; on the contrary, it speaks of a force and an aesthetic, endowed with great rigor and an extreme awareness of the interstices of the Latin American city.

For it is those in-between spaces of the city that appear surreptitiously in Errázuriz's work as if the key to the artist's specific choices lay in those spaces—as if the bodies trapped in her photographs were there to capture our attention not only because of their peculiar figures but especially due to their backgrounds. Although the subjects are diverse, there is one unifying thread that traces their extraordinary similarities, running through the spaces in a singular visual story.

Paz Errázuriz presents us the image of a certain Chilean place that we *latino* bodies know so well, with the moving and unstable harmony of our cities and our dreams of urban glory.

(1992)

Translated by Sowmya Ramanathan

Presentation of *El Padre Mío*

I met El Padre Mío in 1983. The visual artist Lotty Rosenfeld accompanied me on an errant investigation that began in 1980 around the city and its margins, in which we had already passed through multiple hostels, neighborhoods with brothels, and various scenes of vagrancy that Lotty Rosenfeld documented on video.

I use the term investigation in a very broad sense because in fact, it was made up of outings in the city without a structured agenda, just an orientation toward and fixation on worlds traversed by energies or meanings that were somehow different from the visible social and cultural system.

I was especially looking to catch and capture an aesthetic that generated cultural meanings, and I thought of the vital movement in those areas of the city as a kind of negative—akin to the photographic negative—necessary for configuring a positive—the rest of the city. These excluded territories were there to preserve a social fabric woven together by strong and sustained hierarchies.

Attempting to delimit and delineate an aesthetic point of view, the world of urban vagrancy seemed exemplary, in part, for theorizing a critical order that passively transgressed the institutional fixation on refuge in private space. With the advantage and disadvantage of appearing in those areas without having studied sociology or anthropology, I had to establish a wide margin for speculation and trust that craft of narrative would allow me to weave or unite creative distances, liberating the analogical flow and aesthetic charge embedded in the bodies, gestures, behaviors, or fragments of a way of life.

Relying on creativity—and particularly on narrative montage—it became possible to capture the vagrants' dramatism. Their dramatic tension found its material embodiment in how these figures were placed on display on the city's streets, plazas, and corners.

Their individual presences, characterized by pure appearance, reflected a complex and ruptured cosmetic order. They offered a glimpse of a layered signification—composed of the multiple additives—that had reduced them to a violent exteriority.

This exteriority comes from the accumulation of waste and a disposition to cobble together a baroque corporeality whose excess incites fear. Their saturated garments gave off the dirt-stained carnality of the earth, scabbed over with a layer of filth that challenged the stereotype of a sanitized body, dressed in accordance with the standardized logic of composition.

They carried all their belongings in sacks, bags, boxes, or packages, bundles that were also pure appearance: the simile of individual property and, moreover, the copy of a personal history full of possessions that testified to a past existence. In that way, the elaboration of meanings was only legible through the sum of each external symptom at play.

They shared in common the fact that they were all subjected to appearance and exteriority, beyond the particularities of each individual. From this perspective, it was possible to develop impressions that allowed me to perceive my own cultural arguments based on the alterity that these errant bodies assumed in the city.

This is (s)cult(p)ure, I thought.

They were sculptures scattered on the margins: negating architecture's interiority, façades, pure ornaments after a cataclysm.

Observing their transformation into sculptures—I'm using a metaphor—allowed me to develop a form of thinking that could support a project on appearance and exteriority. It thus became possible for me to arrive at the conclusion that they were arranged this way to be seen—to attract the gaze of the other or of others—and that their baroque style concealed the need to be looked at and admired for the radical difference of their existence.

Because they were situated outside the system of economic production, their appearance was their only labor, something that repeated incessantly in each and every figure. Theirs was a solitary and excessive labor whose fragments evoked a visual baroque that was thoroughly *latino* in its particular form of poverty.

Copies of themselves, emptied of interiority, the insubordination of those demanding urban bodies exuded a vigorous libido, held in check by the fractured symbolism that walled them in—perhaps forever—and kept them from unleashing their pent-up desires.

As urban creators of desire, they acted out the spectacle and the cost of that spectacle; they physically embodied a passionate liberation from the world of labor, choosing passivity instead. Their bodies thus became their only asset, all they could offer to the gaze of others. Desire and pleasure fused in those shells of bodies that were incapable of any exchange not triggered by their aesthetic impact.

Self-fetishized, emptied, vagrant within culture, their (s)cul(p)tures rose as a negative in the city, on an endless sectoral journey, thus providing balance to the polarity between sanity and insanity.

Somehow it was possible to imagine on their bodies the imprint of others—institutional others—who sentenced the vagrants to a potentially alarming fate for transgressing the limits of the city's temporary law. The vagrants permanently occupied public spaces and avenues at the expense of a voluntary, existential exposure.

As urban vagabonds using and abusing the city, they could only fulfill their nomadic destiny by fully assuming the paradoxical mode of appearance, that is, of pure exteriority. Their provocation lay in their reversal; as dispossessed subjects they could be abysmally anonymous and yet, still harbor desire.

Desire became transferred irrevocably to these silhouettes that, ultimately, mobilized the silhouette of desire.

Having established my observation of them, also passive, I could perceive that they were practically dispossessed and devoid of oral language. The range of possible verbalizations had fueled the energy that their bodies harbored, foreshadowing the failure of words to name things and name themselves. Their artistic bodies seemed chained to an eternal present, to the instantaneity of the gaze, and to an obvious oblivion in their eyes, ready to devour and dissolve everything.

Yet El Padre Mío was different. His dizzying, circular linguistic presence had neither a beginning nor an end. The Baroque had implanted itself in his dynamic tongue, causing it to explode.

I met El Padre Mío in 1983. He lived on a vacant lot in the neighborhood of Conchalí. His manner of appropriating space attested to an already lengthy stay in the place, with clothes hanging in the bushes, old newspapers, stones from a bonfire, and a large jar full of water, all of which delineated a nexus that the man I call El Padre Mío traversed time and time again.

Lean and rigorously thin, his emaciated physique displayed the effects of exposure to varied and intense climatic conditions. He lived permanently in the elements.

I must emphasize his extraordinary capacity for survival, given that his mind was fixed on a single point. Emptied of its reality, his mind was dedicated to devising a way to decipher his painful and definitive truth. Terrified in the midst of a conspiracy, a deadly power stalked him, turning him into a subject detached from everything, even his own name.

In each of the encounters we had, El Padre Mío was in a total state of delirium, and despite this, he could take care of his own vital necessities.

This book relays three encounters that took place in 1983, 1984, and 1985 respectively. In each one, my intervention has been limited to the faithful transcription of his three monologues recorded in the deserted lands of Conchalí.

I have obsessed over one question that has held up this publication for almost four years: How do I situate this book? This has been a continuous, fundamental question, whose answer, I sensed, was already contained in the very moment of the recording. Recovering his speech, therefore, had to follow its own logic, its desire to be rescued for publication, *this* publication.

The primary question that puzzled me was how to frame his speech, especially since his manner of speaking touched upon many possible approaches from formalized disciplines that were foreign to me, such as psychology, for example.

I had to position myself, once again, in a diverse place. I had to occupy his space in a way that did not attempt to reverse or cure anything, but only insisted upon the moving effects of his speech and the aesthetic relationship to his words, emptied of all meaning other than anguish of a syllabic persecution: the echoing, chain-effect of his rhymes, the vital situation from which he spoke, and the rigorously real existence of the city's margins and that marginal scene.

In sum, I chose to act from within narrative, from within literature.

Viewed through the lens of literature, this *story of a story* contains words that gesticulate until they become paralyzed, a monologue of evidence that cites names—the names of power—and repeats them to a tragic and burlesque extreme.

I evoked the anguish of the internal, literary monologue, that urgency and depth to speak the *true* truths of the character shielded by the formal spectacle of reproducing thought. When I heard El Padre Mío, I thought of and evoked Beckett, traveling wrathfully through words behind a reclusive mother buried on the page.

After Beckett, another image appeared to me:

This is Chile, I thought.

All of Chile is in pieces in this man's illness: shreds of newspapers, fragments of extermination, syllables of death, false pauses, commercial phrases, and names of the deceased. This is a deep crisis of language, an infection of memory, a disarticulation of all ideologies. It's a shame, I thought.

Acknowledging that words *speak* to me when they speak to me, that in general oral language ensnares me, that I am seduced by and committed to the unexpectedly precise speech that I received or found in the city, today, I remember thinking: this is literature, this is like literature.

Having recognized a certain equivalence to the Chilean situation under dictatorship, El Padre Mío's speech—its emergence—seems to exercise both a provocation and a demand to live on as a testimony, although strictly speaking his testimony is devoid of any explicit, biographical information. He himself says this in one part: "But I should serve as a testimony myself. I can't be hospitable because there they deploy the tactic of complicity" (From his "Third Speech").

Plucked from the city's wasteland, the merit of his speech lies precisely in his close relationship with the place; this makes it more than a mere medical case. Positioned on the margins of all cases, his surviving, speaking presence constructs him as a persecuted orator or the marginal victim of a conspiracy that, curiously, makes him seem simultaneously present and absent from all institutional matters.

El Padre Mío no longer inhabits that part of the city. I returned to the area on various occasions. I asked around for him. He left, they answered.

The publication of this book allows me to share his influence, leaving other identifications open. And it, especially, allows me to attenuate his absence.

(1989)

Translated by Sowmya Ramanathan

Travel Diary

(Friday, August 7, 1992)

I had seen the photographs days before.

Now, Paz Errázuriz and I are traveling in the direction of the psychiatric hospital in the town of Putaendo, built in the 40s to treat tuberculosis patients and, after the mass production of the vaccine, converted into a mental hospital for patients from various psychiatric centers all over the country: indigent patients without civil identifications, cataloged as *N.N.* As we travel, the landscape becomes progressively more mountainous. The light casts its brilliance over everything when an imposing building appears, cutting across the mountain peaks. Two hours from Santiago, the structure seems too urban to me. It's as though a small piece of the city fled on its own—as though in a psychotic fugue—to form a surprising scene.

First, there is a gate, then a security checkpoint, followed by the gardens and, still further, the building. When we cross the gate, I see the inmates. Neither their bodies nor their faces are unexpected to me (as I said, days before I saw photographs). It is only their happiness that I find disconcerting as they yell, "Aunt Paz, Aunt Paz is here," time and again as if they can't believe it. They hug and kiss her more and more, while I, too, am kissed and hugged by men and women from whom I must conceal my feelings of deep shock at the precarity of their destinies. I'm not referring to their faces or bodies, but rather to our common, yet divergent, destinies.

What would it take to describe, with words, the mute visuality of these figures that have been deformed by narcotics—with jarring physical tics and an avid shine in their eyes—as they look at and through us, giving us a glimpse of a bifurcated horizon in their pupils. Is it worth insisting on how their bodies carry so many social signs, limping,

twisting, or falling dangerously to the side as they wander cheerfully alongside Paz Errázuriz, who is now their relative?

She's the auntie that takes the photographs that prove, even to them, that they are alive, and that despite everything, they conserve a small piece of being, despite living as chronically ill patients in one of the most legendary hospitals in Chile, the psychiatric clinic in Putaendo, now called Philippe Pinel. I read that name on the building's façade. We are surrounded by the insane, which in a parade may seem amusing, but is also inexcusably striking, of course. Beyond the laughter, hugs, and kisses—and even though a woman takes me by the waist, puts her mouth next to my ear, and calls me "Mamita" for the first time—it is a truly dramatic scene. I, too, now form part of the family: the mother of lunatics.

We enter the building this way, open to the depths of our own insanity, surrounded by material bodies that seem more and more concrete to me even with all of the noticeable deviations of their figures. As we cross the door, I experience a new impact: I hear something like a song that spreads throughout the entire pavilion. The music is executed by a feverish and continuous movement of the tongue that reminds me of the sounds of the Berbers, nomads of a desert I've never been to whose sound I recall vaguely thanks to some film or forgotten recording. I recall the music from the desert, impressed by the force of the throat as it leads me toward the first staircase. There, I am confronted by the hospital's first corridor and window, which lead me directly to the first sign of confinement.

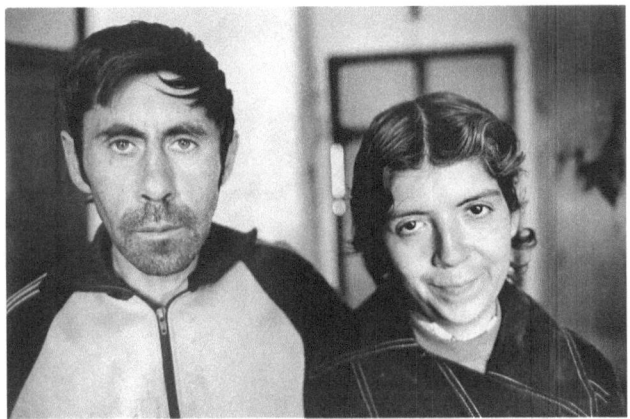

Paz Errázuriz knows the pavilions well: the gray pavilion, the green one… No, I don't know. I can't retain the colors that delineate each unit. We must notify the authorities of our presence. We walk to the offices and enter the administrative area. The psychiatrist welcomes us and tells us of some five hundred patients. (Did he really say five hundred?) Paz Errázuriz has been there so many times that it is not necessary to resort to further formalities. We have free transit through the diverse wards. However, along with reviewing the protocol and permissions, the Deputy Director gives us some curious news: that same day, the hospital is celebrating one more year of its existence. I finally understand the colored balloons in the hallways and the doctor's neat composure and attire. Along with comprehending that we are on the verge of a celebration, I am confused by the news. The hospital's staff, local authorities, and some distinguished guests from town will meet at noon to begin the festivities. The doctor invites us to the party, but what do Paz and I have to celebrate? We are both stuck in the middle, standing on the sidelines. We face the dilemma of having to continuously cross boundaries, and we must reckon with being at a crossroads, divided between the staff and the patients. Touched by a sudden resignation, we hurriedly say "yes, of course, yes," as we abandon the offices. I know that some occasions make it especially difficult to understand the differences that mediate between chance and fate.

When I leave the office, the world seems to split in two as if everything were divided into two blocks: staff and patients. It seems like

a broken world that remains connected solely by the light that filters through its windows. The patients sunbathe. We begin our pilgrimage, which consists of nothing more than climbing up and down, up and down stairs, surrounded by hallways, the typical beds of state hospitals, and patients that keep kissing us. Somewhere amidst the repeated kisses, the idea of love comes to me. I am there, in the hospital, due to my love of the written word and because of the passion that words continue to awaken in me.

When it is no longer possible to harp on the denigration of these bodies, when I know I can never fully account for the limits within which human life unfolds, and when I am certain that the words I possess are simply insufficient, the first pair of lovers appears. Paz Errázuriz introduces us. All this time, I have walked while supporting the weight of a woman who grabs me by the waist and who, when I stop, puts her head on my shoulder or rubs it against my neck, repeating in her mostly indecipherable tongue, "Mamita, Mamita," as though I have raised a spoiled daughter. This child of mine barely speaks. Through signs and gestures, she demands that I meet her needs. She wants my shoes, my watch, my wallet, almost everything I have. I look at this daughter of mine. How old is she? I think maybe fifty years old, no, perhaps sixty, no, forty. Why am I even worried about that detail? I greet the first couple. I think seriously about love. But the truth is, I don't want to think about it.

Further ahead—from corridor to corridor, staircase after staircase, and in the middle of the patios—I greet the second, third, and tenth

couple. There are so many lovers that I am already losing count. "He gives me bread and butter." "I take care of her." They feed and care for each other as best they can, and somehow, like an x-ray, I see the great metaphor that confirms all couples: one's entire life annexed to another's by a cup of tea and bread with butter. They—the chronically ill, destitute, lopsided, lame, mutilated, with fixed gazes, walking through the property with bundles on their backs—are living an extraordinary love story while locked up in the hospital. They are Chileans, forgotten by God and delivered unto the rigid charity of the State.

Seated on a bench in the hallway, one of the lovers opens his shirt and partially unzips his pants, showing us the bandage that covers a recent operation. He is engrossed in his bandage. "Ulcers," he says, and he continues looking at it while pointing to his stomach with the pride of a soldier wounded at war. His partner laughs as if she is pleased that her man has something to show for himself—is she envious, jealous, nostalgic, accusatory?—but then she immediately shows us her own scar that runs down from her navel. In that instant, I realize I am witnessing the obligatory, historical mark that's hidden on the bodies of some female inmates: the women that lost all possible family battles. When she shows us her scar, what she is truly showing us is the trace of sterility from an old, nonconsensual operation that forever severed her reproductive capabilities. Due to her madness, her children now transit only within her mind, defying her own anatomy even as she stubbornly affirms that she was recently pregnant: "*Gorda*", she says, "Two

or eight months along." She says this with her pants still unbuttoned and her gaze fixed, while her partner, also with his pants unzipped, softly caresses his bandage. Lost in different reveries and consumed by a wide-ranging delirium, the two remain seated on the bench, clinging to an inexplicable closeness, tightly connected by a knife's passage through their stomachs. This makes them both perfect and solely for one another, as they face the end of their genetic species both in terms of the operation and their endless confinement. What to say? I must say this: the operation weighs on me. It hurts me. Yet clearly, this is about a total, unique love, a mad love. André Breton floods my memory, and I forget my own thoughts.

I begin to confuse the couples. There are so many lovers. But are there lovers? Margarita with Antonio, Claudia with Bartolomé, Sonia with Pedro, Isabel with Ricardo, and the list goes on. Yet what is the language of this love? I wonder as I observe them, since they don't even possess full words. Perhaps they only have the errancy of a terribly fractured syllable. So, on what terms? From which moment? What amorous aesthetic moves them? I see before me the matter of inequality as they rupture established models. I witness beauty allied with ugliness, old age tied to youth, the paradoxical relationship of the lame and the one-eyed, of the literate with the illiterate. There, in that breakdown, I find the core of love. I understand, in an exemplary fashion, that the object of love is always an invention—the maximum deprogramming of the real—and at the very moment, I must accept that these lovers possess another vision, one that is mysterious and subjective. After all, human beings fall in love like crazy. Like crazy.

"Night before last, last night, and this morning… night before last, last night, and this morning," sings one of the patients while walking through the corridors. She sings a tune that seems symmetrical to her expanding body, twisted by a lateral paralysis. This body is partially disabled but no less affectionate for it. She sings with a soulful voice that overwhelms me. Moved by her singing, I greet the last couple of the morning. They don't remember how long they have been together: "A long time...very long," they say. They don't know how to tell time. They don't know how to read. They don't know how many years they have been hospitalized. They know nothing of their family members. Yet he gives her tea and bread with butter, and she takes care of him.

We enter the room where the anniversary party is taking place. I observe the long, candlelit tables. On one side is the stage for the orchestra. The local authorities and doctors are in the center of the room while various administrative officials sit at the edges. The nurses and orderlies serve the food. I can't help the fact that my head is filling with thoughts. Paz Errázuriz and I don't even discuss the situation. Sitting next to each other, I perceive that we are overcome with similar sensations, some so evident they aren't even worth discussing. We are now eating in the hospital, participating in a celebration that isn't for us: guests turned mute witnesses.

The staff and authorities never seem entirely happy. There is something terribly elusive about this celebration, as if a fraction of a second has become disjointed from the rhythms of a pocket watch. They don't talk or look at each other. They eat amid a silence that can be interpreted in many ways. In the back, a group of young staff members try, unsuccessfully, to change the tone of the meeting by shouting and rehearsing various jokes. Yet it's in vain; they fail to elicit even a smile from the area where we are seated. Maybe later, when the musicians set up, and when we—the party's outsiders—are back to going up and down staircases or sitting briefly in the patios, those faces—the staff's

appearances—may join together on the dance floor, show cheerfulness, and laugh as colleagues. Maybe they'll act as public employees who celebrate the anniversary of their work and forget, for a few hours, that they are representatives of the State that attend to the chronically ill with no form of escape. Those numerous patients ended up in this rural enclosure through an entrance that is now who-knows-how-far-away. Maybe that will happen or maybe this party doesn't have even the slightest hope either. Paz Errázuriz and I get up early from the table. When we leave the room, the light opens us to a new dimension. Without the slightest ambivalence, I am pleased to leave that human canvas behind, dedicated to representing one of the most complex possible jobs: the guardians of a psychiatric enclosure. They are the guards of a mysterious, symbolic disorder that even the most splendid medical science still can't decipher. We exit into the light, and there they wait for us. Yes, Pedro with Margarita, María with Ismael, Rosario with Juan, Carmen with Fernando… They wait, and what they really wait for is Paz Errázuriz's lens that captures them in their few sacred moments.

We are on a patio that isn't a patio. It's a large extension of land with some manicured gardens in front. Behind that, I manage to make out a grove of orange trees. In my pocket, I have two oranges that Juana and Aníbal gifted me, a gift delivered to me by the most destitute beings on earth. They have gifted me with two oranges, picked in accordance with an incredible honor code that seeks all possible ways to avoid the ultimate humiliation of the body: hunger; or at the very least, to eradicate the hunger from within this extensive mental and physical territory marked by countless privations.

The afternoon progresses peacefully. We continue wandering through the patio, sitting at the edge of a small ditch. I remain next to two women who embrace me, one my arm and the other my right leg. I observe Paz Errázuriz also with her faithful daughters. We don't speak. We are simply sitting, taking in the winter sun amid the murmur of the patients around us. The women who have taken over my right side demand that I look at them now and then, and when I do, they give me such full and glorious smiles. "Mamita" becomes even more familiar and natural, and I respond, yes, of course, behave yourself, I don't have cigarettes, the afternoon sun is nice and warm. I say this to the elderly woman who hugs my leg, who has a face that's round like a drawing of the full moon. Ricardo looks at Isabel. They hold hands. She gets angry and pushes him. He asks me to lend him my glasses and puts them on. Isabel laughs and observes him while Ricardo, very focused, raises his face to the sky, lost in thought like a solitary, nocturnal navigator counting the stars.

We must return to Santiago. The light that has accompanied us throughout the day begins to wane. Paz Errázuriz is the one who performs the farewell ritual. She takes her camera, and I see a love for images erupt within her. I am the witness to a moving photographic session as Paz, with extreme delicacy, moves from group to group, responding to the most diverse requests. She permits the flow of multiple and unexpected poses, as if she has been hired for a wedding in which all the guests were godparents, the bride or groom, or the child of a popular baptism. Paz Errázuriz turns her eye into a gift for the inmates. In her photographic gaze, she gifts them with the certainty of their images. When she captures their poses, she confirms for them the relevance of their figures. When she smiles at them, she recognizes the divinity of their bodily behaviors. When she leans forward, in search of the right angle, she dedicates all her professionalism to them.

Yet we must return to Santiago. It will be a silent journey. We will hardly exchange a word. The landscape that had so impressed me in the early hours of that morning will pass by in vain at sunset. I will think of love. I won't think of love. What will occupy me is that kind of fluid love that erupts and spreads within the interior of that vacant lot of a

public hospital. I will remember that a year before, when we spoke in Mexico, Paz Errázuriz told me of her extensive work taking portraits of the patients and lovers of the hospital in the town of Putaendo. I will feel that the words have been spinning around my head for a year and yet, despite that, on my return journey I will be silent, empty.

I will return to the city trapped in the madhouse of my own mind, and afterward, I will walk back and forth for a while, up and down stairs, staggering through corridors and across patios, carrying those bodies in a part of my brain. I will go from one place to another carrying those bodies with the strengths and misfortunes of an aching soul.

(1992)

Translated by Sowmya Ramanathan

Chalk It up to Their Circumstances

(Collective Bathrooms of Female Patients
at the Philippe Pinel Psychiatric Hospital)

1.

There are certain terrible and confusing scenarios. There is also the *idea* of terrible and confusing scenarios: the unbearable image provoked by water, its indiscriminate flow, its violence.

There are surely scenes in which fear crouches in the mind's crevices. I want to think about a slice of fear lodged in the retina, a rumble of fear hiding in the ear or in the unexpected grinding of the skull; or a massive fear that spreads through all areas of the body and grips us with terror, just about to terrify us; or fear that we inhabit. In that way, we become permanently addicted to panic.

Addicted to panic, to the body as panic: we transform ourselves into a body of fears that circulate at a dangerous and tireless speed until we are openly out of control. We find ourselves amidst the limitless fear of a body that is out of control, where all possibilities of controlling its own signals are lost.

Vital signs are altered, provoking a disorder that is suddenly blown out of proportion. That disproportion motivates our fear.

Therein lies the anger and the rage that fear provokes. Yet almost magically, anger and rage turn into fear. The terrifying fear of water.

The whole body, its flesh and blood. The fear of a whole body that is no longer visible because it is a prisoner to fear. Going out, in the flesh, into the cold water, into a fearsome jet of ice water that brutally washes fear from the body. To bathe in icy water at the peak of winter, in unbearable cold, to get rid of fear with freezing water. To withstand the onslaught: the frontal shot of a powerful jet of frigid water.

Yet other scenarios with water also exist: the water that purifies, cleanses (sin), and gives order to the body (within a bourgeois archetype, it must be said).

A smooth, bourgeois body: masterfully adorned by water that makes it function and installs an order that moves smoothly from baptism to bath, bath to beauty, and beauty to pleasure until fully delivering the body unto fashion: a fashionable bath, a bubble bath with bath salts. Salty, sunned bodies. An exciting, bourgeois tickling in the body.

Bourgeois bodies united with water.

Although, suddenly and unexpectedly, cold water begins to fall. A hose-full of icy water spurts and upon this, a scene emerges—or surfaces—of multiple bodies that display and are undoubtedly repressed with water. They are sharply attacked by water that resembles tear gas, rocks, pieces of glass, anything sharp. This threatens the bodies, which manifest their discontent to get away, back up, or flee before the fearsome lashes of the water's troubling attack on the body.

2.

Paz Errázuriz's photographs bear witness to a terribly troubling scenario. It is a scene governed by water: water and bodies. They show the naked bodies of a number of women confined to the Philippe Pinel psychiatric hospital and subjected to the common bath: a rite, a ceremony that combines bathing and ritual. This is a highly conflictive meeting where naked bodies appear. Bathing and ritual. And violence.

The challenge is to think about these bodies following the realization of the photographic act. In my opinion, after publishing these photographs, the question is how to truly reflect on the limitations of the body or on the body at the limit.

This group of naked women, controlled by water, make up one of the most *damned* visual scenes of Chilean photography. They make up a nudity—as nude women—that is neither realist nor naturalist, strictly speaking, but which gradually configures a social model. This social form undresses completely and drapes itself over these unclothed bodies, revealing the limits and limitations of a segment of Chilean society.

The female protagonists' naked bodies speak in a multifaceted way in this series of photographs. They speak of the photograph's porousness. Following Guattari, they speak rhizomatically of the body's cultural state and the repression of the gaze. One can't continue gazing at the photographs without recalling black clouds of ominous birds, circling thirstily overhead, in search of dead and decaying flesh.

Paz Errázuriz's lens conjures these naked bodies as evidence of a terrible social weight that has fallen over and settled on the bodies of those photographed. An extremely negative social situation inscribes its archaic traces on these bodies, which were previously relegated to a more secret, stealthy gaze that, furtively, intrudes in the obligatory, collective bath; this practice continues to congregate these naked women.

We now have a series of images through a social corpus of photographs that recounts an untold story of the body under the effects of water. This is an unprecedented history of the body, of a wholly unprecedented body, of figures completely disrupted and pierced by certain, complex processes that ended up disrupting anatomical geometry's harmonious lines.

These nude and photographed bodies—anatomically disturbed, devastated, blown up by their surroundings—recall other images of naked bodies that were also captured precisely at the limits of what nudity can convey: the point at which an attack on an incalculable and irreversible bodily fate produces agony. In short, I wish to allude to the instances in which a form of gradual and cruel death is consummated within the subject, and to a collective nudity that overwhelms and annihilates subjecthood.

There is an immediate connection to the social memory of Jewish bodies and the circulation of photographs of bodies either on the verge of death or immediately after being subjected to the horrific practice of extermination. These social photographs capture the baseless injustice of official powers, that is, the power to accumulate bodies and obligate them to share one final, lethal nudity—precisely in a moment that annulls modesty due to death's impending arrival.

We already know that when it comes to discourse, culture, and bodily trauma, modesty turns into the true robes with which to cover the body. However, in Paz Errázuriz's photographs, we witness an obscene nudity. I am referring to the obscene impunity that power carries as it dictates an inescapable order—a bodily ordinance—whose objective is to force it to forget modesty. Therein lies the existence of specific political maneuvers exerted on the body to debilitate and dominate it, whose articulation is only possible if one renounces dominant cultural discourse.

Paz Errázuriz's photographs capture the subjugation of bodies to the programmatic, systematic obligation of shared nudity.

They capture the accumulation of naked bodies forced to gather *as* naked bodies. That is the violence: the order to strip as opposed to the will to undress. It is a forced nudity that is identical to a forced labor sentence, which reveals the discourse of the body (and its modesty) as a violation.

One could signal or argue that these images contain a double violation: I am referring to the additional violation produced by the intrusion of the photographic lens. However, I think that the camera progressively reveals—in the most technical sense of the term and as its objective—the precision of the operation being carried out on naked bodies.

Through them, the series of photographs shows us a practice of power, a tradition, a routine, and the inexcusable imposition to which these imprisoned bodies must comply: routine, order, obligation, massive and indiscriminate submission to water—to the sustained jet of cold water. This is a form of official violence exerted with, through, and amidst terribly icy water to cast these bodies aside and push them into their most radical state of corporeal nothingness.

It is this violence that Paz Errázuriz's photographs reveal. But it is a covert and defensive violence, whose particular form hides behind an aseptic, curative, and preventive discourse that "cleans" the bodies, removing their infections, bacteria, and discharge, thoroughly disinfecting them with the help of cold water's traumatic impact on their limbs.

Marquis de Sade already made one of the most significant contributions to culture by focusing on the treacherous and crucial function that power could yield when mercilessly applied to bodies. Sade alluded to routine forms of human control framed by the perspective of a particular bodily pedagogy.

This is a severely disturbed pedagogy.

Sade's relentless, engrossing work, which lacked the slightest hint of concession, revealed that behind bodily violence—I am referring to institutional violence—a disturbing form of pedagogy circulates frequently in search of an exemplary social morality.

Bodies are examples, anatomies that should be exemplary (for others). The bodies photographed by Paz Errázuriz send us to a sphere in which the most intransigent political theories originate, bringing pedagogy closer to extermination.

I am referring to torture carried out in Chile for almost 17 years as a social discipline, or to the well-known images of famous political leaders performing forced labor on Dawson Island, or to the existence of archives containing information about lobotomies carried out on common prisoners in state hospitals as part of an experimental prison program.

Paz Errázuriz's photographs are inscribed within this social logic and within dominant systems that agree upon classified procedures, such as rehabilitation, political sanitation, or hygiene. This logic never resigns, and at one pole of these different pedagogies, there is water: the notorious ice bath and the infamous bucket of cold water.

3.

This group of naked women, who are the protagonists of the series, are photographed in a moment of compliance with a regulation: hygiene. They are captured by the lens as they follow a procedure that seeks to disinfect them, together, *once and for all*.

Obliquely, Paz Errázuriz's series of photographs is inscribed among other visual works that present a kind of nudity that bears an uncommon relationship with the female body.

Since the female nude is a recurring photographic practice that, as we know, has produced poses, fashions, models, measurements, borders, and overflows, it has also generated the immeasurable reproduction of photographic nudes that circulate and move between the harmonious, artistic image to the commercial pages of hardcore pornography.

The female nude is culturally established as a provocation, represented by a speaking body. This is the social discourse attached to a body that, in reality, is not a body—in the biological sense—but rather the theatricalization of a sum of socio-corporal signs that have been orga-nized according to culture's sensibilities and erotic demands.

The politics of the female nude have massively manipulated the canonical body's pose—consider the social specificity of a model body's design—emphasizing the secrets of its erotic and sexual zones. These bodies have been undressed to be "penetrated" by the desire of the mas-culine gaze that governs culture.

However, other photographic nudes—minoritarian and desexu-alized—have also formed part of photography's vision, such as nudes from autopsy rooms or extermination camps.

These naked bodies, driven mad by oblivion and neglect, show how bodies can be reduced to a *lapsus,* an error, to the simple and perhaps pitiful end of the hygienic task.

I want to emphasize neglect and oblivion within this cultural dis-course that ideologically *dresses* the diverse anatomies grouped together in these photographs. The absence of cultural discourse heightens the impact on the eye since the silence appears permuted by the feral pres-ence of bodies that are overly material. The only desire they produce within the viewer—I refer here to the cultural gaze—is the scandalous and immediate need to evade and eliminate the irreverent condition of these totally naked bodies.

This is about forgetting the power that the body exercises when, without the slightest concession, it transgresses the pose, the mold, or the fashion of nudity.

Within hegemonic social settings, the female nude lacks a body. In reality, it is the model of a body: a copy, a simile, the result of a social imaginary draped over the female body to perform the desire for nudity there. This model of bodily domestication develops precisely by inject-ing itself into the body's model, nudity, erotics, and the aesthetics of the feminine.

The bodies photographed by Paz Errázuriz already live outside of those discourses. These nudes, in an archaic state, reveal a social flaw, a fracture that unfolds when a series of signs uncloak nudity as a labori-ous construction.

The bodies of naked women taken during their common bath, dic-tated by regulation, signal that what they hide—their public secret—is a crack, a rift through which the gaze filters toward a zone that is not necessarily genital. Instead, it filters toward a zone of silence, covered by a thick, opaque and sturdy screen with which each and every institution dresses us.

The eye is doused with cold water. It awakens. It begins to move. It rolls backwards. It slides into the unbearable emptiness of itself.

(2008)

Translated by Sowmya Ramanathan

Too Bad You're a *Rota*

Juan Domingo Dávila's painting summons the eye to form an astonishing cultural look at the maelstrom of signs that come together in symmetries and dissidences within its tightly woven fabric. The body—his work's privileged material—emerges as an astonishing (hi)story whose remnants give rise to an apparent (only apparent) chaos, in which it is possible to perceive the boundaries that circumscribe it.

Juan Domingo Dávila has produced bodies to the point of exaltation. He elucidates this pictorial body with his exalted brushstrokes, which require an alert, multifaceted, and decodifying eye that can easily transit within popular, media-based culture before becoming intelligible to the most erudite of academicians. By way of tightly woven micro-murals, Dávila restores entire histories by piecing together traces of dissimilar visual stories, echoes of antiquated cultural disputes that are still relevant today and can be recognized underneath the cosmetic procedures that attempt to conceal them.

In this exhibition, it is the mobile body of the *roto*—a legendary figure in our cultural repertoire—that occupies the visual stage.[31]

Who is the roto?

An initial answer could be: the people.

---

31 The word "roto"—literally meaning "broken"—is a term commonly used to refer to lower-class Chileans with a particularly negative connotation. As Eltit explains later, the term was popularized during the War of the Pacific (1879-1884), in which the roto represented the common man who gave everything for his country. In other words, despite the predominantly negative connotation, it is important to note that the roto is also celebrated as a national hero, an ambiguity or ambivalence that Eltit recognizes in Dávila's work and plays with in her own essay.

The people are represented in a threatening and impure body that exposes its violence through the rags or remains it wears. Barefoot and defiant, transgressive and delinquent, the roto carries signs of degradation—rags, clearly racialized markings, an undeniable expression, and bodily imperfections—that configure him as an ailing allegory of the popular. He is a liminal figure. His ambiguity is the same one that lies within the nation's matrix, because the Chilean roto also corresponds to a heroic image of the War of the Pacific—the war that marked the end of the world—in which the brave, national roto was consecrated as fodder for all the cannons.

Too early on in the history of our republic, the roto became anchored within the social imaginary as an anonymous, crude, and heroic soldier upon whom the nation sustained itself. But beyond its wartime context, the roto was the name, nickname, alias, and slang that synthesized an abjection associated with scarcity: a multidirectional abjection that united concrete realities with an assigned symbolic order. Visually (politically) configured as the material of a caricature, the roto went on to become a popular icon of great significance due to his ability to transcend fragile social structures (since we are very familiar with every social structure's considerable permeability).

Thus, the roto became one of the metaphors that upheld the preeminence of a certain class. Like a *criollo* Frankenstein, festive and carnivalesque, the roto is a father's son, forged artisanally by the dominant classes, a hybrid product consigned as illegitimate by a set of historic powers that—in addition to their condescending guffaws and revelry—reveal the fear inherent in their obligatory coexistence with the subversive massiveness of the other, of otherness, of the roto. A figure constructed from within political interests, the roto also appears as a plague that can spread and contaminate even the class that created him, because his broken body remains crouched—ready to jump out—in every part of the country and (even) in the possibly illegitimate parentage of local subjects' fractured psyches.

The roto is thus an ambiguous figure in terms of what he attracts and repels, a fissure traversed by class-based desires. The desire to socially ascend flows like crazy within him, turning him into a victimized and a victimizing focal point of the social scene. As a metaphor for the people, the roto appears in a visually erratic way. With no space for him in institutional life, his only vitality appears to come from his body's eternal wandering. Graphically presented as an idle trickster, cheater, or *ladino,* the roto as a popular construction is politically deactivated through the powerful social allegory with which he, and others like him, are socially positioned.[32] His vacant and alienated image is turned into a placeholder for diverse, mutating conventions. Constructed as distinct from the disciplinary system of the people he comes from and represents, the roto becomes a speculative figure that marks the limits, forms, and risks of the class system.

Yet in reality, the roto speaks to the hegemony of a single class, a terror, and a singular limit. The roto is the paradigmatic figure of non-belonging. The one, consistent class that confines and classifies him in unnamed territories also expatriates him to the limits of an absent vagrancy without a social horizon. He only acquires prestige, paradoxically, when he defends the interests of the dominant class—when war has already been declared—and only then does he become epic, as a body consigned to death: "Hail Caesar, those who are going to die salute you."

But who is the roto?

A possible answer could be: one who is roto. To be roto alludes to a practice of *roteria:* the nostalgic prototype, a breaking with custom, reprehensible actions that smash the city's agreements and pacts to bits. Diluted behind improper gestures, within a fearsome allegory of the untouchable, lies the phantasmatic image of the true roto. Thus, the roto transcends his own raciality to reincarnate within the Chilean subject's interior spaces—spaces that speak to different destructions, distinct tatters—making it possible to perceive his bastard affiliation. In that way, his hidden nature (fractured, worn, and precarious) reappears in the broken actions and fragments of moral abjection that are married to this figure, stigmatized by class culture.

Like an abstract but no less definitive law, he who is roto is fatally destined to reproduce the fracture, the altered and altering gesture of a

---

32 "Ladino" refers to someone who is astute or clever in his or her actions, but historically has also described Jewish people that were expelled from the Iberian Peninsula during the 16th century.

conduct that charges and reveals him as the representative of all ideological genealogies of imperfection. As a symptom of moral degradation, *rotería* registers the existence of another kind of degradation, this
time racial. As a *raza* of rotos, they only practice *rotería* as a form of
social exchange, exposing the fissures in class norms.[33] Yet in those fissures lies the power of the class that, upon censoring, classifies.

The *roto*'s form is dynamic, invasive, and varied. As the result of a
powerful social agenda, the *roto,* that which is roto, and *rotería* form
a tight body of meaning that uniformly repeats a single binary: inferior opposed to superior. In this way, roto and *rotería* allude to inferior
spaces, to an irreparable social injury that marks the limits between
high and low, pure and impure.

This is how the roto comes to participate in a broad and indelible
classification that immediately places him within a zone of censured
inferiority. He occupies a shifting border that leaves a sinuous and unas-
suming trace; it touches interiors and exteriors, traverses economies and
presences, and indicates customs and actions. On the margins of honor,
the roto appears as a borderline subject midway between dishonor and
mere criminality. One who practices *rotería* is cataloged, classified, and
identified as a roto, and curiously, the label is both a punishment and
an excuse, since it ascribes an essence or nature that absolves him of all
responsibility. Hence, the roto, that which is roto, and *rotería* speak of
an essence that transcends will or social construction. This essence is
inscribed in his soul, carried in his (impure) blood, the deviant product
of deified design already inscribed as immutable.

Juan Domingo Dávila works with the roto's image, circulates his
figure, and the word that names him, because the roto—and that which
is shattered and fractured—alludes to multiple and diverse meanings.
Histories are broken, objects are smashed, bones are fractured. From
what is shared to what he shows to be in disrepair, Juan Domingo Dávila
transforms everything into an object for visual reflection. Utilizing
the well-known icon of the roto and its sociohistorical alterations, the
painter progressively reveals the arbitrariness of cultural constructions.

---

33 "Raza" is the Spanish-language word for "race," but can also be used to mean
"tribe" or "group."

The first image of the roto that Dávila recovers shows an animalized subject whose grim face and clawed feet offer the greatest proof of his barbarism, as an anomalous monstrosity that cites and incites a clear aberration. This first, fiercely allusive caricature confronts the newer face of the roto, now devoid of animalistic features, a softened popular presence that oscillates between a light quarrel and the festive and mischievous uselessness of a failed subject, embraced by the permanent lack of productivity bequeathed by his origin.

Between those two images—or rather, in the union of the two images—Dávila starts to elaborate on the Chilean social and cultural horizon's breakages, fractures, and dissidences. Through an intelligently constructed itinerary, Dávila organizes a fragmentary story told by the roto(s) who—like theatrical prompters—monitor and guard the flow of representation, earning them a well-deserved textual protagonism.

"Rota" is the enigmatic and ironic title of his show. Is the show itself *rota*? Does the name refer to the roto's often-forgotten female partner, a secondary figure in the cast? Does it refer to the broken historical matrix? This multiplicity of meanings speaks to an aperture or to fissures that split open within the spectator's imagination, calling upon and exposing his or her own fractures, which themselves shape reading gestures.

Yet without a doubt, Dávila's transgressive gesture consists of the dual operation of circulating the mechanisms that sediment social parameters as given: a dual task of construction and deconstruction. On the one hand, he deconstructs the figure of the roto and, on the other, he recovers and utilizes it as material for his work, which mocks attempts at classification that conceal real violence. Making the roto the foundation of his painting, he places it alongside sacred and market-sanctioned visual objects like Valenzuela Puelma's "Perla del Mercader," an early classic of Chilean painting with which Juan Domingo Dávila enters into spectacular dialogue. The roto poses in place of Puelma's female slave at a public auction, waiting on the hand of the best and only bidder. In this way, the roto displaces the classic image of the enslaved woman and rematerializes within a feminine image, whose body and flesh are marked by an equally enslaving form of commerce. By appealing to traditionally feminine trades, Juan Domingo Dávila emphasizes that the roto belongs to a minor gender. Embroidery, weaving, and manual backstitching are the protagonists of this sewn, patched-up, warped femininity that occupies the center of Dávila's political tapestry, which grants and filters social locations, eliminating its own threads by transforming the other—the roto—into yet another shred, the touchstone of culture, of sewing.

The roto's feminization is the oblique gesture that Juan Domingo Dávila utilizes in this fascinating and brilliant show to illuminate a subalternity—the classification imposed on and for the body—as well as the violence that circulates, socially, with this image. The roto, as the symbolic property of a specific class, goes up for sale on the open market of representation. This is a symbolic sale repeated incessantly since the roto is an emanation, the production of a name that—like a piece of bait on a fishhook—traps bodies, gestures, and behaviors in a broken, impertinent, inappropriate tidal wave.

(1996)

Translated by Sowmya Ramanathan

Latin Scenes in New York

Moved by a mixture of curiosity and the cultural challenge, I've decided to accept Ángel's invitation to witness a *santería* ceremony in the Bronx, an area where an important part of the Puerto Rican community lives. I know that the Bronx is a symptom and a symbol, socially and publicly positioned as a space marked by poverty and violence, beset (and fore-shadowed) by countless cinematic images, which is to say, U.S.-made films, where a series of crimes take place on screen.

I go to the ceremony with Ángel Lozada, a Puerto Rican student of mine who attends the literary workshop I teach at Columbia University, along with another participant, Miriam Morales, an exiled Chilean living in Mexico who's in New York for the semester. In addition to carrying out his doctoral studies at the university, the young writer Ángel Lozada is also training to be a *santero*. In the subway car, he begins to teach us about the ceremony to which he has invited us, a hasty lesson I have trouble responding to because my eyes are captivated by the bodies that occupy the subway car. I dwell on the *Latino* figures,[34] whose bodies speak through their clothing, communicating more than they actually say through their random use of English and Spanish, occasional

---

34 Typically, the term latino refers to inhabitants of the United States who have cultural ties to the Spanish-speaking Americas. However, latino is also used by many Chileans to refer to themselves as part of the broader community of Spanish speakers beyond strictly national borders. The term has many meanings but is used here for the common resonances between U.S. and Chilean linguistic contexts. It is worth noting, however, that since the writing of this text in 1998, the inclusive language movement has disputed the relevance of the term latino and proposed other alternatives such as latine, latinx, and latin@ to remedy the tendency to privilege the masculine gender in the Spanish language.

sullen poses, festive and animated conversations, and thin cords from the walkmen that hang from their ears before getting lost in their pockets. The subway stations pass and there are more Latinos, more eyes, more gazes, and more chat from Ángel Lozada who is dressed entirely in white—already exhausted by the amount of written work he must produce during his doctoral semester—and who names African divinities and other gods that I am vaguely familiar with. He also tells us that his *santero* godfather has told him that Ángel's destiny as a writer has been preordained by the saint that will one day correspond to him.[35]

I listen to Ángel, and from his words, I begin to understand that he maintains living ties with a popular sector of his community. Despite his graduate studies, which make him a subject of the *lettered* universe, so to speak, his cultural soul summons him toward traditions expressed by popular expressions like *santería*, practiced widely in Caribbean countries.

Though I have already witnessed *santería* ceremonies and rites in Cuba and Mexico, this time I know the ceremony has another air to it simply because the young man, Miriam, and I—connected through our literary practice—are in New York. It will be shaped by a different linguistic context and a distinct landscape, strategic and inescapable, that makes us into people who experience a foreignness incapable of resolution: Miriam, living in Mexico after a forced exile, whose speech is chock-full of Mexican idioms, and me, also intensely foreign in the midst of a brief stay. Yet clearly, without a strain of doubt, Ángel's foreignness is more tense and intense, and much more complex due to the variegated signs of his national history, which continues to unfold.

Ángel, dressed in an unabashed priestly white, is curiously not unique within that subway car, occupied by minoritarian bodies in which the minorities that appear most frequently during the trip, without doubt, are Latino and African American citizens. At one point of the trip, a boy of about nine sitting next to me reads the list of songs from the CD his mother carefully passes to him. Intrusively and from the corner of my eye, I observe that it is by the 60's and 70's Argentine singer, Yaco Monti. The child shows me my own foreignness, since I am unsure from

---

35 While the word "saint" has been chosen for this translation, Eltit refers to the orishas of Yoruba religion of West Africa and the African diaspora.

the tone of his comments if he belongs to the Cuban, Puerto Rican, or Dominican community, and I know that the category of *latino*—that complicated, leveling category—often lends itself to the annulment of uncertainty. It doesn't cancel it out, but it does divert uncertainty toward a more comfortable point that's, as it occurs to me, perhaps less political. The small Latino boy has a Yaco Monti CD in his hands, that Argentine singer pulverized by the feverish times of the record, reborn, singing once again within my own memory in the subway on the way to the Bronx. We have already left the sophisticated, diverse, powerful Manhattan—to delve deeper into the cliché—for the outskirts, where the area's fame is configured by the frequency at which felonies and crimes occur.

We leave the metro and make our way through homogeneous streets. I immediately recognize that neglected, architectonic homogeneity that marks (inhabits) working-class areas, except that this architecture is different. I'm referring to a dearth that is equipped with technology and, because of this difference, I don't recognize it to the point that it keeps me from drawing any parallels with vulnerable sectors of Santiago. Thus, I resort to pondering its differences from other areas of New York. My comparison's effects turn out to be abysmal in their inequalities. On the sidewalks, above the heating vents, there are homeless people stretched out with thick, padded clothes, half-drunk cans of Coca-Cola, and one or two who have a relatively modern radio at their side. Ángel Lozada continues to lead us confidently toward the house. We enter at the same time as a gang of young Puerto Rican boys. Dressed identically—in black leather, with shaved heads and tattoos, and armed—their physical appearances are neutralized, and they lose their threatening aura the minute they enter the house where the ceremony has already begun.

The place is the low-ceilinged basement of a building, which is home to more than one hundred people from the Puerto Rican community. At the front of the room is the young man who is being initiated as a *santero*, accompanied by his *padrino* and a group of *santeros* dressed in a meticulous white.[36] Before the initiate are the drummers and dancers. The number of attendees prevents comfortable wandering because, on

---

36 The "Padrinos" or "godparents" are those who take on the responsibility of leading a younger or prospective santero through the process of initiation.

the contrary, the space seems insufficient for such a turnout. The ceremony begins around three in the afternoon. In the enclosed space, the profiles of the attendees grow sharper.

Without a doubt, the atmosphere is recognizably Latin American, and by this I refer to a familiar, effusive energy. However, the differences from other possible Latin American traditions are also visible because a clear distortion travels through the space, bodies, and enclosure, one that exceeds the language that flows successively and simultaneously, giving way to a bilingualism endowed with an unimaginable velocity. Assembling code upon code, I note that another kind of rigid order is present. It signals an elusive atmosphere, which I perceive originates in a perhaps just partially Anglo-Saxon culture, whose rationalist and almost Puritan tics are there, operating, despite the Latin American crowd, their clothing, and their effusiveness.

It is also evident that many of the men in attendances are gay, and it is Ángel who tells me that in New York's *santería* there isn't so much as a remote trace of antigay exclusion, which is why the most traditional masculinities coexist in this place with men that bear strong feminine characteristics. Without daring to question what Ángel tells me, I surmise this is a special political loophole, since sexual exclusion is a dominant form in main systems and is doubly exclusive in Latin American cultures. Yet those feminine men are there, anchored in male bodies, and the heterosexual participants' openness toward them does not seem to be in question, despite the obvious differences. Or perhaps this has to do with the external order that traverses the participants, making them comply fully with the written laws of coexistence until they become literal. Perhaps, in that way, they act entirely as an exception during a ceremony where the *santeros* speak in "tongues," marking the inclusion of new linguistic codes from an African language. Behind the African litany, multiple expressions in English and Spanish can be heard greeting and welcoming the numerous invitees who seem to have known each other for a long time.

Ángel introduces me to his *padrinos*, a married *santero* couple that will guide and sponsor him. The crowd dances to the beat of the drums and follows their litanies speaking in "tongues," and I can't help but watch a man who enters the house, dressed in an impeccably cut suit with a well-cared-for mustache. His shirt is unbuttoned, revealing a thick gold chain that hangs from his neck and compliments a flashy watch, also gold, shining on his wrist. The man—a prime example of a Latin American macho—drops reverentially to the floor in a ritual form to greet the initiate and the *santeros* that gesture to him. After this, he rises and greets his friends, patting them fiercely on the back.

Then the man offers an animated hug to another tall gentleman, who is dressed in a bright, phosphorescent, red suit, with his face entirely shaven and made-up, pierced by a femininity that becomes even more ambiguous when he embraces the man with the gold chain. They exchange words in English and Spanish with no particular hierarchy. Immediately, next to the man with make-up, I see a young brunette woman dressed in a skirt with a starchy petticoat underneath that gives the skirt some bounce. She wears unmissable golden earrings that spell her name in big letters: "Betty." The young woman sings, dances, and at times speaks with a young man with a small baby, just a few months old, in his arms. The baby follows her dancing with its eyes, lost in concentration, as his young father dances and rocks the child while answering in English to the words that Betty directs to him in Spanish. A woman approaches them—she turns out to be the young man's mother—and coos at the baby. She then continues dancing and musing the African words of the *santero* chant as the drums get stronger, energizing the atmosphere and activating the bodies that move faster and still faster, in sync with the rhythm of the drums.

The gentleman who is being initiated that same day as a *santero* looks haggard as he stands tall among the group of *santeros* that accompany him. He is very young, brown, and of a short stature. He is barefoot, dressed in what looks to me like a distinctly medieval-looking red costume. He holds a golden crown on his head and carries a kind of scepter in his hands. Despite his pallor and obvious fatigue, he maintains a solemn, sacred pose while impassively receiving the homage each guest pays him. It seems to me that some of them have different kinds of status within the *santero* system. They lie face down on the ground to pay tribute to him.

Ángel explains to me that there are approximately 20 families of *santeros* gathered inside that basement, and that becoming a *santero* costs around five thousand dollars, because the initiate has to pay for the drums, dancers, the details of the preparations, and the food that will be served later—a Puerto Rican meal with various kinds of meat that is being prepared at the back of the basement at that very moment. He says that the saint that corresponds to the future *santero* will forbid him from eating certain kinds of meat, and, because of that, this is the last time the boy can consume whatever he wants.

Suddenly, a woman goes into a trance, causing great excitement among the attendees, and Ángel explains that a saint has descended upon her. The *santeros* circle around her and protect her from any possible blows or nudges because her trance deepens through feverish movements and leaps which elevate her almost to the level of the ceiling. One of the *santeros* removes her glasses while the woman, eyes closed, remains completely out of it. I listen to the satisfied comments from people around me. I also observe Ángel's satisfaction as he comments that some of the possessed even swallow lit cigarettes when saints descend upon them, and for that reason, they must be protected from all harm, like being hit or falling. One of the *santeros* puts honey on the ecstatic woman's lips and then the attention on her fades, for a new dance occurs that will unleash another series of possessions.

Ángel's *padrina* explains that the man dancing in one of the corners is a Russian that she is guiding and who has joined the Puerto Rican community. She tells me the Russian has traveled from Pennsylvania especially for this ceremony. It would be obvious to anyone that the rhythm of the man dancing in the corner doesn't match the sound of the drums at all. The godmother adds that the Russian is staying at her house. She also says that the *santeros* meet every two weeks in various parts of the Bronx to perform their ceremonies. She also invites me, in a warm tone, to visit her house when I return to New York.

As the chants progress and as the sound of drums deepens, the number of visitations increases. One by one, the young and old begin falling into trances—always violent and spectacular—including two of the young men with shaved heads dressed in black leather. One of them seems to be in a trance for too long: he lies on the ground, pale, with his eyes half-open, surrounded by *santeros,* while a group of women exclaims in English and Spanish, alarmed, worried that the boy could die in the trance. Yet most of the attendees continue dancing and invoking the saints, in the African language, inviting them to descend and visit the bodies, forcing them into an extreme, frenetic dance. Ángel remains serene, and we direct ourselves to the entrance where a group of smokers gathers.

The smokers talk amongst themselves and about their different trades. From time to time, women and men turn to us to comment on the poisonous effects of cigarettes and offer alarming examples of aunts, uncles, and cousins dying from lung cancer. The ceremony seems about to end, and after putting out the cigarettes, we return with Ángel to the center of the room while the young man dressed entirely in leather continues to lie on the ground, attended to by the *santeros*. A large group of children, wearing their Sunday best, wander enthusiastically among the adults. I say goodbye to the *padrinos* and other guests with whom I have chatted occasionally during these hours. It is about nine o'clock at night and we abruptly exit into the darkness of the exterior.

Outside, the dim lights reveal small groups of Puerto Ricans on the street standing in front of some open bars. There is a grim air to this part of the city, one that is exacerbated by the bad lighting, the deterioration of the houses, the neighborhood's reputation, and the heaping piles of garbage in front of each building. We arrive at the subway station after walking for several blocks, and Ángel asks another Puerto Rican man waiting at the station about which line to take, but the man doesn't answer and turns the other way. When the train arrives, we get into a car, and I realize that the atmosphere has already transformed now that it is past nine at night. The gloomy faces feel pervasive. Ángel's attempts to get some information about the subway line we need to take are unsuccessful, as if people have come to some kind of agreement. None of the passengers answer his questions, resorting to an aggressive indifference. It is only Ángel's intuition that guides us closer to the right direction.

The journey, almost an hour long, is about to end. As we get closer to our destination, the human landscape changes once again, and with that change, new codes appear. Gone are the ceremony and the ceremonial bodies. Gone are their strategies, modified memories, perforated tongues, and cultural madness. I leave behind what seems to me to be a form of politics: an astonishing mode of carrying out a contaminated, cultural resistance.

All hail the new *santero* of the Bronx.

(1998)

Translated by Sowmya Ramanathan

Nelly Richard:
Locations and Dislocations

The critical influence of Nelly Richard's work underscores the importance of a form of thinking that impacted and left its creative stamp on Chile's and Latin America's cultural evolution over the past thirty years. It would be impossible for me to present this book from the *outside*, that is, to read it without the intensity of also being a witness[37]. In that sense, my reading is not merely biographical—I have known Nelly Richard for thirty-six years—but also radical, since I consider myself a witness, among others, qualified to understand her work's conditions of production. From this perspective, those specific conditions of production bestow on her work a certain "aura," as Walter Benjamin would say, or a very special condition in space and time.

The early days and spaces in which Nelly Richard's writing took shape were marked by great complexity: in a trajectory impeded by numerous obstacles, her work intelligently integrated the multifaceted tensions associated with consolidating a cultural career. Her work became known for raising questions in uncharted critical territories or in spaces devoid of consensus, even if dissent was prevalent.

Of course, one of the conditions of her critical practice was the production of texts under dictatorship. With this statement, I am pointing to two facets. On the one hand, we had a dictatorship with all its, let's say, rhizomatic and endless effects. But on the other hand, she had the desire to generate cultural criticism that was obligated to accept the permanent State of Exception as the norm under which to produce, select, and think through the insubordinate nature of the works she critiqued.

---

37   Eltit is referring to Nelly Richard's 2013 book, Crítica y política.

This was a multi-sided critical task because precisely in a context that also functioned as a material text, the pervasive microphysics of power—as Michel Foucault would say—demanded a nonstandard form of writing that could de-standardize to generate a plurality of meanings through the written word.

I must emphasize, in a special way, that Nelly Richard has always refused the mirage of transparency. Her politics of signs never abandoned the semiotic task of disseminating and twisting the axes of discursive normalization. This is how she constructed the peculiarity of her proposal, which would not only generate decades of appreciation but also resistance to her discourse.

Thus, the center of her work is staked not only on its emergence under dictatorship, which certainly marks its historical location, but also on its ability to raise a critical discussion traversed by opacities and generate analytical frameworks to approach an uncomfortable and unprecedented territory.

The emergence of Nelly Richard's work was greeted by caricature, negation, or polemics systematically launched against her autonomous, public thought. I, myself, participated in these debates, and while I maintained partial disagreements with some of her critical operations, I was always guided by the certainty that what was under discussion was the passion of her proposals.

To reframe this in Benjamin's auratic terms, a cut or suspension came with the publication of *Margins and Institutions*, in my opinion, because that book brought together the dispersed flows of her gaze that had taken shape over several years. The text brought together artistic territories that hadn't been critiqued and gave texture to forms of cultural production that lived at the edges of the scene and that, if not marginal, were certainly disaffiliated.

The so-called Escena de Avanzada is a category born of the theatricality of Nelly Richard's thinking. The idea of the scene is not accidental; it channels her aesthetics of naming and reading. The creation of a concept, Escena de Avanzada, also generated other scenes amid an equally intense backdrop. In a highly influential way, Nelly Richard put on the table a kind of *mother name* that would fuel decades of debate.

It is interesting that later, several years later, a debate would break out—with an intensity, both strange and extreme—about the works

Nelly Richard addressed in her critical narrative. In a societal frame, I was interested in the belated re-reading of works that had always been around, such as *Margins and Institutions*. I continue to believe that the struggle to debate a reading of that book and re-refresh the works exceeds its own critical perspective and is based in aspects associated with what Pierre Bourdieu calls—to put it another way—"male domination." Of course, this is because what's in dispute is the indisputable critical power that Nelly Richard's work has generated.

It's telling that a group of local thinkers' search for critical legitimacy may be established through re-tracing her thinking—a revision that is always corrective and normative—and, even more, of her aesthetic gaze. This revisionism, in some cases, harbored a destructive impulse related to Nelly Richard's theorizing. The "Mellado Case" is important because he used and abused the violence of his attacks as justifications to authorize himself;[38] he was unable to channel his envy creatively, to transform it into admiration, as Melanie Klein convincingly argued.[39] That particular envy (the "Mellado Case") also speaks to the power of Richard's writing in a cultural atmosphere marked, like all spaces, by gender asymmetry and disputes in a territory determined, in part, not only by geographical but also symbolic narrowness.

Beyond these episodes—all predictable and, of course, forgettable—one of the most relevant aspects of the book *Crítica y política* is how it gestures toward retracing Richard's work from the vantage point of her own memories and her present reality. This conversation—it must be said—organized brilliantly by Alejandra Castillo and Miguel

---

38   Here, Eltit refers to an essay published by Justo Pastor Mellado titled "Escena de Avanzada," published in 1977. In his essay, Mellado zeroes in on Nelly Richard's classification of the Escena de Avanzada using semiotic theory. He refers to the classification "problematic" and states that the "crítica desatenta no realiza las distinciones de rigor" / "the negligent critic does not follow a rigorous analysis."

39   Austrian-British author Melanie Klein wrote extensively on the relationship between envy and admiration, arguing that envy often hides the admiration for or desire to be like the object it focuses on. To read more, please see *Envy and Gratitude and Other Works* (1957).

Valderrama—illuminates the many fronts that Nelly Richard's cultural work has traversed. Its position at the margins can be felt throughout the entire text, which exudes movement and a noticeable desire for critical wandering that rejects institutionalization and, even more so, essentialism. Instead, it proposes dissent where rebellion settles and becomes normalized, and in this sense, the text reveals the strategies of a kind of cultural nomadism.

I would like to dwell here on a fact that might seem bizarre, but that seems pertinent to remember in this context because of the power of what it proposed. In 1989, two centuries after the commemoration of the French Revolution, Félix Guattari believed that the French Minister of Culture at the time, the socialist Jack Lang, could use his position to raise new perceptual networks capable of generating deeper and bolder axes of meaning. It was then that Guattari proposed to Minister Lang that the state commemorate the bicentennial of the French Revolution with a meeting of all the world's nomadic peoples. Félix Guattari thought that those people, wandering through the world's geographies as nations structured through movement, could offer signs, forms, and a powerful resistance capable of altering the common sense of dominant cultures. Naturally, his proposal was not heard by the socialist Lang because it was too decentralized for the state's rigidity. However, I still think it's one of the most poetic and political proposals I've heard of.

I include this digression to celebrate and recognize the strength of the nomadic as a way to introduce another one of the post-dictatorship period's most eloquent cultural productions, the *Revista de Crítica Cultural*. In an ambiguous time governed by rampant consumerism, the imperative of consensus, and the denial of analytical and critical positions, the *Revista* promoted tense forms of discourse rooted in deconstruction and reflection on Latin America's new societies, which were entranced by the neoliberal promise of global capital.

Conceived as a manifestation of the discursive avant-garde, the journal did not neglect the relevance of the visual scene nor the encounter between artistic practices and critical voices; it was a medium that mobilized the discourse of thinkers linked to the academy but stripped of their academic trappings, exposed, and appearing in a journal imagined outside of institutions. I have no doubt that the *Revista de Crítica Cultural* will be the point of reference for reading how the nineties unfolded, a measure of national debates, and a forum that allowed us to contrast those debates with the journal's approaches. From the beginning, Nelly Richard raised the crucial question about memory as a zone of multiple disputes, not only against oblivion but also against memories inhabited by stereotypes.

We should note that the book *Crítica y Política* includes photographs and cultural memories of the author herself, as well as critical writings about Nelly Richard's work that show the *hand* behind the *writing—la letra de su letra*—or the precise space in which reading becomes writing.

The book also shows how, now in the 21st century, a project called "Imaginarios Culturales para la Izquierda," led by Nelly Richard, sparked controversy within the pages of the same publication that featured it, *The Clinic*, which characterized her approaches as obsolete and outdated. Rafael Gumucio's writings slammed the initiative, arguing in favor of a present founded upon the acceptance and benefits of the neoliberal model. This was paradoxical and interesting because the allegations were published just before the massive anti-neoliberal protests began in the country in 2011.

The book closes with a final conversation, perhaps the most open of all, that refers to the political and to politics, and in which nomadism reappears: that journey through a dynamic left, unsatisfied yet alert to its own signs of conformity.

I wouldn't wish to end this text without affirming that *Crítica y política* demonstrates Nelly Richard's extraordinary discursive solvency and will be an indispensable book. As the witness that I am, I want to note that the author's cultural journey as an outstanding intellectual has been difficult despite the recognition and satisfaction she has obtained. Put another way, each step along her trajectory has cost her plenty, or as someone from Mexico might say, *le ha costado un chingo.*

(2014)

Translated by Sowmya Ramanathan

The Queen of the Block

Pedro Lemebel's death a year ago implied a disruption in the local cultural scene of the last few decades. Although he published some initial short stories, his cultural work came to be inscribed with a sharp, underground force upon the emergence of Las Yeguas del Apocalipsis, the public intervention collective founded at the end of the eighties alongside the writer and performer, Francisco Casas.

Later, in the 1990s and during the start of the transition, Pedro Lemebel's writing took on the *crónica* as a genre and performance as a medium.[40] *La esquina es mi corazón*,[41] published in 1995 by the renowned publisher Cuarto Propio, ushered in a form of writing that appealed to the baroque to pursue a self-aware and highly manufactured aesthetic. He sought to implement a coiled and contorted kind of writing, rooted in the desire for a style that could account for a range of themes: from the political to lower classes, it lingers upon the endearing landscape of *la pobla* in a special way.[42] He validated his writing both as

---

40 The crónica is a distinctly Latin American genre that consists of a typically first-person (though not always) narration of events, which contain historical references but can be read as fiction and structured in diverse formats. The genre has undergone a long evolution and it is notable that many cronistas appealed to the genre as a form of critique, sometimes militant, of social, political, and cultural issues. For this reason, Eltit emphasizes Lemebel's writing of crónicas as linked to Latin American cultural resistance.

41 This is Pedro Lemebel's first book of crónicas, and its title means "On the corner of my heart." Eltit plays with the notion of the street corner in a popular neighborhood in this essay.

42 "La pobla" is a colloquial word used in Chile to refer to marginal neighborhoods or areas that lack direct access to public services. It is short for "población"

a sign and as an emblem by taking shelter within a critical tradition tied to political memory, class resentment, and humor as devastating and inescapable instruments.

Lemebel made the *loca* a public, intense, biting, and ironic weapon.[43] I must point out that I always thought he drew a clear relationship to Manuela, the protagonist of José Donoso's *El lugar sin límites*— an extremely "queer" character (speaking in current terms). However, Pedro's imaginary appealed to a transient loca, moving from city to city, liberated and full of desire. I also thought about the Argentines who were victims of AIDS: Néstor Perlongher, militant of homosexual writing, and about Batato Barea, the mythical performer and founder of the group Peinados Yoly.

Pedro Lemebel's stiletto heels were crucial for him to embark on a challenging trajectory within a social space, which even to this day, is very much characterized by the most conservative, dictatorship regulations. His *crónicas* emerged on the scene precisely in the mid-nineties when hyper-frenzied consumerism seemed like the only anesthesia for escaping anguish, blurring the lines of memory, and proclaiming an impossible form of reconciliation.

Yet his sharp-tongued writing never ceased to denounce the wake of destruction generated by the dictatorship's atrocities. Nor did he hesitate to mock social climbing, prevalent in the nineties as a formula for redemption, with the razor-sharp precision of his queer gaze: *ojo de loca no se equivoca*.[44] I think it is necessary to stress that he never

---

which is used to refer to shantytowns.

43 As Melissa Gonzalez argues, "loca" is "roughly analogous to terms like sissy or (flaming) queen," but is used all over the Spanish-speaking world with different connotations. Regardless of variance, it refers to "some form of feminine gender nonnormativity and can be used in a derogatory sense." Lemebel is widely recognized for having reappropriated this term to describe a specific sector of the Chilean, working-class population, and Eltit's use of the term here upholds Lemebel's original intent at resignification.

44 This phrase literally means, "the loca's eye makes no mistakes" but has also been used as a way to suggest that those that belong to queer communities have specific talents in recognizing one another.

stopped denouncing the open segregation experienced by a large segment of the Chilean population.

He raised his waxed eyebrows on many occasions to expose what he called "his difference" as a proud choice in its own right. He never stopped exposing his divergences, even within the landscape of differences. Each of his appearances inspired not only admiration but also the fervor of the crowd that followed and applauded him.

He was clever. He was daring. He was controversial and a total diva. He remained on the corner of his imaginary *pobla* after counting, one by one, each and every stumbling block placed on his corner by the State. He didn't give up. He didn't comply. The Queen's heart may have stopped, yet his corner of the block continues beating.

(2016)

Translated by Sowmya Ramanathan

Ethics, Aesthetics, Politics

There exists a long-standing debate and prolonged discussion between academics in the North and South. I do not intend to put an end to those tensions here, but my idea is to avoid the extensive series of clichés that have characterized certain voices that endlessly reproduce stereotypes. I am referring to rigid thinking that circumscribes our spaces themselves and fails to recognize zones of porosity or diversity and the politics that bodies transmit beyond their territorial attachments.

At the same time, I think of Chilean public universities. They have faced a distressing weathering and an obligation to raise private money to obtain a significant part of their financing. These obligations not only shaped how knowledge is disseminated, but they also endowed knowledge with an economic component. In the case of private universities, a considerable group views overt profit as their métier, even if they disguise this through gimmicks and deals.

Thus, the student who pays for his education is considered something of a mix between a *customer* and an *investor*, a user who, in turn, exercises a kind of self-directed leadership. The student-client materially invests in himself as one product among many. Then, in the mid-to-long term, his spending turns into earnings since the university degree is not only a consumer good but also a weapon that intensifies consumption, thereby justifying a substantial trail of debt as part of the process. This so-called higher education is central to the functioning of the market. Both the university and labor markets are synchronically complicit in intensifying education as consumption—not as a right—under the stifling neoliberalism in which we live.

From this perspective, it becomes evident that all academic production has been affected by the violence of this situation. I refer here to the influence of particular forms, conducts, and requirements that were implemented and then normalized as truth because of the U.S. and perhaps European models. Within the critical territory of literary studies, the obligation to the "paper," to publish, to appear in indexed journals, and to follow the rigid monotony of the academic essay format must be understood under this prism. In the end, in many cases, this demand has prompted some hasty and, most dramatically, irrelevant work. Articles and even complete books have lost their most poignant critical weight and turned into a kind of post-thesis obligation or a basic requirement for reaching a higher rung on the ladder of the labor hierarchy.

As an illuminating site for pondering cultural problems and offering unexpected and sound readings, the essay has been affected by a retail-style overproduction that obeys the neoliberal structure's mandate and forces the subject, ultimately, to exploit himself.

From my perspective, the robotic format imposed on the texts suggests nothing more and nothing less than a rigid kind of guardrail against the possible and necessary overflow that these writings could transmit. This is an anesthetizing type of pedagogical format that wipes out the writing itself, placing it back in primary school, radically distanced from the idea of the literary essay as a zone of rigor, or a site of new experiences and freedoms.

I have asked myself who writes the rules of a game that can't be played. To what do these rules conform, or why are they obeyed? I have asked myself this many times because I believe that, due to their commercial instability and intellectual ability, the humanities represent a critical space for thinking and rethinking the most complex areas of life. Yet if writing itself is held captive by rigid legislation, how can it be conceptually liberating while seemingly imprisoned by the requirements imposed upon it?

Some writing emerges from a virtual reality—very literal and material—that disorganizes spellings, creates new anti-academic grammars, breaks rules with surprising constancy, generates deliberate disorder, alters sense, and fragments meaning. However, Chilean academic writing insists on establishing limits that lead to the asphyxiation and dangerous isolation of its own field of production.

Ultimately, I wonder: for whom do we write in Chile? One possible answer is: we write for the regulations. Thus, the aesthetic impact, inflections of a new century, and any possible (and necessary) discursive openings are consigned to a self-absorbed professionalism that neither radiates nor modifies its own structures. I refer so repeatedly to Chile while imagining similar situations in other countries, not only because that is where I am a citizen but because it is the Latin American country that was established as a laboratory of extreme neoliberal practices. Due to this generalized appropriation of the social model, the effects of regulations also become partially visible within essay production, which is characterized by a recognizable uniformity in many cases.

The task now is how to continue thinking about what Pierre Bourdieu might call this field of Latin American literature—which ultimately comprises a limited community of voices despite spanning diverse territories—beyond its reversals, renewals, or reiterations.

Yet what I seek to emphasize here is that in spite of or against regulations, a series of well-consolidated exchanges already exists and flows, not only within the study of Latin America and its literatures, but also with the *field* in the United States (to continue with Bourdieu).

Thanks to the materiality of that flow, which maintains the energy of an active community, we gather from South to North in this legendary academic center.

I want to join the Townsend Center for the Humanities and the Departments of Spanish and Portuguese and Comparative Literature at the University of California, Berkeley, in paying tribute to the dear and respected Francine Masiello, one of the most outstanding scholars in the Latin American cultural field. I do not intend to turn Francine Masiello into our object of analysis here, much less account for her trajectory—which is spectacular by the way—but I cannot fail to point out the political-aesthetic elements that her texts and her figure transmit. For I would define her, as always with the hesitation and suspicion that all classifications entail, as a Joycean: a sharp and risk-taking Joycean who reads and rereads, thinks and rethinks categories, moves vertiginously between the centuries, deploys readings on the body and its symptoms: power and the body, the power of the body, the market and the body, and writing and the body.

She is a Joycean who moves through areas of turbulence like Dublin: territories like Argentina and Chile that exist within the broad margin between domestication and revolt. Francine Masiello has thought about these territories in a special manner and written about them conclusively. Of course, Masiello's work exceeds Argentina and Chile, sailing through authors and themes from other geographies. In that sense, she is more.

Yet today I want to relive a very personal and important chapter for me and that I will hazard to share with you. I remember in either 1988 or 1989, I was asked for the first time to collaborate on a cultural piece for the only opposition newspaper circulating at that time in Chile, *La Época*. It was interesting, but highly traumatic because it was not a minor task by any dimension. On the one hand, there was (and continues to be) a negative reputation around me for being unintelligible— or for having unintelligible writing—and in that sense, writing for a newspaper involved a challenge and a risk. On the other hand, without ignoring that I was worried about appearing out of place in the newspaper, the most pressing matter was how to account for the national context: the dictatorship still hadn't materially ended, but the signs of its defeat were already visible—even though I must say here that to this day it has been a very relative defeat.

I admit, as I said, that writing for newspapers intimidated me, and in a certain way, I was affected by what was said about me in my field. It was one thing to write an unintelligible book, but it was another thing altogether to write an incomprehensible text in a newspaper with a large national circulation. Of course, I didn't and still don't agree with the classification I carry, but I must admit that I felt—and perhaps still feel—a bit guilty. However, I considered that the newspaper was changing and transforming into a space in which I felt it was necessary to participate.

In reality, without ignoring the impact of the rumors, I consider myself a fighter from a literary perspective. Beyond the talk, it was crucial that I was searching for a way to use that space politically, from a cultural point of view, of course. I wanted to allude to the problematics that traversed us: the monotony of living and coexisting with a severely injured psychic and emotional portion, in the face of a repeated, incessant, inhuman set of situations that we literally had to swallow and that were—and I feel in my case, still are—bubbling underneath the surface.

In this way, clinging to small gestures of resistance—those that are microscopic, planned and carried out alongside numerous cultural companions over the years—I thought about what I would write as my first journalistic experience. It's not that I overestimated my presence in the newspaper. On the contrary, I wanted to legitimize my presence in that medium. I felt that I was crossing into a new territory and had to politicize this new experience as much as possible, because any other way, it would be completely meaningless.

Yet, of course, we were still living under a State of Exception. The most important thing was censorship: this was as well-known as were the forms of wading through it. It was then that I found my topic, specifically in an article by Francine Masiello that discussed post-dictatorship Argentine culture and articulated the precise undertones that the Chilean cultural context was already beginning to experience. I spent my column commenting on her article. My first writing for the newspaper was on Masiello, and beyond the quality of my text, I felt I had done the job, that it had met my own expectations.

At that time, I hadn't read Francine's work, except for that illuminating essay, and I certainly didn't know her personally. However, somehow it became forever imprinted as part of my trajectory. From that moment on, naturally, I was attentive to her trajectory. What I want to emphasize before concluding this episode is that in her essay, Francine Masiello read the "state of affairs," so to say, with special accuracy, because ultimately her text accounted for a matrix: a core problem that triggered a detonation of outbursts, latencies, or prolongations of a larval state. That was precisely what allowed me to read, in so many words, Chile in Argentina. Beyond what we understand as a simple similarity, Masiello proposed the intelligent form of what could be called—or more precisely, of what I could call—a "modulation."

Yes, because when reading and re-reading some of her texts, I realize that, rather than definitive statements, Masiello deploys a more subjective or singular field around which multiple voices appear. They appear at a crossroads in which the author has formulated the question of sense *and* nonsense, sense *or* nonsense. There, fiction writers, poets, theorists, and art critics form a mobile community that finetunes its own melodies. They generate a particular noise, not necessarily a chorus, but a modulation that Masiello produces as a critical strategy.

I already said that she seems like a Joycean to me. I would say that this position allows her to transition from *The Odyssey* to *Ulysses*, but of course, in a distinct way: forked or *bífida*, as she would say. For, in the end, she is a Joycean woman. And in that precise condition of a woman—and as a woman, forked or bifurcated—she is a critic with knowledge (in the Foucauldian sense) that moves through divisions or seams, transiting unwaveringly through history, ethics, and aesthetics. In a different register and from other conditions of production, she reminds me of the Austrian writer Elfride Jelinek. In her novel *Wonderful, Wonderful Times* (1980), Jelinek proposes a *post*-scene to relive traumas and repetitions, and she returns to these traces time and time again. This is because the matrix remains, formatted within her, and generates other scenarios: present scenarios that drag the wake of antiquity behind them.

I read Masiello's essay "Plaza" about the Zócalo, the famous Mexican plaza that provided a performance venue for the "naked" photographer, Spencer Tunick. Masiello perceives the deliberate depopulation of the Zócalo, that matrix—a site filled with history, a current space for precarious commerce, and a place of native languages—to host an event of notable commercial proportion, in so many words. Nevertheless, the displacement or expulsion of small merchants in favor of the ideology of mass consumption does not overwhelm her text. Instead, it is about establishing and reestablishing a journey through various squares, using the Zócalo as a matrix to produce modulations, rhythms, and cadences, which arise not to negate Tunick's occupation, but to decenter it. This permits, as an analogy, precarious vendors from other Latin American plazas to set up their own stages. The same vendors that were displaced from the Zócalo—I mean, as "others"—modulate that which Tunick's work doesn't allow for due to its stridency. Francine Masiello's journey is fascinating to me because of this intelligent construction or reconstruction of diverse plazas, spaces that are ultimately for literary texts that can only inhabit these historic public squares, where citizens' bodies and histories are spun together, as highly vulnerable vendors.

Yet her territory is also that which is most tangible: the body. The body and its senses appear as another one of her authorial concerns. The body of writing is a material site of production: in varied states, it enters the body through the body of the written word in order to detonate itself with tangible effects. In or between those bodies—I am going to continue abusing the concept—there are essential modulations that produce a material encounter that displaces their symptoms and functions as an expansion of meaning.

Francine Masiello thinks about the loose interwovenness between the written word and the senses. In writing, she glimpses the somatization of history. It is not about transmitting emotions through the written word, following the term's most common notion, but rather about a presence that can contain the relationship between body and catastrophe, writing and catastrophe, graphic trace and catastrophe: not as a simple meaning, but as a site activated by the senses and, therefore, completely corporeal.

Francine's critical work covers three centuries in-depth, 19th, 20th, and the start of the 21st: the 19th century Argentine woman as raw material for the nascent republican State, the woman as "angel of the home," and the working space that Marx failed to glimpse as one of capitalism's most profitable unpaid areas, relegated as it was to the category of unproductive work. Francine examines the "angel of the home" only to turn what is understood as private space on its head and illuminate how it is singularly politicized by the female body in order to restore and contest the erasure of that body and its contributions in public space. Because ultimately, the great masculine decisions that have shaped political and economic models—their forms and their intensities—have always or almost always been made *behind closed doors,* in the most private sector of the public, such that one may think of them as *domestic* decisions. Thus, Francine Masiello deconstructs the category of woman in the 19th century, a time—like all other times and their powers— marked by disputes over the empire of a single gender as the protagonist and manager of conflicts.

Thus, the particular administration of knowledge—I refer to a kind of consistent audacity—has allowed Francine Masiello a mobility that remains focused on strategic places that can redefine what may be understood as minoritarian. In this way, her critical gestures have broken with the most didactic and routine schemes and agendas to reformulate the gaze and reframe problems. From this perspective, she re-politicizes the field. She distances it from petrification since she intensifies her forked tongue and uses it as a foundation for thought and action.

Yet Francine is also an academic who is well-known, admired, and recognized by the many students she has trained and who somehow contain her within their own thinking, in their writings, and in the direction of their gazes. Andrea Jeftanovic, the renowned Chilean writer, intelligent critic, and a dear young friend, always conveyed this to me with accurate words that combined affection, respect, recognition, and admiration. For my part, I must point out that my first stay as a visiting professor outside of Chile was right here, at Berkeley.

I had already personally met Francine and my dear Gwen Kirkpatrick in Chile. Of course, I was simply terrified by the multiple challenges that this trip implied for me. Yet beyond my fears and my already chronic insecurity, I traveled, and right here in Berkeley I was able to directly witness Francine's political work. She maintained active ties to La Peña, a political-cultural space made up of Latin American exiles, especially Chileans, and this is not common. On the contrary, it is completely rare, since the U.S. academy, apart from valuable exceptions, remains within the academy and doesn't establish links to the surrounding community. On the other hand, in 1996, Francine maintained these relationships and established concrete, markedly effective exchanges with the participants of La Peña who had dedicated their lives to various trades. Thus, Masiello's personal ties also extended to the outside world, as a gesture of recognition and solidarity with the various political experiences triggered by the darkest times.

That political practice was one piece of a larger whole because, at the same time, I was part of a group that held inter-academic meetings with other professors, including Gwen Kirkpatrick and Mary Louise Pratt, who was a professor at Stanford. They invited me to one of their meetings where I recognized not only a powerful intellectual energy but also an equally unusual political situation that broke with convention again. This is because they generated a union of academic women from powerful institutions that did not compete enviously with one another but rather joined together, fracturing some of the reductive stereotypes associated with the feminine. I thought of a kind of super-strong "academic front" that collectively intensified its knowledge and, in this way, strengthened its critical presence as a body that unfolded, rhizomatically, to amplify the scope and power of their voices.

I am sure that there are other aspects and a large sum of strategies in Francine Masiello's administration of knowledge, elements that are inscribed in her politics of presence, acts of writing, and the critical decisions she has made. I am certain that my intervention is an insufficient accounting of her comings and goings, of her transit through geographies and bodies, of the forked and passionate aesthetic explorations contained in her acts of reading, and in the inevitable and dizzying act of thinking. I also imagine the joy writing produced within her, and I can envision each of the stumbling blocks she has had to circumvent. I can glimpse her fulfillment every time she identified a thread of meaning or finished a book.

I know how and to what extent literary work is addictive.

After this very necessary and exciting day in which we pay tribute to her clear trajectory, I would like to go out, why not, with Francine Masiello and walk arm in arm, as she accompanies me to the HO store to buy a blouse for the Chilean summer. And while we walk, arm in arm, like the *comadres* we've become, I want her to speak to me with her passion that I know so well, about the cadences of the latest poems she admires, of the blank spaces, of texts to be written, of the most emotive lines of her new book, of the aesthetic connections that arise between language and a sonic trail, which only a forked Joyceana like her is capable of modulating.

Thank you very much, dear Francine, for all your time and your work.

(2015)

Translated by Sowmya Ramanathan

At the Edge of the Written Word

Half boy, half dog. Intelligent animal. Panting. In the novel *Patas de perro*, the Chilean novelist Carlos Droguett invented a figure that seems lucid and provocative to me. He wrote about difference drained from a body forced to negotiate between the irreverent signs of a pack of hounds and a solicitous domestication.

Yet of course, ultimately unsubmissive, he had to disappear after his pack. He chose to fade away into the pack's most profane barking, losing himself in the night.

I evoke the boy-dog, Bobi, since he stands as a metaphor that challenges us to this day. I want to allude to his distance, his resistance. Yes, resistance. For the boy-dog always perceived his canine deviation as something more, an attribute and a gift there to increase a double potency, at once extraordinarily human and dog.

Obstacles launched themselves at Bobi with an undisguised fanaticism. The most decisive powers tended to be biased against him, unleashing prejudice and a countless sum of judgments. They passed judgment on him. Between the foaming of a mouth too prone to thirst and two powerful paws, he faced hunger and beatings. His body became a site of incessant punishment.

However, protecting himself, he was already shielded within his own resistance.

With decisive lucidity, he understood that there was never even the slightest possibility of resignation. His body, branded as monstrous, was a scandal, and yet he knew it was entirely his. There he was: Bobi passing by.

Possessed by a form of fear that was intertwined with serenity, he confronted the intransigence dictated by officialized programs. Early on, he knew that something in him inspired feelings of entangled anger and guilt. Rage and guilt were embedded within the very institutions that expelled him because he represented an acute desire that hegemony didn't dare to claim as its own. Bobi embodied a consolidated dream of insurrection that the system was forbidden to yearn for, even in its wildest dreams.

In this way, Bobi resembled a nightmare taking place in broad daylight. Only the butchers seemed destined to recognize him, and for that reason, they threw him pieces of meat from their damp and blood-stained counters to humiliate him and highlight the animal matter they knew so well. Of course they knew—the butchers.

But Bobi was inscribed as an emblem, because Carlos Droguett managed to create his novel by appealing to an imperious, eager, non-stop, feverish writing. A writing that forces its most concentrated readers to alter their breathing rhythm in order to merge and reemerge with it, contaminating themselves with an accelerated, doglike reading.

The novel and its disturbing writing remain there, cornered, perhaps left behind on a hyper-solid, although surely less ostentatious bookshelf. In his novel *Patas de perro,* Carlos Droguett's extraordinary contribution continues its creative, mysterious, and challenging trajectory to show us that yes, yes, perhaps there is a body that doesn't and shouldn't unite with others just for the sake of it.

I want to thank everyone who works at Casa de las Américas and, very especially, the president, Roberto Fernández Retamar, for the honor they have bestowed on my books by dedicating this week to them. Of course, I thank my friends and literary critics for their presence on this unique and incomparable occasion, in this unique and incomparable space.

As we know, Casa de las Américas is already inscribed within the literary imagination of the continent as one of the most consistent and insistent projects on behalf of the promotion and production of dialogues between diverse and plural literatures.

Of course, I cannot help expressing my admiration for baroque Cubanism, recognizing that its most extremely codified linguistic network is an indisputable milestone. I refer not only to its new, defiant, and acutely Caribbean repositioning of Góngora enacted by Lezama Lima—which the divine Sarduy read in an outstanding way—but also to the adhesive and adhering baroque humor that assaults us, sheltered behind a tangled intelligence, to permit an eruption of laughter and dilute the reservoirs of resentment.

I take the liberty here of annexing and evoking Roberto Fernández Retamar's creative Cuban laughter—legendary and unforgettable for me—and on a strictest note, his poetry and his well-established theoretical contribution.

So, what to do, what to say, what to write? In these circumstances, what could I contribute?

It is pertinent, I'll say, to hesitate, to permit myself a few digressions without fear of stirring up diverse and divergent meanings, even at the risk of spouting nonsense.

This invitation, which seems too generous to me and the most prestigious I've received in the now extensive years that make up my literary activity, is extremely stimulating, yet also—I must say—difficult to accept. As Jorge Fornet understood very well, any statement by an author borders on absolute irrelevance. Thus, I hide behind the provisional and the tentative to try to expose some of the problems that, from my perspective, function as triggers in the act of writing literature.

In truth, I believe it is necessary to specify that each book that I have managed to finish has been the product of its particular process, because even when I know how much intense concentration it required, it always had to emerge from its own momentum. I allude to the written word and its considerable material weight.

I myself feel, in part, like a foreigner to those books that abruptly cease to belong to me at the crucial and inescapable moment in which they detach themselves from my hand in order to go off, with their dog-like paws—their *patas de perro*—salivating and rushing outwards. They leave, searching for a hole or a fissure in the wasteland of an eye that may pick them up.

I have never felt like a professional writer. I'm closer to an artisan of the imperfect written word; its impossibility and irrefutable flight amaze and captivate me. A ludic trap is set by a written word that presents itself as apparently available, and the critical challenge lies in following the most strained dictation of that word, chasing it, tongue hanging out, hard-headed, within an uncertain search for producing little more than an aesthetic and political flash.

Elsewhere, I have referred to the possibility of establishing a politics of writing, transforming the written word into a perhaps risky political sphere, always evolving, through lateral pathways. That's precisely it:

being barricaded in each turn of the written word without abandoning the turn. Remaining there, turning over and over, illuminated by the doubtful hope of inhabiting its twists. Yet, actually, this is about capturing hope. It's about focusing on the desire to twist and turn.

For, in reality, there is joy: that nontransferrable and astounding joy provoked by an extreme proximity to the written word, a joy that reneges on and rejects writing's professionalization. Rather, the horizon seems to complete itself when a hint of a tremor can be felt, or with the latent danger of a shipwreck that will never end.

I have always considered, with extreme clarity, that it is the written word that must find its place because what arises, in an unstoppable way, is the exactitude of a space for the precise place of the letter. Though I understand the emergence, and perhaps necessity, of the author who puts body and soul into operating his or her own production, I am instead theoretically and politically interested—without resorting to romantic idealizations—in the *non*sense(s) that literature carries and in its most subversive capacity for dispersion.

Yet of course, today the written word is, as I perhaps perceive it, trapped in a corner. In the same way that the law does not necessarily lead to justice, literature seems to shy away from its unofficial work with writing. It avoids this due to ultra-capitalism's strict mandate, embodied in the editorial industry, which turns the book into a productive source of entertainment or legitimates a kind of frivolousness. That's fine. The critical point lies in how the industry's mandate depoliticizes the written word and converts it into a mere referential zone, a simple illustration of a determinate, opportune reality that turns out to be convenient and functional for the commercial project that surrounds and constrains us today.

We know, of course, that a part of literature has always inhabited a minoritarian field, which is interesting. Yet today, the triumphant eruption of the free market's subsidiary book-market constructs sensibilities that reduce and alter the most complex problems by generating stereotypes that, when solidified, solidify the system. I think that the general and indiscriminate development of the literary market is neither innocent nor incidental. Beyond the pseudo-commitments of its content, the market acts as the incentive of a large agenda to depoliticize the written word.

It could seem like an extemporaneous undertaking to invoke the specificity of writing as a critical interrogation of the material foundation of storytelling. Put another way, the dominant sensibilities currently frame their rejection by presuming anachronism. However, denying the spatiality and density of the written word in all its material dimensions—as well as the range of intricate relations it summons—implies adhering to what Pierre Bourdieu calls "de-history," and in this case, literary de-history. This makes the desocialization of literature possible. This is one of neoliberalism's primary tools for validating itself.

It is not my purpose to put neoliberal literatures in their place, nor to question their authors. Rather, my focus is on the possibility, in the limited borderline spaces at hand, of bringing the written word closer to writing without any profit motive other than its shock and its infinite internal permutations. I am referring to a kind of productivity anchored in the passionate rigor of continuing to think of the literary as a shrinking trade, to thus refute the spectacularizing expectations that the free cultural market promotes.

For it seems to me—and I admit, without reservation, to the margin of errors that my impressions may carry—that if we give ourselves up to the seductive side that writing carries, we foster a hegemony similar to the powerful television network CNN, which, under a supposed pluralism, forms opinions at the cost of repression, suppression, and informative distortion. In this space, I cannot fail to refer to the contexts that history provides us with today, a history that—as we know—has always carried an inexhaustible source of tensions. This history has demonstrated, to the point of exhaustion, that it strives at all costs to avoid any kind of respite.

However, it is impossible to ignore how an extreme and turbulent social scenario is currently taking shape which, for the moment, seems undeniable. This is a scenario that validates pure violence and moral outrage in order to hide or conceal its rapacious, warlike claws that—shielding themselves behind a humanitarian discourse—drill holes to extract the maximum possible amount of oil reserves and obtain massive control over gas pipelines.

Today, mosques have been stigmatized as a new symptom of a colonization that, yes, has too many precedents. And even so, mosques have been stigmatized.

Just as long ago, gold served as the foundation for discourse to dismantle the first inhabitants of the Americas, who were subjected to an ideology that dismissed their conditions as human. Today, we see how the cold determination that seeks to illegitimately possess petroleum and gas turns the Muslim into its prisoner. What a shame.

Yet there's more: we see the interference with the complex and agitated geographies of Colombia and Venezuela, the prolonged siege of Cuba, the exemplary punishment experienced by Argentina.

The wars of the twentieth century, produced with the same characteristics as the script of a Hollywood film, take place before spectators on the world screen, a screen that cannot be deactivated even if we close our eyes. Even if we close our eyes, it continues on and on.

Citizenship has taken a nosedive. We are but spectators. Yes, we have become spectators even of our own devastating lives because communication technologies, supposedly destined to promote active integration for participating healthfully in the world, just reproduce and communicate with themselves, intensifying or moderating the spectacle.

In this way, a reality passes by that ends up becoming disposable. It is an acute recycling that pushes us to the next shot. And yet, we perpetually forget what the next shot will be. The rapid invasion of Afghanistan seems as distant as though it had unfolded in a remote past.

I ask myself: what must the journey have been like for the Taliban prisoners now that they are so close, and yet, so far, relegated to the military base in Guantánamo?

Elsewhere, as if the screen could be split, there are bombings of Palestinian houses—the explosion of the houses of suspicious relatives—while Ariel Sharon transports the weight of his deformed humanity (though I don't wish to make fun of his body). It is Sharon's body that singles out his Christian capital sin on the screen: I am referring to gluttony. His eager will is to take over the desert and govern even its smallest grains of sand, converting the abused Palestinian people into dust.

How is it possible that this paradoxical, dramatic resolution is underway right now: when one of the most moving events, that sorrows historical memory, is constituted by the deliberate machinery of death that was utilized against the Jewish people, operated by a Nazism that found its echo within a sick system that convinced itself that such a massacre was possible.

Yet now, to deepen the contradictions, on two parallel screens, Ariel Sharon and George W. Bush congratulate each other and pose for a now belated posterity in front of the White House.

There is a medieval flavor to this feudalist form of alliance. The eras are indiscriminately mounted on top of one another. Forced into the passion of investing, multitudes of bodies increase the ample poverty line when the market falters.

Yet it is necessary to strengthen the market's good health through a sharpening contempt for the unfortunate, straggling multitudes.

However, despite considerable limitations, framed within a narrow horizon, Brazil, the most powerful and populated country of the continent, chose a former metal worker as its President. Not a businessman, no, but someone who once worked as a metal worker. It is stimulating and interesting how, within the most radical forms of control, lines of flight are organized that defy the logics and shatter the parameters of what is possible.

I realize that I have already diverted the course of the written word, that I've exceeded my own format. I return, then, to position myself in the literary terrain.

Of course, how to return if literary territories are correlated with other literary terrains, and also with the textuality that history imposes, rather than offers. I entered the narrative field while a fierce dictatorship was going on in Chile. Like millions of my compatriots, I carry an active memory and am aware of how much thinking is violated when multiple, diverse forms of violence are legalized, even in terms of the smallest acts of daily life.

At this point, in the vein of asymmetries and their quota of violence, it may be opportune to refer to the open problem of gender and literature. The market has already appropriated this dilemma. Under the prism of difference, the ghetto has been intelligently redesigned. In reality, it's not about women's literature—I mean, the possible and complicated unraveling of its figuration—but rather producing a literature apt for women's consumption. I am referring to stories that make the proliferation of the consumer model viable, which is how the literary field is divided into segments to maintain hegemony. In this way, Literature (with a capital L) and its conservative agenda remain unscathed. And on another shore—which can't be anything but comprehensive—there is an agglomeration of what is understood as women's literature as an appendix, thus simply appealing to the sociology of the written word.

We are witnessing the biologization of culture, that cosmetically and politically relevant quota that requires a segmentation and classification of the markets with the goal of intensifying its sales.

However, beyond all projects, the enigmatic device of the written word remains.

I think that this extraordinary meeting calls into question precisely that enigma. On this occasion, it has befallen the books of which—up to a point—I can claim authorship. These books, as I said before and reiterate now, are imperfect and unstable.

Yet in some part of my head, I have the certainty that a literature anchored in the depth of the written word gives us life. It sustains us.

We resist. Half children, half dogs.

Thank you very much.

(2002)

Translated by Sowmya Ramanathan

In the Intense Zone
of the Other Me

José Guillermo Barrera Barrera, Blanca Esther Valderas Garrido, José Calderón Miranda, Manuel Antonio Maldonado, Alejandro Bustos González, Enrique Patricio Venegas Santibáñez, Luis González Plaza, and Daniel Navarro, who lived in various towns in Chile and the areas adjacent to Santiago, survived their executions carried out in 1973. In different places, each one of them was part of a group of citizens who were clandestinely shot on the edges of cliffs by representatives of the Chilean State. Though, from a different perspective, they didn't survive. After more than thirty years, Enrique Patricio Venegas says: "But the only thing I know is that they killed us on the slope." And Daniel Navarro affirms: "They executed me in Chena."[45]

In this way, these citizens oscillate in an ambiguous condition: they live their lives as deaths, and they are witnesses to their own deaths in life. This is perhaps an aside, but a very significant one in the Chilean tragedy since it is not about mere "survivors," but inhabitants captured or encapsulated in limbo. Within historical records, they are *los fusilados,* the executed. They live in an unprecedented, unusual, *other* situation that produces a displacement of both life and death. They stand as the protagonists and witnesses of macabre scenes in which they provided endearing solidarity to their comrades in the final moments of the massacre. This is how journalist and historian Cherie Zalaquett records the events in her book, *Sobrevivir a un fusilamento,* published in Santiago in 2006. What is fundamental to me about this book is that

---

45   Please see Section 1's chapter, "They executed me in Chena," for a more in-depth look at Eltit's reading of Zalaquett's book.

the testimony can even testify to one's own death and at the same time, be a witness to the death of (an)other, and others.

Alejandro Bustos endowed Orlando Pereira, in his inhumane death, with the genuine status of human: "I don't know how the waters carried us to the shore or how I was able to drag him to that sandy bank. And there he told me: 'Put on my sweater so that it covers your body because I'm gonna die.' I could see blood gushing from the little holes in his chest where the bullets were, and blood running down his arms: 'Lay me down, please, lay me down.' I held him in my arms, and his mouth filled with blood. He lay shivering on my lap. He whispered to me to ask his wife and children to take care of themselves, and especially, of his daughter Sarita, whom he loved so much. Then he drowned in his blood. It came like a spurt, and he died in my arms." Luis González recounts: "At that moment, Jaime Bastías, who was a 17-year-old boy,[46] crying, terrified, hugged me in the middle of the gunfire." These Chilean citizens—all of working-class backgrounds and inhabitants of a vital situation that could be called post-human—experienced an irreversible condition emanating from a moment they couldn't have foreseen. Daniel Navarro lived a confusing, incomprehensible moment: "It was Sergeant Soto of the Carabineros, who had previously been in Huelquén; he liked soccer and always invited me to play for his team. 'Sergeant Soto, sir, why don't you help me?'" Yet Sergeant Soto was already someone else, and not only was he *not* going to help, but he was there to execute Daniel. This is the crucial moment in which the codes burst, opening a fissure, a hole, or an abyss, in which an extermination scenario is unleashed, incapable of containing itself.

As the reader I am, Cherie Zalaquett's book is, in my opinion, an essential text because it moves through such a forceful limit, so that what we understand by *horror* occurs again and again in speech, altering the most familiar categories.

In the work of the important writer Primo Levi, cited by the Italian philosopher Giorgio Agamben, the final witness, the fundamental one, is impossible, because he is dead: "[...there is] no one [who] ever returned to

---

46   Original text specifies "17 años" in this quotation, which differs from the 2015 "In the Intense Zone of the Other Me" where the boy is described as 16 years old.

describe his own death,"[47] Levi affirmed. And of course, he is right. This is totally true if we think in biological terms. Yet in my opinion, from the more material perspective encapsulated by the symbolic, these Chilean witnesses *returned* in a dual sense. They returned as double witnesses, as much to speak of their own deaths as the deaths of others. Furthermore, they recognize themselves as murdered and they are contained and classified in the files of the Chilean massacre as executed—*los fusilados*.

I wanted to start my intervention by acknowledging this book that seems exceptional to me, in the greatest sense of the word. As an inhabitant of the dictatorship period, I belong to the so-called *inxilio* or interior exile, and I experience a social mourning I know will never end in the face of the human catastrophe that erupted in Chile, pulverizing all pacts of coexistence. In my case, that extreme time—with its human costs and multiple, rhizomatic, totalitarian contingencies—transformed into tight knots that pushed me to read forever (I mean until the present day), in a much more acute and dizzying way, about how domination operates. In other words, I read in search of the folds and unfoldings in which various powers administer and exercise violence.

Now I want to speak as the writer I am. I have always thought of literary writing as a political sphere. In my particular case, I use this expression in a less traditional sense, since I am not referring strictly to literature that merely refers to politics, but rather to writing that works with signs, moving and removing them to generate a favorable space for developing scenes and scenarios less ruled by the sum of public and literary discourses that cynically inscribe bodies and produce imaginaries. I reiterate that this is a personal position and not intended to present itself as truth or dogma for others, but I have always envisioned writing as a blade that even cuts through the publishing market's consensus and its advertising mechanisms. To formulate an image akin to what I seek to conceptualize, I am interested in producing something of an *Okupa literature*.[48] I fully understand that this image can be controversial due

---

47   Giorgio Agamben, *Remnants of Auschwitz: The Witness and the Archive*. Translated by Daniel Heller-Roazen, New York: Zone Books, 1999), Page 33.

48   By using this term, Eltit refers to the Okupa movement, of those who occupy abandoned houses or other spaces as a response to economic difficulties and

to the social sanctions against acts that are considered illegal, but my literary imagination works by sliding through concepts. To repeat, my desire is based on a kind of *Okupa* literature that is lodged and dislodged within the abandoned and the transitory, and that survives by appealing to a low-intensity flow in perpetual movement. I mean to say, without a stable anchor neither in the market nor in the state.

It would be absurd to say that my literary work lies in a simple rationalist and even pragmatic *will*. This is not the case, because my literary politics emanates from the indisputable territory of desire and the multiple complexities that intervene in its configuration. I am referring to tracing an irrepressible journey through the written word that, of course, is neither absolutely spontaneous nor entirely controllable. I have written several novels. Beyond their aesthetic results—or in other words, their inevitable failures or possible achievements—I have asserted and inserted my body in every one of those texts. I know I did this, but I have also forgotten which body I inserted. I know I maintain distance from all my novels, and yet the most concrete time of my life takes place within them; although, of course, it's already another life—the life of the novel—which is displaced in a body that I can no longer recognize as my own.

It was inevitable that my literary journey would pass through peripheral areas, and that I would remain a tightrope walker: on the edges, at the edges. Of course, I recognize that it has been a truly unique privilege to remain close to my desire to write beyond any notion of obstacles, even something akin to total disaster.

However, at times, I also found it necessary to depart from fiction—or from a series of possible fictions—to enter other spaces filled with stories and events that did not belong to me and that, nevertheless, inhabited me in a truly powerful way.

Because we are on the important topic of testimony, I wish to testify in a partial manner, with an uncertain certainty, to the tremors, hesitation, doubts, and certainties that accompanied me during the creation of two books. Though these projects exceed me, they caused me

---

the lack of social protections, specifically housing. Some branches are connected with Anarchist or Communist movements.

incessant—let's say—political-aesthetic questions which, in turn, generated commitments in me that I refused to renounce.

I would also like to specify that for more than two decades I have read a set of critical literary texts that interrogate some Latin American testimonial productions and question their mechanisms of production which, according to their critics, reveal asymmetries. I know that these pensive texts transmit some questions that are legitimate and others that are perhaps, I'm not sure, feigned. To use Pierre Bourdieu's expression, I also understand that it is necessary to interrogate the "literary field" to thus produce the necessary agitation that mobilizes discourses, renews models, and prevents conformist monotony. Nevertheless, without forgetting or silencing the controversies that are necessary insofar as they generate contributions—or generate nothing; who cares?—my intention is to bring to light the elements I relied on to prepare these two books, different and distant from one another given the inescapable characteristics of their circumstances.

Since my childhood, I've been a wanderer of the streets: *una callejera*. Transiting through parts of the city has allowed me to hear multiple voices, witness unexpected scenes, imagine fragments of existences, and to think and stop thinking about myself in order to see others. Beyond the fleetingness of these encounters, I have experienced a sudden affection that triggers simultaneously whole and fragmentary images of people I do not know, but understand, or believe, or perhaps want to understand. I speak of unique scenes that appear and disappear amidst a brilliant wake of shock and protest. That is the subjective street that I have truly walked throughout my whole, long life.

Precisely in the most oppressive years of the dictatorship, that city—the guarded city—became even more intense for me. My strolls through the streets became populated with more *callejeo*—more wandering—perhaps as a way to recover myself. Later, I thought that there, in the street, I could find a way—I didn't know which one—to free myself from the prison of my own writing, which has always seemed insufficient to me, in one way or another, and at times exhausting.

My friend Lotty Rosenfeld, the great visual artist and fellow member of CADA, generously accompanied me to various places without questioning the unstable ambiguity that moved me in the slightest. She accompanied me *just because*, even though I was never able to precisely explain the exact reason we went to certain places that seemed necessary for me to visit. The truth is that I didn't have much clarity about why we were going from one place to another. I only knew that I was following a quest that existed without a rational or programmatic blueprint.

Callejeando, wandering the streets, is how we met the man who years later would be called "El Padre Mío." When that moment transpired, everything—the suspense of those times and the pieces of my own story—made sense. I knew that I hadn't only found him, but also the most exact core of my wandering, vagabond self.

It was the end of the search and what quenched my thirst for the street. It happened in 1983. We went back to look for him in 1984, and there he remained, speaking. He was still speaking dizzyingly in 1985. When we returned in 1986, he was no longer there, but thanks to my companion Lotty Rosenfeld, I had his recorded speech. However, what could I do with his speech? This was the most complex aspect. I had found a language that seemed essential to me, and yet I couldn't visualize a space to contain it. He lacked references, but still, he kept repeating his literary, hyper-poetic, and tragic speeches in my mind. During the three encounters, he was always delirious but kept himself out of the psych ward. I must say that we never had a conversation, let alone even a hint of an interview, since he remained an orator who spoke his truths while Lotty and I witnessed as his only audience.

In a manner of speaking, he had built himself a place in a world he had constructed and that belonged to him, on that little piece of wasteland on a devalued city bend. He had some blankets hoisted up with a stick in the manner of a flimsy tent. He had a campfire and a jar of water. He had a dog. However, the most crucial thing is this: he had his own powerful language, plagued with multiple meanings—and I had his language.

Later, when he was gone, I thought of a book for the first time. I also thought that I had never read such a book. I thought that without recognizable references, nobody would publish it. I thought that I was too nuts and that I was going to be exposed. Yet I also thought (and that was the only thing that mobilized me with certainty) that it was a poetic and political act to transport that destitute voice—full of alterations, twists, and turns—to the consecrated cultural space of the book. That's what it was all about. I was convinced that it was necessary and, moreover, urgent, because he perceived the relationship between money and extermination in an amazingly accurate way, based in a complex poetics. He read the history of the world with a crazy and simultaneously lucid accuracy, and he specifically read Chile. I thought about how to show my respect for him.

I thought about respect in an integral sense: how to respect his person and respect his speech. I understood that I had to take care of him and take care of myself. I went back and forth many times in the process until I finally spoke with Francisco Zegers, an independent editor and friend, who said yes to me beforehand, prior to becoming familiar with the text. He did it with a certainty that, to this day, I consider a supreme gesture of trust. Then, the book was underway. It was real, and I had to place it in motion. I knew I simply had to transcribe and present the language integrally, without intervening, without making any cuts. It was during the final days of the typewriter. My daughter Dani, then a teenager, transcribed the tapes and then my work materially began. I reviewed the transcript very rigorously, so as not to miss a single one of his words. I listened to his speeches to the point of memorizing them. The papers began to pile up on the table.

Yet, how to move from speech to writing? That was one of the dilemmas I had to face. Under which grammar should I organize his words? I wrote his text over and over implementing different nuances: with separating periods and without. I debated about the use of capital letters. I remember that the versions I typed repeated and repeated from a place of microscopic detail, because in some way, that written discourse required a certain visuality, or at least, I thought it needed an exact visuality that could allow for the brilliant and captivating flow emanating from his speeches.

It's an extraordinarily short book, yet I took months to complete its final version, focusing on minute details in order to assess which form would be conducive to the visual strength of its organization. Afterwards, I wrote an introduction to his speeches. I wasn't and still am not sure about that writing. I go back and forth like a pendulum, ceaselessly wondering if it might have been a concession for me to facilitate a possibly more understandable literary life for both of us. Yet I wrote that introduction about which, decades later, I continue questioning myself. In it, with every possible emphasis, I sought to extol his importance. *His.*

Finding a title for the book was another truly crucial aspect of that time. For me, within the title was another nucleus of the respect to which I have already alluded. In the encounters we had, he constantly referred to three characters who starred in his story and focused his anguished condemnation: Señor Colvin, Señor Luengo, and El Padre Mío, as he defined this third protagonist.

From his speech, I was able to choose the title *El Padre Mío*. The book's cover indicated my authorship—my name—and signaled him as my father. That exact father/daughter cover allowed me to provide restitution and generate a fair exchange, from my perspective. For on that cover, I recognized a lineage and discursively affiliated myself under the wing of his speech. It was an exciting day when I was able to forge a connection between his paternal name and mine. It was also a work focused on an aspect I am passionate about, which is listening to certain voices and allowing some ways of speaking, turns of phrase, or expressions to filter in and accompany me permanently in my aesthetic imagination.

"El Padre Mío" is literally my father in some remote sense, and his words are close to mine, I know this. Yet it is he who continues speaking, with his indisputable singularity, of that which must be endlessly and stubbornly condemned in this world—as he masterfully does—like the banks, interest rates, weapons, and extermination that always endures. Despite calculations, rules, analyses, and even good intentions, his appropriation of the city demonstrates that there are people with a marvelous drive to survive who opt for a form of admirable autonomy without refusing suffering and self-exclusion.

As an author, I experienced one of the most fulfilling moments in my literary history with the book's publication in 1989, and this has nothing to do with its reception, which was limited and almost non-existent at the time, of course. Instead, it had to do with the meanings generated by the small, almost negligible political-literary gestures in which the precarious and so arduously flattened "you" utters "I" in a supremely powerful way and then, as they say, it (im)prints.

Three years later, while I was living in Mexico, my friend—the great Chilean photographer Paz Errázuriz—came to visit me for a few days. She told me that she was taking photographs of patients interned at the

Philippe Pinel psychiatric hospital,[49] a name chosen in honor of the French doctor recognized today as the founder of modern psychiatry, or at least one of them. The hospital was in the mountainous city of Putaendo. She told me that it was an establishment serving both men and women, where many romantic partnerships formed and where she was taking photographs. She told me she thought we could do a book together. I pointed out that it would be interesting to draft a text in which writing and photographs shared a common site—the book—but preserved considerable independence in the storytelling. She said yes. Before her return to Chile, she asked me again if I was on board with the possibility of writing a book on the couples at the psychiatric hospital. I answered that it seemed imperative to me.

This is how the book that would later appear with the title *El Infarto del Alma* was conceived. I wrote to the loyal and supportive Francisco Zegers. I only told him about the project's formal elements, which included photography and literature, because I had nothing to say in detail except that Paz and I had agreed upon a book that would exceed both literary and photographic discourse. He answered me immediately, was determined to publish it and, even more, proposed to design it.

Yet I want to share with you now the doubts and even stress that accompanied me at that time. I had visited the Psychiatric Hospital in Santiago before on a few occasions and perceived its operating model in general terms. Furthermore, it is important to note that I do not share the "compassionate" gaze of Christian instruction. In fact, I am an atheist. I carry even less of a balanced outlook when faced with any kind of diversity, and if I do, it is akin to the self-pity I can occasionally experience myself. However, what I do have—thanks in part to my communist mother—is a political backbone. It is this foundation that has permitted me to maintain a position of parity, which makes me aware of the spaces marked by scarcity or difference: their strengths, faults—whenever present—aesthetics and the historical resistance they bear.

---

49 Eltit also refers to her work at this hospital in another chapter in this section, "Chalk It up to Their Circumstances."

I was living in Mexico. I was going to write a complex book already visually written by photography—photographs that I was still unfamiliar with. I was in the process of writing a book about nothing other than *mad* love, as the saying goes. It was a completely inverted path to *El Padre Mío*, which was founded on the anarchic poetics of personal freedom, among other things, through which his speech's complete explosiveness flowed.

I had to produce a literary text endowed with a certain wholeness that could signal a diversity of meanings. Although it sounds contrived and perhaps pompous, my mind entered the Chilean psychiatric hospital—a facility with which I was unfamiliar, located in a town completely foreign to me. I mean to say, the most unregulated part of my mind—the part that writes—locked itself within confinement, disease, history, and love in that space of isolation and pharmaceutical drugs. My mind positioned itself within the concentration camp of a madness that had already been stripped of delirium. I knew that all the order and strict routines that enabled the establishments' operation were guaranteed by powerful, constant antipsychotics and very precise medications used to pacify.

Though the place was politically adverse to me, I thought that the formation of couples partially subverted its own assumptions: inside, beyond all the medications, the patients produced alliances that surpassed mere survival. I also considered the bodies to be partially *outside*, in a non-literal sense, because of Paz Errázuriz's photographs. That's how I understood it. I just had to think about what I would write, what writing I would undertake, or rather, what I was undertaking and how I would do this.

I had a double responsibility: on the one hand, my commitment to Paz Errázuriz to produce a book. On the other hand, most crucially, I had the challenge of writing to address a scenario in which a form of rebellious and necessary romanticism coexisted with an indissoluble alliance of terror, persecution, and chaos that thrived under circumspection. I already knew that the capture of these bodies came about through a dramatic acceptance and adaptation due to a long, and in many cases, chronic history of confinement. Yet nothing made writing easier for me, until my own doubts and even the repudiation generated in the face of confinement and medications gave way, thanks to my insistence on generating possible approaches to the book. Thus, we began plotting a possible route on the horizon.

I thought about love. Rather, I thought that if all love is mad, how would love between mad people take place inside a psychiatric hospital? I thought that this precise, different, mobile, changeable, fleeting love was perhaps the most poetic of all loves due to its conditions of production, as Karl Marx would say. I thought I must read.

The first thing that moved me was a need to research how love had been configured at the dawn of the Spanish language. I want to say that my interest lay in the images that were set in motion and the expressive intensity that configured amorous emotion at the language's beginnings. I read a lot of poetry: *jarchas*, Mozarabic poetry, and medieval romances.[50] I reviewed those poems carefully because I imagined that there, at the dawn of the written language, it would be possible to read not only the past, but also perhaps some diluted vestiges of meaning in the present.

It was exciting to go over the images emanating from those poems, which were repeated in all the scenes of romance. However, the fine threads of the past had a particular way of expressing an overwhelming melancholy for the beloved subject, and several texts repeatedly alluded to the skeleton or bones. The beloved one was always in the process of arriving, leaving, or dying, as a permanently absent other that belonged only to writing. A series of signs emerged seeking to express how love madly navigates its embodiment in words.

I knew that those inaugural poems did not only *reproduce* loving emotions. Until today, the most important thing for me is that they *produced* feelings of love. That was the commitment that mobilized me: amorous poetry as a producer of love. That is why I tasked myself with discovering the dawn of the love story by reading its first poems in the Spanish language.

I wanted to find a foundation in the medieval period of language: one branch of what could be considered high culture because I needed to take my own images to an extreme and wrap them around those

---

50 Jarchas, also written kharja, are a lyric genre of Al-Andalus and are often about love.

bodies that lacked not only prestige but also rights. The walls of the hospital seemed analogous to the plague-ridden medieval fences that kept sick bodies away from the outside. It was necessary to recover a lost aura, to make them exclusive and powerful. I wanted to generate the images they deserved; to incorporate the respect to which I have previously referred. I was searching for an aesthetic that could contain them. It had been years since I had read Michel Foucault's *The History of Madness* and Susan Sontag's *Illness and Its Metaphors*. In those days I read *Love in the West* by Denis de Rougemont.

Certainly, I read about the history of the Chilean hospital itself. In its beginnings, it was an establishment to treat patients with tuberculo-sis, because the mountains, light and sun favored healing of the lungs. It was considered "a beautiful French castle" by the inhabitants of the town of Putaendo in the forties. In 1968, it was redeveloped into a psy-chiatric hospital and chronically ill patients from different parts of the country were transferred there. However, it was a tuberculosis hospital first. I thought of tuberculosis as Romanticism's most prized disease. Moreover, it was a desired disease. I quote the Almerían poet, Francisco Villaespesa: "you coughed so much that day / that your handkerchief turned red: / and jumping for joy / you said, upon giving it to me, come / and look. Thank the heavens / I'm consumptive as well."[51] Unlike other diseases, tuberculosis produced an aesthetic attraction in the world of art and leisure, a rebellious response to the exacerbation of manual labor and the imperative of exhausting work used to exploit and annihilate.

I thought about the foundations of Romanticism and its configu-ration as an artistic movement of anti-rationalist rebellion. I believed there was a connection there: in the early hospital's specific fate and its transformation from tuberculosis to madness. It seemed that there was a certain oblique thread linking romantic rebellion—synthesized in a contemplative listlessness caused by disease as an opposition to classifi-cations and regulations—with the love of these couples who lived in the Philippe Pinel Hospital, unknown to a significant part of the outside

---

51   These lines from Francisco Villaespesa's poem have been rendered into English to privilege literal meaning, thus sacrificing the Romantic characteristics of the original Spanish.

world. I thought that the hospital itself, as a crossover point, signaled a curious territory of exactitudes.

I'm not sure why, but I read some books related to hostelries during the first part of the 19th century in Spain. Today, I can assume I was following the route of language and the collapse of colonial control. Yet what I do remember reading in those texts was the stage and state of poverty and indigence, through lives that hung in the balance of the entire social structure's extremely insecure charity. I knew the Chilean patients were of destitute origins and to a great extent, lacked family support. Many of them even lacked formal state identification. When they were admitted in 1968, the hospital authorities had to arbitrarily give them names, surnames, and birthdates.

In another place that was no less real, I supposed that something poetic had invaded my own life. I lived far away, in Mexico City, and yet a part of me continued to be absorbed in the town of Putaendo, thinking about the most subtle way to literarily enter the psychiatric hospital—not to undo it, but yes, to differentiate it slightly.

During one of my trips to Chile, Paz Errázuriz and I went to the town of Putaendo and entered the hospital. We were there for a day. I partially knew and had partially already imagined the suffering, glimmers of happiness, distance, or the most overwhelming precarity that ran through that space. I was ready. Yet without the slightest doubt, I lived those hours as a witness, and, at the same time, as but another imprisoned inmate. I continue to live with images of that day embedded in my brain.

I returned to Mexico and the book's writing began. I had finished the series of readings I had planned and had already prepared some options. I understood that I had to avoid a linear path and take an alternate route toward those bodies. I already knew I had to appeal to discursive fragmentation, a multiplicity of tones, and a mix of writings to give a conceptual and political account of a dislocated love that, as I said before, was produced under specific conditions.

I let the styles enter. I turned to the multiplicity of poetics: the literary devices of the epistle, the personal diary, and the literary essay—which I used freely. I reviewed word after word, and despite all my work, I know that I achieved neither the tone nor the force that had taken over my imagination.

At the time the texts were written and while I was still in Mexico, letters functioned as a form of periodic communication and exchange between me and Paz about the book. Very occasionally we would try out the novelty of the fax machine. In one of her letters to me, Paz Errázuriz told me that one of the patients told Paz that her soul had experienced a heart attack. I thought it was a perfect title. Paz agreed. Thus, the book had its title, *El infarto del alma*—Heart Attack of the Soul.

I understood that all I would be able to express was a certain poetic flow for bodies bound together by the fatal equation between madness and poverty. I knew that I was going to trace a set of verbal signs that would insufficiently account for some of these captured existences that resisted and survived largely thanks to the mirage of the other and of others. I felt the full weight and scale of my fragility. I lamented my limitations.

When I was back in Chile in 1994, the book was published. I valued the political and aesthetic alliance that Paz and I established in terms of gender and genre because, in the end, we formed just one more couple. Chile is truly, very difficult for women writers and artists. After all, we were two women with our own cultural production who were able to unite and establish an equal relationship, mobilized only by the impulses in each one of our respective imaginaries, and aimed at a common task: the book.

Later, of course, I returned to fiction, but without abandoning a certain melancholy that this book makes me feel to this day: the sensation of a daydreamed literary universe that I have still been unable to access. Since the literary imagination knows no bounds, I still hope for a whole book to materialize out of my long-standing love for writing: a book that lives within the part of my mind that continues clinging, I already know, to a mad hope.

Thank you very much.

(2015)

Translated by Sowmya Ramanathan

Freedom is Always
the Freedom
of Those Who Dissent

Rosa Luxemburg's love letters, selected and gathered in this book, cannot be separated from her resounding theoretical work, articles, or
extensive correspondence in favor of the party. As a whole, her writing
provides access to her biography, a life crisscrossed by affective, political, and cultural references that permit the visualization of various contexts in which one of the most influential thinkers of Marxism spent
her life. Passionate and dazzling, her life trajectory ushered in a unique
political trajectory in which she established—within the framework of
the same Marxist matrix—the necessary differences that constitute her
inalienable singularity.

Born in Poland in 1871, Rosa Luxemburg pursued a doctorate that
covered economics and philosophy while simultaneously remaining
committed to relentless political activism and theoretical writings that
pursued forms and principles for undoing bourgeois structures. In line
with rising European leadership, her political position led to her impris-
onments. The first was in 1903, but her longest time in prison spanned
from 1915 to 1918—covering virtually the entire period of the First
World War.

A militant of the Polish Social Democratic Party, she belonged
to the Spartacus League, which later gave rise to the Community
Party. She maintained an internationalist, anti-war position, in favor
of popular dissent. She was a spontaneous thinker within a revolution that included everyone from the *lumpenproletariat* to
artists. Her tenets marked a point of tension with the great Marxist thinker, Lenin: "The ultra-centralism asked by Lenin is full
of the sterile spirit of the overseer. It is not a positive and creative

spirit,"[52] Rosa Luxemburg affirmed in a critique contained within her *Selected Works*. Her differences from Lenin are widely known—populating the texts of both thinkers—and in turn, have been central to Marxist analyses in several moments.

Beyond systematically refuting and debating with Luxemburg's texts, Lenin publicly expressed his respect for her despite their theoretical divergences: "Distinguished figures of the revolutionary proletariat and unfalsified Marxism such as Rosa Luxemburg had an outright appreciation of practical experience and its critical analysis in assemblies and the press." On the other hand, in his book *My Life,* Leon Trotsky recognized a theoretical proximity to the Polish thinker: "With pleasure, I can attest that the point of view Rosa Luxemburg developed in the name of the Polish Revolution is very similar to mine."

Inevitably, her proposals and perspective generated crises to the extent that they focused on the production of unique, independent thinking, causing fractures within her own organization. In this sense, political differences with Karl Kautsky inspired his many followers to raise an ongoing conflict with Rosa Luxemburg. In a letter written to August Bebel on August 8, 1910, the influential Austrian leader Victor Adler refers to Rosa Luxemburg in the following terms: "The poisonous bitch will yet do a lot of damage, all the more so because she is as clever as a monkey." On August 16, 1910, the German leader replied: "With all that damned woman's spurts of venom, I wouldn't want her to not be in the party."

August Bebel published *Women and Socialism* in 1879, a text that is considered a classic in the arena of the emancipation of working women to this day. Yet his opinion regarding Rosa Luxemburg shows a paradox or, rather, allows us to see how she accomplished a powerful entry into a political world marked by what could be considered a masculinity bordering on totalitarianism. Due to the structural nature of the organizations of her time—inhabited and controlled by men—it is evident that the thinker's outstanding intelligence, positioned at the center of one

---

52 Translation of Rosa Luxemburg's "Organizational Questions of the Russian Social Democracy" from https://www.marxists.org/archive/luxemburg/1904/questions-rsd/ch01.htm.

of the most important and significant political scenes, was not exempt from her colleagues' fear (always *machista*) when faced with her abilities.

From this perspective—that of gender—it is necessary to consider as paramount her close friendship with Marxist and feminist Clara Zetkin, a promoter of International Women's Day, who dedicated her life to proclaiming equality between men and women and, of course, to achieving universal suffrage. In 1907, alongside Clara Zetkin, Rosa Luxemburg directed the First International Conference of Socialist Women. In a letter to Luise Kautsky written in 1911, she affirms: "Imagine this, I've become a feminist." This precise aspect has generated controversy, since while certain feminist histories redeem Rosa Luxemburg, others indicate that her contributions always upheld Marxist political theory.

After Rosa Luxemburg's assassination in 1919, the feminist Clara Zetkin wrote, "Rosa gave to Socialism everything she was, all she was worth: her personhood, her life."

Without a doubt, Rosa Luxemburg's various correspondences circulate through cultural spaces as necessary texts, documents, and even proof of a journey. This is because the letters were thought of increasingly as a significant cultural product. Moreover, they were fully integrated into literary studies under the title of "referential genres." Thus, they inhabited and populated aesthetics since the letters maintain a form or protocol. They convey forms that enable a reading of the times and their rituals. Their transits make it possible to access social dilemmas. They break public silences, sharpen styles, play with their own signs, intensify yearning, and reveal paradoxes.

It could be said today that the letter is dead; that it was extinguished and displaced in the 20th century by the new communication technologies praised for their speed, ushering in a new, frenzied temporal condition. These are instantaneous products that incorporate new formats with distinct discursive strategies that remain outside of formal studies. These forms of writing remain in a cybernetic space, waiting to be incorporated into different media and included in academic research. Old letters and their seals only persist today, in large numbers, as strictly bureaucratic messages.

Yet the old-fashioned letter, founded on anticipation, continues to intensely inhabit culture as a reference in order to continue pondering the inexhaustible traces between the body, history, and time. From this perspective, old letters from artists, writers, politicians, and various public figures are of special interest for contemplating contexts, alliances, tensions, or specific constructed forms of thought. Nevertheless, today, letters from popular spheres are deposited into a multiplicity of archives that permit a reading of the signs of the times, their rituals, and the identification of the social marks of emerging discourses. It is possible to consider letters as a kind of *crónica*, texts that address an active self that moves within the written word, realizing, through multiple images, the psychic state of the present.

Rosa Luxemburg's love letters focus predominantly on her lovers—all connected to her political work—but they also account for her remarkable wisdom as a literary reader. They describe her painting practice and linger upon the feelings that nature provokes in her. Thus, reading this correspondence confirms that the author communicated a broad aesthetic sensibility that expanded and circulated through diverse spaces.

Although the Marxist author married Gustav Lübeck, their marriage only fulfilled a contract to obtain German citizenship. In that sense, their amorous relationships unfolded freely, and while perhaps not secretly, certainly privately.

In a television interview, the philosopher Simone de Beauvoir said, while referring to her decisions: "I have never lived with a man nor had any children." This path was chosen previously by Rosa Luxemburg. Of course, the lives of both women were radically different. However, there is a fine thread that runs between them, uniting them by living in a space occupied by masculinity. Rosa Luxemburg never lived with a man, nor did she have children.

The most prolonged and significant exchange of love letters was with Leo Jogiches, born in Russia in 1867, who was her great comrade in her political career. The sentimental connection between them lasted between 1893 and 1907. Both founded the Polish Social Democratic Party and participated in the Spartacus League. They undertook shared editorial projects, traveled, were political prisoners, witnessed major events, and shared a social landscape permeated by the problems of their time. Their romantic separation didn't break their political and partisan ties. When Rosa Luxemburg was murdered by the Freikorps, a German paramilitary group, Leo Jogiches threw himself into finding the culprits. Two months later, he was taken prisoner and murdered in jail without the slightest hint of a trial.

The letters to Leo are multifaceted. They are passionate, recriminatory, professional, disenchanted, and urgent. Yet beyond their emotional breadth, they reveal an intense and extensive relationship that gradually experienced a wear and tear.

In Rosa Luxemburg's letters, neither her childhood nor family are central. Yet in a letter to Leo, she refers intensely to the loss of her mother: "Especially when I lie down to sleep, my mother's death immediately appears before my eyes, and I have to wail aloud from the pain." This remark uncovers the degree of trust they came to share, though there are also frequent reproaches or signs of urgency to take the relationship to a degree of greater intensity: "Look how low and vile you are. I have a feeling that every word about the dumbest political issue interests you twice, ten, a hundred times more than when I pour out my heart over you."

Over almost two decades, the relationship that Rosa Luxemburg maintained with Leo Jogiches was perhaps the most important, harmonious and real one of her lifetime. She names him as "husband" in a symbolic sense. In her letters, she expresses the desire to settle down, mentions the lack of a child, and understands that these zones of affinity are powerful and fruitful: "No other couple in the world has as many chances to be happy as we do," she tells him. However, it was those same affinities that gradually generated the distance insofar as she began acquiring growing prestige as a Marxist orator and theorist, while her partner was recognized as a great organizer, yet was incapable of writing his political guidelines. Thus, a form of competition was unleashed between the two: "There isn't a single thing that worries me and about which I write to which you do not respond with lessons and advice," he reproaches her. But the lovers' relationship spanned the test of time because political assassinations—of which they were victims in 1919, just two months apart—inscribed them together in the tale of a great social history.

The exchange of love letters with Kostja Zetkin (1885-1980)—son of her great friend, the German Clara Zetkin—gave rise to passionate texts: "Beloved, I desire you greatly!" At the same time, it revealed Leo Jogiches's jealousy of the new relationship: "Yesterday Leo was here, and it is clear that he wants to accompany me on my trip so that, in case he finds you, he can shoot you and then commit suicide." The relationship with Kostja was secretive, known to Leo but apparently unknown to her friend Clara. The loving finale with the young man did not put an end to the friendship between them, which lasted for some time.

In the letters to Kostja, Mimi the cat—her great companion of those years—appears, revealing the feline affinity she shared with Lenin: "She greatly impressed Lenin, who said that only in Siberia had he seen such a magnificent creature. He said that she was a *barskii kot*, a majestic cat." Mimi the cat is a protagonist in her surroundings and in her exercise of painting. Beyond the passion that Kostja Zetkin inspired in her, the correspondence offers a glimpse of a particular pedagogical disposition: her formative decision to suggest books and itineraries, and push him to study economics and politics, though Kostja ultimately dedicated himself to medicine. For Rosa Luxemburg, this was an open relationship until its end, which was elaborated with subtlety and elegance: "You forced me to love you with your love, and if your love were to fade into nothing, the same would happen to mine."

Paul Levi (1883-1930), her defense attorney, became Rosa Luxemburg's lover. A militant and leader, the letters speak of a union founded mainly on partisan issues and the crises generated within leadership. Yet, as one of her letters indicates, she still hides their relationship from her former lover: "When your telegram arrived, the man with the great mustache (Leo Jogiches) was here; however, I was careful not to talk about you, and when he later asked me if I liked my lawyer, I gave him an evasive answer." Rosa Luxemburg's relationship with Paul Levi was characterized by the political emergencies and continuous ruptures within the organization itself. Her rather brief letters address one political situation or another based on growing differences of opinion: "In the Party Committee, I was treated like a criminal."

The letters to her lover, Hans Diefenbach (1884-1917)—though according to some sources, this was a platonic relationship—focus on her own moods and on the nuances of her time in prison, despite maintaining echoes of her past. These letter-readings contemplate and analyze literature, and in them, she displays her interests: Shakespeare and Kipling, among other figures. Yet she also takes aesthetic positions: "I don't want to hurt his feelings, although as always, I prefer to be honest:

the book seemed very brave and agreeable to me, but more like a pamphlet than a novel," she affirms in regard to Romain Rolland's work.

The texts reveal an intense admiration of nature. Shock and awe intensely blend together before the landscape, the birds, and the weather. It is possible that the years in prison intensified her perception of the outdoors, making her see nature's power with a meticulous gaze: "In two weeks it will already be a full year since my imprisonment here, and if you don't count the short intermediary period, it will actually be two full years." Hans Diefenbach died on the front lines during the First World War.

Reading this correspondence today reveals Rosa Luxemburg's amorous world as inseparable from a form of thinking aligned with equality, freedom, and the search for an inhabitable space for the working class. It exposes the passion of her debates and makes it possible to affirm that her figure transgressed the barriers of gender and genre. This contemporary publication reveals the paradox of *el paso y el peso del tiempo*—the passage and weight of time—highlighting the structure of an existing, prevailing form of writing that deposits sediments of what the future may hold. It confirms that while the crime of the German ultra-right ended Rosa Luxemburg's material life, it failed to assassinate the far-reaching survival of her mind.

(2021)

Translated by Sowmya Ramanathan

National Prize for Literature Acceptance Speech (2018)

Good day. I would like to greet, of course, the authorities present and to remember the people who made it possible for me to be here today: my mother and grandmother. They are not here, but they are within me. They live inside my body and, fortunately, they speak to me daily.

I would like to point out that cultural life, in my case, began within what we call *inxilio,* that is, internal exile. We lived in one of the most painful, dramatic, and unforgivable times in the history of the twentieth century: the long history of the dictatorship. In fact, I even think that that dictatorship extended beyond that time because the dictator remained in command of the army and made himself a Senator of the Republic.

Within Chile, we shaped culture. I worked. Many people worked. There are some here who accompany me in what could be called resistance, from the cultural point of view, obviously. I send my regards to those people. Many of them aren't here today, but they continue to live on in our memory.

At the same time, I must point out that, precisely because of the importance of my mother and grandmother in my life, I am committed especially to women, to the terrible history of inequality they face in each and every area of life. Especially today, I ask myself when and how parity of wages will materialize, considering that women earn less than men for the same work. As I have said on other occasions, being paid less means, socially, that we are worth less, because if not, we wouldn't be paid less. I will continue to work tirelessly for women.

Chilean writers are doing fundamental work. Today, several of them are here and many are not, but they have been not only spectacular in their presence and participation in the great literary debates but also fundamental for understanding that the written word is social.

I would also like to consider here that I come from a Palestinian migrant family, and, therefore, I will always enthusiastically greet anyone who arrives in Chile, remembering precisely that my relatives arrived, carved a path, started families, and generated culture, among other undertakings.

My family is of Palestinian origin, so I receive this award with the understanding that it goes beyond me. It is an award that, in some way, recognizes more peripheral literatures, those that I have followed with great pride. I have never claimed a place other than my own. I'm very happy, and, more than anything, contact with others is what matters to me.

I will continue to engross myself in thinking about the inequality that governs us today, about the people who live on the margins, about vulnerable families, their dramas, and their debts in a society in which subject and object become more and more similar.

I will continue to advocate for social equality because, for me, sincerely, each and every single one of us is worth the same. Yet that must be reflected in our social apparatus.

I know the literary world is aligned with that thinking. I will remain absorbed in writing my books, in the same way I have done all this time, using the literary word to create what we need: an important literary community that goes beyond individual differences. Ultimately, we can think differently, but we can also find common ground on basic points.

I thank my family, who have been very supportive, the rector of Universidad Tecnológica Metropolitana (UTEM), who received me for 30 years and allowed me to write. I thank the rector of Universidad Católica, where I did my undergraduate degree. I was telling him how interesting it was to live through the moment of reform of La Católica. I then moved on to Universidad de Chile, whose vice-rector is also here today.

Of course, I will continue advocating to undo any milestone or event that jeopardizes, rejects, reneges on, or attacks sexual diversity because intolerance is simply unacceptable. Our children will have their social identity, and they have every right to harness it as they see fit. We are here to support, not destroy our children.

Thank you very much.

(2018)

Translated by Sowmya Ramanathan

About the Author

Diamela Eltit (1947) is a Chilean writer. From 1994 to 2017, she was full professor at Universidad Tecnológica Metropolitana in Santiago, Chile and was granted an honorary doctorate by the same institution in 2023. Between 2007 and 2019, she was distinguished global professor at New York University. She has held visiting professorships as the University of California, Berkeley, Columbia University, Stanford University, and the University of Pittsburgh, among others. In 2015 she held the Simón Bolívar Chair at the University of Cambridge, England. In 2010 she received the José Donoso Ibero-American Literature Prize for her outstanding literary career. In 2018, she was granted the Andrés Sabella Prize by the city of Antofagasta, Chile; in 2020, the Carlos Fuentes Prize for Literary Creation (Mexico); and in 2021, the FIL Prize by the University of Guadalajara. Her literary work has been translated into English, French, Portuguese, Italian, Greek, and Finnish. She has published twelve novels, three volumes of essays, and numerous journal articles. Her first novel, *Lumpérica* (1983), turned forty years old in 2023.

About the Editors

Michael J. Lazzara is Professor of Latin American Literature and Cultural Studies and Associate Vice Provost of Academic Programs in Global Affairs at the University of California, Davis. He is the author of *Civil Obedience: Complicity and Complacency in Chile since Pinochet* (2018), *Luz Arce and Pinochet's Chile: Testimony in the Aftermath of State Violence* (2011), and *Chile in Transition: The Poetics and Politics of Memory* (2006), translator of José Carlos Agüero's *The Surrendered: Reflections by a Son of Shining Path* (2021) and Ana María del Río's *Carmen's Rust* (2003), and author of numerous articles and edited volumes on topics in memory, human rights, and culture.

Mónica Barrientos is academic coordinator of the Doctorate in Social Sciences at the Autonomous University of Chile. She has a Ph.D in Hispanic Languages and Literature from the University of Pittsburgh. Her line of research is on contemporary Chilean and Latin American textualities and the relationship with space, visuality, and activism. She is the editor of *Catedral Tomada: Journal of Latin American Literary Criticism* from the University of Pittsburgh and president of SOCHEL (Chilean Society of Literary Studies). Among her publications are: *Valoración múltiple sobre Diamela Eltit* (2021), *La pulsión comunitaria en la obra de Diamela Eltit* (2019), and *No hay armazón que la sostenga: Entrevista a Diamela Eltit* (2017).

María Rosa Olivera-Williams is Professor of Latin American Literature and Cultural Studies and Head of the Spanish Section in the Department of Romance Languages and Literatures at the University of Notre Dame. She is the author of *El arte de crear lo femenino: Ficción, género* *e historia del Cono Sur* (2012; 2013) and *La poesía gauchesca de Hidalgo a Hernández: Respuesta estética y condicionamiento social* (1986), and co-editor with Rodrigo Caresani of *Escenas de traducción en las literaturas de América Latina* (2023), with Cristián Opazo of *Humanidades al límite: Posiciones en/contra de la universidad global* (2022), and with Mabel Moraña of *El salto de Minerva: Intelectuales, género y Estado en América Latina* (2005), and author of numerous articles on modern and contemporary literature and culture in Latin America. She is currently completing the monograph "Tango Imagining National Roots in the Maelstrom of Modernization in Argentina and Uruguay," for which she received a J. William Fulbright Research Grant.

About the Translators

Michael J. Lazzara (See description p.279.)

Catherine M. Brix is Assistant Teaching Professor of Hispanic Studies at William & Mary. Her research focuses on Southern Cone testimonial literature of the Dirty War and interdisciplinary approaches to literary criticism and peace studies. She is the author of "La justicia social en la educación penitenciaria: Una estrategia católica" in *Humanidades al límite: Posiciones en/contra de la universidad global* (2022) and translator of Olivier Morel's 2018 documentary *Ever, Rêve, Hélène Cixous*. She is currently writing her first book, *Trauma and Testimonio: Memories of Hispanic Women Prisoners under Dictatorship*.

Carl Fischer is Professor and Chair in the Department of Modern Languages and Literatures at Fordham University in the Bronx, New York, where he teaches courses on Latin American visual culture, film, and literature. He is the author of *Queering the Chilean Way: Cultures of Exceptionalism and Sexual Dissidence, 1965-2015* (2016) and co-editor (with Vania Barraza) of *Chilean Cinema in the Twenty-First-Century World* (2020). His writing has been published in *American Quarterly, Revista de Estudios Hispánicos, Hispanic Review*, and *Comunicación y medios*, among other academic journals. He previously worked as a translator for the Chilean government.

Sowmya Ramanathan is Visiting Assistant Teaching Professor of Hispanic Studies at William & Mary and a scholar of 20th and 21st-century Latin American literature and culture. She is currently at work on her first book, *Moving Encounters: Forays Into Feminist Praxis,* and has published articles on affect and social networks in Chile, Latin American feminist magazines and cultural resistance, and the uses of humanistic methods for evaluating contemporary shifts in sociocultural narrative. Her previous translations include *La poética de la fragilidad* (2016), a transmedia project by artists Lata Mani and Nicolás Grandi, and subtitles for Mani's film *The Earth on its Axis, We in Our skin: The Tantra of Embodiment* (2015).

Index

About the Latin America Research Commons

Latin America Research Commons (LARC) is the first open-access publishing press dedicated to the publication of monographs in Spanish and Portuguese. It is an editorial project that originated in the Latin American Studies Association (LASA), and its main goal is to ensure the widest possible dissemination of original monographs and journals in all disciplines related to Latin American studies. It is oriented to making sure that scholars from around the world are able to find and access the research they need without economic or geographic barriers.

In Translation: Key Books in Latin American Studies is a LARC series dedicated to publishing classic Latin American books which have never been translated before and to reaching new readers.

www.ingramcontent.com/pod-product-compliance
Lightning Source LLC
Chambersburg PA
CBHW060601030726
47498CB00005B/1484